The
CROSSING
OF INGO

THE CROSSING OF INGO

by

Helen Dunmore

HarperCollins *Children's Books*

First published in hardback by HarperCollins *Children's Books* 2008
First published in paperback by HarperCollins *Children's Books* 2009
HarperCollins *Children's Books* is a division of HarperCollins*Publishers* Ltd,
77-85 Fulham Palace Road, Hammersmith, London W6 8JB

www.helendunmore.com

3

Text copyright © Helen Dunmore 2008

Helen Dunmore asserts the moral right to be identified
as the author of this work.

Isbn 978-0-00-727026-2

Printed and bound in England by Clays Ltd, St Ives plc

TO JODI AND GABRIEL

CHAPTER ONE

"I see that the guardian sharks have returned," says Ervys. Both he and Saldowr glance upwards. Far above them, shadowy shapes patrol, gliding across their territory and then turning with a whip of the tail.

"Yes, they are back," says Saldowr. His face is watchful. "They gave you no trouble on your journey to the Groves of Aleph?"

"No trouble at all," says Ervys with cold satisfaction. "The sharks and I know each other well."

"Perhaps a little too well," murmurs Saldowr.

Ervys doesn't reply. His powerful tail stirs as if he'd like to lash out at Saldowr, but he does nothing.

"The sharks also know it is their duty to guard the Groves of Aleph," continues Saldowr, still watching Ervys closely. Ervys's face remains expressionless, but his broad, muscle-packed shoulders give a small shrug. Saldowr lets it pass.

Ingo needs every drop of strength that Saldowr possesses now. Ervys grows bolder day by day. The wound that almost killed Saldowr when the Tide Knot broke has been slow to heal, but he cannot allow himself to relax for a second. Ervys has lost one battle, but this is war and there are many more battles to be fought. He has more followers now than ever. Already too many of the Mer are forgetting what they owe to the human children who ventured to the Deep, fought the Kraken in all his shape-shifting terror and defeated him. They listen to Ervys rewriting the past and telling them what their future should be. Saldowr has his own spies hidden among Ervys's supporters. Ervys sways the crowd with his speeches just as the sea sways great ropes of oarweed.

"Human beings have always longed to rule over Ingo! We know from the gulls that humans are growing ever more ambitious and greedy for Ingo's wealth. They are no longer content with polluting our world and killing its inhabitants. Now they scheme to trap the tides and give themselves the tides' power. They plot to build metal monsters and plunge them down through the waters of Ingo, so that their arms can beat the sky and destroy the birds that travel over Ingo. Who knows what humans will plot against us next? They must be driven out of Ingo! If we are forced to shed their blood, then so be it!"

Saldowr knows how Ervys's voice thunders out over the crowds, and how they roar back their agreement.

"Fight for what is ours by birth and by blood! Defend Ingo! I offer myself to you as a leader who will sacrifice the last drop of blood in his body for the Mer and for Ingo that is ours by birth!"

The crowd roars again. Saldowr's spies make sure to join in the applause. They gaze at Ervys with a look of blind faith, so they won't stand out from the crowd as Ervys's gaze sweeps over it.

"Follow me, and I will make you free," declares Ervys. "You will rule your own lives. You will not need Saldowr or those half-and-halfs who dare to meddle in the affairs of the Mer." There's a murmur of protest, but Ervys is on to it immediately.

"You say that they saved your own little ones from the Kraken? You think that's a reason to be grateful to them? I tell you, the Kraken only woke in the first place because it felt the polluting presence of humans in Ingo. I tell you again, the Kraken is sleeping now. His lair lies deeper than the trenches of the Deep. You have no cause to fear him any more. The Kraken will not wake. Saldowr tells you stories to keep you afraid, so that you will cling to him like children. But you are Mer!"

"Yes, Ervys, we are Mer!" bellows back a hand-picked group of Ervys's closest supporters.

"Then will you join with me to cleanse Ingo of humans?"

Again the group yells its answer: "Cleanse Ingo of humans! Cleanse Ingo of humans!"

More and more of the crowd join in. But not everyone, Saldowr's spies tell him. Not yet.

"The time has come to fight!" Ervys's voice thunders above the tumult. "If we are weak, the humans will take over Ingo as they have already taken over the whole of the dry world. We must fight for what we love! Fight for what is ours by birth and by blood!"

"Ours by birth and by blood!" roar his supporters.

As the clamour swells Ervys holds up his hand for silence. Instantly there is a hush.

"Will you take me as your leader?"

A second of silence, and then a crash of voices: "*Ervys! Ervys! Ervys!*"

And now Ervys is here in the Groves of Aleph, in Saldowr's own domain. He is growing bold – or more likely, he wants something. Saldowr will not challenge Ervys yet. The tide is running too strongly in Ervys's direction, sweeping too many of the Mer with it. This thing must run its course if Ingo is not to be torn apart.

"So tell me, Ervys, exactly why you have come," says Saldowr aloud. He speaks calmly, and a flicker of scorn crosses Ervys's face. He wants a fight, but Saldowr refuses to give him one.

Ervys tosses back his thick mane of dark hair. Light ripples over his body, emphasising the blue tinge of his skin. His eyes glitter.

"I am here because it is time to gather the cohort of young Mer who are of age to make the Crossing of Ingo," says Ervys. "The Assembly must choose which of them will make the Crossing."

"Indeed," agrees Saldowr. "I am not forgetful of my duty, Ervys. I shall make the Call as I have always made it, and the Mer will hear it as they have always heard it."

"As you have always made it," Ervys repeats. His eyes flash mutinously. "Saldowr, I have come to the Groves of Aleph alone, without protection. I have shown trust in you."

"I am honoured," says Saldowr politely.

"I have done this so that you and I can speak frankly. There is no one to hear us. We two can drop the pretence that things now are *as they have always been*. The world is changing, Saldowr! The Mer must change with it. They must learn to find the old in the new."

"You are right," says Saldowr. His eyes gleam with mischief as he notes the surprise that Ervys cannot quite hide.

Then Ervys's expression darkens. "*You* are no friend of change, Saldowr."

"I tell you, Ervys, *you* are the one who wants to shut the door against the future, not I."

"It's time for the Mer to have a leader who has their true interests at heart," replies Ervys.

Saldowr laughs softly. "Is that the sum of the change you are talking about, Ervys? A leader? And who might that be, I wonder? We Mer have never needed *leaders*. We have had our guides and Guardians, and they have served us well. The Mer were glad enough to accept my guidance when the Kraken woke and their hearts were cold with fear."

"But the Kraken is sleeping now. There is nothing more to fear from him."

"Tell me, Ervys, what makes you so sure of that? Everything that sleeps knows how to wake again, except the dead. The Kraken, I think, is alive."

The Groves appear to have grown darker. Perhaps heavy black clouds have swept over the sun, high above in the Air. A restless current ripples the folds of Saldowr's cloak. Faro, hidden behind a heap of rough boulders, presses himself flat against the sand. He must not move. If Ervys even suspects that he's here, listening...

And Saldowr must never know. He sent Faro away to the borders of Limina, to give company to an ancient Mer woman who was about to leave Ingo and enter the other world, from which no one ever returns. Fithara had always liked Faro. She used to pop sea grapes into his mouth when he was little. Saldowr said, "Stay there with Fithara until I send for you."

Faro sat with her for a while, until Fithara grew tired and closed her eyes. He had never disobeyed Saldowr before. He knew he ought to stay, but fear had been gnawing in him all day. Saldowr had tried to get him well away from the Groves of Aleph. Faro was sure there was a reason for it. Saldowr would never have sent him so far away just because he wanted to be alone. If Saldowr ever seemed to need solitude, Faro would vanish in the flash of a tail.

There must be some danger that Saldowr didn't want him to share. But if there really *were* danger, Faro's place was at Saldowr's side. Even if it went against Saldowr's command, he must go back.

As he swam down towards the Groves he came face to face with the guardian sharks who patrolled against intruders. Faro was used to them. He'd known them since he was too young to talk, and they knew him. They understood that Faro had his duty with Saldowr. The sharks knew about duty because theirs was inherited from their ancestors. They must challenge any stranger who might threaten the Tide Knot or its Guardian.

But today the sharks seemed to have forgotten that Faro wasn't a stranger. Instead of giving way immediately as normal, the lead shark blocked Faro's way and stared at him with a cold, malevolent eye. However well you think you know a shark, there is a place inside it that you can never reach. Faro knew that. Sharks are not swayed by sympathy or pity. They carry out their duty without emotion. For a few seconds, as he gazed into the eye of the lead shark, even Faro was afraid. The shark's jaws moved, as if he were thinking. Faro hung still in the water, his heart racing. Slowly, very slowly, the cold eyes seemed to remember who he was. Grudgingly the shark moved aside to let him pass.

Everything in the Groves appeared silent and deserted. For a moment Faro wished he had not come back. Saldowr would be very angry at his disobedience. *But*, thought Faro, *I am Saldowr's* scolhyk *and his* holyer. *I have to be with him if he needs me.* Cautiously Faro swam forward, keeping in cover behind weed, boulders and the uprooted trunks of huge branching weeds. For once he was grateful for the devastation left behind when the Tide Knot broke. It hadn't all healed itself yet and the debris gave him plenty of hiding places. He glided from thick, tangled weed to the shelter of a pile of rocks, and settled himself to wait, his tail curled under him.

Faro did not hear them coming, but suddenly they were there, close together, in front of Saldowr's cave. Ervys and Saldowr. Faro's fists clenched in shock and anger. How had Ervys dared to return to the Groves of Aleph? And why was Saldowr talking to him so calmly? Ervys had no right to be there after the way he'd plotted against Saldowr.

Saldowr should have banished him when he had the chance, thought Faro. *Ervys was weak then, after we defeated the Kraken. If Saldowr had used all his powers, we would never have seen Ervys again.*

But he must not be disloyal to Saldowr, even in his thoughts. Whatever Saldowr had done or not done, he had good reason. *It will be part of a pattern that is too big for anyone else to see*, thought Faro hopefully.

Ervys looked formidable. Resolute. His defeats seemed to have done nothing but polish his anger and his hunger for power. Faro looked at the tall, powerful figure, and dread rippled through him. But Faro refused to be afraid. He was about to fling back his head defiantly, but just in time he remembered that he must be still and silent. There would be plenty of chances to confront Ervys, he told himself. Now he must watch, and listen, and wait...

"...the Kraken, I think, is alive," says Saldowr, and Faro watches the Groves darken.

"Are we going to talk about the Kraken for ever?" demands

Ervys. "It's time to move on. The Kraken is sleeping."

"Let us hope he does not turn over in his sleep and remember us," says Saldowr. "But you are right in one thing, Ervys. It is time for me to make the Call. It takes many days to bring together all the young Mer who wish to make the Crossing of Ingo. "

Ervys swishes his tail. "There are many among the Mer who will not answer when you blow the conch," he says, putting the faintest emphasis on the word "you".

Faro has to dig his nails into his palms to stop himself from crying out in protest at this insult to Saldowr. But a small, reluctant part of his mind knows that Ervys is telling the truth. Many of the young Mer in Faro's own age group have turned away from Saldowr and everything he stands for. They follow Ervys now. They want what he promises them – freedom, independence, an end to this mingling with humans. Pure-blooded Mer must unite and build a future together. If that means that they have to fight, then so be it. Only old people and has-beens say that the Mer must resolve all their conflicts peacefully. Ervys is a real leader, a man for our times.

Saldowr's silence goads Ervys into recklessness. "Many among the young Mer no longer recognise your authority, Saldowr," he says.

"I am aware of that," answers Saldowr quietly.

Why won't he fight? thinks Faro, burning with anguished fury against Saldowr. Why doesn't he destroy Ervys now that he's got him here alone? *Saldowr could do it; I know he could.*

"Then let us act on it," says Ervys smoothly. "Let us make the Call together. You will call your people, and I will call mine."

"They are not *my people*," says Saldowr with sudden anger. "I am privileged to be Guardian, no more than that. The Mer belong to no one but themselves."

Ervys looks at him consideringly. "Do you agree that we should both make the Call?"

Saldowr appears to be thinking deeply. His cloak swirls around him, his hair flows across his face, hiding it. At last he draws himself upright, pushes back his hair and says, "We will each blow the conch in turn. But hear me, Ervys, everyone in the age group for which the conch blows must be free to answer its summons. No one shall be prevented, understand me? *No one*."

The power than Faro has longed to see is alive in Saldowr now. His eyes burn with inward, hooded fire. Ervys moves back, just a little.

"Of course," he says, with the first touch of uncertainty in his voice.

"I want to hear none of your talk of pure blood, and half-and-halfs. Neither from you nor from your followers. Ingo can only be healed when it accepts that it is not complete in itself. Do you understand me?"

Ervys raises a hand in protest, and then slowly his hand drops to his side. *How can he understand?* Faro wonders. *Even I don't understand what is in Saldowr's mind now.* But after a long hesitation Ervys bows his head in agreement.

"Wait here while I fetch the conch," says Saldowr with all the old authority in his voice.

Saldowr swims to his cave entrance and disappears inside. Faro watches Ervys closely. The man's face is knotted with concentration. He is thinking something through, and Faro wishes he knew what it was. When Saldowr emerges with the conch in his hand, Ervys shakes his head as if a shoal of tiny fish were nibbling at his skin.

Faro eases himself a little way further around the side of his boulder, holding a bunch of weed in front of his face to camouflage it, and peering through the strands. The conch is as big as a man's head. It is full of lustrous, changeful colours: dark at the tightly whorled tip, pearly at its broad base. Saldowr lifts it high and flings back his head. His lips touch the lip of the conch. Water pulses through it, building up pressure, and the conch begins to sound.

At first the Call is no more than a palpitation of the water. Faro is disappointed. He has heard the sound of the Call before. Even though he was always too young and he knew that the Call was not meant for him, his whole body had thrilled down to the tip of his tail. Perhaps the Call doesn't sound the same if you are too close to the conch.

But the Call grows. It begins to beat the water like a whale's tail, sending waves of sound to crash against Faro's ears. Now he hears it truly. It enters his body and vibrates against every part of it. The Call is in his muscles, in his bone. It is inside his heartbeat. It grows louder and louder until his whole body shivers with the impact. He wants to leap through the water, to turn a thousand somersaults, to fly down the currents like a dolphin. This time, the Call is for him.

Faro curls up tight, tight, hugging his tail. He must not be seen. If Ervys and Saldowr knew that he'd watched this...

The Call thrums through him, on its way to the ends of Ingo, on its way to the ears of the young Mer who are ready to hear it. Elvira hears it as she sorts red weaver-weed to make dressings for wounds. Her skin prickles and her eyes grow brilliant. Girls diving with dolphins hear it and backflip, stunned, listening. Boys surfing wild currents hear it and fight their way out of the surging bubbles, shaking their hair out of their ears. The Call flows over the rocky cradles of Mer babies. Ancient Mer shake their heads and smile, remembering the past as the Call rushes past them. Mothers press their young children close, glad that it's not yet their time for danger and adventure. The Call races through Ingo, into every underwater cave, through the hulls of sunken treasure ships, into coral reefs and gullies where conger eels live, through kelp forests and shadowy underwater caves, searching out the Mer who are ready to make the Crossing of Ingo.

The Call is like a snatch of music thrilling through Ingo, so irresistible that those who hear it will do anything to hear it again. It's time, the Call says. Time to leave your family and your home behind. Time to say goodbye to all the places where you've played and learned and slowly grown up. Time for your own journey to the bottom of the world and for your own adventure.

At last, Saldowr lowers the conch. "Your turn," he says, passing it to Ervys.

The conch must be much heavier than it looks. Ervys's shoulders sag as he takes its weight, and for a second it looks as if the conch will fall to the sand. But Ervys braces himself and lifts the conch to his lips.

The Call is different this time. Ervys blows a harsh, blaring sound. It is loud, but it does not touch Faro. He hears Ervys blow on the conch, and feels nothing. *But some of the Mer will answer it,* thinks Faro. *Some of them, who won't answer Saldowr, will answer Ervys. They'll come to the Assembly chamber and present themselves as candidates for the Crossing of Ingo, because Ervys has blown the conch.*

It's an ugly thought. Faro doesn't understand why Saldowr even let Ervys lift the conch. He could have smashed Ervys's skull with it. *If I'd been holding the conch, that's what I would have done*, thinks Faro. Ervys's body would have drifted down to the sand, his tail limp and his blood making red smoke in the water. Faro's eyes sparkle as he considers the defeat of his enemy.

But he's getting cramped, hiding behind these rocks. Surely Ervys will leave now that he's got what he wants. Ervys lowers the conch. Saldowr swims forward and takes it. He seems to hold the weight without effort. Faro thinks that the lustre of the conch looks less bright now that it has been blown. It will be put away and it won't emerge from Saldowr's cave for another five years, when the next group of young Mer is ready to take on the challenge of the Crossing.

But if Ervys gets more power, everything will change. He won't blow the conch for the whole of Ingo as Saldowr does. He'll blow it, but only for his followers. Instead of a whole age group of the Mer travelling to the Assembly together, there will be angry arguments. Fights, maybe.

Faro's fists clench again. He wants to leap through the water to Saldowr's side and fight for him. Now's the time to stop Ervys, while he's alone and before he can grow any stronger.

It's already too late. Ervys turns with a twist of his broad, powerful shoulders, and strikes off through the water with a blow from his tail. In a surge of bubbles he is gone, and Saldowr has done nothing to stop him.

But Faro is still stuck behind his rock. He can't come out now. Saldowr will know that he saw and heard everything. His fingers tingle with cramp, and he unclenches his fists. His tail aches for free water.

"Come out now, Faro," says Saldowr.

Faro's heart jumps in his chest like a fish on dry land. Saldowr has turned to face the rock where Faro is hiding. His face is stern. Faro braces himself. This is the worst thing he has ever done. He has spied on Saldowr and eavesdropped on his conversation. How could he have been so stupid as to believe Saldowr wouldn't sense his presence? Saldowr had only kept silent until now to shield Faro from Ervys's fury. Cold, heavy trepidation fills Faro. He's not afraid of any punishment, but if

Saldowr says that Faro can no longer be his *scolhyk* and his *holyer*, he would rather die. He can't imagine a life where he doesn't serve Saldowr, and where Saldowr no longer teaches him and prepares him for the future.

All these thoughts flash through Faro's mind in a couple of seconds. Already he's swimming out from behind the rock. He won't make Saldowr call him twice. He swims to within an arm's length of Saldowr, and then the Guardian of the Tide Knot holds up a hand.

"Why did you disobey me, Faro? I told you to stay at the borders of Limina with Fithara until I sent for you."

Faro bows his head. He could argue, but he will not.

"You should not have seen me blow the conch. One day I would have shown you, but not this time."

Perhaps Saldowr is going to bar him from making the Crossing. Faro bites his lip, staring at the sand.

"Look at me, Faro."

He looks up.

"You are loyal. You want to serve me."

Faro nods.

"You must believe that there is a pattern in what I do. You were angry because I did not attack Ervys. But if I had done that, Ervys's followers would have risen up in fury. They would have said that their leader had been killed by my treachery. That I had invited an unarmed man to come to my cave alone. That I did not care about the Mer, only about clinging on to my own power. Understand me, Faro, I would have lost my influence with the Mer. Without their trust I can do nothing. Even those who follow Ervys, I think, still trust me in their hearts. Do you understand me?"

"Yes, Saldowr," says Faro reluctantly.

"You want to fight." Saldowr's voice is warmer now. There is humour in it, and affection. Faro looks up, full of hope. Perhaps Saldowr is not going to send him away. Perhaps he is not going to bar him from following the Call.

"You must wait, my son. There will be a time to fight, and we must be ready for it. If we act too soon, we destroy all our chances."

Saldowr is still holding the conch as easily as if it were one of those fluff feathers that drift down from under a young gull's wings and lie on top of the water.

"You heard my Call," he says.

"Yes," replies Faro.

"You will answer it. And there are others who will answer it. Your friends. They will hear the Call but they will need your help to reach the Assembly chamber. You must go to them, Faro."

"To Sapphire and Conor?"

"Of course."

The echo of the Call seems to thrum through Faro. Sapphire and Conor will hear it too. Their Mer blood will dance in their veins as his does.

"We'll come to the Assembly together," he says eagerly. His blood tingles, turning a hundred somersaults in his veins. "All of us together."

"Listen carefully, Faro. Your friends are called not only for themselves, but for the healing of Ingo. If those who come from the world of Earth and Air, and who have both Mer and human blood can be called and chosen, and can complete the most important journey in the life of the Mer, then there is hope that Mer and human will come to understand each other in peace. But where there is a great prize to be won then there is also great danger."

"Ervys will try to stop us."

"Yes. You must be prepared for that. Now go to Sapphire and Conor. Quickly, Faro."

CHAPTER TWO

"**I** wasn't born with a duvet-washing gene just because I'm a girl," I shout up the stairs to Conor.

Saturday. I tick off a list on my fingers. Laundry, do the vacuuming, clean the bathroom. Dig over the potato bed. Go up to the farm for eggs. There's my maths homework, and I'm supposed to be handing in my project on climate change after half term and so far all I've done is download some photos of deserts.

Saturday morning. Work, work, work. I might as well be at school. And we're coming to the end of all the food Mum stacked in the freezer before she and Roger went to Australia. Shepherd's pie, chicken casserole, homemade soups, lemon drizzle cake (my favourite) and gingerbread with almonds (Conor's favourite). Mum made more cake in a week than she usually makes in a year. Roger called it guilt cooking, and he put a stop to it when he came in the morning before they left and she was baking cakes and crumbles for the freezer instead of doing her packing.

"You've got to stop all this guilt cooking, Jen."

"What do you mean?" Mum asked fiercely, her eyes bright as she wielded the flour sifter.

"You've no call to feel guilty. These kids *want* to stay here, surely to God you've heard that from them enough times. I know I have. Sapphy's a great little cook and Conor's no slouch. You go on upstairs and finish your packing or you'll end up in Brisbane without a bikini, which is a crime under Australian law."

I couldn't help laughing, just as I couldn't help liking Roger when Mum put down the sifter, rubbed her hand over her face (leaving an extensive trail of flour) and smiled reluctantly.

"Come and help me pack, Sapphy?" she asked.

Mum and Roger have been gone for a month now, and we've eaten all the dinners Mum left in the freezer, apart from some grey frozen parsnip soup.

"Conor! You need to wash your sheet and your duvet cover."

"I'm still in bed." Conor's voice floats down from the loft, blurred and sleepy. "It's Saturday morning, Saph, for God's sake."

"You can't be asleep if you're shouting at me. It's ten o'clock, Con. I need to get the washing on or it'll never dry."

I am turning into Mum. I sigh and start sweeping the floor while Sadie pads round me, thumping her tail against the flagstones. She's desperate for a real walk. I took her out for ten minutes when I first got up, but she wasn't impressed.

"Oh, Sadie." I throw the broom down, drop to my knees and wrap my arms around Sadie's warm neck. She whines sympathetically, rubbing her head against me. "Shall we leave all this and go for a long, long walk?" I ask her. Sadie's tail whacks against my legs. "Walk" is her favourite word.

Just then Conor staggers downstairs, still wrapped in his duvet, clutching a bundle of sheet and pillowcases. He drops the duvet on the floor, flops down at the table and puts his head in his hands.

"Are you OK, Con?"

"I got up too quickly."

Got up too quickly! I have been up since eight thirty and I've already cleared the kitchen, done the washing-up and scraped a layer of grease off the stove.

"You could at least take the duvet cover off the duvet."

Conor looks up in surprise at my tone. "I'm going to, I'm going to. Relax, Saph, it's Saturday."

"It doesn't feel like Saturday to me. It feels like Monday morning." A wave of self-pity sweeps over me. School all week, cooking every evening, chopping wood for the stove, homework, taking Sadie out, washing, cleaning, digging the garden... It all takes so long and there's never any free time. I have to admit that usually Conor does half of everything, but this morning I've had enough.

"I'm going down to the cove."

Conor looks up. "What about my duvet cover?"

"You can mop the floor with it for all I care."

Conor leans back, tilting his chair. "Rainbow's coming up later, maybe Patrick too. I'll cook dinner."

"We mustn't forget about Mum this time."

Last time Rainbow and Patrick were round for the evening, we lit a fire outside and sat round it for hours, talking, working out chords for a new song and trying to tell each other's fortunes. We didn't hear Mum call. At the weekends she usually calls late in our evenings, which is early in her mornings. She calls from an Internet café about ten kilometres from where she and Roger are staying, and then we call her back. I can't believe how early that café opens, but Mum says it's the way things happen there, because the middle of the days get so hot.

We've got a webcam and Internet calling, which Roger installed on his state-of-the-art computer before they left. There will be no escape from communication! This is both good and bad. It's lovely to talk to Mum, but when I'm tired or not in a great mood it's hard to hide it from her. Conor reckons that Mum calls when it's late in the evenings here to check that we're both safely back at home.

People say how amazing communications are these days, because you can feel as if you're in the same room as someone in Australia. But you don't really feel that way. You keep telling each other news about your lives, but it feels false. Conor is better at it than me. Sometimes I find myself wishing the call was over. At home we never sit down face to face for fifteen minutes with Mum and talk about everything we've done that day. We might wander into the kitchen and chat a bit. Often I prefer just being quiet with people.

Seeing Mum's face on the flat, cold screen of a computer makes it seem as if she has already gone far, far away from us, much farther than the thousands of miles she has travelled physically. She looks different. Her skin is deep brown from being out in the open all day long instead of working in the pub as she does here, and her hair has light streaks in it. It's late spring in Queensland, and Mum says it's much warmer than a Cornish summer. Mum looks more relaxed than I've ever seen her. She and Roger are staying in a little beach house, which someone has lent to them. It's very remote. Mum gets up with the sun and pretty much goes to bed when the sun goes down, except when they light a fire and sit round it. The stars are enormous, she says.

It makes me feel as if Mum isn't the same as the Mum I know. She is meeting a lot of people out there. She knows all Roger's colleagues in the diving project, and their friends. She says Australians are amazingly friendly, and they are always getting asked to parties and barbies. Mum and Roger have already got a whole new Australian life together. It feels very, very weird, as if she might suddenly announce that she likes it so much out there, she's decided to stay for ever.

Get a grip, Sapphire. You chose to stay here. You could have gone with her.

"Don't swim outside the cove," says Conor.

"You sound just like Mum."

"You know what I mean."

I know what Conor really means. Stay where it's safe. Don't go to Ingo without me.

I sit back on my heels. Sadie's warm, questioning brown eyes gaze into mine, wondering what I am planning. A long walk over the Downs, maybe? A rough scramble along the cliff path? Her mind buzzes with a map of a thousand smells – farmyards, rabbit holes, flat stone boulders where adders come out to sun themselves on the warmest autumn afternoons...

"Do snakes have a smell, Sadie?" Sadie barks.

"You can't not take her out now, Saph. Look how excited she is," says Conor.

"All right, Sadie, this is the deal. You and I will walk for one hour max, then you promise not to whine and scrabble at the door and look pathetic when I go to the cove and you can't come."

The way down to the cove is too steep for Sadie. Besides, she would hate it there. Our cove is a gateway. Most human beings wouldn't guess it but dogs can sense what's really going on. Sadie would know straightaway that the smell in her nostrils was the smell of Ingo.

Sadie gives me a wise, impenetrable look. I decide to believe that she's agreeing with me. "Walk, then be good at home," I repeat firmly.

I open the door, cross the garden, lift the latch of the gate and kick it where it sticks. Sadie bounds through. "Wait, girl."

I look up at the sky. It's a perfect October day. You would think it was still summer, except that the sun is lower in the sky and there's a clear, tingling taste in the breeze. A few bronze leaves stir on the rowan tree by our door. I'll swim without my wetsuit today. The sea still has most of the summer's warmth in it.

At that moment there's a slash in the air above my head. Something hurtles past me, raking my hair with its claws. I flinch and throw my hands up to protect my face. The gull squawks loudly as it soars back into the sky.

"Conor! One of those gulls went for me again."

Conor comes to the door and squints up at the roof. A second gull sits squat by the chimney, watching us with its hard yellow eye. The first gull wheels round from its attack, glides back to the cottage roof with one powerful stroke and alights, folding its wings. I brace myself in case it dives again. It gives a mocking screech, but stays up on the roof.

"Every time we go out of the house, they're waiting."

"I know," says Conor.

"I'm worried about Sadie. Mary Thomas's cat had to have ten stitches in its back. It was the worst gash from a gull the vet had ever seen. Do you think a gull would attack a dog as big as Sadie?"

"They're territorial," says Conor.

"Only when they're nesting. They can't be still nesting at this time of year. It's too late."

The gulls shriek, as if they're laughing at us. A third gull circles way above the roof, like a police helicopter over the scene of a crime.

"They never used to settle on the roof like this," Conor says.

"No. It's only since Mum and Roger left." As soon as I've said the words, I want to call them back. The gulls frighten me. They watch the human world, and report back to Ingo. I remember how one of them slashed my hand down by the cove. I thought then that it was one of Ervys's spies.

Conor flaps his arms and shouts at the gulls. "Go on, get out of it!" They squawk back in derision. Sadie barks furiously, but the gulls take no notice of her.

"I'll get the ladder," says Conor. "I'm going to check if there *is* a nest up there."

"No, don't, Conor!" If he's up the ladder and the gulls attack him, he'll have no chance. He'll have to put up his hands to shield his face, and then the gulls will get him off balance. In my head I see Conor slowly toppling backwards. "Mum'll kill me if you fall off the ladder."

The gulls screech again, as if they're imitating me. Slowly, in their own time, they take off from the roof. They wheel above us, mocking our Earth-bound anger with them, and then they take aim at the horizon and fly straight out to sea. They are as sleek as rockets homing in on a target.

"Imagine being able to do that," I say, shading my eyes and squinting after them. "They can go from one world to another whenever they want."

But Conor's not listening. "Saph, look. They *are* building a nest. Look up there, by the chimney."

"But it's the wrong time of year."

31

"They're building it, all the same. I wonder why."

"I don't like them. They patrol that roof like prison guards. Every time we come out or go in, they're watching."

"That's crazy, Saph. They're just birds."

"Sadie! *Sadie!*" I shout. She's gone into the ditch again. It's always full of rich, smelly mud, even when there hasn't been rain for weeks. She's definitely going to need a bath now. "Sadie, you bad girl."

But I'm glad really. Bathing Sadie will stop me thinking about the gulls. I fetch her zinc bath and lay it on the gravel. I fill saucepans with water and put them on the stove to warm while Conor unwinds the hose. Sadie stands watching, quivering with excitement. Sometimes she hates her bath, sometimes she loves it.

Today she's decided to hate it. She keeps trying to escape and she sloshes water all over us. Conor helps to hold her while I wash her with special dog shampoo. She whines piteously, as if we're torturing her.

"Sadie, if you keep on jumping into ditches you'll keep on having to have baths."

"Cause and effect, Sadie girl," says Conor, passing her towel. I rub her hard all over. She likes this part. By the time she emerges from the towel, golden and gleaming, Sadie looks extremely pleased with herself.

"You know you're beautiful, don't you?" I ask her.

"Of course she does," replies Conor.

"She's the most beautiful dog in Cornwall... Hey, Con, we

could take Sadie to a dog show! She'd be sure to win a prize."

Conor raises his eyebrows. "She'd hate it, Saph. Think about it."

I think about it. Lots of poodles with pink ribbons around their necks, mincing past the judges – and Sadie bounding around the ring, chasing imaginary rabbits. Maybe not...

"I *am* going to get that ladder," says Conor. "While the gulls are out of the way it's a good chance."

"Don't, Conor. What if they come back?"

"I don't like the way there are more and more of them all the time," says Conor quietly.

He is right. It was just one gull to begin with, and then two, but sometimes there's a whole row of them standing motionless on the spine of our roof now. They watch everything. They know that Conor and I are alone in our cottage.

"I counted eight yesterday evening," says Conor.

We're not really alone, I tell myself quickly. Granny Carne told Mum she'd watch out for us. Our neighbour Mary Thomas and everyone else in the village "keeps an eye", which can be quite annoying at times. We go to school as normal. But at night we're alone in the cottage.

Don't be so pathetic, Sapphire. You can manage fine. Look at how Rainbow and Patrick cope when their parents are away in Denmark for weeks on end. They just get on with it.

The trouble is that I spent so much time and energy convincing Mum it was safe to leave us, that I forgot about how I might feel once she was gone. As soon as Mum and Roger's taxi had bumped away down the track and I saw one gull watching from the roof, I began to feel uneasy. If Mum had known about Ingo, or the forces that were gathering there, or the battle between Ervys and Saldowr, or any of a hundred things that Conor and I know and have kept from her so carefully, then she would never have left the cottage.

Saldowr said we would see Dad again, when the Mer assembled to choose who would make the Crossing of Ingo. Dad will have his own free choice too, one day – to decide whether to stay in Ingo or return to Air. He'll be able to decide his own future. What if Mum knew that?

It's strange how different it feels now that Mum isn't here. Even Roger's absence changes things. It's as if we are boats which were held safe by an anchor, and we never realised it. Now the anchor has been pulled up and we might drift anywhere. When it gets dark the wind roars around our cottage so loudly that it feels like being in a boat at sea. You can easily believe that you have already left the Earth and are halfway to Ingo. Winter is coming. The dark is growing stronger every day.

"I'm going to see if I can reach that nest. Help me get the ladder out of the shed, Saph."

"You can't destroy their nest, Con! What if there are babies in it?"

"I won't do anything to them. And why would gulls try to lay eggs at this time of year anyway? The chicks wouldn't have a chance of survival."

"What if they come back and attack you?"

What if the gulls are spying for Ervys? is what I want to say, but I keep quiet. Conor will think I'm imagining things as usual. But to my surprise he says what I'm thinking.

"I don't want them spying on us."

"Do you think they *are* spies, Con?" I ask, lowering my voice to a whisper.

"Whatever they are, I don't want them there."

"Don't get the ladder, Con. *Please.*" I've lost Dad – or as good as lost him. Mum's gone to Australia. My brother's got to stay safe.

Conor's expression changes. "Don't panic, Saph. I'm not planning to fall off the roof and break my neck. You hold the bottom of the ladder and it'll be fine."

The ladder is heavy. We drag it across the garden and hoist it against the wall. It's the one Dad used when he painted the outside of our cottage. I remember the last time he did that. The fresh white against the storm-battered old paint.

"Hold it like that, Saph. Lean all your weight against it."

"Be careful, Conor."

He goes up the ladder quickly. Con's used to ladders because his bedroom is up in the loft.

"Can you see anything?" I ask.

There's a pause. Conor is at the top. He hasn't got anything to hold on to now. He braces his feet on the top rung and leans forward, then carefully stretches to his right, towards the chimney.

What if they come back? If they strike at him now, when he's off balance, he'll fall. I turn and scan the horizon. No black dots of gulls. I turn back to Conor. "Is it a nest?" I shout up.

"Yes." His voice sounds strange. He's leaning right across to the chimney. His hand is almost in the dark mass of the nest. He's taking something out of it. Now he's looking at what's in his hand.

Conor freezes. Sadie and I stare upwards in suspense. Slowly Conor's hand closes around whatever he's found. He teeters as if he's forgotten he's at the top of a ladder. For a second I think he's going to lose his balance. At my side, Sadie lets out a volley of warning barks. I turn around and see dark specks on the horizon, growing bigger as I watch. The gulls.

"Conor! Get down quick! The gulls are coming."

Conor scrambles down the ladder one handed. As he jumps to the ground, Sadie leaps around him, barking protectively. The sky is suddenly full of gulls. A cloud of beating wings hides the chimney as they circle the nest, screeching out their anger.

Conor's holding a handful of seaweed. "Is that what the nest is made of?" I ask.

He nods. "It's all woven together."

"But gulls don't make nests like that."

Conor shrugs. He is very pale. He pushes apart the strands of weed and I see a pale, glistening oval, about the size of a fingernail.

"That's not a gull's egg."

"Look at it, Saph."

I look at the egg. It is translucent green. Inside it there is a tiny creature, moving. A creature with fins and a tail. A fish. I shudder.

"The nest was crammed with them," says Conor.

"But if they hatched, they wouldn't be able to breathe in the air."

"I don't know what they are," says Conor. "Touch the shell, Saph."

I put out a finger reluctantly, and prod the egg. It is rubbery. There's liquid inside in which the little fish can swim. I snatch my hand away. There is a ringing sound in my ears. My mouth turns dry.

"Why have they put the eggs on our house?" I whisper to Conor.

"They're just trying to scare us."

"Do you think *he's* behind it? Ervys?"

"Probably."

"What are we going to do with this horrible egg thing?"

"Feed it to Mary Thomas's cat."

I laugh, but my spine crawls with horror as I imagine fish hatching out of the eggs and swarming all over our roof. I know what Ervys is telling us. *You human creatures are coming into my world. I have my powers too. I can make Ingo come to you.* It's happened before. Fish swam in the streets of St Pirans after the Tide Knot broke and the sea flooded the town. Ervys thought that was a great victory for the Mer, in the battle between Ingo and the human world.

The gulls have settled on the roof again, in a long line, watching and waiting.

"What are we really going to do with the egg?" I whisper.

"I don't know. Bury it?"

"No. That's what they expect us to do. Let's give them a surprise, Conor. Let's take the egg down to the sea and release it."

Conor looks at me, eyebrows raised. "You're very peace loving all at once, Saph." But he gives me the egg in its nest of weed. I am just putting it in the watering can so it won't dry out before I can take it down to the cove when there's an explosion of wings and silent, furious, stabbing beaks.

"Sadie!"

We both rush to her, screaming at the gulls. They fly off, climbing steeply into the sky like planes after they've dropped their bombs. Sadie stands silent, quivering all over. On the golden fur of her back there is a long, ugly wound. Her blood wells and spills down her coat.

"Sadie!"

She is too shocked even to bark. I rub her face, calling her name.

"Bastards," says Conor. "Quick, Saph, help me get her into the cottage. I'll call Jack's and ask them to help us get her to the vet. She needs stitches."

It's early evening. Sadie is asleep on the hearth rug. I've lit a fire, and the reflection of flames dances on her coat. The vet has stitched her wound and dressed it, and given Sadie an injection against infection. Conor spent his savings to pay the vet's bill.

Mary Thomas said we'd have to get someone up from the council to do something about those gulls. We just nodded.

Rainbow and Patrick will be here in half an hour. Rainbow is bringing some pasties from St Pirans, because we told her what had happened to Sadie and that we hadn't had a chance to cook.

Conor reaches forward to put another log on the fire. "So are you still going to release that fish back into the sea?" he asks. His voice is harsh.

"Yes," I say.

"You're crazy, Saph. Mary Thomas's cat should have it."

"No," I struggle to explain. "If we act like them – like Ervys – it will never end. There'll be one revenge, and then another, and then another..."

"I get the point. There's another solution, though, Saph. We could walk away."

"What do you mean?"

"We get out of it. Turn our backs on Ingo completely. If you don't feed your Mer blood by thinking of Ingo and going to Ingo, it'll grow weaker. In a few years' time you might not even remember that it's there. You'll look back and believe that Ingo was one of those things you used to be interested in before you grew up."

"How can you say that, Conor? Ingo is real."

"Of course it's real. But it doesn't have to be real *for us*. Look at Sadie. That happened because of us going to Ingo. Do you really want to live like this, Saph?"

"Conor, I can't believe you—"

And at that moment it comes. A low, thrumming sound that is sweet and piercing at the same time. It seems to begin deep in the shell of my ear, as if it's growing from inside me. But it's not just inside me, it's outside me too. It beats the air like a bell, but it's not an Air sound at all. It's salty, full of tides and currents and vast undersea distances. It sounds like the sea beating on the shores of my understanding. It's a summons, an invitation, a command.

Conor hears it too. The log rests in his hand, forgotten. The sound grows until there is nothing else in the room, nothing else in the whole world. Every cell in our body vibrates to it, and now, suddenly, I grasp its meaning. I am hearing the Call. I am being invited to come to the Assembly chamber as a candidate for the Crossing of Ingo. It's what Faro told me about, but I never thought it would feel like this. I glance down at the bracelet of woven hair that is always on my wrist. My hair, twined so close into Faro's that you can't tell where one ends and the other begins. My *deublek* bracelet. Faro's voice comes back to me. *And then, little sister, we will present ourselves to the Assembly, and say that we are ready to make the Crossing of Ingo.*

The Call thunders through us. Faro will hear it too in Ingo. And Elvira. The log falls to the floor as Conor reaches out and grabs my hand. I've never seen Conor look like this. Lit up, like a face with a torch shining on it, except that the light is coming from inside him.

"Saph," he says, "you hear it too, don't you?"

"Yes."

"I was wrong. Everything I said was wrong, Saph. We've got to answer the Call."

CHAPTER THREE

All yesterday evening Conor remained lit up with excitement. I was sure that Rainbow and Patrick would sense the Call thrumming through him, even though they don't know about Ingo. Maybe Rainbow did, in a way. She was very quiet, and she kept glancing at Conor when he wasn't looking, and then away. Rainbow likes Conor; really likes him. Sometimes I wonder what might have happened if Conor had never seen Elvira. Conor almost never talks to me about Elvira, but I know he thinks of her. He keeps her talisman around his neck. But whenever we're with a group of friends it seems that Rainbow and Conor will end up sitting together talking. Conor's face is full of warmth and life when he's with Rainbow. They laugh a lot, but it's not as if the rest of the world has vanished into nothing, as it is when Conor's with Elvira. Rainbow isn't dreamy like Elvira. She's always aware of other people.

It was a good evening, but because of the Call it felt as if Conor and I were on one side of a sheet of glass, and Patrick and Rainbow on the other. I think they felt it too. We chatted about music for a while, and then everyone lapsed into silence. Patrick had brought his guitar, but he didn't play. We built up the fire because it gets cold when evening comes down, and sat around it watching the flames. You know how it is with watching a fire: you don't have to talk. The flames twist and pucker round the logs, never making the same shape twice. It made me think of the fire I saw once, when Granny Carne showed me the passage that runs to the centre of the Earth, from the standing stones. A log hissed and crackled. I suddenly thought, *There's never any fire in Ingo.* It sounds so obvious, but I'd never realised it before. Faro had never sat by a fire and watched the flames and dreamed, and he never would. Faro watches baby fish flicker in rock crevices and dark red sea anemones quivering. He would scorn the idea of fire. *Humans are very strange. Why should anyone want to change the temperature of their world? Why not live in it as it is?* It would be impossible to explain to Faro about shivering with cold on a winter's night. He's never felt anything like that. He's in his element, slipping through it, part of it. Faro would hate this fire.

Conor's eyes were shining with dreams. I saw that Rainbow was watching Conor, not the fire. I couldn't work out her expression. Rainbow is someone who understands much more about you than you ever tell them. Conor felt Rainbow's eyes on his face and he looked up and smiled. Rainbow smiled back. They are so similar, even though Conor is dark and Rainbow has hair the colour of sunlight. They have the same warm-coloured skins. They are responsible in the same way.

"Conor," said Rainbow, "Patrick thinks he can get you a Saturday job at The Green Room, don't you, Pat?"

The Green Room is the surf shop where Patrick works. Everybody wants to work there because they pay over the minimum wage and you have an amazing reduction off all the stuff. Conor leaned forward eagerly. "D'you think you really can, Patrick?"

Patrick nodded. He is a person of few words. Then I saw Conor remember, and the eagerness faded from his face. The sound of the conch thrummed in my head and I knew that Conor heard it too. It drowned out everything.

"I'll call in one day," said Conor awkwardly, and I saw the surprise and disappointment on Rainbow's face. She'd expected him to seize the chance of the job. But I couldn't think about Rainbow too much, because my mind was full of Ingo. The flames of the fire made shapes like waves. I listened and I could hear the swell beating against the base of the cliffs. The tide was high, almost at the turn. Ingo was coming close. I saw Rainbow shiver.

"The sea's loud tonight," she said.

"You always hear it like that up here," said Conor quickly. "It must be the way the wind blows."

"It never sounds as loud as this in our cottage," said Rainbow.

"And we're closer to the water than you are," said Patrick. "The tide comes almost to the door. Or *through* the door sometimes." He was thinking of the flood and the way their cottage filled with sea.

"It won't come like that again," said Conor. He threw another log on the fire and the sparks shot upward. Rainbow leaned forward, holding out her hands to the flames.

"I love fires," she said.

I know, I thought. *You love fires and horses and dogs, and everything that belongs to Earth. You've never heard Ingo calling and you never will. You're not half one thing and half another. You're all Earth, like Granny Carne. You don't have to choose because the choice has already been made in you.*

The sea boomed against the cliff. I felt it ebb, then surge forward and smash on the rocks. Rainbow was right. Ingo was very close tonight. Faro was there somewhere in that deep wild water, and my father, and my baby half-brother, little Mordowrgi, and all the others. Soon I would be there too, and Conor. Excitement raced through me like an incoming tide.

But this morning everything is flat and gloomy. The rain is coming down in a thin, steady drizzle. The hilltops are hidden in mist. The only thing that is sharp and clear is the impossibility of our dreams.

How can I leave Sadie? She trusts me and believes that I'll always be here to take care of her. I think of Sadie padding up and down, whining, sniffing the air, scratching at the door, waiting for me. I can't abandon Sadie. Besides, there's Mum. She'll call us, as she does every day, and we won't be here. She'll call again and again, and still we won't answer. How much human time does it take to make the Crossing of Ingo? Mum will panic and get on the next plane back from Australia.

We have to think about school as well. They'll notice our

absence, and Mum has given them contact details for everyone who is supposed to be responsible for us while she's away. In practice that means they will contact Mary Thomas, because Granny Carne has no phone. Mary will come over and find an empty house. In less than an hour the entire village will be searching for us. They'll remember Dad's disappearance. They'll whisper, *"God forbid it's another Trewhella lost to the sea."* They'll scour the cliffs and coves and all the deserted places where we might have fallen or become trapped. In my mind I see the searchers moving steadily forward, beating at the furze on the cliff tops. I see divers with waterproof torches scanning the backs of caves. They'll risk their lives to find us. We can't let them do that.

Even if we managed to fix school, it's impossible to fix the whole neighbourhood. If you cough at one end of the churchtown, someone the other end will ask if you have a cold.

But we *must* go. We have no choice. I can't hear the Call any more but the memory of it is twined into every fibre of me. It won't let me alone. You only hear that Call once in your life; if you ignore it, it won't come again. Faro will turn his back on me. He'll rip off the bracelet he made from our hair, and he'll never call me "little sister" again. Dad will be at the Assembly. It's our chance to see him again.

Ingo needs us to make the Crossing. We are mixed in our blood, Mer and human. Ervys hates us for it: he wants nothing human in Ingo. I used to hate it too because I wanted to be one thing only, instead of being torn two ways. But now I'm beginning to understand that to be double adds things to you as well as taking them away. I've been to Ingo so many times and there's still so much I don't know. I will never know Ingo truly unless I make the Crossing. Saldowr believes that the Mer world and the human world can come together, and stop fearing each other and trying to destroy each other. If human blood can make the Crossing of Ingo then maybe there is hope for a different future, where we're not all battling for what we want and trying to destroy what is different from us.

Ervys will do anything to stop us. He wants Mer and human to remain apart. Fear and distrust is what drives his followers, and gives him his power.

I've got to go, but I can't... I must go, but how can I...?

By ten o'clock this morning my head felt like a hive of swarming bees, full of thoughts that couldn't live together. I was so desperate for distraction that I even dug one of my school set books out of my bag. Now I'm sitting at the kitchen table, trying to read *Pride and Prejudice*. The words dance and dive. If only Jane and Lizzie realised how lucky they were. All they had to worry about were their embarrassing parents and the embarrassing men who kept trying to marry them. They were never going to go to Ingo in their shawls and long dresses and elaborately curled hair...

Sadie is under the table, asleep. She's been trying to hide under things ever since she got back from the vet's. I keep telling her, "You're safe now, Sadie girl. No gull will ever come into our cottage." I wrap my arms around her neck and kiss her cold black nose, but she looks at me with scared eyes and I see she doesn't really believe it. Even in her sleep, Sadie twitches and whimpers. She's dreaming of gulls with cold yellow eyes and beaks that stab at her flesh. I'll never let it happen again. I'll throw myself on top of her so that they can't get to her.

Conor has gone back to bed. In his view sleep is the best thing to do with a rainy day like this. I tried to talk to him about the Call but he was grumpy and monosyllabic – "Yeah, all right, Saph, we'll work it out" – and then he dived back under the duvet. I've got to wake him up at one o'clock because we're due at Jack's house for Sunday dinner at one thirty.

When the knock comes at the door, I shout, "Come in, it's open," and quickly shove a heap of ironing off the table into the laundry basket. Some of our neighbours are all too curious about "How those two younguns are coping with their mum off in Australia". They come round with a pie or a bunch of onions and their eyes dart round the kitchen, checking every heap of unwashed mugs.

It's Granny Carne. Her old brown coat is dark with rain. She takes off her boots at the door and steps inside. Fortunately she has no interest in dirty crockery or unswept floors.

"Those gulls are thicker'n ever on your roof, my girl."

"I know. Do you want a cup of tea?"

"Cup of tea would be good." Her eyes burn on my back as I fill the kettle. "You want to do something about them," she says.

"Yes," I reply.

"I hear they hurt your Sadie."

"We took her to the vet. She had to have stitches, but she's

OK now, except she's been asleep most of the time since. She doesn't want to come out from under the table."

Granny Carne bends down and whistles softly. Immediately Sadie stirs. Shaking her head as if to shake away a bad dream, she creeps out from her shelter and rubs against Granny Carne's long skirt. Sadie trusts Granny Carne more than anyone except me, ever since she almost died and Granny Carne healed her.

"She's not looking so good, spite of what the vet's done for her," observes Granny Carne. A pang of dread goes through me.

"She's all right. The vet said she was."

"All right, is she?" asks Granny Carne. I look at Sadie. Her tail is down. She's huddling against Granny Carne as if she wants to make herself disappear.

"She's still scared that the gulls will get her," I say.

"With reason good," answers Granny Carne. "A dog can't stay in a house all day long, cowering under a table. It's not in her nature." She bends down and strokes Sadie with a strong, reassuring hand. "It's not in her nature, what's going on here. You let me take Sadie, my girl."

"*Take Sadie!*"

"You let her come up to my cottage where she'll be safe. There's no shadow of a gull there." Granny Carne looks up, straight at me, hard and clear.

"But... but I look after her. I won't let anything hurt her."

Granny Carne glances down at Sadie's back. She doesn't say anything about the injury. She doesn't need to. "Listen, Sapphire.

Nothing of Ingo is going to come close to where I am. Sadie can walk on the Downs with me and be free. Those gulls lifted off your roof the moment they saw me put my foot to your threshold. But once I'm gone, they'll be back, and more of them each day. You want your dog to be frightened out of her life? You give Sadie to me and no harm will come near her."

Sadie is watching Granny Carne's face very closely, following the conversation. She whines deep in her throat, as if agreeing.

"But I can't. She'll miss me too much." *I'll miss her too much*, is what I don't say. "Sadie needs me."

"How will you look after Sadie where you're going?" asks Granny Carne. Her face is stern, intent. There is no point trying to pretend I don't know what she means.

"How do you know?"

"You've been called to make that Crossing. You remember I told you once, my girl, neither hell nor high water would stop you once your heard that Call. And your brother too. Look at your face. Look at those gulls gathering. There's some in Ingo don't want you to make it, seemingly."

"But we can't go. Sadie – Mum—" Suddenly the reality of it hits me as hard as a blow. I am only going to hear that Call once in my life. If I don't go, I'll feel as if something has reached inside me and ripped my spirit down the middle like a piece of paper.

"Some things, if you don't do them, they follow you all your life, whispering in your ear," says Granny Carne. She faces me sternly as if she's judging me. "You'll find a dozen good reasons why you pulled back from the Call, and you'll even fool yourself that you had no other choice. But in your bed at night you'll curse yourself for a coward."

I stare at her in astonishment. Why isn't Granny Carne trying to keep me here, as she's always tried before? It feels like a cold wind whistling through me. Granny Carne isn't going to stop us. The choice is completely ours.

I hear the creak of Conor's loft ladder. He's heard voices and he's coming down to see who is here. The door opens and he ambles into the room, yawning and wrapped up in his duvet as usual.

"Granny Carne." A slow, warm smile spreads over Conor's face.

"Yes. I've been talking to your Sapphire. The two of you are going out into the world, seemingly." Conor shoots me an accusing look.

"I didn't tell her. She knew," I say quickly. "But, Con, I can't see how we're going to do it. There's Sadie, and Mum, and everyone else. They'll think we've – we've disappeared."

"Like Dad," says Conor. He frowns, thinking. Conor is logical. He always looks to find a path to a solution. Usually it works, but this time logic isn't going to help. Granny Carne isn't going to help either. She stands there, watching, waiting.

"There'll be more than those gulls wanting to stop you," she observes.

"I know," says Conor.

"I've no rowan berries for your protection this time. You'll have to go alone."

Without meaning to, I glance down at the bracelet on my wrist. My *deublek*. Granny Carne's gaze follows mine. "Earth can't help you in the Crossing."

"We're not helpless," says Conor hotly.

"I know that, my boy." Granny Carne's ancient, hardened face remains impassive, but her eyes soften as she looks at Conor. "I can't give you anything. No berries, no touch of fire. There's no Earth magic where you're going, only what's inside yourselves." She pauses. Her owl eyes are lit up now, fierce and bright. "But never forget how strong that is. Come here, give me your hands." She takes Conor's outstretched hands and presses his thumbs together. "Think of what's strongest for you here on Earth," she whispers. "Let it come to you. Don't force your thoughts now."

Conor closes his eyes. I look away. I feel as if I shouldn't spy into his thoughts. There is a long silence, then Conor opens his eyes again. He looks surprised, as if what came into his mind wasn't what he'd expected.

"Now you, Sapphire." My thumbs touch. It feels like a connection being made. "Think of what's strongest for you here on Earth," she says. "Let it come to you."

I don't even have to think. Sadie leaps into my mind, bounding down the track towards me. Her eyes glow, and her golden coat shines in the sun. I hear her bark. My thumbs feel as if they have fused, like legs into a tail.

"If you forget Earth, touch your thumbs together like this and press. Sure enough it'll come back. Wherever you are, however deep in Ingo you travel, you can't lose what's deep inside you," says Granny Carne.

The pressure is released. I let my hands drop to my sides. The Sadie in my head vanishes. The real Sadie is watching me with scared, questioning eyes.

"I'll take your Sadie with me now," says Granny Carne. "Best I do that. As for your mother, you'll find a way. A Call with as much power over the pair of you as that, it'll make its own path through your lives. You and Conor have good brains between you. I won't wait for that tea now, my girl, I'll be on my way."

"But, Granny Carne..." I can't believe she's just going to go like that. I'd expected her to stand in our way, as she did in the lane long ago when she stood between me and Ingo and wouldn't let me go. But now she's stepping aside.

Granny Carne has her hand on Sadie's collar, steadying her. Objections whirl in my head. I've got to stop her going – why won't Conor stop her?

"But what about Sadie's food bowl – her food – and there's her lead—"

"Sadie and I can manage. Say your goodbyes, Sapphire."

I kneel down at Sadie's side. There is a shaved place in her coat where the vet put in the stitches. The gash went deep. The vet said he'd never seen a wound from a gull as bad as that. There is still a faint smell of antiseptic. I don't ever, ever want Sadie to be hurt like that again. What if the gulls had gone for her eyes?

"You'll be safe with Granny Carne, won't you?" I whisper.

Sadie's beautiful shining golden coat is a blur. I swallow. I don't put my arms around her body in case I touch her wound. Instead I rub my face against her soft, cold nose. "Goodbye, Sadie darling," I say, keeping my voice as steady as I can. "You'll be fine. Granny Carne will look after you. Be good now."

Sadie doesn't make a sound. She pushes her nose into my cheek. She knows what's happening. I feel terrible. It would be better if she protested.

"I love you, Sadie," I whisper. "Don't forget."

I stand up again. I want Granny Carne to take Sadie away now, quickly, before I have time to think about it. Granny Carne seems to understand. She moves to the door and opens it. "There's no gulls now," she reassures Sadie. She bends down and slips her hand though Sadie's collar reassuringly, then says over her shoulder to Conor, "Your mother has a second cousin somewhere upcountry, Plymouth way. Could be it's time for you and Sapphire to pay a visit there, with your half term holiday coming. Anyone in the village who asks, that's where I'll tell them you are."

One moment an old woman is looking at us over her shoulder, the next moment her outline blurs and trembles. I see a young, strong woman with ropes of gleaming earth-coloured hair. The outline shimmers and vanishes. I see an owl with fierce, unblinking eyes. Its wings are spread, ready to fly off into the dark. The owl fades. Only its eyes remain, deep in Granny Carne's weather-beaten face.

The wind blows. The door bangs. Granny Carne is gone.

At first the day went on quite normally. We went up to Jack's, and his mum made one of her classic dinners with roast beef, Yorkshire puddings and what she calls roast-pan gravy. Jack's dad talked endlessly about whether he would get a government grant for re-laying a stretch of Cornish hedge. Jack kept trying to change the subject. He thinks his dad is extremely boring most of the time, but I didn't mind. Hedging is as good to talk about as anything when there's a storm raging in your mind.

We're back at the cottage now, and it's almost ten o' clock, the time when Mum usually calls on a Sunday. But it's not Sunday for her, it's already Monday morning. While we are still enjoying the last hours of the weekend, Mum is in a world that's going back to work.

Mum's face comes on screen. Her hair is pulled back into a ponytail. She's wearing a dark red T-shirt and she looks tanned and cheerful, but apprehensive too.

"I've got some news for you guys." *You guys*. Mum sounds more like Roger each day. She pauses. We can see her taking a deep, steadying breath. "We've got the chance to take a big trip north, up the coast. It's a mate of Roger's who runs these trips into the bush. He's offered us a freebie if we go as chief cook and bottle washer to the paying customers."

"Bottle washer?" I ask.

"Doing all the stuff tourists don't want to do for themselves," says Mum succinctly. "It's for two weeks, though, and we'll be way out of contact. We won't have access to a phone and anyway there's no signal up there. How would you feel about not getting calls for a while? Listen, you can be straight with me about this, Sapphy. Nothing's fixed yet. I won't go if you're not happy about it—"

"Of course you've got to go," says Conor immediately. I know my brother well enough to be sure that he's not even thinking about how brilliantly this all fits in with our plans. Mum and Roger not calling us for two whole weeks! Nothing could be more convenient. Conor goes on, "It's the chance of a lifetime, Mum. A trip like that would cost a fortune if you had to pay for it. You have to go."

"You'd love it out here, Conor. Next time you two are definitely coming with us."

Next time? What is going on? Mum sounds so full of life, as if Australia has turned on a switch in her which has been off for years. Since Dad went, maybe. *No, be honest, Sapphire. Mum wasn't like this even when Dad was at home.* She's changed. She's stronger, bolder, more alive somehow. I'm not sure that I want her to change too much more – I don't want Mum to become someone I don't even recognise...

I lean forward and open my mouth, but as I do Conor grabs hold of my wrist under the table, out of sight of the webcam. He squeezes tight, warningly. "Two weeks is nothing. We'll be fine, won't we, Saph?"

"Ye-yes."

"Are you sure?" asks Mum eagerly. She really wants to make this trip, but she's worried too. The deal was that she would see us and speak to us every day unless it was completely unavoidable. In a minute another switch will turn on inside Mum: the guilt switch.

A Call with as much power over the pair of you as that, it'll make its own path through your lives.

It's happening this minute through the Internet as Mum waits for our answer. The Call is making a path for us. Mum's eyes search my face.

"Of course we're sure," says Conor. "Everything's fine here. No problem."

"Except that Conor needs to learn where the washing machine is," I say. Mum's face relaxes.

"As long as you're both well and happy."

"We had Rainbow and Patrick round last night," says Conor with apparent casualness. Mum looks even happier. She likes Rainbow and Patrick more than any of our friends. She senses that Rainbow is like her, that's what I think. Someone who will anchor us to Earth. And Patrick's ambition to become a doctor is exactly the ambition Mum would love me to have. I'm sorry, Mum, but it's never going to happen.

A big trip north, into the bush... Poisonous spiders, king cobras, crocodiles... "Be careful up there, Mum. Crocodiles are really cunning. They use their tails as levers to spring out of the water and get you. If a croc chases you, you have to run in zigzags because that confuses them. And there's loads of snakes in the bush too. You can't walk around in flip-flops."

Mum is laughing. "Is this my daughter talking, or is it my mum?"

"I'm serious, Mum."

"I'm sorry, Sapphy, I didn't mean to laugh at you."

Mum seems so real that I feel I could put my hand through the screen and touch her face. But I can't, and in a minute her screen image will disappear. People get lost in the bush. They die because there's no water. I take a deep breath. Mum will be with Roger, who probably knows how to dig a bore hole if need be, and kill a fighting cobra with one karate chop. Mum will be fine. What a role reversal. Mum spends her life worrying about us, and now I'm panicking about her.

"We'll be completely safe," says Mum earnestly. "Roger's mate knows the bush. He wouldn't take tourists anywhere dangerous."

But Mum knows, as I do, that nowhere in the world is ever completely safe. Your life can change in the blink of an eye, on a calm and beautiful Midsummer night. You lose what you love while you think it is still safe beside you.

"I know, Mum," I say. "You'll have a great time."

Mum smiles back, reassuring and reassured. "I know I can trust you two – to take care of everything," she says, looking at Conor. He looks straight back.

"I'll look after Saph, Mum, don't worry."

"And I'll look after Conor's underpants."

"Is Sadie all right?" asks Mum quickly.

"She's fine." I nearly add, *She's just in the kitchen,* but pull myself back. First rule of deception: *Never lie when you don't have to.*

"I'm so glad you've got Sadie. A dog in the house is good protection."

"For God's sake, Mum," says Conor, "you sound like the mum in that film of Peter Pan." I nearly laugh, thinking of Sadie padding round the house like Nana, pulling us back from Ingo by the seat of our pyjamas. I know why Conor sounds sharp. Guilt. He's not exactly lying to Mum, but he's certainly misleading her. Mum, however, doesn't realise any of this. She thinks that Conor's just cracking a joke, and she laughs with her new Australian lightheartedness.

"Don't go flying out of any windows," she says.

"We won't," I say, looking Mum in the eye. Just for a second I feel a surge of guilt, as if I'm the parent lying to her child for its own good, so that the child won't be afraid. The mark of the Call must be blazing across my face. Doesn't Mum see? Can't she guess?

But no. Mum notices nothing, and we say goodbye.

CHAPTER FOUR

Conor lifts the globe from its place at the back of our living room's deep windowsill. He pushes it with one finger so the globe turns a slow circle on its stand. The land is dark brown, with the names of countries written in close, spidery writing. The oceans must have been deep blue once but they have faded and now they are a pale blue-brown. *The Indian Ocean... The Northwest Passage...*

I used to trace the names with my finger when I first learned to read. They were the oceans Dad used to talk about when he said, "One day, Sapphy, I'll take you to see the world. We'll cross the five oceans. North Atlantic, South Atlantic, the Indian Ocean, South Pacific, maybe even the Southern Ocean. Or we might go north, way up here through the North Pacific until we come to the Arctic Ocean."

"But that's not five oceans, Dad, that's seven."

"Ah well, the North and South Pacifics really only count as one, same with the Atlantics."

If Mum was there she'd frown with annoyance. "Filling the child's head with crazy ideas, getting her excited about things that will never happen. Why do you do it, Mathew?"

"Who's to say what will happen and what won't?" Dad would murmur, touching the globe again to make it spin.

I believed every word he said. The oceans seemed to belong to me already. I imagined Dad and me in the *Peggy Gordon*, cutting through the brilliant waves of the Southern Ocean. We'd discover a rake of tiny islands scattered across the water like stars in a deep blue sky. We would catch fish to eat and when our jerry cans were empty we'd steer for a green island to fill them up with fresh water from a little bubbling spring. We would pull the *Peggy Gordon* up on a beach at evening and maybe curious people would come down to talk to us. We'd eat and drink with them, and Dad would trade songs with the island singers...

Conor traces a line between Cornwall and the huge continent of Australia. His finger travels around the western bulge of Africa, past the Cape and eastwards across the Indian Ocean. How easy the journey looks when you've only got to turn a globe. To the bottom of the world and home again in a few seconds. But it won't be like that for us.

"It's so far," I say.

"I know," replies Conor.

"It's quite – quite scary, isn't it?"

"Yeah. You know that time I went climbing on the cliffs with Jack up by Godrevy, near Hell's Mouth? I never told you what happened. We got stuck. Couldn't go back, couldn't go on without kind of jumping and throwing ourselves on to the next handhold. The sea was boiling down below."

"You should have told me," I say.

"Yeah, well, I didn't want to scare you. In the end we had to do the jump. Jack was in front of me so he went first and I had to watch him. Worst moment of my life. Well, nearly the worst."

"But he didn't fall."

"Course he didn't, idiot. He's still alive, isn't he? After that bit, it was easy."

"So once we set out it'll be easier."

"Maybe."

Later, when Conor has gone up to the farm for the eggs, I go to the chest where Dad stored his prints and negatives. The chest has six long, shallow drawers which glide in or out at the touch of a finger. I go to the fifth drawer down and slide it open.

I haven't looked in this drawer since Dad went away. Nothing's changed. Dad's drawers were always kept ship-shape. I slide my hand to the very back, and my fingers touch a familiar, fragile roll of parchment. It just fits the shallow drawer.

I take out Dad's map. I don't know why I call it "Dad's map" really because he always called it "the Trewhella map" or "our map". But I associate it with him because we spent so many hours together poring over it. It's very old. A length of faded black tape ties the rolled-up map. The parchment is yellow brown and stained. I used to think the brown stains were blood, but Dad said they were just where sea water had darkened the parchment. *This map has travelled the oceans, Sapphy. It's been in our family for hundreds of years.*

We can't display the map on a wall because it has to be kept away from the light, which would quickly fade the outlines and the writing. Besides, Dad always said such a map is a private thing. You don't want outsiders to ask questions, or tell you that it ought rightly to be in a museum. *This map was made by Trewhellas, Sapphy. It's to be kept with the Trewhellas.*

I untie the black tape. I know what's inside so well that I wait for a moment, not unrolling the map but letting every detail of it rise to my mind. It's a map of the world, but not like any you could buy now. At each pole there is a vast prowling mass of icy land. In the centre of the Arctic mass a jagged black rock rises sharply from the whiteness. It is marked *The North Pole.* Our map was drawn at the time when people thought there was solid land at the North Pole, not a mass of frozen sea.

Australia doesn't appear on the map at all. Where it should be, there's a sheet of empty ocean. The shape of South America is wrong, much shorter and wider than it really is. California is an island. The British Isles are drawn out of proportion, and there are beautiful tiny drawings of sailing ships making way out of London and Bristol. The European part of the map is detailed and complete with rivers and mountain ranges, but the northwest of America and the east of Russia and China are vast unmarked territories, enclosed by uncertain lines. It looks as if the mapmaker was guessing at the boundaries.

When I first saw the map I didn't question it. It was Dad's map, so it must be correct. I even told my teacher that the world map on our classroom wall was wrong, but he said that mapmakers these days had satellite photographs to make their maps absolutely accurate. The next time Dad let me look at his map I felt as if it had tricked me. I said, "Dad, they've got it wrong on your map. Africa doesn't go like that. And look, they haven't even put Australia and New Zealand in."

Dad said, "Those men who risked their lives to make this map weren't stupid, Sapphy. This is their world. They drew what they knew."

"But they've put sea dragons in the ocean. And look, there's a man spouting water and blowing on a seashell."

"That's Neptune, Sapphy. God of the sea."

"But maps ought to show real things. There aren't any real dragons." I was at the age when you're proud of knowing that there are no such things as dragons and fairies.

Dad said, "Maybe there were dragons then. Don't make the mistake of thinking that your ancestors knew less than you do, Sapphy."

"The map's wrong, though. We've got satellite pictures nowadays. We know what the Earth really looks like."

Dad laughed scornfully. "You don't learn what the world is like by looking at a picture that's been sent from a piece of metal and plastic orbiting miles above the Earth's atmosphere. Think of all the salt seas they fought across to make our map, and all the storms they weathered in a wooden ship that you wouldn't believe could sail as far as France."

The map is old and very fragile. Even the careless touch of a human hand can damage it, Dad used to say. Carefully, as he taught me, I unroll it and spread it out on the table. A piece of paper falls out. Not old parchment like the map. Twenty-first century paper, folded. My heart jumps with excitement. All at once I'm certain that this is a message, hidden by Dad for me to find. I was always the one who wanted to see the map, not Conor. I pick up the paper and unfold it, my fingers trembling. But there's nothing to be excited about. Just a few scribbled figures.

22 30 7 6
23 00 9 6
23 15 15 6
23 30 19 6

It's Dad's handwriting. The sight of it hurts me. I don't want to think about Dad's hand picking up the pen and writing these figures. It must have been important or he wouldn't have bothered to put the paper inside the map. I look at the figures again, trying to add them up and guess their meaning. They refuse to give up their secret.

I turn back to the map, and weigh down its corners with the smooth pebbles Dad always used for the purpose. Automatically my gaze goes to the place where we live. The coast of Cornwall is beautifully drawn by someone who knows every cove. The mapmaker has made Cornwall look a lot bigger than it really is in proportion to the rest of the British Isles. Dad said there was a reason for that too. *If you're making a map, you might make more of something that's important to you.*

As I bend closer I see something I am sure I've never seen before. In the blue-brown waters off the west coast of Cornwall there is a new word, written in tiny, exquisite writing. It looks exactly like the handwriting on the rest of the map, but the ink is new. Not faded brown, but sharp and black.

Ingo

Ingo. A shiver runs over my skin. I seem to hear the wash of the waves in the coils of my ears. No one else can have written that word except Dad, before he left us. I scan the map again. Yes, there is something else that wasn't there before. How could I have missed it? In the corner of the map, where the known dissolves into the unknown, there is a small figure. Dad always drew well. This is one of his best drawings. It shows a Mer woman. Not a mermaid with long golden hair, a scaly fish tail and a comb in her hand, but a Mer woman like those I've seen in Ingo. She has long dark hair and a strong seal tail.

When Dad drew this he couldn't have known that Conor or I would ever find our way to Ingo. It was a clue, maybe, left for anyone who was capable of understanding it. Just one word, Ingo, and one figure. If this map went to a museum they would say that the Mer woman was a mythological figure. Someone would pore over the word Ingo, and maybe decide that it was a local name for one of the reefs.

But this map is never going to a museum. It is private and it belongs to the Trewhellas, because we are the only ones who truly understand it.

I look around for the pot where Dad kept his best pen. No one has touched it since he went. Mum took all Dad's clothes to the charity shop in St Pirans, and she sold his camera and the digital printer he used for his work. But she kept the personal things for me and for Conor.

I take out the pen and unscrew the cap. The pen has a fine nib which is good for drawing. I bring pen to paper, and hesitate. It feels like sacrilege. I am breaking a rule that has been drummed into me since I was first allowed to see the map. But as the first line flows it feels entirely right. I am meant to be doing this. I am a Trewhella and this map is for the Trewhellas, to show us what the world is like.

Close to the word Ingo I draw four tiny figures. They are as small as I can make them without losing definition. Two are Mer and two are human. The Mer figures have strong seal tails and flowing dark hair. The girl wears a bodice of woven sea grass. The human figures are dark-haired too. They could be cousins to the Mer figures, except that they have legs instead of tails.

I understand now what Dad was trying to tell me about the mapmaker who made it. This map is about a person's experience of the world, not about what a camera sees as it blinks in space.

I finish my drawing. The piece of paper with Dad's writing on it is still lying open. I glance at it again, casually, wondering if it's worth putting it back into the map before I roll it up. My glance sweeps over the numbers, and suddenly I realise that they are not part of a calculation. It was the layout that confused me. If Dad had put in the dots, I would have seen their meaning immediately.

22.30 7.6

23.00 9.6

23.15 15.6

23.30 19.6

They are times and dates. Half past ten in the evening on the seventh of June. Eleven o'clock on the ninth of June. Quarter past eleven on the fifteenth of June. Half past eleven on the nineteenth of June. Dates and times which were so important to Dad that he must have noted them at the time. So important that he hid the paper inside the map. He didn't think anyone else would ever guess what they meant, but I know. I know which June it was. It was the month that Dad disappeared.

These must be the times and the dates when he heard Mellina singing. It was Dad who wrote the word Ingo on the map because even then he knew – or suspected – what Ingo was. My heart beats faster. Maybe these weren't just the times that he heard Mellina sing. They might have been times when he went down to the cove, and met her, and fell so deep in love with her that he knew he would abandon everything for her.

I am not sure why he left a record of these times. Perhaps it was a clue for whichever Trewhella might come to read it one day.

My eyes sting. I so wish I could go back in time. If only I could come in and find Dad while he was writing those figures. He must have felt completely alone. Ingo was pulling him, the way the Call is pulling us, and he couldn't tell any of us about it. All he could do was leave a message almost in code, and hope that maybe one day somebody would understand.

I roll up the map very carefully with Dad's piece of paper inside it, exactly as it was. I wrap the faded tape around the parchment, and tie it so that the bow won't loosen even if it has to wait for years before it is undone. I slide the scroll to the back of the drawer at the left hand side, where it fits perfectly.

I've left my own message now for whoever comes after me. I wonder if one day in the future some girl who looks a little like me will unroll the map and look at those four little figures, and understand what they mean.

CHAPTER FIVE

"Watch out, Conor, I'm going to throw it."

"You're crazy," grumbles Conor. "I told you, you should have given it to the cat."

I take a small plastic bag out of my pocket, and shake out the bed of weed which is wrapped around the fish egg. The little fish is still alive, swimming inside its rubbery membrane. I shudder, draw my arm back and throw egg and weed as far away from us as I can into the waves.

Sea water swirls around my legs, almost knocking me off balance. I grab Conor's arm and we stand together, waiting, watching the horizon. The Call is alive in both of us. It's like music rising at the start of a crescendo, but it hasn't got there yet. We are waiting for Faro.

The sky is dark today. The wind chops off the white crests of the waves. Even inside our cove, where the water is protected by a curve of cliff and by the rocks that guard the entrance, the sea is wild.

A wave sucks back, tugging at us, wanting to pull us with it. We manage to stay upright, but we have to fight for balance.

"There he is!" shouts Conor.

Faro's head shows through the wave crests and then vanishes again. Next time he rises he is only fifty metres from shore. He waves, and we plunge forward. I dive through the first wave and then the next, cutting through the water with Conor beside me. We are not in Ingo yet, but the water feels like home.

We reach Faro. His head is above the surface and he is breathing air. He is pale and his face, like the sea, is stormy. I wonder if the air is hurting him. I thought it was growing easier for Faro to make the transition.

"Are you all right, Faro?" I ask.

"I was pursued," says Faro, and anger blazes in his eyes. "Look." He flips over so that we can see his tail. There is a gash in it at the base. "I am losing blood," says Faro. "I have called my sister but she is with a child who was thrown against the rocks by a rogue current. She will come when she can."

"Faro! It looks deep," I say.

"It is deep. It was intended to be deep. Mortarow pursued me. The sea bull has gored me."

"He did this to you?" demands Conor, and a fury equal to Faro's flares in his face.

"Ervys's followers have taken up arms," says Faro. There is deep anger in his voice as he shakes back his hair defiantly. "He has taught the Mer to arm themselves against their brothers and sisters. He has defied the law of the Mer. Saldowr shall hear of this."

"Faro, can you climb up on to a rock?" I ask him. "We aren't healers like Elvira but if we press hard on the wound that might stop it bleeding."

"It will weaken me more to leave the water. I came to tell you that in two nights we will answer the Call. But Ervys's followers are waiting for us. They will pack the Assembly chamber if they can. They will try to turn the Mer against us so that we are not chosen to make the Crossing. They fear what will happen if we succeed. They don't want peace: they want war, and victory."

"What time? When shall we come?"

"Be here when the moon rises. I will come for you. You will know when the time is right, because the Call will grow so strong in you that you hear nothing else. This is what I have been told by those who have made the Crossing. I will be here for you."

"But you're badly hurt, Faro!" I stare through the water and see a cloud of blood around Faro's tail. "Will you be strong enough?"

"Strong enough!" says Faro, looking at me as if I am Mortarow trying to stop him. Then his face softens. "Are you wearing our bracelet, little sister?"

"Of course." I lift my arm to show him. "Faro, what kind of weapons have they got – Ervys and his followers?"

"They have taken up spears fashioned from the wood they find in drowned ships, and from sharpened stones and coral."

I look anxiously at Faro's tail. I know that people often get blood poisoning from coral wounds. "Was Mortarow's spear tipped with coral, Faro?"

Faro turns aside and spits into the water. "Mortarow has taken human metal to tip his spear. He has been rummaging deep in the belly of a wreck and has found human weapons." He spits again. "And our sea bull says that he is upholding the pure traditions of the Mer." He's very pale. Anger gives him energy, but he needs Elvira's help, and quickly.

"Go, Faro, you've got to hurry. Are you strong enough? Shall we come with you to find Elvira?"

Faro shakes his head. "In two nights I shall be here for you." He turns. There are no dazzling somersaults this time, or glittering plunges into deep water. Faro dips his head beneath the surface and swims down, down into Ingo until he is lost to sight.

"We shouldn't have let him go, Conor. That wound was deep."

"He'll be all right, once he gets to Elvira." Conor turns and wades back to shore. I catch up with him. "Only two nights to wait," he says.

"Yes."

Conor glances at me, his face sombre and thoughtful. "Aren't you afraid, Saph?" he asks.

"Of Mortarow, you mean? But Saldowr wouldn't let him hurt us... would he?"

"Mortarow has just struck at Faro, Saph. He knows that's the same as striking at Saldowr himself. They've lost their fear of what Saldowr can do to them. Listen Saph. Do you really still want to make the Crossing?"

I stop dead in the shallow water, grabbing Conor's arm to

make him stop too. "How can you say that?"

"I'm not even sure that I should let you go."

"*Let me go!* Conor, you're my brother but you're not my keeper. Don't you understand? I've got no choice. I've got to go."

Conor sighs. "I keep thinking what Mum would say if she knew."

"You can't think like that."

"You're my sister, Saph. My real sister."

I know this is a dig at Faro. Conor doesn't like it when Faro calls me *little sister.* "I know," I say, "but I still have to go. And so do you, don't you? You heard the Call." Conor nods. "Ingo needs us," I go on.

"You don't have to tell me that, Saph. I've seen what Ervys can do. We've got to stop him. I just wish I could go alone. Being afraid for another person is much worse than being afraid for yourself."

I shiver. "I'm so cold, Conor. Let's get home quick."

As we climb up the rocks I look back. The cove is filling. The tide's coming in. A wild tide, full of anger. Next time we come here the moon will be rising. We'll walk into the water and our journey will begin.

Rainbow is at the cottage. She has tethered Kylie Newton's pony Treacle to the gatepost and he is munching placidly at a clump of grass. I glance up at the roof. The gulls attacked Sadie; they might go for Treacle too. Every hour of the day they are there now, watching. Sometimes they change guard as one posse flies out to sea and another flies inland to perch along the ridge of our roof. I wonder what else they have got in their nest now. As if it feels my thoughts, one of the gulls stretches out its neck and screams down derision.

I could have given your stupid egg to the cat, but I didn't. You should be grateful, I tell them in my mind, but I don't think the gulls can read my thoughts.

"They can't be nesting at this time of year," says Rainbow, puzzled. The biggest gull is staring at her and Treacle with its yellow eyes. Suddenly it looks aside, like a bully pretending to have lost interest when he spots that someone's not going to be intimidated. He struts along the roof a little way, then flies upward in a wide circle that keeps well clear of us. One by one the other gulls lift off, squawking out their protests, and fly out to sea. For the first time since Granny Carne visited there are no gulls on our roof.

"I won't have them on our roof," says Rainbow as if she has perfect gull control.

"Don't you like gulls?" asks Conor.

"I used to, but they've changed. They've become really aggressive. I don't mind them dive-bombing to take food off people because that's their instinct. They're scavengers by nature. But the last year or two I've seen them attack for nothing. They went for my neighbour's dog one day – you know, Sky. And she's tiny, she's only a Yorkshire terrier.

I had to beat them off." She strokes Treacle's neck reassuringly.

"Does Kylie ever get a chance to ride her own pony?" I demand. Rainbow laughs.

"You know Kylie," she says. "If she can get someone else to exercise Treacle for her, she will. She likes the idea of having a pony but she doesn't like the work."

I stroke Treacle's nose while Conor goes in to make tea and rummage through the larder to see if we've eaten the last of the last Guilt Cake.

"Kylie is unbelievably lazy," I agree. "If I had a pony I'd want to do everything for it."

"They're going to take me on at the stables on Saturdays," Rainbow says.

"Which one?"

"Tregony. It's mainly mucking out and leading the little ones out on rides. I don't get paid but I'll get two hours free riding and I can use the jumps any time I want."

"It'll be good for you to get up on something a bit more exciting than old Treacle," I say. Rainbow's a good rider.

Rainbow pats Treacle protectively. "How can you say that? He's got the best temperament. You could put a cat up on him and he wouldn't shy."

"And he gallops exactly like his name."

"Don't listen to her, Treacle." We both laugh. Conor comes out with a clutch of mugs in one hand and a plate of biscuits.

"No more cake?" I ask.

"No more cake." He smiles at Rainbow. "You're growing your hair."

I hadn't noticed, but he's right. Rainbow's bright hair is curling down over her neck now. She blushes a little. "I just felt like it," she says, looking down at the mug of tea Conor hands her, rather than at him.

"It's nice," says Conor.

"But where's Sadie?" asks Rainbow abruptly.

"She's gone to stay with Granny Carne for a while," I answer, not looking at Rainbow.

"We've had a call from family upcountry," says Conor.

"Mum's second cousin," I put in quickly. "They want us to go up there for half term, and maybe stay on for a week afterwards, because of Mum being away. We're going to write to our schools for permission to miss the time. But we can't take Sadie because they live in a flat."

Too much information, I realise as the words gush from my mouth. Second law of lying: don't put too much icing on the cake. Silence falls, an awkward silence.

"In Plymouth," I blurt out.

Rainbow looks from me to Conor. Her face is puzzled. Her blush returns and deepens. "I didn't know you had any family in Plymouth," she says. "Have you been up to stay with them before?"

"Yes," I say.

"No," says Conor at the same moment.

Another silence falls. Rainbow turns away and starts to fuss over Treacle. "There, boy, good boy, steady there..." Treacle looks surprised but smug, while Rainbow gulps down her tea, even though it must be too hot.

"They're not well," I blunder on. "Our cousin and his family, that is. That's why they want us to go, to help look after them..."

"I've got to get going," Rainbow mutters into her mug. "Kylie will want Treacle back..."

Kylie Newton wouldn't care if you took Treacle out until the middle of next week, I think, but I say nothing. I have the feeling that Conor's got to sort out this mess, not me. The silence drags on painfully. Rainbow puts her mug down on a flat stone, fumbles for her hard hat and puts it on.

"Rainbow," says Conor.

"Yes?" Her voice isn't cold – Rainbow's voice could never be that – but it's constricted.

"Rainbow, I'm sorry. That wasn't true, what we said."

"I know."

"Saph and I do have to go somewhere. But we can't tell you any more than that. We can't tell anyone. If our schools think we're with family there won't be any trouble."

"You didn't have to lie to me," Rainbow says.

Neither of us knows what to say. Colour rises under Conor's brown skin. He frowns and his lips tighten. I hope Rainbow doesn't think he is angry with her. He's furious with himself, and with everything that's forced him to lie to Rainbow. "I was stupid," he says quietly.

"Yes, you were." Rainbow is frowning too. *Elvira would have melted into sympathy by now*, I think. But Rainbow's not like that. She thinks a lot of Conor but she expects a lot from him too. They take no notice of me. In fact they've probably forgotten that I'm here. Rainbow is trying to work out what can have made the Conor she knows behave so much out of character.

Suddenly she gets it. Light breaks on her face. "Is it to do with your father?" she asks. I follow her thoughts. She believes that maybe we have been right all along. Dad is still alive, and we have managed to trace him. Conor hesitates. He can't – no, he *won't* – lie to Rainbow any more, but he's got to give her some kind of explanation. It would be cruel to leave her thinking that we don't trust her.

"In a way it is," he says carefully.

Another flash of insight. "You're going where he is, aren't you?"

"Yes," says Conor. You can see how relieved he is to be telling the truth. "But we can't tell anyone else. It's vital. People could get hurt."

"Is it dangerous, then?" It's an odd question, given all that Rainbow doesn't know. It's as if she understands what is going on by instinct.

"It could be. But Saph and I haven't got any choice."

This is where I have my own moment of inspiration. "Granny Carne knows," I say.

Rainbow's expression clears. "She knows where your father is?"

"Yes."

"And she hasn't tried to stop you?"

I think of Granny Carne standing in the lane a long time ago, keeping us from Ingo, giving us blackberries that tasted of Earth. She stopped us then, but time has moved on. We're not strangers to Ingo any more, or visitors who can plunge beneath the skin, surf a few currents and come out unchanged. We've become part of it, even Conor, whether we want to be or not. Our future is tied to Ingo's. That's why Granny Carne won't stand in our way this time, and why she can't give us any protection. I see her in my mind's eye, her red scarf flying in the wind, her feet planted on the Earth, her far-seeing eyes fixed on me. One of her hands is lifted. I don't know if she's greeting me or saying farewell. Her other hand rests on the hoary grey of a granite standing stone, while the adders – her nadron, the children of Earth – twist and twine at her feet. The vision is so powerful that I almost hear the snakes hiss.

I come back to myself. Rainbow is watching me curiously.

"Granny Carne hasn't tried to stop us," Conor confirms. "She's the only one who knows where we're going, though. You won't tell anyone else, will you, Rainbow? Not even Patrick?"

"Not if you don't want me to."

Rainbow unhitches Treacle's reins from the post and leads him away from the wall. He stops, placid and foursquare as ever. She puts her foot into the stirrup, and springs on to Treacle's broad back. Her legs are way too long for him, but Rainbow is light and no burden.

"That animal's more like an armchair than a horse," Conor

says, trying to lighten the atmosphere. Rainbow remains serious.

"You said it might be dangerous."

"Yes," says Conor.

"You will—" Rainbow clears her throat. "You will come back, won't you?" The light is behind her, shining through the bright rim of hair beneath the hard hat. Conor puts his hand on Treacle's neck. He is serious, too, as he gazes up at Rainbow.

"I'll come back," he says. "I promise you that."

CHAPTER SIX

Faro was right. When the time comes, we can no more resist the force that is pulling us towards that Assembly chamber than we could stop the blood flowing through our veins. The Call isn't just one note blown on a conch: it's a summons. Ingo wants us, needs us, and demands that we come *now*.

It's a clear, still night, thick with stars. The moon will rise soon after nine o'clock, Conor says. It's coming up to high tide. The salt tide of Ingo rises in me, growing stronger every minute.

We turn out the lights and lock the cottage door. A gull mews like a cat out of the darkness above our heads. Another answers, and then I think I hear wings. Conor stares up, trying to see what the gulls are doing. "Are they still there?"

"I think one flew off."

"Do you think they've guessed where we're going?"

"I don't know."

We are both whispering. Now that my eyes are getting used to the dark I can see the pale shapes of the gulls standing on the roof, silhouetted against the moonlit sky. There are six of them.

They make no more sound. Their silence seems more sinister than a flurry of angry squawking.

"Come on," says Conor.

We cross the garden, open the gate and set off down the track. Our feet crunch more loudly on the hard surface than they ever do by day. I glance back. I can still see our home by starlight, although the moon hasn't risen yet. The gulls are there, watching and waiting. *They can wait there as long as they like*, I think, *but they'll never be able to enter. The rowan will keep our home safe.* I can just see the rowan tree's shape against our door. *No evil can cross a threshold which the rowan guards.*

Lights glow through curtains from the scattered cottages where our neighbours live. In the morning they'll see that no lights are on in our cottage. They'll think we've left early to catch the train up to Plymouth. Granny Carne has told our neighbour Mary Thomas about Mum's cousin, and the news will be around the village by now.

Down the track, down the path. The dew has already fallen and it's cold. The air smells of autumn, of mushrooms, bracken and the sea. We don't talk. The power that is taking us into Ingo now is too strong for words.

We're almost at the place where the little hidden path curves away off this one, to the lip of the cliff where we'll scramble down to our cove. Faro will be waiting—

Conor stops dead. I almost fall on top of him. "What's wrong?"

"Listen."

I listen, expecting to hear the sound of the sea or maybe the Call again, or maybe my own name carried on the wind from the sea, as I heard it once before:

Ssssapphiiire... Ssssapphiiire...

But there's nothing.

"Conor, come on, we've got to hurry."

"No. Listen, Saph. I'm sure I heard something."

The night breeze lifts my hair. Prickles of fear run up my neck. Ervys can't leave Ingo. But what if the gulls attack now, out of the night sky? They will be able to see better than us. There are hundreds of gulls roosting in the cliffs.

"Listen."

This time I hear it too. A muffled groan. It could be an animal but I'm immediately sure that it's not. It's a human sound.

"Is anyone there? Are you hurt?" calls Conor. His voice is much too loud.

"Conor, don't!"

"Answer if you can!" calls Conor, ignoring me. Again, a faint moan carries towards us. "It's close. I'm going to shine the torch."

We weren't going to shine the torch until we needed it for climbing down to the cove in case its light gave us away. Conor flicks on the beam of light and passes it slowly and thoroughly over the dense mass of brambles, bracken and furze. The sound comes again.

"It's down here!" Conor pushes forward, down the little hidden path that goes to the cove. I'm close behind. "Stop, Saph! Here! There's someone here."

He shines the torch down. A figure huddles on the path. There's something else – two long pieces of metal reflecting in the torchlight. Conor kneels down. "It's Gloria Fortune," he says over his shoulder. "Hold the torch, Saph."

I take the torch. "Don't move her if she's injured, Con."

"I'm not stupid."

I recognise Gloria Fortune now. The metal things are her crutches. She must have slipped and fallen.

"She's soaking wet," says Conor.

"Oh my God." She has done it. Somehow she has crawled down over the lip of the cliff, down the rocks to the sand. She has got to the sea.

"Don't shine the torch in my eyes," says Gloria. Her voice is faint but steady.

"Are you all right? What happened?" asks Conor.

"I'm not hurt. Just – tired. Had to lie down a minute."

"You were groaning. Are you sure you're not hurt?"

"Cold, that's all. Got to get home – Richard'll be back soon. He'll think s-s-something's – happened to me."

"Something *has* happened to you," says Conor grimly.

"I should never have gone down there," mutters Gloria.

"Can you get up if Saph and I help you? Your crutches are here. We'll get you back home, it's not far."

"But, Conor!" I burst out. I can't go back again. We're more than halfway to Ingo. The pull has become so strong my whole body is possessed by it.

"We've got to, Saph."

Gloria is moving. Slowly, painfully, she rolls over and struggles up on to her knees. She waits, gathering strength.

"Maybe we should get Richard. If you've damaged your leg any more you'll need a stretcher," says Con.

"No!" says Gloria. "He mustn't see me like this. Help me up." One on each side, we support Gloria under her arms and help her up. Her clothes are soaked with water. She smells of the sea.

"What happened?" asks Conor.

"I thought – thought someone was calling me. Into the water. Don't know how I got down there... found the way somehow. I think I was on the rocks... A wave came over me and then I was afraid." Her voice drops to a whisper. I lean close. "There was something in the water that hated me," I hear her say.

I feel both horror and relief. Gloria hasn't been to Ingo. Her Mer blood must be strong enough to take her to the gateway, but not to allow her to enter Ingo alone. There was no Faro there to guide her. What if she had gone into the water and found Mortarow there – or Ervys?

I thought Granny Carne was protecting Gloria and keeping her safe on the Earth. It must be the Call that is making Ingo so powerful tonight. No one would have seen Gloria go. No one would have missed her, until Richard came home. Gloria might have been found days later, washed up miles down the coast. No one would ever guess what really happened. They'd say it was a terrible accident.

"You must never do that again," I say protectively. I can help Conor take her back to her cottage. It will only delay us for a few minutes, and what does time mean tonight anyway? Soon we'll be in Ingo time, and human clocks will mean nothing.

"Got to get home – Richard..." mutters Gloria, sounding like an exhausted child rather than the strong woman I know she is.

Slowly, step by step, we get Gloria home. She is shivering with shock and cold, but it's not far. The air is still but I feel as if I'm pushing into a strong wind with the effort of turning my back on Ingo. Their rented cottage is only a couple of hundred metres from ours. I don't even glance at our cottage. I don't want to see if the gulls are on the roof, or if one of them is flying off to deliver the message to Ervys that Gloria has survived. I remember Faro's words. *They don't want peace, they want war, and victory.*

Gloria's cottage is dark. "Thank God, he's not back yet."

We push open the unlocked door. A wave of warmth enfolds us. Conor switches on the light, while Gloria slumps into a chair by the stove. "You need a hot shower," I tell her.

"In a minute." She opens her eyes, reviving. For the first time she cracks a faint smile.

"We'll stay with you until Richard comes home," says Conor.

"No! He'll know something's wrong if he sees you."

To be here in Gloria's cottage is torture. Faro is waiting for us. The Call is dragging at me. The time is now. But Gloria is cold, wet, weak. People die of hypothermia.

"We're not going until you've had a hot shower and got into warm clothes," I say decisively.

Their shower is downstairs. Gloria moves slowly but she seems stronger now she's in her own place. I wait outside the door, listening to be sure that she's all right. I hear the shower running, and after a few minutes Gloria comes out wrapped in a blue dressing gown. Conor brings her tea and she settles herself by the stove again, in the opposite chair because the first one she sat in is damp with sea-water.

"I'll be all right now." Gloria is an adult again, competent and calm.

"Promise me you won't ever—" I begin, then stop. I don't think I have any right to ask Gloria for promises. But she looks straight back as if she understands exactly what I mean.

"Never again," she says. "Never, ever again."

It's safe to leave her now. As we close the cottage door and turn away down the track we see headlights bumping down off the main road. Richard is on his way home.

"He'll look after her," says Conor.

"Yes."

"They should move," Conor goes on angrily. "He should get her right away from here."

I have nothing to say. I want Gloria to be safe. But denying her Mer blood isn't going to make her safe, not for ever. There has got to be another way. Not Ervys's way, with Mer and human battling and Ingo and Earth deadly enemies.

CHAPTER SEVEN

The cove is brimful of tide. No jumping down from the rocks on to clean pale sand tonight. "We'll have to climb right out over the rocks until we're sure we're above deep water," whispers Conor. I don't know why we're whispering, but we are, and we don't call for Faro either. He may not be the only one of the Mer who is watching and waiting for us tonight.

The rocks are sharp and slippery. The starlight is strong enough to guide us as we lower ourselves into gullies then climb the steep rocky sides of the cove. We need to go right out, almost to the cove's mouth. I follow Conor, reaching for handholds, and fitting my feet into the rock's crevices. He hasn't switched on the torch since we left Gloria Fortune's cottage.

"Face the rock and let yourself go down backwards," he whispers. "I'll go first." I glance down. In the starlight I can see Conor's outline pressed against the rock. He lowers himself carefully, and then lets go and slides to the next foothold. The rock slopes at about forty degrees here. It looks dangerous. It *is* dangerous. If Conor slips too far he won't fall in the water, he'll fall on rock. But once he's down, there's a ledge above a sheer drop. It'll be safe to dive from there.

"I'm down. Come on," he calls softly.

I turn to face the rock, and press against it as Conor did. My fingers dig into a narrow crevice. I let go of my safe finger-hold and let myself slide. There's no foothold or handhold. I scrabble desperately, my jaw cracks against the rock, I bite my tongue. But my foot jars against a spur of rock. I'm not sliding any more.

Foothold, slide. Handhold, slide. Suddenly, with a jolt, both my feet hit rock and Conor's hand is behind my back, steadying me. "You've made it, Saph. You're on the ledge. Turn round slowly."

I shuffle my feet around cautiously, and turn to face outwards. At that moment the moon rises behind the curve of the cliff. First the rim, then the broad curve, then the whole moon floats free, lighting up the cove so brilliantly that it seems as if day has come. Below us the sea bulges, black and oily looking. There is hardly any wind, but a big swell. The water breaks as it enters the cove, slapping against the rocks with a hollow boom.

For the first time in my life I'm afraid of the sea. Even when the Tide Knot broke, the fear was different. Then, the sea came out of its bed, out of its element, and tried to take over the land. It was natural to be afraid. But this is different. It feels as if the sea is prowling below our ledge, waiting for us.

How I wish Faro would come. The fingers of my right hand

have gone to my bracelet. I touch the *deublek* made of our woven hair. Of course Faro will come. We have to go to the Assembly chamber together.

The water is empty. No Faro. *In two nights I shall be here for you.* Faro has never broken his word to me. Something must have prevented him. Maybe the wound on his tail was more serious than he thought.

"It looks as if we're going to have to find the way to the Assembly chamber ourselves. Do you think you can remember the way, Saph?"

I think of the narrow passages Faro took me through. "I'm not sure, but if we follow the Call it's bound to take us there."

"Can you feel the Call now?"

"Ye-yes, I think so." But the truth is that I can't. It has faded abruptly, as if the mass of rock that surrounds us is blocking out its signal.

"I can't," says Conor. "I'll have to rely on you."

What if something bad has happened to Faro? "We've got to get to Ingo quickly, Conor." The water heaves beneath us. There is a path of moon on its surface. Tonight even the moonlight looks sinister.

"We'll have to dive right out," I say.

"Let's dive together. I'll count."

I can't get into a proper diving position because of the rock face behind me. The drop is about four metres. I've dived from higher points than this. My toes curl over the edge, gripping it. Diving in moonlight isn't the same as diving in daylight. You can't judge distance so well. If I push off as hard as I can, I'll be all right.

"Ready, Saph? One – two – three – *GO!*"

We dive in the same second. I enter the water at a steep angle, down, down, down through the blackness. As soon as the sea touches me I know I'm not in Ingo. The sea is cold and hostile. I can't breathe in it. I kick hard, swim up until I break the surface, and push my hair out of my face. I tread water, looking around. "Conor?"

"I'm here."

We are both whispering. Rocks loom above us, the cold sea drags at us. Behind us the cliffs bulk high against the moonlight.

"Saph, swim out! Swim to the entrance of the cove! The tide is dragging us to the caves."

He is right. I'm not swimming but the rock face is moving, gliding past me. It's like being in a rip, but there aren't any rips here inside the cove. I turn seawards and swim as hard as I can for the channel between the rocks.

Conor is a few metres to my left. I'm swimming with all my strength but I'm barely moving. Cold, strong water has got me in its grip. It hates me. It wants to destroy me. It will carry me to the back of the cove, smash me against the cliff, drag me into the underwater caves where no one will ever find me...

Dark despair crawls over my skin. Where is Ingo? Why wasn't Faro here to greet us as he promised? A wave surges over my face.

"Why struggle?" says a voice which is so close that it seems to be inside my head. "Why not let go? There's no hope of escape. If you stop fighting, it will only hurt for a little while and then it will all be over." The words seem to echo around the cliffs and the rocks. They are waiting for me to give in. Our cove has become an enemy.

There was something in the water that hated me.

Gloria said that. She felt it too. The wave tried to get her but she escaped. She fought her way up the cliff on her crutches. Crawling up the steep, rough rock, dragging herself, dragging her crutches. Doing what no one would ever believe could be done by a woman with a shattered thigh-bone who is waiting for a hip replacement operation.

The gap between Conor and me has widened. He's being pulled back too, but in a different direction. I kick my way as hard as I can through the hostile water. I'm not going to look at the sheer sides of the rock, bearing down on me, or at the cliffs behind. Only at my arms sweeping the water aside, and Conor's head on my left. He's fighting too, beating his way forward.

You must never, ever swim out of the cove, Sapphy. The currents are dangerous. Stay in the cove where it's safe.

Dad drummed those words into me for years, but tonight I'm certain that they aren't true. Getting out of the cove is our only hope. Once we are in the open water, then Ingo has got to come to us. Or else—

Don't think of that. Just swim.

The feeling of hatred is growing stronger, as if whatever has possessed our cove knows that we're about to escape it. I'm swimming as hard as I can, but my limbs are so heavy that they can hardly push the water aside.

"Saph! Look! I think – I saw Faro – out there – " Conor's voice comes in gasps. We are both exhausted, but Faro's name sends a pulse of hope through me. If he's there, then Ingo is close.

A few more metres, that's all. Those rocks aren't really closing in on us from both sides. It's an illusion. The thing that hates us wants to frighten us into turning back. Remember how wide the mouth of the cove really is. Remember how easily the *Peggy Gordon* used to sail out. It was wide – safe...

"We're through!"

The drag on my mind and body has disappeared. I'm free. The sea buoys me up, salty and welcoming. It feels neither cold nor warm. It feels – it feels...

The surface parts, and lets me in. I swim down, and moonlit bubbles stream from my hands. I know there are no air bubbles streaming from my mouth. Down, down, down, through the live, velvety water. I catch a faint, far-off sound, like the boom of sea in a giant shell. I am in Ingo.

"Greetings, little sister."

"Faro! Why didn't you come?"

Faro swims close. "Speak softly. There are spies everywhere."

Conor swims towards us. "What happened, Faro?"

"Ervys has made your cove into a Porth Cas. I could not enter it or warn you."

"What do you mean?" I ask.

We are in the moonwater, and there's enough light to see the anger on Faro's face.

"You know that we Mer can enter each other's thoughts, Sapphire? You know how the Mer reach decisions in the Assembly chamber, by thinking together? Ervys has taught his followers a different way of using that power. They think together and make their hatred into a weapon. It becomes like a living creature, which can be kept in one place until it grows strong enough to change the nature of that place. They have made their Porth Cas at your cove. They knew you would enter Ingo that way."

"Couldn't Saldowr have stopped them?"

"No. He's at the Assembly chamber now. Ervys is trying to prevent our people from entering, and Saldowr is there to protect them."

"Where's Elvira?" asks Conor. "Is she all right?"

"She's in no danger. We will see her at the Assembly chamber."

Our people. Dad will be there among them. I am sure of it. He will come to see his own children present themselves as candidates for the Crossing of Ingo. I will see Dad there, among the ranks of the Mer. Saldowr promised it.

I can promise you that you will see your father again, and soon... at the next Assembly, when the young Mer who think they are ready to make the Crossing of Ingo will come forward... Your father will surely be there...

"Have you fallen asleep, little sister?"

"No – I'm sorry, Faro, I was just thinking—"

"You hide your thoughts from me today. Why is that?"

"Because they're private, Faro."

"Private! There is no yours and mine between us," says Faro with an air of grandeur that makes him look like a prince. But there are no princes and princesses in Ingo.

It is so good to see Faro again. In spite of the dark and danger it feels like old times. Any minute now he will flip into a series of outrageously dazzling somersaults, calling, "Watch me, little sister!"

"Faro, is your tail all right?"

He shrugs. "It's fine." This probably means it isn't fine at all, but Faro's tone stops me asking any more.

"We must close our minds as we go to the Assembly chamber. You will be all right, Conor, since you open your mind to no one in Ingo." He shoots Conor a glance which makes me think, for the first time, that perhaps Faro is disappointed by Conor's lack of warmth towards him. It's not that Conor doesn't like him. I wish Faro could understand that. But Conor doesn't entirely trust Faro, not as I do. All the same, Faro's wrong. Conor *does* open his mind to one person in Ingo: Elvira, Faro's sister. I wonder what Faro really thinks about that?

"I'm certainly not going to play mind games with Ervys or anyone else," says Conor.

"Ervys will believe in the power of his Porth Cas," goes on Faro, "but he may have laid other surprises for us just in case you two got into Ingo another way. And now *we* will surprise *him*."

"Do you think… Is he waiting around here somewhere, Faro?" I ask.

"No. He and his followers will have gone to the Assembly

chamber. They want to be sure that all the young Mer who follow Ervys are accepted for the Crossing. If they can, they will stop those who follow Saldowr. But let any of the Mer dare to interfere with the Call!" Faro tosses back his hair. "They will learn what it is to break the laws of Ingo. Let them feel for themselves the hatred that they try to call down on others! Let the spear in Mortarow's hand become the spear in Mortarow's heart!"

"Faro!"

"What?"

"You sound so – so vengeful."

"You have not seen my vengeance yet, little sister," says Faro. His voice is very quiet. He is not boasting, but promising. "He tried to kill you there in the cove, with your *deublek* on your wrist, as you came to answer the Call of the conch. Every law of Ingo is outraged. And Conor too," he adds quickly. Conor laughs.

"You find it funny?" demands Faro.

"Chill, Faro," says Conor. "It was just the way you put it. I'm on Ervys's case as much as you are."

"Chill?"

"It's like *Give me five,*" I put in quickly.

"Ah, I see! Conor, give me five!" And everything else is forgotten as they laugh and slap hands.

Excitement is building in me now. Faro's descriptions of the Crossing glitter in my memory.

I've heard such stories, Sapphire! There are fish that fly and fish like rainbows and fish that walk on the floor of the sea, and whales bigger than any we see in these waters. There are lost cities too, Sapphire, which were in the

Air once and which sank down into Ingo long before our great-great-great-grandmothers went to Limina. Think of it, little sister! We are going to the bottom of the world…"

"Aren't we supposed to be at the Assembly chamber?" I ask.

CHAPTER EIGHT

As we swim closer to the Assembly chamber we see a stream of young Mer approaching it. Faro has brought us round by the south, to my relief. I wouldn't want to face the narrow tunnels we had to pass through last time, not after the Porth Cas. We swim easily, but I notice that Faro is not as fast as usual. Whatever Elvira put on the wound has worked well, but Faro's tail hasn't completely healed yet. The Call echoes in our ears like a trumpet, stirring our blood. Ingo wants us to be at the Assembly chamber. I am sure of it, whatever Ervys says.

I am longing to see Saldowr. We keep a few metres below to the surface in the moonwater until the moment when we have to dive to reach the chamber. Shadowy figures stream past on both sides now. It looks as if the whole of Ingo is gathering. I thought Faro would take us to join the current of young Mer, but he doesn't.

"We are not going to use that entrance," he whispers. My heart plummets. Just as I thought we'd missed the tunnel, we're going to have to go into it.

"But, Faro, we can't go back now!"

"I don't mean the tunnel, little sister. Follow me."

I remember how the main entrance to the chamber lay directly above the Speaking Stone, high in the rocky roof. Faro swims sideways, through the dark water. He can see better than I can. I follow closely, with Conor at my side. Now we can't see any other Mer.

Faro slows, and swims along the face of the rock, testing it with his right hand, patting, feeling. He goes a little farther and then stops. "It's here."

I can't see anything. The rock looks solid.

"Conor, give me your hand," says Faro. He guides Conor's arm. Suddenly Conor's hand slides behind the rock. He pulls it out quickly.

"You try, Sapphire."

The rock looks solid but there's a space behind it about as wide as my two hands held finger-tip to finger-tip.

"Saldowr told me about the gap. None of the Mer know of it."

"Can we get through?" Conor asks.

"He says so. We'll have to squeeze in sideways. If we can get our heads and shoulders through, then our tails will be no problem." It's the first time Faro has ever forgotten that we are not Mer.

Faro turns and peers at us through the gloom. "Conor, you go first. You'll have to feel your way. And then you, Sapphire. I'll keep watch. Once you are through, you'll find that you are on a ledge above the Assembly chamber, hidden by a veil of rock."

"How far do we have to go?" asks Conor.

"It's only a short way."

"Can I go first?" I ask.

"Let me. It might be dangerous," says Conor.

"No, Con!"

They move aside for me. I feel my way into the space. It is very dark and very narrow. I turn so that my shoulders are at the narrowest possible angle and push myself forward, head first. My head scrapes rock. I must have got the angle wrong. I try again, moving parallel to the rock, and this time it seems to open up for me. I edge sideways with my hands flat against the rock. It's very tight. If it's tight for me, it'll be even worse for Conor. And then I see space ahead of me, and light – a greenish glow. Sea worms, thousands upon thousands of them, lighting the chamber.

There is the veil of rock, as Faro said. I can hear the vast murmur from the Mer crowds. The ledge is broad enough for three of us. I press my face against the dark passage from which I've just emerged, and whisper: "I'm through!"

I count until Conor comes to stop myself thinking of him wedged there, unable to move backwards or forwards. *Thirty-one – thirty-two...* It's half a minute already. Surely it didn't take me that long? *Thirty-eight – thirty-nine...*

Conor emerges. I can't see his face properly but I can hear the relief in his voice as he says, "That was a bit tight."

"Did you get stuck?"

"Just my head for a few seconds."

"Will Faro be OK?"

"He's coming now."

In a moment we are all reunited, pressed close together so that the rock veil hides us. I don't suppose anyone will look up, but we've got to be careful. Conor swims a quarter stroke forward, and sculls himself into a place where he can peer around the edge of the rock. "I can see them!" His voice vibrates with excitement. "They're coming in past Ervys's men!"

"Let me look." I join him.

Faro swims above me so that we can both see. The huge chamber is alive with people. I scan the crowds, trying to pick out Dad's face. Rows of Mer are seated below us in ranks that rise way up the sides of the chamber. I scan up and down the ranks and then across. I think I see him behind a pillar, and then the figure moves and it's not him.

"Conor," I whisper, "can you see Dad?"

"Shut up, Sapphire, I'm looking..." Conor sounds edgy. He's been as sure as me that Dad would be here. I'll search for Mellina too. If she's there, Dad will be close. But there aren't any babies or small children here. She wouldn't leave Mordowrgi behind.

"There!" says Conor suddenly, pointing.

"Pull your hand back!" Faro whispers urgently.

I've already seen where Conor's pointing. All the other faces vanish into a blur, and one face shows up as if a spotlight is on it. Dad is high up in the top rank. He's looking intently towards the chamber entrance. He looks different. Older. His face is drawn. *But that's natural; he's been injured*, I tell myself quickly. You wouldn't expect him to look the same. His hair flows around his shoulders like the hair of the other Mer. It has grown very long. His chest is bare. Like Faro's, his upper body melts into a strong seal tail. I can look at nothing and no one else. My father, so close that if I called he would hear me.

The two times that I've seen him in the flesh since he disappeared, he has been alone. When he rose out of the pool I didn't even see his Mer body. I couldn't bear to. It seemed too monstrous. When he swam in to warn me on the night the Tide Knot broke, he was a distant figure in a wild stormy sea. I saw his face and heard his voice, but no more.

I knew that Dad had become Mer. I even saw his Mer body in Saldowr's mirror, but I still refused to accept it. It seemed like a nightmare that had swept over us all. I believed that one day we would wake up from it, and Dad would return to himself.

Now that belief fades until I can't feel it any more. Dad isn't alone. He isn't a stranger here. He belongs. He is seated in the ranks of the Mer, as if that's his rightful place. He looks at home in this Assembly. Another Mer man leans over to speak to him. They confer for a few moments. It's clear that they know each other well. Dad has a life apart from us of which we know nothing. When I held my baby half-brother Mordowrgi in my arms, I thought I understood that. But it's only in this moment, when I see Dad turn casually to a friend in the Mer Assembly chamber, that I realise fully what he has become.

I thought everything would be all right, as long as Dad was

given his free choice, but I was wrong. A wave of bitterness washes through me, tasting of defeat.

Conor is watching Dad too. We glance quickly at each other, but say nothing. We are probably having the same thoughts.

I feel very tired, as if I've run a long, long race and at the finish there is no tape, just an endless track going on into endless distance.

I can't look at Dad any more. I must hold on to what we came for: the Crossing. Deliberately I focus on the Speaking Stone, set into the floor of the chamber. I will block Dad out of my mind.

The stone flashes opal in the reflected light from the thousands of sea worms that cling in clusters to the rock face. The chamber is like a vast theatre, humming with excitement and expectancy.

Our hiding place is high up, just below the main entrance and looking directly across at it. Ervys's men are there, clustered around the entrance. They are not blocking the way exactly, but they float in ranks on either side of it. Some of the young Mer pause and shrink back as they enter the chamber and see what's waiting for them. I am not surprised. These are full-grown Mer, powerful and full of menace. It must take a lot of courage to swim forward if you don't follow Ervys.

I recognise some of them – Talek – Mortarow... And there, closest of all to the entrance, still and brooding, is Ervys himself. A shiver of dread runs through me. He looks as if nothing could prevent him from being here, where he wants to be, or doing what he wants to do. Why are so many of the Mer still following him? They know he couldn't save them from the Kraken.

"The Mer hate the fact that it took humans to save them from the Kraken," Faro whispers in my ear. "Ervys gives them their pride back."

"But going to the Deep had nothing to do with pride! We didn't do it because of Ervys. It was because we didn't want the children to be... hurt." I mean "killed" but I don't want to say it.

"Everything is to do with pride where Ervys is concerned," says Faro.

I remember what it was like to confront Ervys last time I was in this chamber. When you're close to him, you see just how strong he is. His arms rippled with muscle; his tail lashed from side to side, like a tiger's before a kill. One blow from that tail could have killed me. But most frightening of all was the way his eyes measured me so coldly. I was a thing that had got in his way, not a person.

As I watch him, Ervys puts his hand on the shoulder of the man next to him. He turns. Ervys says something and smiles, showing his teeth. A jostling ripple spreads through his followers. There are so many of them now...

"Hagerawl," murmurs Faro, "Morteweth, Gwandrys..."

"Why are there no Mer women? Doesn't Ervys want them as followers?" asks Conor.

"Ervys thinks that only men should fight for him. Women can heal and feed and tend the children."

"So why do any women support him if that's what he thinks of them?" I ask.

"Those who like being slaves support him," answers Faro.

I watch the incoming stream of young Mer swimming past Ervys and his threatening supporters. I can't see any weapons, but perhaps they have them hidden. Spears tipped with razor-sharp coral, or with metal taken from shipwrecks. I shudder, thinking of the gash in Faro's tail.

But there's another figure floating between the Speaking Stone and Ervys. He is facing away from us, towards the entrance. His long cloak flows around his body, hiding it, but I would know him anywhere. He is upright, his head flung back commandingly as he faces Ervys's followers. His right arm is outstretched, his hand held up like a barrier. It's Saldowr. His eyes are fixed on Ervys's followers, watching every move they make. They would like to surge forwards from the entrance and block the way to the Speaking Stone, but they don't.

Saldowr stands alone. Alone, by force of will rather than by weapons, he's holding back Ervys so that *all* the young Mer can reach the Speaking Stone.

"*Only the Call knows who is chosen,*" whispers Faro angrily as if he's quoting something.

"I thought that the Mer chose, in the Assembly," says Conor.

"They give the sign of agreement, but the decision is already made, and not by them. It is there in the face of the boy or girl as they swim up from the Speaking Stone."

Suddenly one of the Mer around Ervys swaggers forward.

Deliberately, he looks across at Saldowr as his broad, squat body blocks the way of a Mer boy. The boy stops swimming. Even from here we can all see his fear and confusion. Angry uproar rises from the Mer benches. Some rise in protest, others jeer and beat the heels of their hands together.

Saldowr's voice cracks out. "Let him pass to the stone."

Ervys's follower holds his ground, glancing around for support. No one else comes forward.

"Let him pass to the stone." Saldowr's voice is quieter now, but more penetrating. It makes me afraid, even though I'm not Saldowr's target. Ervys's follower turns and we see his face. He opens his mouth, and then closes it again. He looks for backing from the ranks around Ervys, but no one stirs. Sullenly, he swims back to his fellows at the entrance.

"Ervys will choose his fight," comments Faro.

"What do you mean?" I ask.

"That boy wasn't important enough. Ervys is waiting for something more.

For us, maybe. Perhaps he knows by now that we broke out of his Porth Cas. The gulls could have brought word to a follower close to the surface. Ervys will guess that we'll come straight here.

The boy swims until he is above the Speaking Stone, then quickly and neatly he dives down in the sheer dive that no human can ever equal, touches the stone, and comes up to face the Mer. Immediately, without looking at one another, the Mer respond. A single word ripples around the chamber.

"Chosen... chosen... chosen...chosen..."

But not all the Mer speak. Many remain silent, arms folded, resisting. Ervys has his supporters on the benches too.

"This breaks our custom," whispers Faro angrily. "We speak together or keep silent."

I wonder who will speak for us. Even the Mer who support Saldowr may keep silent when we swim up from the stone. *Half-and-halfs*, Ervys calls us. We pollute Ingo with our human blood. How many of these Mer believe that? My stomach knots with tension. Before long, we'll find out.

The boy has already gone. A girl approaches the stone, and then another. Each has their moment, but that moment passes so quickly that the line of waiting Mer never stops moving. *But even so*, I think, *it would take weeks for all the young Mer to come to the stone*. Surely every single Mer in our age group can't make the same journey to the same chamber? How big is Ingo, anyway? Does its power stretch all the way around the world?

"Faro, are there other Assembly chambers?"

Faro looks at me for a long silent moment. At last he asks, "What do you mean?"

"I mean, surely all the Mer in the whole of Ingo can't come here, into one chamber. The oceans are huge. There must be too many Mer, even in our age group. How big is Ingo?"

"You must speak to Saldowr," he says haughtily. "Ingo is as it is."

I almost smile, but stop myself. Conor nudges me.

"I only meant, does Ingo cover the whole world?"

"Of course it does. What else could there be? But perhaps there are other Assembly chambers," he concedes.

The young Mer are still coming in a stream that appears endless. Saldowr's cloak billows in the current that they make as they pass him. There is only one of him. I believe in Saldowr, of course I do, but—

"There are many of Ervys's followers," says Faro as if he has heard my thoughts.

"What?"

"Among those coming to the stone. Watch carefully as they pass Ervys."

The next two candidates must be Saldowr's followers because they make no sign as they pass Ervys. But then a girl in a bodice of dark-red woven weed enters the chamber. She looks to her left, where Ervys stands behind his men. Quickly she raises her left hand to her forehead and touches it with the knuckle of her index finger. Nothing more. Her hand drops and she swims forward. The gesture is so fleeting that I'd have missed it if Faro hadn't told me to look out for a sign. She dives to touch the Stone, comes up to face the Mer and is greeted with the familiar word: "Chosen.... chosen..."

"Elvira will come soon," says Faro.

"How do you know?"

"She is in my thoughts. She wants to be with us but I have told her we are hidden. She will be chosen, and then she will wait for us outside the Assembly chamber."

He sounds so confident.

"How can you be sure that Elvira will be chosen?" asks Conor. "There seem to be a lot of Ervys's people. Won't they stop her? They know she's with us."

"The blood of our ancestors runs differently in Elvira's veins. Saldowr has spoken of it to me. She is pure Mer. Ervys still hopes to win her trust."

Faro looks so proud, and so lonely. I hate it. I take his hand so that our *deubleks* touch, and for a second his expression lightens. "If Elvira is not chosen," he continues, "then the Mer are liars and there will be no true Crossing."

We wait, tense. The next girl is not Elvira, nor the next. Neither of them makes any sign to Ervys, but the two boys who follow both make the brief touch of knuckle to forehead. Faro's fingers clutch my arm, digging in deep. I stifle a cry.

"Faro, what is it?"

"It is Bannerys. My friend."

I know so little about Faro's life. I should have realised that he would have many friends among the Mer of our age who are coming as candidates for the Crossing.

"He came with me to hunt the orca," says Faro, his face pale as he watches Bannerys dive to the stone. "He was my brother then – when the orca forgot that we Mer are not seals to be taken for his food." His grip on my arm loosens. Hard anger sets on his face. "Let Bannerys learn what it means to follow Ervys," he murmurs.

"Perhaps he doesn't realise what Ervys is like, Faro..."

"Could *you* look at Ervys and not know what he is like?"

Bannerys has already risen to face the Mer. They choose him and he swims away. Faro remains rigid, fists clenched, until Bannerys has left the chamber.

"Con, what's an orca?" I whisper.

"A killer whale."

I look at Faro with respect. "Elvira is coming now," he says.

Conor pushes forward. And there is Elvira, slight, poised and lovely as ever. She swims gracefully through the entrance, looking neither to right nor left. I notice a stir among Ervys's men, but no one tries to stop her. In one fluid movement, she dives for the stone. When she comes up level with the ranks of Mer again, she looks around the chamber slowly, as if to take in how many are there. For a moment we see her face, which is calm and sure.

There is a pause, and then the voices come: "*Chosen... chosen... chosen...*"

Faro relaxes. A smile of pride lightens his face. I'm leaning forward to say how good it is that Elvira's been chosen when everything that has just happened falls away from my mind. The Call sounds for me. I know it is for me because somewhere in its music I hear my name. The Call reverberates through the chamber, filling it just as the water fills it with salt. It must be an echo. No one is blowing the conch now. But it can't be an echo because it's much too real and clear. Enchanting images rise in my mind: a vast ocean, so blue that it is almost black; fish like rainbows, blue whales, schools of porpoises; no land within a thousand miles, only water...

I move forward. Conor grabs me back. "Saph! They'll see you."

"Wait!" says Faro.

"But I have to go. The conch is calling me."

Conor lets go of me. Faro says, "They say there is no music like the conch when it calls you down to the Speaking Stone. Go, Sapphire."

I slip out of our hiding place and swim along the wall until I'm well away from the niche. I don't want Ervys and his supporters to see where I've come from. I draw up my knees and brace my feet against the wall of rock. With all the force in my body I thrust off, diving down and down until I reach the place above the Speaking Stone.

There is uproar even before I reach it. Ervys and his supporters have seen me and recognised me. They are baying for my blood. The Mer are standing up from their seats, some of them shouting, some of them clapping in welcome. I glance over my shoulder. A supporter is talking rapidly into Ervys's ear. Any moment now they will come over and seize me and everything will dissolve in chaos. Saldowr has turned to me. He is watching me calmly, with a faint smile on his face. In his eyes I read a message: *Go on, my child.*

I jackknife into a dive. Water streams past me, voices blare in my ears and then everything fades as I come to the stone. It glows with calm radiance. Its heart flashes crimson as the wave of my dive throws green reflections over it. I take a last stroke, and touch the stone.

Nothing happens. No tingle or sudden feeling of warmth in my fingers. It is stone, smooth and hard and unyielding. I touch it, and that is all. But for the first time I understand the purpose of the stone. It doesn't speak, or give any secret messages. That would be cheap magic, and what it really does is even more powerful. The Speaking Stone allows us to speak for ourselves. It reveals our own purposes to us, however deep they are locked in our hearts.

I will make the Crossing of Ingo, I say, but not aloud.

The stone does not answer. I turn and swim up to where the Mer wait. Ervys's supporters are slamming their fists into their palms. The water churns with anger. I hear Ervys yell above the tumult: "Are we going to let a human creature take part in the most sacred mystery of our race? Are the Mer so degenerate?"

I am not going to say anything. I scull myself into position directly above the Speaking Stone and face the Mer. I look around the whole circle of faces, as Elvira did. To my right, to my left, ahead and behind. Let them dare to call me a half-and-half now. Let them dare deny what the Speaking Stone has recognised. I know what is written on my face. I know that I will make the Crossing.

Ervys knows too. Out of the corner of my eye I see him struggling against the protection with which Saldowr is shielding everyone who comes forward to be chosen. Saldowr has turned back to face Ervys. From the tension of his body and his upraised arm I can see how hard he is fighting to keep Ervys from me.

I push back my hair. Let the Mer answer me now. I look up at the top rank where my father sits, and find him. He is leaning forward, his eyes fixed on me. He gives no sign of recognition. His face is heavy with anguish.

The voices roll through the water towards me as if they are one voice: *"Chosen... chosen... chosen..."*

I keep my eyes fixed on Dad's face. Not a muscle moves. His lips do not open. He says nothing.

Chosen... say the water echoes. *Chosen... chosen...* But not by my own father. I look away from him. I will not let my eyes return to his face. I let the voices of the other Mer sink into my heart. *Chosen... chosen... chosen...*

It is done, and Dad can't undo it. The Mer have chosen me. Let Ervys fight as hard as he likes. Even if he kills me he will never be able to take away this moment.

CHAPTER NINE

I want to wait for the others, but I must swim away and join the stream of young Mer who have already presented themselves as candidates and been chosen, or not chosen. How terrible not to be chosen: to learn that the Crossing does not lie in your heart. But the stone can only reveal what's already true.

We pass through the entrance easily. It is much wider than it looked from our niche, and Ervys's followers are massed at one side where the candidates enter. I'm afraid they'll try and block my way, but they don't even glance at me.

It seemed to take so long to dive to the stone and to come up and wait to hear the verdict, but it can only have been seconds. There's Elvira, swimming ahead of me. Even though my time in front of the stone was short, I realise that we have been in our hiding place much longer than I thought. Moonlight has gone, and grey dawn is seeping down through the water.

"Elvira!" I call softly. I still don't want to attract attention to myself. She looks over her shoulder, beckons me on, and keeps swimming upwards. When we are some way from the chamber's entrance, she slows and waits for me. Around us, all the young Mer who have already been into the chamber are dispersing. Others are still streaming towards the entrance. I wonder how long the choosing goes on. It all seems a lot less organised than I'd expected. Well, what *did* I expect? Maybe that it would be a bit like the beginning of a marathon, with a starting line and numbers being handed out, and officials walking up and down looking at clipboards and stopwatches, and people swinging their arms and jogging on the spot to warm up…

You idiot, Sapphire Trewhella. Jogging. On their tails perhaps?

"Sapphire!" Elvira's beautiful face is lit up by her smile. "You were chosen. I knew you would be."

Somehow it is faintly irritating to have it taken for granted. I shrug. "The others should be along in a minute," I say.

But now it's Elvira who seems anxious. "Did they come forward? I saw nothing. I am a bit afraid, Sapphire. Not so much for Conor, but for Faro."

"Faro? Why for Faro?" How can she think Faro might be refused? He is far more Mer than I am. No one could be braver or more ready to risk adventure than Faro. He has already visited the Deep, which no Mer had ever done before. He is Saldowr's *scolhyk* and his *holyer*.

Even as I pile up the reasons in my mind some of Elvira's uncertainty starts to infect me. She is twisting the fringe of her bodice nervously as she stares down at the wide entrance to the chamber. "I wish they'd hurry," she whispers.

"Do you think Conor will be all right?"

She considers. "Yes. It is the two of you whom Saldowr

most needs to complete the Crossing of Ingo."

"We are making the Crossing for ourselves, like all the other young Mer."

Elvira looks surprised. "Oh no, Sapphire, it's not like that. You'll understand – but look! There's Conor! Quick, Sapphire, he hasn't seen us!" She plunges down towards him, waving. I swim after her, but not too fast. *Let them have time for their reunion*, I think sourly. Now that she's succeeded in panicking me about Faro, Elvira seems to have forgotten all about him in her joy at seeing Conor again.

When I reach them Conor is smiling too, but there's tension in his face. "I don't know what's happening with Faro," he says. "I'm afraid they've spotted our hiding place. Even though you and I swam along the wall a way, they must have seen the direction we came from. Ervys has only got to send some men around the outside of the chamber. They'd find the gap soon enough."

"They'd be too big to get through."

"There are plenty of young Mer among his followers."

"I can feel Faro in my mind," says Elvira slowly. "He is like this." She spreads out her hands, fingers rigid. "He is waiting. Oh no, Conor! He has closed his thoughts! Even to me he has closed them!"

"Why?" I ask.

"Someone else may be trying to invade them."

More and more young Mer emerge from the chamber and swim away.

"Conor," I ask very quietly so that Elvira won't hear, "did you see Dad?"

"Yes," says Conor in a voice that's like the closing of a door. But I've got to persist.

"Did he – did you see his face when they were choosing?"

"He didn't speak for me. He kept quiet." The bitterness and contempt in Conor's voice makes me wince.

"Nor for me."

Conor says a word I've never heard him use about anyone.

"Conor, don't!"

"Why not? It's what he deserves. I keep giving him another chance, and another and another, and so do you. We've made enough excuses for him. You keep hoping against all the odds that he's going to come home to us. It's never going to happen. He doesn't want to be free to choose. We're pathetic, Saph, and I'm not going to do this any more. I'm going to close my mind to him, like we closed our minds to Ervys."

"I can't do that to Dad."

"So you'd rather keep on hoping for things which are never going to happen?"

I don't know what to answer. Sorrow for Conor, anger with my father and fear for Faro load down my mind. I watch the young Mer coming out of the chamber. Some of them have that familiar look of sureness and calm purpose. Others are blank. One boy passes close to us without even seeing us. I understand why when I see the numb disappointment on his face. He's come all this way, and not been chosen. He's got to go back home and face everyone's pity. What if Faro comes out with that look on his face? It would be unbearable.

That's what Dad chose for us: rejection. Maybe he thought it didn't matter so much because we weren't Mer. A bitter taste fills my mouth. No. I mustn't think of Dad. I must close my mind against him, as Conor said.

"There he is," says Elvira. There's no relief in her voice, only tight fear. As Faro swims towards us I see why. Faro's mouth is set in a line. He is moving slowly and there is no sign of joy.

"Faro!" I had never even thought of making the Crossing without him. Now I touch the depths of disappointment. If Faro isn't with us, the journey will be as grey as this dawn light.

No one wants to question Faro. His grim face forbids it. At last Elvira touches his arm gently. "My brother," she murmurs, as if he's been in a terrible accident. Faro clears his throat and gives us a defiant smile that does not reach his eyes.

"Don't be afraid. I have been chosen."

"Then what...?" asks Conor.

"I had to dive to the stone twice," goes on Faro in a harsh, level voice that makes him sound much older suddenly. "You can imagine what pleasure that gave to Ervys's men."

"But no one ever dives twice," blurts out Elvira, completely forgetting her usual tact.

"Exactly," says Faro. "But I had to do so."

"Well, we're here now, all four of us. That's all that matters," I say quickly, willing the others to stop asking questions. Faro's face softens.

"You are right, little sister. But since you haven't asked me, I will tell you anyway. There should be no secrets between us. I heard the Call. You know how it is." We nod in agreement.

"I dived down and then suddenly I knew that everything was wrong. This was not my time. I rose immediately." He swallows. The agony of that moment is clear in his face.

"Ervys's men shoved forward. They were baying with triumph and even Saldowr could hardly hold them. You should have seen their faces. There were plenty of Mer in the ranks who also rejoiced. I was afraid – not of *them*," and Faro throws out a hand dismissively, as if Ervys and all his spears are nothing "but of the hatred that was in them. And then I knew that the hatred was not outside me, but inside me too.

"Saldowr looked at me over his shoulder for a second – he could not look longer, because it took all his power to restrain Ervys's followers from rushing forward and taking control of the water above the stone. That was exactly what they were looking for: a chance to control it. And in Saldowr's face I saw that I had almost given it to them. When I dived, my mind was not clear. I was thinking of Ervys, not of the Call, not of the Crossing. I had done what my enemies wanted. My heart was full of hatred and the stone could not see my choice."

"And so you dived again."

"I dived again, and this time it was right. I was chosen. Even those who were howling for my blood could not deny the truth when I faced them after the second dive."

"You are so brave, Faro," I say.

"So brave! So stupid. I fell into their trap. I risked all our chances. You could not have made the Crossing without me."

"We'd have tried," says Conor.

"Of course I know that. But you would have left your bones in the oceans of the south, my friend."

"You were so brave, Faro." I tell him, "I'd never have had the courage to dive a second time."

"Well, we are here, as you said, little sister. The four of us. Nothing stands in our way. Let's go!"

"Go?" *What, now?* I want to say. Without any preparation? Don't we have to gather supplies, bring medicines for healing, food? You can't just set out across the world saying "Let's go!" – Conor and I in our old cut-offs, Elvira in her little bodice – although now I look at her more closely I see she has a bag attached to her belt, which is about half the size of my hand. Well, that's fine then. A bag the size of my purse at home must be big enough to hold everything we need for the longest and most dangerous journey we're ever likely to make.

"What's wrong, Saph?" asks Conor.

"Oh, nothing."

"You have a very expressive face, little sister," says Faro with a trace of his usual teasing.

"I was just wondering – aren't there things we need to bring?"

Faro laughs. "You humans! When you cross the world you take a ship loaded down with food and water and metal and weapons. You take a cow to give you milk to drink and sheep to slaughter."

"I'm sure we don't take sheep, Faro."

"Our ancestors tell us that you do. But we Mer are different."
Conor and I exchange glances. How often have we heard this?
"Whatever food we need, we will find on our way. No cows will be
necessary. Come, little sister, we have wasted enough time. Let's go!"

"But which way are we going?" Faro is already swimming away.

"South, of course," he cries. "What other way could there be?"

"It'll be the route the Mer have always taken since time
began," Conor murmurs. "They've not much desire for
innovation, have they?"

South. I summon up my school atlas and its double-page
spread showing the map of the world. How strange: usually the
human world grows dim in my mind once Ingo surrounds me.
But I can see the atlas almost as clearly as if it were in front of
me. The flat map is no good. I need a globe. Dad's globe. The
faded blue of the oceans, the brown of the land.

South, past the Scillies, bearing east across the Bay of Biscay
and down the coast of Spain. Out into the Atlantic, where Africa
bulges into the ocean as if it wants to join up with South
America again. On and on until we reach the Cape, then
eastwards again through the vast Indian Ocean which stretches
all the way to Australia. That must be the way that the Mer go to
cross Ingo, never touching the land. I say nothing aloud. Faro is
always so scornful when I use human words for the oceans. He
must know the way.

At that moment I feel a presence knocking at the door of my
mind – insistent, urgent – asking me if I will let him in. I've

shared thoughts with Faro for so long now that it doesn't feel strange, but this is different. A mind far more powerful than anything I've ever imagined is trying to communicate with me.

Saldowr.

Yes. I must speak to you but I cannot leave the chamber. There are many young ones who need my protection. Don't be afraid.

I sense Saldowr's huge mental power, but he's holding back so as not to overwhelm me.

You have been chosen. Faro and Elvira have told you how important it is to Ingo. You carry something within you that is stronger than the divisions between our two worlds. Mer and human can become one, reconciled. The wounds that tear the Mer can be healed. The Crossing will make you wholly Mer, but your human blood will not weaken. There will be many dangers, and not where you expect them. I cannot predict them for you. Be strong...

My mind floods with Saldowr's warmth and encouragement, and then as suddenly as he came, he's gone. I grasp for his thoughts and find nothing.

"Conor."

Conor's staring at me, looking as shaken as I feel.

"It was Saldowr."

"I know."

"Many dangers..." quotes Conor wryly. "I suppose it's too late to convince you that you ought to go home, Saph."

"Definitely."

We swim on, following Faro and Elvira. The pace of our strokes is steady. We have a long journey ahead of us, and we need stamina, not speed. Faro will find the currents for us. Maybe they'll bring us to the Great Current that he told me about long ago. The currents will sweep us almost to the bottom of the world…

We've got into a weak current which doubles our swimming speed while barely disturbing the clarity of the water. Faro glances back over his shoulder from time to time to check that we are within sight of one another. *This is how it will be for thousands of miles*, I think dreamily. Sometimes Faro and Elvira leading, sometimes Faro and me, or Conor and Elvira, or Conor and me…

The dawn light has changed to blue-green. The sun must be shining up in the Air, lighting up the human world. Its light filters richly through Ingo. We are swimming about thirty metres below the surface, and the sea bed has already fallen far away below us. The water beneath us shades from purple to black. I think of the Deep, then pull my mind away. I wish I could have seen the whale before we left. Maybe she would have given me a message for her daughter who lives at the bottom of the world. I'm determined to find the whale's daughter. The whale has done so much for me; I want to do something in return.

A shoal of mackerel shimmers around us, parting to make way and then closing up behind us. Faro and Elvira, up ahead, vanish in a cloud of black and green and blue and silver. The mackerel flicker past us, almost touching our skin, but not quite. They are friendly, inquisitive and unafraid.

Suddenly the shoal shudders. Within a second it changes direction. The mackerel plunge downward and disappear.

"Isn't that weird?" I say to Conor. "They were all swimming along quite happily and then they just—"

"*Shark!*" calls Faro. He and Elvira stop dead in the water as only Mer and dolphins can. "Quick, sideways, let's get out of this current."

But why is Faro so worried about a shark? I think as I kick free at a diagonal to the current's tug. There are plenty of sharks around here. Basking sharks, porbeagles, even the odd mako, but none of them will harm us as long as we don't upset them. The sharks that patrol the Groves of Aleph are Great Whites, and they scare me even though Saldowr has taught them to recognise us, and let us pass safely.

We're all out of the current now, close together. "Did you see it?" asks Faro.

"No, nothing."

"Up ahead. It will turn soon and come back. That's what they do. They circle, like this..." He draws an oval shape through the water with his hands.

"What kind of shark was it?" asks Conor.

"What did you call the sharks from the Groves, Sapphire?"

"Great Whites. But they know us, Faro!"

"Wait. Look ahead. He is coming again."

It's just a dot in the water, and then it grows towards us like a train first seen way down an empty line. "He's coming straight for us."

"No, he will pass us," says Faro. He does not take his eyes off the shark. As he predicts, the shark swerves left to pass us on our right. He is a Great White for sure – as big as a basking shark but he moves like a knife through the water. I see his closed, underslung jaw, his pale belly and one cold, dull eye. He surges past us like a missile. In a few seconds he is small in the distance, then he disappears.

"He'll pass closer next time," says Faro.

"Doesn't he know us? Isn't he one of the patrol?"

"No."

"Do sharks ever attack the Mer?" asks Conor. His voice sounds steady.

"Sometimes they refuse to hear that we are Mer. They hear that we are seals. This one – I am not sure. I think he knows who we are. He may be a follower of Ervys. I know that Ervys has taken time to make friends among the sharks. But even Ervys – I can barely believe that any Mer would turn a shark against his own kind.

Faro scans the water. There are no fish now. Every flicker of movement has been stilled by the shark.

"He's coming again," says Conor quietly. "Maybe we'd better believe it, Faro."

We turn to face the shark. It passes a little closer this time. If it came nearer – if it even grazed our skin – it would rip it to ribbons. And then we'd bleed – there'd be blood in the water. Blood brings more sharks.

I clench my fists over my chest. I've got to keep calm. Sharks can smell panic. I must not think about its teeth.

"If you hit them on the nose, doesn't that scare them off?" says Conor.

You might as well try to hit the nose of an express train as it thunders towards you. The shock would knock you out. You wouldn't even know when the shark opened his mouth—

No, Sapphire. Don't. I feel sick. My stomach is a knot of terror.

"It's coming again," says Elvira.

"I am going to try and make it recognise me," says Faro.

This time the shark comes so close that its wash hurls us through the water, separating us. I swim frantically, arms and legs thrashing, trying to see where the others have gone. Through a churn of bubbles I recognise Conor's outline.

"Saph!"

"I'm here."

"Faro? Elvira?"

We are all safe. We grab hands so that next time the shark won't throw us apart. But it's not going to work. The shark is huge. It could toss three of us aside like plastic toys, while it turned and seized the fourth. It is taunting us, stretching out the attack so we have time to feel all the terror it wants us to feel.

The terror in my mind is so great that there is no space for anything else. A dark flood of it swallows my brain cells. All I can feel is fear. I picture Conor torn away in the shark's mouth. His screams for rescue. The shark shakes him like a doll, but he's not a doll. He's my brother and he's alive and he knows what's happening until the second that the shark rips him apart. Would I have the courage to fight the shark for Conor, even though I knew there was nothing I could do to rescue him? Would Conor come for me if I was the one the shark took first?

The terror eases a little. Conor would fight the shark and so would Faro, even if they knew it was useless. They would rather lose their own lives than live with not having tried to rescue me. And I'd rather die fighting for them. *Don't think about the shark; think about the others*, I tell myself.

"The shark's mind is closed to us," says Faro. "I can't make him know that I am Mer." His voice stays calm, but there is no hope in it. The shark will circle us once or twice more, and then, when we're stretched to breaking point, he'll close in for the kill. There is nothing we can do to stop it.

"Hold on. When he's ready to strike, go for his eyes. Even if he gets you in his jaws, feel for his eyes. If he gets one of us, the rest must keep fighting."

We huddle together as close as we can, as if we're one body. There's a bit of comfort in not being alone. Faro tries to push me behind him, but I resist.

"I am stronger than you are, little sister."

"No," I say. "My nails are longer than yours. Better for gouging its eyes out."

We peer ahead into the water. Every nerve in my body strains for the first sight of the shark. "He's coming," says Faro.

Out of the distant water a dark shape appears, and starts to grow. But at the same moment the water churns above us. Oh God, it's another shark, attacking from a different direction. We are finished now.

They surge past us, so close their bodies almost touch us. They separate so that some of them are above us, some below, some to our left and some to our right. They are almost nose to tail as they begin to circle us...

Familiar shapes of snout and tail. Glistening bodies, much smaller than the shark's. Small, intelligent eyes. Within a few seconds a cage of dolphins protects us. Now they face outward to fight off the shark.

He barrels towards us, coming in for the kill. As he turns in I see his belly and the gape of his jaw. At this moment the dolphins start to thrash the water. We can see nothing. Shark and dolphins disappear and the water turns white around us. We cling to each other. Our ears thunder as the dolphins beat the sea with their tails. We are hurled from side to side, thrown against each other. Something strikes my arm in an explosion of pain. The dolphins are fighting for us. The frothing bubbles around us are no longer white, but red with blood. We're in the eye of the battle but we're not fighting and we don't know what's happening, or who's winning. I catch one glimpse of the shark, its mouth wide, its rows of teeth so close that I can see the filth trapped in them. The sea convulses, the shark's jaw slices sideways, and he disappears.

I cling so hard to Faro that I don't know if it's his heart

thundering or mine. His hair sweeps across my face, hiding everything. But I sense that the dolphins are still fighting for us. Their strength, determination and courage fill my mind like the beam from a lighthouse, driving away the terror that almost swallowed me.

At long last the storm begins to ease. The blur of the dolphins slows. Now we see them separately. There are at least ten dolphins swimming around us in circles, guarding us while others plunge off in all directions and then return. One dolphin swims slowly back into the circle. There is a deep gash in her side and her blood rolls out into the water, clouding it. There is no sign of the shark.

"Are you hurt, Saph?" asks Conor.

"Only on my arm. It's not much."

"I will look at it for you later," says Elvira.

It seems very strange to hear one another's voices again. In my mind I had already lost them, but here they are. Faro, Conor, Elvira. The four of us are still safe, and still together. The sea no longer drums with terror. The shark has gone.

The sea rings with dolphin music. Long ago, when I first came to Ingo, I could only hear clicks and whistlings from the dolphins. Then words began to come clear, as fish show up against the sea bed once you've spotted their camouflage. Now I hear the full music of dolphin language as they sing to one another.

Wave-Rider struck the attacker on the gill pouch
The sons of the pod fought beside him

The daughters of the pod tamed the blood-shedder

Who is wounded?

Scylla is wounded

Is it her blood that runs in the water?

Her blood runs in the water but she will not die. She beat the attacker on the nose with her snout

Does she wish to be carried to the surface?

No, she has still got strength enough to swim

Then let us greet these little ones whom we have protected

The dolphin with a gash in her side is nudging close to me. I stretch out my arms to her and embrace her. "Dear Scylla. You saved our lives. Are you very badly hurt?"

"Not very badly," answers the dolphin. Her voice is weak, but calm.

"All of you saved our lives," I go on. "We are so, so grateful. Another minute and the shark would have killed us."

"It was not time for you to die, my sister," murmurs Scylla. "You have a long journey to make. You must stay alive."

"I certainly want to," I say fervently, and Scylla starts to laugh then stops because it hurts.

Another dolphin swims up at high speed, and stops with the sudden, brilliant dolphin dead-stop that amazes me afresh every time I see it. I am sure I recognise him. He looks like the dolphin who rode with Faro when we returned from the Deep to the Groves of Aleph.

"I am Wave-Rider," says the dolphin. "Quick, we have gained a little time but not much. We dolphins can hold off one shark, maybe two. But if more come we cannot protect you."

"Do you think they will come?" asks Faro.

"I am as certain that they will come as I am sure that the sun will rise tomorrow," says the dolphin. "That shark may not return, but others will. They will test us and test us until they break through our defences. We dolphins understand the ways of sharks and rarely have to fear them. But these sharks are different."

"They are Great Whites, aren't they?"

"They are Ervys's creatures," says the dolphin, and I learn that dolphins' eyes, usually so warm, intelligent and communicative, can also blaze with anger. "They have gone outside their nature to fight Ervys's battles. They have made you their prey, not from hunger or from any natural desire, but because they do Ervys's bidding."

Elvira swims down to examine the wound in Scylla's side. The flesh gapes red. The gash is so deep that a layer of fat is exposed. It seems to be bleeding a little less now. Elvira pushes the sides of the wound together while Scylla floats patiently, sculling with one flipper to keep herself in place. It must hurt, but Scylla doesn't flinch. Another, older female dolphin swims to Scylla's other side to support her. Gradually, as I stare in fascination, the lips of the wound seem to draw closer together.

"How do you do that, Elvira?" I ask. Elvira does not answer until she has finished stroking together the ragged edges of the red tear in Scylla's side. Her fingers look as if each of them possesses a deep, sure knowledge.

"It will do better now," murmurs Elvira to the dolphin. "You must swim slowly, and keep close to your pod until the wound is completely healed. If you feel weak, don't try to swim at all. Allow the others to support you."

Elvira's healing isn't magical. The gash is still there, but it no longer looks raw and dangerous. It looks as if it will know how to heal itself.

"How did you do that?" I ask again.

"I can't explain it very well. I am only learning. A year ago I could have done nothing for Scylla. I don't heal her myself – you understand that, Sapphire. All my hands can do is to remind Scylla's body of how it wants to be. Not injured, but whole. Sometimes a wound is too serious and I can achieve nothing. Only a great healer like my teacher will succeed with someone who is close to death. Let me see your arm now."

It's only a bruise above the elbow. The skin is blackening already. Elvira feels my arm and then my shoulder. She massages the shoulder joint carefully, and then her hands move down my arm and stroke the bruise from sides to centre with a light, butterfly touch. "Your shoulder will be stiff," she says, "but luckily it was not dislocated. Your arm will hurt, but you can swim. Later I will give you another treatment."

Wave-Rider, who was silent while Elvira treated us, now says, "We must hurry before the shark tells his fellows where we are. The sharks believe that you are going south."

"Of course we must travel south," Faro cuts in. "There's no

133

other way to make the Crossing of Ingo. Since the time of our ancestors..."

"You will never make the Crossing if you continue south," goes on the dolphin. His voice is calm and logical. "If you go south, the sharks will swallow your bones. Even if you escape them – which cannot happen, I think – Ervys will have set other traps in your way. He is determined that you will not make the Crossing of Ingo." The dolphin's skin ripples as he flexes his muscles. "Ervys fears you. If Ingo is healed, and the human world and our world can live without enmity, then the Mer will not need him. This is what Saldowr tells us."

The thought of the sharks hammers at my mind. We've got to get away.

"We could go north," says Conor.

"North?"

"The world's round, isn't it? Surely we can still cross Ingo if we go north."

"North?" repeats Faro with such intensity that at first I think he's angry with Conor. It's another case of Breaking All the Laws of the Mer, I suppose. But maybe it's better to break a few laws than to end up in a shark's belly...

"*North!*" Faro mutters again. His eyes glow. "North, of course! Why didn't I think of that? No Mer ever made the Crossing of Ingo that way—"

"But, Faro, they must have done," I break in. "Don't you remember you once told me that some of the Mer dived under icebergs and met ice bears with claws like hooks. There aren't

134

any bears in the south – at least I don't think there are."

"The bears are only a story for children," says Faro.

"Stories have to come from somewhere," says Conor. "Polar bears only live in the Arctic as far as I know. Maybe long ago the Mer *did* travel that way."

And maybe Faro believes us. "A northern Crossing..." he says as if to himself. Longing and excitement stir in his voice. "It will be an even greater adventure..."

Elvira, by contrast, looks distinctly cross. "But, Faro," she says in a tone of sweet reason, "if the Mer have taken the southern route for generations, then surely that must be because it's the best one? Why risk going where none of us knows the way?"

"Why risk anything at all? Why not go home and let Ervys rule over Ingo?" snaps Faro.

Elvira refuses to lose her temper. "You know I didn't mean that. But we have to be practical."

"Practical? So which do you think is the *practical* choice? Being eaten by a shark, or giving up and going home in shame?" It looks as if we're on the brink of a full-scale sibling row – I wonder what Elvira will look like when she's in a real rage – but Conor cuts through their argument.

"We can go through the Arctic Ocean. How frozen will it be now in October, Saph?"

"I don't know. It starts to freeze up again in August, I think."

"I wonder if we could dive under the Pole. I don't suppose it matters how thick the ice is, as long as there's free water under it. There's a channel between Asia and America – I can't remember what it's called. It freezes in winter, but we can swim under the ice and then south again. We'll be into the North Pacific by then..."

"*North Pacific*," says Faro a little scornfully. *Where is that written on the water?* he'll demand if I say "Atlantic".

"Call it what you like," says Conor impatiently. "We haven't got time to argue. We can't let ourselves be killed. We can't give up. That only leaves one option."

"*North...*" Faro lingers on the word as if he likes the taste of it. "I have gone some way north, but never far. There are currents which will take us there, but they are wild and dangerous. Ervys will not think of us taking the Northern Passage. The whales and the fulmars say that the ice joins together and becomes the Frozen Ocean." I think of Dad's map and the vast, shapeless mass of ice to the North.

"Everyone knows that there are monsters to the North, made of snow and ice," Faro goes on. "They prowl the surface of the Frozen Ocean and sometimes they plunge deep into the water, searching for prey. Ervys will expect us to try again by the south. He will keep his forces there, waiting for us..."

"Let him wait! We'll be long gone by the time he realises!" says Conor excitedly.

Conor and Faro both laugh aloud, showing their teeth. They slap hands as Conor taught Faro to do. How alike they are. Their warm dark colouring, their brown-black hair, the strength in their arms and shoulders and the fierce determination on their faces. I wish I could feel as confident that we can outwit Ervys.

Once he finds out that we haven't gone south, won't he pursue us?

"What do you think of the North, little sister?" Faro asks me.

"I prefer it to the sharks."

Faro laughs again. "What about the ice monsters?"

"I don't believe in them," I say firmly. "They are mythical creatures." And then I think uncomfortably, *As I believed the Mer were before I came to Ingo.*

"When we come to the monsters I will tell them that you don't believe in them."

Faro's face gleams with delight. He seems to have thrown off the memory of the sharks as a seal's skin throws off water. For the first time since his injury, he throws himself forward and executes a slow but perfect somersault.

"We will escort you past the Lost Islands," says Wave-Rider as we swim away together. "We will keep company with you westward until you are well beyond these sharks' territory. But there we shall have to leave you. We have young ones who cannot travel farther, and Scylla needs time to recover from her wound. Keep well out of land. There are nets which have trapped many of our people. They hold us beneath the water and we drown. Swim on until there is no more land to the west of you. Then listen until you hear where north is. From there, you must find your way."

CHAPTER TEN

The dolphins have left us now. It was hard to see them go. I pressed my cheek against Scylla's face and told her we'd never forget that the dolphins had risked their own lives to protect us from the shark.

Just before they left, the dolphins made a circle around us as they did when the shark attacked. They wove in and out of one another, plunging and somersaulting. They leaped upwards, breached the surface, then crashed down through the water. They rushed towards us, stopped dead so that the sea surged around them, and nuzzled us gently with their snouts.

"Goodbye, dear Scylla."

"Goodbye, Wave-Rider."

"Goodbye, Amaris."

"Goodbye..."

We stared after them until we couldn't see them any more. The last of their calls faded into the sounding of the sea. We felt very alone without dolphin music all around us.

We've been alone for three days now. At first we were on edge and looking out for sharks all the time. We've seen plenty of basking sharks, and a pod of minke whales passed us and greeted us, but there's been no sign of a Great White. We're beginning to relax, but we don't sleep much. One of us is always on guard while the others float, resting. I dream a lot, but I don't sleep deeply. A part of my mind is always alert and watchful.

It's strange when it's your turn to stay awake while the others sleep. The sea is never still and never silent. You jump at a shadow, but it's only a shoal of fish. You hear a distant calling of whales, but can't make out what they are saying. Moonlight filters down, making ghostly blue glimmers on the others' faces.

None of us rests for long. We've got to keep swimming, and besides, you don't seem to need much sleep in Ingo. We don't need to eat much either. Faro and Elvira have showed us all the edible weeds and sea grasses. Sometimes we find sea grapes, and there's another type of fruit which only grows in fast-flowing water. Elvira calls them current berries. They look like frogspawn and they feel slimy when you swallow them, but they are very filling.

Faro and Elvira know every plant, but they won't touch even the smallest shrimp. They can't imagine eating a fish, let alone another mammal like a seal. It's as barbarous to them as eating a baby would be to us. Once, when I first knew Faro, I made the mistake of saying that mackerel have to be eaten quickly once they're caught or they go off. Faro looked at me with fascinated disgust. "*Go off,*" he repeated and shook his head. "Why not eat them when they're alive, then?"

"Faro, that would be horrible!"

"So killing them isn't horrible?"

The Mer have other ways of nourishing themselves besides eating. If we grow tired Elvira tells us to rest and draw the sea deep into our lungs so that the nutrients and minerals can pass into our bodies. It's a wonderful feeling. I imagine breathing pure oxygen must be like this. You feel a rush of energy and power. Your heart seems to pump more strongly, and you can think more clearly. I never really feel hungry in Ingo.

"Isn't it strange that what drowns you in the human world is what feeds you here?" I said to Conor once.

"*Our* world, you mean," he answered sharply. Conor moves as easily through Ingo as I do now. He never struggles for oxygen as he used to do, as if he was having an underwater asthma attack. That was so frightening. But even though Conor's as much at home physically as me, mentally the human world – Air – is always home to him.

We've been travelling west, as the dolphins instructed. We are a long way from land now. You can smell land when you're in Ingo, just as you can smell it when you're out sailing and you catch the first scent long before you see the smudge of a cliff on the horizon. It's a sharp, mineral smell, quite different from the smell of Ingo. You can smell the pollution too: all the filth that humans pour into Ingo, as Faro expresses it. I'd hate to swim near the mouth of an estuary where there's a big city like London or New York. The taste of the water would make me gag.

Even way out in the Atlantic we find plastic drifting through the water. You have to be careful with small pieces of plastic and with plastic bags. They can get lodged in your throat and choke you. Faro says many creatures die that way every year.

I love it down here, just deep enough to feel safe but not deep enough to be swallowed up by darkness.

"It'll be time to turn north soon," says Faro.

"Faro, do you think Ervys is going to send some of his followers after us?" I ask.

Faro frowns. "The young Mer who make the Crossing in Ervys's name will all take the southern route. No shark will stop them. Ervys will not want his supporters to scatter too far. The North is wide and they would struggle to guess our route."

"But it's possible, Faro."

"I think Ervys will not attack us when we expect it, little sister. He is too cunning for that. He was defeated in the Assembly chamber, but he must have been sure that the shark would kill us. Now he wants us to forget to fear him. Only then will he strike. But I promise you, little sister, Saldowr and the dolphins will be doing everything in their power, every moment, to protect us from Ervys and his forces. It is a hard task. Ervys is as wily as he is strong."

"You seem to know him really well."

"Saldowr has taught me to know him."

The two of us are swimming together, ahead of Elvira and Conor, who are having one of their deep discussions about nothing of interest to anyone else. I am keeping an eye on the

Conor/Elvira relationship. They swim very close together, but the last time I dropped back and casually listened to a fragment of their conversation, Elvira was telling Conor how to articulate a damaged tail spine if the injury were close to the fin – *Of course, with a higher vertebral injury the manipulation would be quite different* – Conor appeared to be listening attentively, but did I detect a slightly glazed look in his eyes? I put on speed, and came up alongside Faro again.

"Elvira's very dedicated, isn't she?" I observed.

"To what?" asked Faro.

"To healing, of course."

Faro grinned maliciously. "I wasn't sure what you meant."

The farther we get from the sharks, the lighter our spirits. Already it feels as if we've been travelling for weeks, not a few days. I wonder how much human time has passed, then I put the thought aside because it's no use worrying about that. The truth is that I'm not really worrying at all. Ingo is so strong around me. My human life still seems clear – it hasn't vanished into a fog as it's done before when I've been in Ingo – but it has the clarity of a brilliant painting or a perfect description. I have to remind myself that human life is something real which I've experienced myself.

Faro is teaching me to whistle. It's quite a different skill from whistling in Air. You make sound by blowing the water harshly from the back of your throat or softly against your palate. It's one of those things that would be easy if you'd grown up doing it, but is frustratingly tricky if you try to learn it later on. I'm getting a better sound already. At least, I think so. It makes Faro laugh quite a lot.

"It's easy for you," I protest. "I'm always trying to do Mer things and you never have to try human things. I bet you wouldn't make such a great goalkeeper."

Immediately, I wish I hadn't said this. Faro is so intensely curious, and he'll want all kinds of technical detail about football which I won't be able to supply. And besides, Faro would probably make a brilliant goalie, swiping the ball away with his tail in an exhibition of power and finesse which no two-legged creature is ever going to match. Except of course that football matches are not held underwater...

"What are you thinking about, little sister?"

"Nothing."

"Shall I try to open your thoughts?"

"No, Faro, you're not allowed to—"

But at that moment Faro's face changes completely. "Hush, Sapphire."

He stops dead, seizing my hand to stop me with him. The others almost swim into us but Faro doesn't even notice.

"Faro," I whisper as cold dread steals over me, "is it the sharks?"

"No. It is a Mer voice. Sapphire, he is calling..."

One of Ervys's men. We were too confident that they

wouldn't follow us. They must have guessed about the northern route and swum after us to cut us off—

"... for you," says Faro.

"I hear it too," says Conor.

I listen. Through the water, faint and faraway, comes a voice that is terribly familiar and terribly out of place.

"Sapphire... Sapphire..."

"He's calling for you," says Conor. His voice is without emotion.

"Dad?" I say very quietly, so only the others will hear me.

"I think it is your father, Conor," says Elvira, but for once Conor takes no notice of her.

"Do you think he's followed us, Con?"

"How else could he have found us? But we're not in the Assembly chamber now. He can't stop us." Conor sounds as if Dad is a stranger, and a hostile one.

"Shouldn't we answer him?"

"You can if you want."

"I'm just as angry with him as you are, Conor. Dad didn't speak for me in the chamber, either."

Conor just shrugs. "You'll never be as angry with him as I am, Saph."

"Sapphire... Sapphire..."

He's coming closer. We could still escape if we swam fast, but my arms and legs won't move.

"You'd better answer him then, if you're going to," says Conor. But I don't need to. A figure comes swimming towards us through the gloom of the dark green water. My first thought is that Dad looks much older. He's swimming strongly but there is none of the joy I remember from our days at the cove, when he would dive and swim and play in the water all day with me and Conor until the tide came in. He slows down, searching our faces. His hair has grown even longer. It is a thick tangle of weed that spreads out behind him. At his temples the hair is grey.

"I've found you at last," he says. "I was so afraid…"

The moment when I should have hugged and kissed Dad has already passed. The truth is that I feel nothing. It's as if I've hidden all my love for Dad so carefully that now I can't find it, even when I want it. He is such a stranger. The powerful tail, which is so beautiful and natural on Elvira and Faro, looks like a deformity when joined to my father's familiar torso. Dad's face looks different too. It's not just older, but heavier, too. When Dad used to wake us up in the mornings when we were little, we always felt that something exciting was about to happen. We'd go out in the *Peggy Gordon,* or we'd learn to set a crab pot, or Dad would teach us how to frame the image when we took photographs. Or he'd tell us crazy stories about what all the old respectable people in the village had been up to when they were little, or he'd buy marshmallows and we'd spear them on sticks over a fire—

I mustn't think of all that. *This* is Dad, now.

"Thank God I found you in time," says Dad.

The four of us have drawn close together.

"In time?" I say.

"The dolphins told me that you were going north."

"You can't stop us now, Dad."

"I'm asking you to return with me."

"For the sharks to kill us? Or perhaps Ervys?" says Conor.

A flash of Dad's old spirit shows as he says, "Don't back-answer me, Conor. I'm your father. I will not let you die on this crazy journey. Why else do you think I was silent in the chamber? I had to protect you. You don't understand how ruthless a man like Ervys can be. You've got to go home, back to the Air, while you still can. If Ervys can be sure you will not come back to Ingo, he will leave you alone."

Conor and Dad look very alike as they glare at each other. Conor has grown so much taller since Dad left. Soon they will be the same height.

"It's too late for that," says Conor at last. His tone is not angry as I expected, but it is final. "We might have been little kids when you went away – well, Saph was, anyway – but we're not now."

Words prickle in my head like thorns. *You weren't there for us, were you, Dad? We had to manage without you, and now we can. We don't need you any more.* I keep silent. There's too much distress in Dad's face for me to add to it.

"I can't let you go," says Dad, but his expression reveals that even he doesn't really think he can stop us. No one answers. "Or perhaps I could come with you."

"You are too old to make the Crossing of Ingo," says Faro. I am sure that he doesn't intend to be cruel, but Dad flinches.

"I've come a long way to talk to my children," he says coldly, as if Faro is some stranger at a family gathering. I'm afraid Faro will snap back, but he holds his temper. Elvira takes her brother's hand and draws him aside.

"I can never forgive myself for what I've done to you," says Dad in a low voice.

"But, Dad—" I say, shocked.

"No, Saph, let him say what he wants to say."

"I know how angry you are, Conor. I can't ask you to understand what's happened. If I could go back and change things…"

But would you, Dad? I wonder. Would you really want little Mordowrgi never to have been born? Would you really want to lose Mellina? I've seen the tenderness in your face, and in Mellina's, when I looked into Saldowr's mirror and watched you greet each other. Even the baby waved his little fists to greet you. They are your family; I understand that now. The words still hurt but I can't pretend that they aren't true.

You are Mer now. Even if you could undo it, you'd never be able to wipe out all the memories of your Mer life. You'd wake at night and long to hear Mellina singing again. Or you'd hear the cry of a gull and think it was Mordowrgi crying for his lost father.

It's taken me such a long time to get here, Dad. I never thought I'd understand you, let alone feel sorry for you. All I could think about was the wrong you'd done to the three of us – Mum, Conor and me.

"What's done is done, Dad," says Conor. "Even Saldowr can't

make time run backwards." He tries to smile, but it doesn't work. "Let's deal with things as they are," he urges Dad. "Saph and I *have* to make this Crossing. It's part of… well, it's part of everything that's happened since you went away. Maybe it's the final part…"

"Don't say that!"

"Oh, Dad, I don't mean final as in we're going to die. But the Crossing of Ingo is so huge – we can't go around it, we have to go through it. If you'd been young – if you'd been in Ingo when you were young, I mean – if you'd been able to make the Crossing then maybe none of this would have happened. You'd have *completed* something and you'd have known where you were, instead of marrying Mum and still not knowing and always wanting something you hadn't got. I don't want to be like that, Dad! I want to know where I am. I want to know *who* I am. When I've made the Crossing, I'll know. That's what it's about. Besides…" He hesitates, and then I know that he's not going to tell Dad the deep reasons that we've got to complete the Crossing. Instead he lets his voice tail away.

"And does Sapphy think the same?" asks Dad in a low voice.

This is one time when I'd prefer Conor to speak for me, but he isn't going to. I haven't really stopped to consider *why* I am making the Crossing. I've heard the Call, and answered it. Now, because of what Saldowr's told us, I know we have a mission that goes beyond our own journey. I'm impressed by what Conor says about completing things and knowing where he is and who he is, but I have to admit none of it had crossed my mind. From the first time I heard about it, the Crossing of Ingo just felt... inevitable.

"I don't know what I *think*, Dad. The only thing I'm sure about is that my Mer blood won't let me do anything else."

Dad stares at me, then at Conor.

"Go home, Dad," I say as gently as I can. Now, for the first time, I feel no horror of his Mer nature and his Mer body. I want to put my arms around him and hug him until that terrible lost look leaves his face. "Please go home." As the words leave my mouth, I realise that I don't mean "home to Mum" any more, or even "home to the human world". I don't know exactly when it happened, but at last I've accepted that his home is here in Ingo, with Mellina and Mordowrgi. Maybe Saldowr got it wrong and Dad doesn't have a choice to make any more.

"Mordowrgi's lovely," I say aloud. "I can't wait to see him again."

A gleam of hope shines on Dad's face.

"You'll be in my mind and my heart day and night," he says.

Not very restful for Mellina, I catch myself thinking, although my throat aches and I can hardly bear to look at him.

"See you, Dad," says Conor. He puts out his hand as if he's intending to shake hands with Dad – which would be improbably weird as the two of them have never shaken hands in their lives – but halfway through the gesture he changes his mind, or else Dad changes his. Something happens, anyway, because for a brief second Dad's arms are around Conor and Conor isn't fighting free.

"Goodbye, Dad," I say. I daren't kiss him or hug him now in case it breaks my resolve.

"Goodbye, my girl," says Dad. He hesitates. I hesitate. There's so little water between us but it feels like an ocean. I can't move. I never feel the cold in Ingo, but I'm frozen now.

It's Faro who breaks the silence. He has left Elvira's side and drifted close to me again. *Sapphire*, he says very quietly, *he is your father.*

No one else responds. It's as if Faro hadn't spoken, and all at once I realise that he said nothing aloud. His thoughts have touched my thoughts, as they've done so often.

I know, I answer silently, *but—*

You don't know. He'll be gone, and you might never see him again. You know the risks that lie ahead of us. If you haven't said goodbye, it will hurt you.

I am taken aback by the certainty in Faro's mind. How does he know these things?

Because it happened to me.

But, Faro—

There's no time for buts, little sister. Say goodbye to him.

Dad is looking at me with such hope in his face, and such pain.

"Dad..." I say aloud.

I don't have to do any more. His face lights up. I don't even see him move but the next second his arms are around me, crushing me so tight that my ribs hurt. I've been so afraid of his Mer self but when he hugs me I don't even notice that he is Mer. His body is different, but he is still Dad.

"Sapphy," he mutters in my ear.

"What?"

"Come back safe. Promise me you'll come back safe."

"I'll be all right, Dad."

I can tell he wants to cling on to me, but he lets go. I am back with the other three again, and Dad is separate.

"You'd better go now," he says to all of us. He doesn't want to swim away. He doesn't want to be the one who leaves, not this time.

"See you later, Dad," says Conor as if he's going up to Jack's for a couple of hours.

"See you later," says Dad. He used to say it like that when he walked off up the track on a summer evening for a drink in the pub. But this time we are the ones who move. I stretch out my arms and kick through the water. First one stroke, then the next, and then the next. This time we're heading north through unknown waters, and Dad is the one who stays behind. I look back over my shoulder as we swim away, gathering speed. I look once and then a second time. The last time I look it's hard to see him, but I know he is still there, not moving, looking after us until we are out of sight.

CHAPTER ELEVEN

"I have always longed to see the world of ice," says Elvira happily.

"Have you?" I look at her in surprise. I've never thought of Elvira as adventurous. But her usual rather annoying air of mysterious calm has vanished. Her eyes sparkle with suppressed excitement. For the first time, her expression is like her brother's.

Elvira goes on eagerly, "Yes, Sapphire, always. When I heard stories about the North, it was like listening to tales of somewhere that I had travelled in another life."

"But when we first suggested going north, you didn't seem too happy about it."

"That is because I thought we should not break with the tradition of the Crossing of Ingo. But now I believe that we have no choice, and so I'm free to think of the North." Elvira laughs, showing her perfect teeth. "My mother would tell me about Mer people who lived in the North. Their hair was silver and their skin was as pale as the moon. She said they had learned to see in the dark because their world was dark for months on end in winter. When the light came back in summer, they never slept because the sun never slept either. I was so curious. I wanted to make friends with a Mer girl like that. I was only little and did not understand how far away the northern ice was, so one day I thought I would set out to find the world of ice for myself. I went off alone – I did not even tell Faro. I was about six years old. But perhaps Faro has told you about it?"

"No, he never has."

Faro and Conor are up ahead, discussing our route again. Faro believes there is a very strong current about two days journey from here, which will take us directly east of a great frozen land mass. Conor and I think this means we'll be travelling east of Greenland, towards the Arctic.

"I swam away silently while my mother was sleeping," Elvira continues.

"Your mother?" My curiosity burns. I want to hear more about their mother. Faro never talks about his parents.

"Yes, Sapphire." Elvira smiles the sweet, gentle smile that has infuriated me so often. "Has Faro never spoken to you about our mother?"

"No, not really," I say reluctantly. I don't want Elvira to think Faro doesn't confide in me.

"He does not wish to speak of her. I understand that."

"Why not, Elvira? Is she… is she dead?"

"Yes, she is dead," says Elvira, still smiling at me. A surge of frustration goes through me. Elvira must have feelings – why does she hide them all the time? Or perhaps she only hides them from me.

"She died when we were seven."

We? "You were both seven? You mean you and Faro are twins?"

"Of course. It is very common among us Mer." Faro never told me that, either.

"She was ill for a long time, and then she went to Limina," goes on Elvira in her silvery voice.

"That must have been so hard for you – and for your father," I add, thinking that perhaps Elvira will tell me more about her family. I know nothing of their father either. Why haven't I ever asked Faro? I know so little about him in some ways. And yet I know him so well – I understand him as if I really were his sister.

"We had no father," says Elvira. "Saldowr is our guardian."

Of course you had a father, I want to say. The word makes me feel raw. In my mind I see Dad watching as we swim away. Everyone has a father, even if they don't see him or know him. Not to have a father is *an-at-om-ic-ally im-poss-ible*, as Faro told me when I first met him and suggested that he might be a "mermaid". But Elvira's sweet silveriness has a core of steel to it, and I don't ask any more questions about her father.

"That must have been hard for you," I repeat lamely, and then I remember that Elvira hasn't finished telling me about her escape to the North experience. "So what happened when you ran away – I mean, swam away on your own? How far did you get?"

Elvira laughs. "Not very far. A dolphin who knew my mother found me wandering and brought me home. I was so angry, but I didn't dare to show it. And when we got back, my mother hadn't even noticed I was gone. She thought I was with Faro."

We both laugh. It reminds me so much of the times I used to storm off in a temper when I was little, and hide under my duvet making secret plans to run away so no one would ever find me, and then they'd be really sorry and wish they hadn't been so horrible to me... I did run away once or twice, but only as far as the end of the track. Elvira's story makes me feel quite fond of her, for the first time ever.

At this moment there's a yell from the boys. "Current! Current up ahead!"

"I thought it was two days away," I shout back.

"Quick, we need to keep together! *Elvira! Sapphire! Come on!*"

As I reach them I see the current, about a hundred metres away. It's a bright, glacial green, pulling at speed through the darker Atlantic water. Faro is assessing it with the kind of attention a canoeist might give to white-water rapids.

"Is it the current we want?" I ask.

"It's definitely going north," mutters Faro. "I'm not sure we can risk it, though. It's very fast – and look how the flow keeps changing." He's right. As I watch, the current gives a wicked swerve as if it's taking an invisible corner at top speed.

"It is unstable," says Faro. "That is where the danger lies. As we go north they say there are mountains of ice that sail with their heads in the Air and body and tail deep in Ingo."

"Icebergs!" says Conor.

"Icebergs – is that what you call them? They are mountains. The part that shows above the water is far higher than any of your cliffs. Here in Ingo they are ten times as large. The current must take us safely between these ice mountains. If we are hurled against them the ice is as sharp as coral. It would kill us for sure," goes on Faro in a matter-of-fact tone. "I am not sure that we can trust this current..."

Faro talks about the current as if it's a living creature, and perhaps it is. We all gaze at the sinewy race of it. It looks as if it is rushing north because, like Elvira, it has always dreamed of the world of ice. Perhaps it will turn into ice when it reaches the Arctic. I agree with Faro. I'm not sure we can trust it to keep us safe. The current is stretched out like a rope, but inside itself the strands coil like a serpent. Now I'm studying it I can see that the green colour is made up of thousands of different streams, some almost white, some emerald, some a bright, cold turquoise. I understand why Faro is scrutinising it so carefully. It might be deadly.

"It will take us where we want to go," says Faro at last.

"Are you sure?"

"Sure? What is *sure* when you are making the Crossing of Ingo?" he mocks me. "This is not a tame current. Even if we lie in its heart, we may be battered by its force."

"Do you think we should risk it?" asks Conor.

"Yes," says Faro.

"Saph? Elvira?"

"If Faro thinks so," I say. Elvira says nothing. She's deep in contemplation of the current.

"It is so beautiful," she says quietly. I watch the flash and turn of the water. It reminds me of jewels – diamonds and emeralds – but no jewels have so much life in them.

"We'll take that as a yes, then," says Conor.

We decide that we'll dive one by one. As each dives, the other will follow immediately. Once we are in the current we must swim to its heart. I know from past experience that currents are like storms. All the fury is on the outside, but in the heart, or eye, there is stillness.

Faro will dive first, then me, then Elvira and Conor last. We must keep close and not hesitate because if the current gives one of its sudden, wicked-looking swerves, one or more of us could be left behind.

"What if we get separated?" I ask.

"Keep going north. Ask every creature you meet if it has seen any of us. But be careful of the orcas, little sister. Remember that sometimes they refuse to hear that we are Mer. They may not hear that you are human and prefer to believe that you are a seal." I shiver.

"Keep going north..." repeats Elvira dreamily. Conor looks at her, frowning slightly. Elvira looks a million miles away from us, lost in her own world. But we have to be alert. We have to keep together. This is real.

"Are you ready?" asks Faro. The muscles in his shoulders tense. His tail lashes from side to side, gathering power. His arms go back, and his tail whips up and then down. He plunges forward and vanishes into the current. Instantly, without thinking, I follow him.

I'm inside, looking out. A veil of a million shimmering particles hides me. *It was easy*, I think with a surge of joy and relief. *I've dived straight to the heart of the current.*

The green Atlantic rushes past me at a speed I've never known before. This is a new world, where mighty currents sweep from ocean to ocean, grazing continents as they go. Faro told me about the Great Current once. This can't be it because the Great Current goes southwards. But this one deserves to be called great, too.

Faro is ahead of me. His arms are pressed to his sides, like mine. We can't speak to each other because our voices would be drowned in the roar of rushing water. I open my thoughts and try to find his. *Faro?*

A surge of exultation hits me. Faro is loving this. The force of the current and the excitement of the journey flood his mind so that there's no room for anything else. But I want to talk to him.

Faro? It's me, Sapphire.

Slowly, reluctantly, his thoughts make room for me. *Sapphire?*

Isn't it amazing, Faro? As soon as the thought leaves my mind I know it's stupid. He doesn't need me telling him it's amazing, because he knows it with every fibre of his body. I'll leave him alone. I'll let go, let the current take us, and stop thinking.

But it's too late for that. Faro is restless now. *Look behind you, Sapphire. Can you see the others?*

I am doubly stupid. I haven't even bothered to check that Conor and Elvira are safely in the current. But it's hard to turn round against the rush of water. Slowly, centimetre by centimetre, I twist my body until I'm lying sideways, and I can look back and down my body.

I'm staring into a green tube that coils round and round on itself with dizzying speed. A crush of bubbles hides everything. There's no sign of Conor or Elvira. Maybe it's because I'm ahead of them. I could see Faro clearly because I was behind him. Probably the others are just hidden by the surging coil of the current. I wish I could share thoughts with Conor, but I've never been able to – at least, only in the ordinary human brother-and-sister way. As for Elvira's thoughts, I've never even tried to enter them. She is so different from me that I've always been sure I wouldn't succeed.

But what if they're not there? What if Faro and I are rushing on faster and faster and they are left behind? We mustn't lose one another. Whatever happens, we must be together.

Nightmare images dance in my mind. Conor knocked sideways by the power of the current, losing sight of us. A prowling killer whale, forgetting that Conor and Elvira are human and Mer. Or perhaps Ervys's followers, swimming steadily north, catching up with us—

Sapphire. Faro has broken into my thoughts. *Listen. I will have to close my thoughts to you while I try to find Elvira. She is far away and I need all my strength. Don't be afraid, little sister. I am still here, even if you can't communicate with me. Don't lose sight of me.*

I've lost touch with how long we've been inside the current. It could be an hour or a hundred years. All I hear is the thunder of the Atlantic pouring past me, and the deeper, serpentine roar of the current that has hold of me.

We were travelling so fast that everything we passed was a blur. It hurt to look at it. I knew I must look ahead and fix my eyes on Faro. His shape shimmered and dazzled up ahead of me. Sometimes I thought I'd lost sight of him, and a wash of panic went through me, and then I found the outline of his tail again through millions of dancing green and silver and turquoise particles. Sometimes he seemed to dissolve completely, as if the current had swallowed him. I couldn't find him with my mind. I had to keep on believing that he was there, up ahead of me, and I wasn't alone.

If I let myself think about Conor I felt the kind of terror you experience when you're standing on the edge of a cliff and a buffet of wind hits your back and you feel yourself start to sway so that the churning water far beneath you seems to rock towards you – and poor Elvira, dreaming of the North and the ice. She was longing to make this journey and now perhaps she's been separated from Conor as well as from me and Faro. She might be alone, terrified…

The water we sped through was growing darker. Either night was coming, or we were being pulled deeper. At that moment the current whipped round so sharply that I felt as if I was going to break in half. The rush of speed stopped, the current convulsed and I was flying through the dark water alone. In the distance I saw the thick green rope of water pounding on without me.

I'm alone. *But not in the Deep alone*, I tell myself firmly in case panic sets in. The water has darkened but I can still see my own hands moving through it like ghosts. I've never seen such clear water. It's as pure as crystal. I'm afraid to look far and see the emptiness. Conor left behind, Elvira vanished too. I don't know what's happened to Faro. Everything has failed. We haven't kept together and now I'm alone somewhere thousands of miles from home. I will never be able to find my way back.

I can sense a huge shadow on my left side. I won't look. I won't give it – whatever it is – the satisfaction of knowing that I'm icy with fear. Orcas – killer whales – Faro says they sometimes forget that you are human. They're not the only ones. I'm not sure that I'm human any more. I'm not sure where I am or who I am. I was so confident, telling Dad that my Mer blood wanted me to make the Crossing and I had no choice.

Now I don't feel either Mer or human. I just feel... lost.

"Little sister?"

"Oh, Faro. Oh, Faro."

He's behind me, swimming towards me faster than I've ever seen him swim. I'm almost sobbing with relief as I swing round towards him. We grab hold of each other. I can hear his heart thundering and I am sure he can hear mine. "I thought I'd lost you," he says.

"I thought *I'd* lost *you.*"

"I know. I'm sorry. I should never have closed my mind to you. I thought I'd never find you again."

"Me too."

I realise I'm clinging to him. But he's clinging to me too, as if we've found each other in a shipwreck. We let go, and smile shakily at each other.

"That was awful," I say.

"I shouldn't have trusted that current."

You're not to blame," I say quickly. "It was the current – and maybe we didn't hold on tight enough to each other in our minds. But, Faro," I go on very quietly, in case whatever is making the huge shadow might hear us, "can you feel something? Over there to the right?"

"I think it is an ice mountain."

"How do you know?"

"Look at it, Sapphire."

I turn reluctantly towards the shadow. It has come a little closer, drifting noiselessly towards us.

"Look down," says Faro.

He is right. Far below me there is a mountain range of ice. Spurs as sharp as daggers reach up towards us. There are dark blue valleys and long slopes that glisten in the dimming light. So this is an iceberg. It looks like a whole country made of ice.

"It's going to pass us," says Faro. "It's heading south."

We watch, hypnotised, as a great wall of ice glides closer.

"We must get out of its path," says Faro. "Swim left."

The vast mass of the berg is on our right, but one sheer side will pass close to us. Too close. It looks as if it's coming straight at us. As we start to swim it drifts nearer, turning just a little. I kick out, stretching for clear water. The berg looms behind me, monstrous, spreading its shadow through the water like a stain, catching up with us—

"Hurry, Sapphire."

I throw myself forward as Faro grabs my arm and I feel us surge through the water. His tail drives us forward with a power no human can match.

"It's going to pass us," gasps Faro in my ear. One more stroke and his grip on my arm loosens. "We've made it."

As we turn to watch, the outer edge of the iceberg slides past us less than ten metres away. It moves silently through the water, towering hundreds of metres above us, majestic and pitiless. The mouth of an ice cave gapes at us. Half the cave is sealed with ribs of ice, like fantastic tree trunks. It is as dark as ink inside, as if it goes back for ever. High above, the iceberg soars, dizzyingly vast. Its flank is broken by cliffs and gullies, each one ten times bigger than any I've seen in the human world.

"I should like to swim inside that cave," says Faro thoughtfully.

"Faro, you can't—"

"It would be like swimming in and out of a whale's ribs after its spirit has gone to Limina. We could discover what's inside the ice mountain. Think what an adventure that would be, little sister!"

"Especially when part of the berg breaks off and traps you inside. Or crushes you." And then you'd be there for ever, imprisoned inside a mouth of ice. Would you freeze solid, and become part of the berg? Some human explorer might break our bodies out of the ice with a pickaxe. They wouldn't believe that Faro was real, when they saw his tail—

Don't be stupid, Sapphire, I tell myself quickly, suppressing a shudder. Icebergs don't stay frozen; they melt as they drift south.

Faro sighs, looking after the berg with regret as the last of it glides past us. He really did want to explore those caves. I wish I could be free of the dread that creeps into my mind like a cold fog, paralysing it.

"Faro..."

He turns to me, his face still bright with longing. "What is it, little sister?"

"Nothing."

But the spell that the iceberg has cast over him is broken. "They will see the ice mountain. They will have time to avoid it," Faro says, as if arguing with himself.

"You mean Conor and Elvira?"

"Of course."

The iceberg has distracted us, but now its shadow fades into the distance and the reality of our own situation sharpens. Night is coming. The others are somewhere out in the darkness. We don't know where they are, and we have no way of finding them.

CHAPTER TWELVE

Night has fallen. There's so much night here in the North, and so little day. We rise close to the surface, where blue, mysterious light filters down through the water from the moon and the stars. I gaze upwards and wish that I knew how far north the current had taken us. I force my mind back to everything I know about the Arctic. *Concentrate, Sapphire, this is important.*

It was the start of half term when we left home, so late October. I remember reading that daylight disappears for months on end in winter at the North Pole. So we can't be that far north yet because there's still some daylight. The nights will grow longer the farther north we go, until the sun never rises at all. We'll have to rely on the moon and stars. When I look up I can see the distinct shape of the moon through the water. It's about three-quarters full. I hope that the moon is waxing rather than waning. We'll need all the light we can get to find the others and then travel onward.

A sudden decision forms in my mind. "Faro, I'm going to go through the skin."

"But why?"

"I don't know. I feel as if I've got to. I want to look at what this world is like, above the surface."

"I'll come with you."

"Don't, it'll hurt you."

"You know it's not so bad for me to pass into the Air these days, little sister," says Faro quietly.

I wonder if Faro is going to let down his defences at last, and talk about the human blood he fights against so fiercely, but he doesn't, and I say nothing either. Slowly we rise through the pure, glimmering water. There is the skin above me, where Ingo ends and Air begins. I point my arms above my head as if I'm diving, and kick upwards.

My head breaks the surface. I look around me at the black, moonlit, silent sea. The water is so calm that a circle of ripples spreads outward from where I came up. A long swell rolls quietly beneath the surface, looking like an oiled muscle in the moonlight. Stars glitter above me. I float on my back and watch them. They seem so close, as if I could reach out and touch them. Constellations flash and glitter. There's no light pollution to hide them, and no smog or smoke either. I'm looking at the stars and seeing what my ancestors must have seen thousands of years ago. The moon shines so brilliantly that when I lift my hand, a moon shadow moves on the face of the water.

My body is still in Ingo. I haven't breathed air yet, but now I must. I push back my hair and take in a long, freezing breath. Cold as it is, it burns its way down my lungs like fire. A knife jabs under my ribs. I steady myself. The first breath is always the worst. I breathe again, treading water, and this time the air slides in more easily. I cough to clear my throat and the noise bounces, echoing across the silent sea. I scull myself round in a slow circle and survey the world of ice.

Far away, faintly lit by the moon, the iceberg that passed us is drifting into the distance. But there's another on the horizon, and another. Wherever I look I see the hulk of a berg moving south. It looks as if the whole world of the North is drifting in slow motion. As well as the bergs there are ice floes, rough and uneven, coated in moonlight. My eyes are getting used to the light. I scan every floe, every stretch of open water. There's no trace of life. No sign of Conor or Elvira.

Faro's head breaks the surface beside me. I look away as he struggles for his first breath; he won't want me to watch.

"It doesn't hurt as much," he says at last, wiping sweat from his forehead.

"I can't see the others, Faro."

"Did you think they'd be here?"

"I don't know."

Faro turns very slowly in the water, scanning the seascape through 360 degrees. Suddenly he's still. "What's that?" He points to a lump on the nearest ice floe. At first I think it's just a rough heap of ice. But as I look more closely a familiar shape shows against the background. It looks like a seal hauled out on the ice. It looks so familiar – so *safe* – that I find myself smiling. Maybe it's a Cornish seal who's also decided to make the Crossing of Ingo.

"It's a seal, Faro!"

"Yes. Come on."

We swim towards the floe. Even though we're breathing air, I think we must still be partly in Ingo. I can't feel the cold of the Arctic water.

Faro reaches the floe first. The seal is already sliding backwards off the ice, ready to flop into the water. Clearly it doesn't think we are either familiar or safe.

"No, don't go!" I call softly. "We won't hurt you."

It's not a common seal or a grey seal, like we have at home. Its fur is thick and white with black patches. It turns a dark face towards us, opening its mouth, and I see pointed teeth. It is still afraid of us, but now it's curious too. Faro raises his hand in greeting.

"He will know that I am Mer and that my people have never killed his people." I hope the seal will not also know that my people have often killed his people. He raises his head and regards us.

"Greetings," says Faro.

"Greetings," says the seal in a gravelly voice. His eyes turn to me.

"This is not one of your people," he says suspiciously to Faro.

"My friend is Mer enough to make the Crossing of Ingo." The seal throws back his head and gives a bark of laughter.

"The Crossing of Ingo! I have heard of it. But you are heading in the wrong direction, my friend. You must travel south, as I am doing."

"We must travel north," says Faro. "There is danger for us in the south."

"From hunters?"

"Yes, from hunters," says Faro, and I shiver, remembering Mortarow's spear thrust in his tail. Ervys is suddenly very real, and close.

"There is danger everywhere," says the seal. "We have had a bad season. The char and cod do not fill our waters as they did in the time of our ancestors. This season's pups are weak, and Nanuq is hungry."

"Faro," I whisper, "what is Nanuq?" But he shakes his head almost imperceptibly.

"Have you seen any of our people on your journey?" he asks the seal. "A girl, and a boy who looks human but lives freely in Ingo?"

"No."

"If you see them," I say eagerly, "tell them their sister and brother are safe and searching for them."

"I must go south," says the seal, "but I am weak and I have travelled a long way already. My brothers and sisters are far ahead of me." We are close to him now. Faro and I grip the edge of the ice floe and look up into the seal's face. His fine, sensitive whiskers are drooping. He is thin, and even in the moonlight we can see that his fur is rubbed away in patches. His body is slumped against the ice as if it will never rise.

"I have no strength left to swim," continues the seal. "This sikurluk will carry me south, and perhaps I shall catch some fish and regain my strength."

We nod. I am flooded with pity for the seal. It's obvious that unless a miracle happens he will never make it south to his winter feeding grounds. The rest of the seals have had to abandon him to his fate.

"Nanuq has had a bad season too. He is hungry and desperate," warns the seal. "He may not choose to hear that you are Mer."

"Tell me what Nanuq is like," says Faro.

The seal laughs his barking laugh again. "You are playing with me, friend. Everybody knows Nanuq. He steals over the ice like a shadow. He is more deadly than a harpoon in the hands of the greatest hunter. His teeth and claws spill hot blood on the ice and melt it. But we Natsiq grow fewer and Nanuq grows ever hungrier."

"He means a polar bear, Faro," I whisper as dread coils around my heart again.

"So the ice bears are hungry," says Faro. "We shall have to make sure that they hear we are not their prey, little sister." The seal gives us a mournful, pitying look.

"To die in the claws of Nanuq is perhaps a better fate than to die slowly from hunger," he observes. "Sometimes I think that if I see his shadow I will not fear it."

I don't share this discouraging opinion. Dying of hunger sounds vague and distant. Being torn apart by a polar bear sounds only too immediate. I glance around. Nothing moves. But would a polar bear be visible against the ice? And do they sleep at night?

Suddenly my hands, gripping the edge of the floe, begin to burn. Cold cuts into my palms. The protection of Ingo is leaving me. A long shudder runs through my body as the Arctic water seizes hold of it. Faro snatches back his hands from the ice. It's happening to him too. The cold of the Air has caught us like fish in its net.

"Quick, we must go back through the skin." Already Faro's teeth are chattering. My hands are so stiff I can barely move them. "Dive, Sapphire!"

"Goodbye," I stammer to the seal. My teeth are chattering so much I can hardly get the word out. He watches as we turn, brace our feet against the underside of the floe, and dive.

It hardly hurts at all as the waters of Ingo enter my lungs and fill my body. The icy grip of the Arctic is broken as Ingo enfolds me. We are back in our own element, safe. I look over my shoulder and see the ice floe growing small above us. I picture the seal drifting southwards, stoically waiting as his island of ice slowly melts around him. He is much too weak to fish.

When I turn back, Faro is already swimming away with the steady Mer stroke and sweep of the tail that he can keep up for hours. Where's he going? Away from the ice floe. Northwards. I plunge after him. "Faro! Stop!"

With a twist of his tail he is back at my side. "Are you hurt, little sister?"

"No, but we can't go north without the others. They'll never find us."

"They will go north too. That's what we agreed. Keep going northwards if we get separated."

I stare at him. "But Faro, we didn't expect this to happen…"

"It has happened, little sister. What do you suggest? That we should swim round and round in this world of ice until they appear, or until we die? I cannot find my sister anywhere. Do you think I haven't been searching for her? I have stretched every fibre of my mind, Sapphire, and there is no answer from Elvira. We must go on and make the Crossing, and trust that they will join us. It's what we agreed."

It sounds so logical, so right. I'm half persuaded, but then the reality hits me. It means leaving Conor behind among these icebergs, thousands of miles from home, maybe drifting injured, maybe alone—

"I know we agreed, but I can't do it, Faro." Faro is silent.

"Can't we give it a couple of days at least?" I plead. "Just to give them a chance to catch up with us, wherever they are?"

"But will you go on with our journey after the two days if they don't come?"

I will have no choice; I see that. To go back without Conor and Elvira will be no better than to go on without them. Faro understood that before I did. Besides, if we go back we'll have lost everything. No Crossing of Ingo. Our failure will prove Ervys right. He will grow stronger, and more and more of the young Mer will follow him. He'll lead them deeper and deeper into conflict. Weapons will bristle throughout Ingo. Those who won't follow will be destroyed. Ingo and the human world will be pitted against each other in a battle that will go on for generations. Everything Saldowr hopes to avoid will happen.

"Do you think it will still count if you and I make the Crossing?" I whisper, because I don't want to say the words aloud and make them real.

"I don't know. I believe it may count for something," replies Faro. "Believe me, little sister, I would much rather stay. I would rather die searching for your brother and Elvira than live without them."

"I know."

"If Ervys gains more power in Ingo, you know what kind of world he will make there. There will be no more gateways between your world and mine. He will set guards on all of them. Every cove will be a Porth Cas. He will hunt down those whose blood is mixed – Mer and human – and he will kill them. Saldowr says this is the world Ervys wants. Ervys tells his followers that Mer and human have separate destinies and must be kept apart. War between Ingo and Air will be inevitable until Ervys gets all the territory he thinks Ingo needs."

Ervys's plans don't leave any space for me. I'm a half-and-half. I don't belong in Ingo and I've got to be hunted out. Nothing we have done for Ingo counts any more. It doesn't count that Conor healed the Tide Rock after it broke. It doesn't matter that we went to the Deep and defeated the Kraken.

"It's the same for me," says Faro.

"What do you mean? Faro, I wish you'd keep out of my thoughts!"

"Then close them against me, little sister. You know what I mean. I have human blood," says Faro. "In Ervys's opinion, even if I were ninety-nine parts Mer and one part human, that one part would still make me unfit to live in Ingo. I have listened to the speeches he makes to his followers. He talks of the pollution of human blood in the Mer race, and how it must be eradicated. He means every word."

I am so shocked that for a while I say nothing. I never thought Faro would openly admit to his human blood. He's fought against it and denied it for so long. Now I partly understand why.

"Do his followers believe it too?" I ask at last.

"More and more believe it," says Faro sombrely. "Think how easy life becomes, little sister, if all the evils of the world can be solved by hating us and wiping us out."

Us. Again, I never thought I would hear Faro say that. *Us.* Whatever the future is for people like us, Faro and I share it.

"Saldowr says that the future lies with Mer and human living together – learning to share their worlds. He told me so. For a long time I fought against it, but my mind has changed. Saldowr says I must hold this knowledge in my heart and build on it, whatever happens to him. I am his *scolhyk* and his *holyer*," says Faro, and his eyes glow with all the old pride. "Saldowr has taught me that Ervys's way leads to destruction, not just for his victims but for all the Mer."

"Destruction..."

"Yes. Evils compared to which the breaking of the Tide Knot

and the awakening of the Kraken are small troubles."

"Oh, Faro, I wish it didn't have to be like this. Why can't we all just live peacefully?"

"Because Ervys exists," says Faro, "and if one Ervys dies, there will be another. We must be strong, little sister. Remember, Ervys will be very happy if we fail to make the Crossing of Ingo. Our failure will prove his point and recruit many more followers to his side. There are Mer who are wavering in the currents now, unsure whether to be loyal to Saldowr or follow a new leader. They will decide for Ervys if we fail."

I know that Faro is right, but there is a cold feeling in my heart, as if some of the northern ice has got into it. I'm afraid that Conor won't understand why we've travelled on without him and Elvira. He'll think I've abandoned him. But surely – if we can search for just two more days – we'll find them.

"I suppose you're right," I say.

"Reach out for Conor in your thoughts," says Faro, "and I'll reach out for Elvira. Keep your mind open. Listen for the smallest sign of their presence."

"But Conor and I can't enter each other's thoughts."

"You humans! All the same, reach out."

We float, half awake and half asleep, for the rest of that night. No current comes near us and I'm glad of it. If we struck a strong northern current, I'm not sure I could keep Faro from surfing it. A few fish drift by. Once I think I hear a whale, but the noise dies away in the distance. I open my mind as wide as I can, feeling through the darkness for my brother's presence.

Conor? Conor, can you hear me? It's me, Saph. I'm here, waiting for you. If you're hurt, give me a sign if you can. We'll come and rescue you, wherever you are.

No sign comes. The Arctic swell rocks us like a cradle. No one seems to be out there.

A late, feeble dawn starts to seep down, lighting the water. We're about twenty metres below the surface. The water's crystal clarity is startling. I thought the sea around Cornwall was clear, but it's cloudy compared to this. I can't smell land at all. We said we'd wait two days. I'm not sure if this counts as the first day, or if it's already the second. If it is, we have to go north tomorrow.

"Maybe we should swim round in a wide circle," I suggest rather hopelessly.

"And exhaust ourselves," snaps Faro. "That sounds a good idea."

"We can't just float here all day waiting for them to find us."

"I know that. But we need our strength. We don't want to end up like that seal— Wait, Sapphire. Hush. Keep still."

"Faro, what is it?"

He points into distant water, up at the surface. I strain my eyes but all I can see is the faintest of shadows.

"It's not a shark, is it?"

"No. *Wait.*"

It's coming closer. I recognise the movement long before I can really see the outline. An unmistakable firm outward sweep of the arms. A slow stroke that conserves energy and lets you swim all day long. Breast-stroke. It's them! "Faro, look, it's the others!"

"No, Sapphire. Look at it." Faro's voice is tense. The creature is coming into focus now. The blunt head, the smooth, sweeping, steady stroke that comes and goes, the limbs spreading and drawing in... "What is it, Faro?"

"Nanuq," he replies.

It is a polar bear, swimming on the surface, its yellowish coat distinct against the rich blue-black water. It's doing breast-stroke so powerfully that in a few minutes it will catch up with us. I stare at it, hypnotised. Its head dips below the water with its next stroke, and it sees us down below.

"Dive!" says Faro. "Dive, Sapphire!" But a shelf of ice has glided beneath us. It juts out underwater from a passing berg. We can't dive out of the bear's reach. Not in time. The bear plunges, diving for us. There's nowhere to go. Faro throws his arm around me as we face the bear. Its muzzle is heading straight for us. I see its eyes, its mouth.

"Know that we are Mer, Nanuq," says Faro. He speaks full Mer, which every creature in Ingo understands. "If you smell human blood, know that you cannot spill a drop of it without spilling Mer blood too. Our people have never harmed your people."

The vast shaggy belly of the polar bear glides overhead, so

close I could touch it. With unnerving speed and grace, the bear turns in a tight circle until it faces us again. The front paws open wide, although the bear's claws remain sheathed. They close around me, not crushing me but holding me tight in a cage of bear flesh. The next second, Nanuq and I are shooting up to the surface.

We come up in an explosion of foam into a whiteness that almost blinds me. The bear rolls over, swimming on its back, holding me. I can smell its breath. The fur is a dirty, sodden cream. In a moment it will unsheathe its claws and kill me. My chest pounds with the agony of being torn through the surface so suddenly. I hear Faro's voice. "Don't hurt her! She is one of us."

Nanuq will kill me, and Faro will see my blood in the water and rush forward to attack the bear, and then Faro will be killed too. Desperately I reach out for him in my thoughts, trying to prevent him.

Go north, Faro! Quickly! At least one of us will escape.

But Faro is rising to the surface. His voice cracks as he cries out, "Nanuq! Hear me! Hear that she is of Mer blood!"

"Mer blood," rumbles the bear's voice, so close to me that it feels as if she's speaking inside my body.

"Yes," I gasp.

"But you are breathing air."

I move my head a little in the direction of Faro's voice. I can just see his face. His lips are drawn back, his teeth bared. He is getting ready to fight the bear. But he mustn't or she'll kill us both.

"You're hungry," I say to Nanuq, and her grip on me seems to ease, just a little.

"Yes, hungry, little one. I have swum many miles from the far North without finding safe ice for hunting, or seals."

"But I am not your prey," I say with all the firmness I can muster.

The bear turns her head from side to side, peering down at me, trying to identify me.

"I must eat," she rumbles again.

I think of the seal floating south. If I tell Nanuq that there's a seal not far away, and that if she swims directly south she'll find it, then maybe she will let me go. No. She'll think I'm trying to trick her. And besides, the seal wants to live as much as I do.

"You can't eat me," I repeat. I don't know where my certainty comes from, but it is like invisible armour that holds me safe even though I'm trapped between the polar bear's paws. "You must hear that I am not your prey."

"Does your Atka protect you?" asks the bear. I have no idea what an Atka is, but decide to say yes. The bear nods her head sorrowfully.

"Nanuq cannot cross the Atka," she says, "and I am so hungry, and I have swum so far. Perhaps your Atka is telling me that I must prepare to die."

My fear is shrinking. I look at the bear closely, meeting her eyes, studying her body. All I saw as she dived at us was a fearsome predator. Now I see a badly healed gash in her shoulder and the hollowness of her flanks. She has been hungry a long time. I wonder how long she's been swimming, desperately searching for food or for somewhere she can rest. I glance at Faro. His face has changed. He knows the bear won't attack me now.

"Go south, Nanuk, where you'll find land and food," he says. The bear releases me and rolls over in the water.

"The seals do not pup as they should," she says, "and the pack ice breaks up. My hunting grounds are shrinking, and my paw is hurt so badly that I cannot run on the ice." She extends her paw. For an odd moment the huge, powerful polar bear looks like an injured dog holding out a wounded paw.

"May I look at it?" I ask.

She growls agreement. It is her left front paw that is injured, and as soon as I examine it I see why she can't run. The paw is swollen around a splinter of metal. Every step must drive the metal deep into the sore flesh.

"How did this happen?"

"In the summer, by the human settlements. I have tried to release it with my teeth but they cannot reach the place." She has torn the flesh too, worrying at it with her teeth to try to free the splinter. Her paw is a mess of half-healed scars.

"Look, Faro. If I had a knife, I could cut it out." I can feel the tip of the metal, but flesh has grown around the splinter. Elvira could do it.

"Neither of us are healers," I tell Nanuq.

"Try anyway," she says wearily. "If I cannot hunt, I will die."

"Keep very still." I brace my feet against the bear's chest. "It will hurt you," I warn her.

I feel carefully for the edges of the splinter. I'm going to have to dig down with my nails to get a grip and try to ease it out. She has driven it deeper, ripping at it with her teeth. My nails grate on metal, then slither away. I try again. A low growl of pain escapes from Nanuq. Perhaps there is poison deep in the wound, but once the splinter is out then the salt water will have a chance to heal it. I try again, pushing down the proud flesh with one hand while I grip the splinter with my nails.

"It's coming. Faro, grab hold of me! Pull me from behind!"

I'd never have done it alone. With all the power of his tail, Faro backstrokes, pulling me by the waist. I feel one of my nails break, but by now my fingers can grasp the end of the splinter. I work it round. Nanuq groans with pain.

"It's coming... "

I get my thumb and forefinger firmly around the splinter, and pull as hard as I can. "Faro, pull me!"

Like a tooth out of its socket, the splinter comes out, slowly at first and then all at once in a cloud of pus and blood. Nanuq gives a deep groan and quivers all over.

"It's done. It's out," I tell her. "Look." I hold up the metal shard so Nanuq can see it. It is half as long as my hand. No wonder she hasn't been able to run.

Nanuq bows her huge, heavy head in acknowledgement. "Thank you, child," she says. "It is fortunate that I remembered you were not a seal."

"Yes," I agree fervently.

I release the splinter. It turns over in the water, once and then again, and begins to dive, still turning, into the clear and endless depths. I rub my eyes, which are strained by the dazzle of light on ice. Already the sun seems to be sinking in a mass of crimson. I've been above the surface too long breathing air. I want to sink down like that splinter into the safety of Ingo. The sea around us is covered in blobs of ice, but they are too light to support as much as a seal's weight, and much too light for Nanuq to stand on and sail south. She will have to swim.

Slowly, wearily, Nanuq turns on to her belly, flexes her strong hind legs, and begins to swim. She doesn't say farewell. She seems to have no energy left for anything but the struggle to survive. Maybe she'll find a seal – *not our seal* – I add quickly in my thoughts – just another seal that doesn't want to live quite as much.

"If you see our brother and sister, tell them to come north! Tell them we're waiting for them!" I call after her. As soon as the words are out of my mouth I'm not sure I should have told Nanuq about Conor and Elvira. Perhaps she'll start to look out for them. She's very hungry.

"Faro, I shouldn't have told her—"

"It doesn't matter," says Faro quickly, but I know he's only trying to make me feel better. He didn't say a word about the others to Nanuq.

We're silent for a while, and at last Faro says reflectively, "We are still in Ingo, little sister, but this is not our home. We must keep silent, and watch, and listen. We can trust no one."

I nod. Faro dips his head beneath the water then comes up shaking it so hard that hundreds of glittering drops fly through the air.

"This is the longest I have ever been in Air!" he announces proudly.

"Yes, but it's not really like being in Air, is it? I don't feel the cold."

"No. Maybe the boundary between Air and Ingo is not so sharp here. This is good Air. It has no human dirt in it."

"Faro!"

Faro grins at me over his shoulder as he prepares to dive. "It's the truth, little sister!"

As I dive after him I think of Nanuq. At least her paw will heal. If she finds land, Nanuq will be able to hunt. Maybe she'll survive.

CHAPTER THIRTEEN

The Arctic days are even shorter than I thought. After Nanuk has swum away, the light fades. A reddish glow lights Ingo for a while, and Faro and I swim in a wide circle, searching, as I suggested. It's obvious that Faro thinks it is a complete waste of time, but it would feel even worse just to float and wait.

We see more harp seals, all on their way south. Most of them look thin and weary. Everyone we meet has the same story. It's been a bad season. There is not enough fish and there are hungry polar bears with cubs to feed. Many seal pups have died because their mothers did not have enough milk for them. A bad season, but perhaps the next will be better, says one old seal philosophically. We keep a lookout for sharks, but so far we've seen none. There's no hint that Ervys's followers are on our track. Maybe the dolphins have decoyed them in another direction – or Saldowr's power is holding them back.

So far we haven't seen any orcas. A beluga whale comes close with a calf at her side, swimming northward. We hear other belugas singing, but we can't see them. The beluga mother swims up to us and asks fearfully, "Have you seen Nanuq?"

"She's gone south," I say, but Faro interrupts.

"The whale doesn't mean our polar bear, Sapphire, she means *any* polar bear."

"Oh, I see. No, we've only seen one, and she's heading south."

"Nanuq has stolen my sister's calf, who was not yet weaned and still spent his life tucked behind her flipper. We fought hard. We thrashed with our flippers and tails and we made a circle to protect the little one, but Nanuq was too quick for us. Nanuq tore my sister's calf away from us and his blood flowed in the water."

Her own calf sticks to its mother's side like a shadow. He's only been alive a short time, and already he's seen his little cousin taken by the polar bear and ripped apart.

"I must stay close to the pod," says the mother anxiously. "We are on our way north for the winter, where the food is rich under the ice-sheets. But my little one was born late. He finds it hard to keep up." The water pulses with whale clicks and whistles. "I must go on." Slowly she swims off, the calf tucked against her flank.

"It's a pity the babies aren't the same colour as the mothers," I say, "then the polar bears wouldn't be able to see them so easily. But at least they're heading north, not south."

"Like us," says Faro.

"Not yet, Faro! We've still got one more day."

"You keep telling me that."

"Everyone in the North seems to be looking for someone or running away from someone. I wish…"

"What do you wish?"

"I was only thinking about the whale – not that beluga, *our* whale. I wish she were here. She could help us find the others. She could use her echolocation—"

But Faro is impatient. "What's the point of thinking about her?" he demands. "We have to help ourselves. No one is coming to rescue us, little sister."

And now night has fallen again. We'd be lost without the moon. Faro is asleep, his hair spread out in the water around him and hiding his face. I am so tired, but I can't close my eyes. All day I've felt as if I've missed some vital clue that would help me to find Conor and Elvira. It's like when a word is on the tip of your tongue, tantalising. I wish I could remember.

Faro's hair drifts back, revealing his sleeping face. I've never seen him as fast asleep as this. It's a little bit frightening. He's gone away into a country where I can't follow him, and I'm completely alone. I'm tempted to nudge him, accidentally on purpose, just to be sure that his eyes will open...

He'd be cross, though. He's having a good dream, I think. He's smiling in his sleep. Maybe he's dreaming that it's all over and we've made the Crossing, and all the Mer are welcoming us home.

His lips move as if he's talking to someone in his sleep. If I woke him up now, maybe he'd remember the dream. No. If I wake him up, all the dangers and difficulties will come flooding back to him: Conor and Elvira lost, the Crossing of Ingo sliding into failure when it's only just started. I won't disturb him.

I stare up through the quiet moonlit water. An ice floe drifts overhead, making a black shadow that looks a little like a person with arms and legs tucked in.

It's lonely here. Faro was right. We may be in Ingo, but we're not at home. Very, very far away I can hear whales singing to each other. I listen hard but I can't make out what they are saying. I wish I could remember what it is that I've forgotten. It's like the answer to the last, vital clue that will complete a crossword puzzle.

Suddenly, as clearly as if I am still gripped between her paws, Nanuq's voice rings through my mind. *Does your Atka protect you?*

Atka. That was it. That was the word I was trying to find. Even though I still have no idea what an Atka is, I sense that it's important. Nanuq thought I had an Atka who was looking after me, and so she didn't hurt me. *Nanuq cannot cross the Atka.* I'm sure that's what she said. I should have asked Faro about it. The temptation to wake him up grows stronger.

No, I'm not going to do it. Faro won't know what the Atka is any more than I do.

"Atka," I say aloud, but not loud enough to wake Faro. "Atka... Tell me what the Atka is."

As if saying the name aloud has given it power, I feel the word begin to come alive. The Atka. *Does the Atka protect you?* The word is mysterious, powerful, even ominous. It's a call that I have got to answer. I know what I must do now. Just as I longed to sink down into Ingo earlier, now I long to rise to the surface and view the world of ice. The Atka is drawing me upwards with an invisible but overwhelming magic.

I nearly let myself go. My arms are poised to sweep me upward, my legs close together ready for the strong kick that I've learned from the Mer. But the moon shines through the water on to Faro's face and my arms fall to my sides as I turn back to him. I can't leave Faro alone here. He might drift away, sleeping. I would never be able to find him again.

A tingle of fear runs through me at the thought of what's so nearly happened. Faro fell asleep trusting me to be here when he woke again. Gently, very gently, I stretch out my hand. Very slowly, so slowly that he will hardly feel the pressure, I close my fingers around Faro's wrist. My fingers touch his *deublek*, made of our woven and plaited hair. Faro stirs, smiles, but doesn't wake.

Very cautiously I start to paddle with my feet. I drift upwards, and Faro comes with me. It is all so strange and dreamlike that I'm not entirely sure that it's really happening. Perhaps I've fallen asleep without realising it and this is a dream. But the *deublek* feels real under my fingers.

Just beneath the surface, I stop. I'm not going to take Faro through the skin. The shock might be dangerous, and it would certainly wake him. Keeping hold of his wrist, I push my head through the surface and take a deep breath of the frigid Arctic air. It hurts less than I'd expected. After a few moments I'm able to look around. The moon is even more brilliant tonight, and the stars flash as if they're about to leave their places and come down to earth.

Faro's weight tugs at me, pulling me back towards Ingo. But I can't sink down yet. Instead I find myself speaking into the silence.

"The Atka," I say. "What is the Atka?"

Immediately an ice floe in the distance gives a shiver, as if the wind were blowing it. It's not very big, only about the size of a table, and a metre or so high. Slowly the shiver changes to movement, as if an invisible hand were pushing the ice floe from behind. It turns towards me, and as it turns I see that there's someone sitting on the scooped-out floe. It's a girl, about my age. Her hair is silver and her skin as pale as the moon.

I blink hard, squeezing my eyes together until they sting. When I open them she'll be gone. She's just a trick of the moonlight. I open my eyes and the girl is still there. Her face is clear and definite, but her body looks as if it's wrapped in a robe of fog. Suddenly I remember what Elvira said about the Mer of the North, with their pale bodies and silvery hair. But some instinct deep in me makes me sure that whatever else this creature is, she isn't Mer. She doesn't look as if she belongs in Ingo. She looks as if she's grown out of the ice.

I feel sure I've seen her face before. She isn't beautiful like Elvira. Her face is small and fierce. Her hair looks as if it's been charged by electricity into a wild silver halo.

"Who are you?" I whisper to myself, not thinking that she'll hear me across the stretch of water that separates us. But she does. She laughs, and each note of her laughter tingles as sharply as an icicle.

"Don't you recognise me?"

"Have I seen you before?"

"Oh yes, I think so. But humans don't remember, do they? All their memories from before they are born are hidden from them."

Is this creature really saying that I knew her before I was born? She must be mad. She's got to be. I'd better humour her.

"I thought you looked a bit familiar," I say lamely. Her hair glitters in the frosty moonlight as she nods her head.

"Come closer," she invites me.

"I can't!" I don't mean to shout, but my voice ricochets against the ice. I'm afraid that there may be more hidden listeners. Ice spirits, tucked away on the floes and in the chambers of icebergs.

"*Can't?*" Her voice is mocking but not hostile.

"No, I—" Has she seen Faro? Can she see his shadow drifting in the water just beneath the surface? I don't feel as if it's safe for her to see Faro. If that fog around her body would stop swirling for a second, I'd be able to see her clearly – but it won't stop. It swirls as if the ice itself is breathing in and out.

"*Who are you?*" I repeat.

She laughs. "I'm your Atka, of course," she answers.

The power of the word thrills through me, and so does fear. I am not even sure that she's real and solid now. If I touch her, and she's a spirit, then my hand will plunge into icy breath. I nerve myself to ask the question, even though I dread the answer.

"Can you tell me what an Atka is?"

"Your Atka protects you. Didn't you hear Nanuq?"

Doubt rolls over me. It could be a trick. If she's supposed to be protecting me, she hasn't had much success so far. Conor's gone, I'm alone in the Arctic, and I don't know where to go or what to do. Only the plait of the *deublek* that links me to Faro feels real.

"Where did you come from?" I ask, trying to keep fear and suspicion out of my voice.

"Oh, I've been here for a long time. I was waiting for you," says the Atka.

"You couldn't have been. I didn't even know I was coming here. No one did."

"Baby reindeer says to mother reindeer: *Where did you find those berries?* Mother reindeer says to baby reindeer: *Under your nose.*"

Hmm. I may not know anything about ice spirits, but I know all about people trying to patronise me. "Have you seen my brother?" I ask her sharply. She opens her eyes wide. Their pupils are sickle moons of black bathed in icy, silvery irises.

"I have not seen your brother," she says with an indifference that chills me. It's clear that it wouldn't matter to her whether Conor were alive or dead.

"But if you're supposed to be protecting me, can't you help me find him? I need him!"

"No. I am *your* Atka, not your brother's."

"Then you're no use to me!" I say furiously. The Atka laughs as if what I've just said is not only inoffensive, but also extremely funny. Her ice floe spins in a full circle, and her hair flies around her like a cloud. She comes back to face me.

"Do you even know what an Atka is?" she demands.

"Obviously not." I'd be tempted to plunge across to her and give her a slap if it weren't for the risk of plunging my hand into icy, living fog.

Faro's weight shifts, and I grasp his wrist more firmly. How can he manage to sleep through all this? Maybe there are more kinds of people living in Ingo than I've ever realised – not only the Mer and a few humans who have enough Mer blood to survive—

"Neither Mer nor human," says the girl. "Just your Atka."

Suddenly I am very, very afraid. She is invading my thoughts. I don't mind when Faro does it: I know Faro.

Alatuk alatuk Atka, Atka amaluk alatuk, croons the girl softly, like a mother bending over a cradle to soothe a restless baby.

"What does it mean? *Who are you?*"

The girl's face is coming into sharper focus. As I watch, lips, eyes and mouth become distinct in the moonlight. Her colouring is as different from mine as a negative is from a printed photo, but it is like looking into a mirror. The Atka has taken my face. But she didn't look like that a minute ago, I'm sure of it. She's mirroring me.

"Don't be afraid," says the Atka. "It's just a song. It means, *"Little one, listen to your Atka,"* that's all. Only your Atka can tell you when it is time to leave the world. Come a little closer so that you can see me properly. There's nothing to be afraid of."

"No," I say loudly. "No. No, I'm not coming anywhere near you."

The Atka raises her eyebrows. "Haven't I told you there is nothing to be afraid of? The Atka protects you. Nanuq knew that. Nanuq knew that only your Atka knows when it is time for you to change one world for another. And I am not telling you that now. You must stay in your world and fight its battles. I am only showing myself to you so that you will know me again, when it is time."

But the Atka is moving closer on her throne of ice. The floe glides across the water towards me, faster and faster. I am frozen. If the Atka touches me, I'll dissolve into terror, like ice into water. And yet at the same time I want to touch her. I want to know what she really is: a dream or a spirit or a living creature. I hang in the water, staring into the Atka's sickle-moon pupils, tempted, mesmerised. The Atka doesn't look like me any more. Her hair is a glittering crown and her fingers are shards of ice. She stretches out one hand, ready to touch me.

But before her ice floe can cover the remaining space of water between us, something else presses against the back of my hand. The *deublek*. Faro's hair plaited with mine. His wrist under my hand. I hear Faro's voice in my mind: *Two together. And strong as we were strong in the Deep*. His words melt the spell that holds me frozen. In the half second before the Atka reaches me, I dive.

Faro is shaking me. My heart is thundering. "Wake up! Wake up, little sister!"

I struggle back to consciousness. "Where is she?"

Only Faro is there, wide awake, watching me with concern. "You had a nightmare," he says. "You were screaming."

"No, it wasn't a nightmare, Faro. It was real. It was the Atka."

"The Atka? What is that?"

"A girl, a girl like me. She had my face but no body, at least I don't think she had a body. There was a fog swirling around her, and then she had a crown."

I expect Faro to laugh at me, but he doesn't. His brows draw together in a frown. "You have been visited by a spirit," says Faro decisively. "I have always been told that the world of ice is haunted by spirits, some bad, some good. Your Atka, I think, was a bad spirit."

"But she said she was here to protect me. I think she was, in a way… but she only wanted me; she didn't care about the rest of you. I wish you'd told me about the spirits, Faro," I add shakily, trying to make a joke of it. "I would have chosen the southern route and the sharks."

"Maybe you were asleep and it was all a dream," says Faro, but I can tell he doesn't really think it was. His expression is clouded. I can't get the face of the Atka out of my mind. Even though I'm still shaking with fear, I want to see her again. I think that Faro is wrong. She wasn't a bad spirit. Just very, very frightening.

You will know me again, when it is time.

"Maybe you've got an Atka too, Faro," I say, but Faro wrinkles his nose in disdain.

"No evil spirit of the ice is going to run *my* life," he says. "If I see my Atka, little sister, I will do – what is that word you told me for not looking at a person?"

"Blanking."

"I will blank my Atka," says Faro grandly.

"Good luck with that, Faro."

I force the memory of the Atka down into the depths of my mind. *Think about* now, *Sapphire. Think about everything you can do to find Conor again. Think about Saldowr.*

"We had no choice," says Faro, and it takes me a minute to know what he's talking about. Our route, of course.

"I know that, Faro. The sharks would have killed us if we'd gone south."

"We will do it this way, little sister. We will not fail," says Faro between his teeth, and I know that he's talking to himself as much as to me. The Atka's words echo in my head. *You must stay in your world and fight its battles.*

Day is coming again. The rising sun sends a bloody stain through the water, and then cloud covers it and the sea turns grey. The light is wan and heavy, as if winter is almost here. It's the second day, the one when we have to go north, but still there's no sign of Conor or Elvira.

"Oh, Faro, I wish they were here."

"So do I."

"There's got to be something more we can do."

Faro doesn't answer. Instead he takes hold of my hands and begins to rub them between his. "You look ill, little sister. When I was very young, I remember my mother rubbing my hands like this. She said it was to make the blood move faster in my body." He looks up with a quick, brilliant smile, then carries on rubbing.

"Faro, stop! Our *deubleks* have got tangled. They'll break—"

"No, they won't." Carefully Faro begins to ease the bracelets apart, but they refuse to separate.

"Two together. And strong as we were strong in the Deep," I say aloud.

"What's that?"

"The *deubleks*, Faro! Maybe they've joined together for a reason. Maybe they know something we don't," I say, excitement rising in me. "Listen, let's try to say it again, together. It might give us a chance."

"Say what? You mean, *Two together*…"

"No, not that! I mean, *I wish they were here.* Say it, Faro, say it. Make the wish while the *deubleks* are joined."

I can tell he thinks it's pointless, but he shrugs and agrees. "If you want it so much, Sapphire."

My voice shakes with hope as I say, "*Now.*"

Both together, we say the words. Nothing happens. "Let's try again."

This time Faro rolls his eyes impatiently, but he repeats the words with me anyway. Again, nothing happens, except that when I look down I see that our *deubleks* are not caught in each other any more. Our wrists separate and drop to our sides.

"Well, that's that then," I say flatly.

I told you so may be trembling on Faro's tongue, but he doesn't say it.

"We must make our plans to travel on, little sister," he says quietly. "We are going to have to rely on ourselves, not on any magic."

I feel as if I've swallowed a stone, but just then my brother's face floats to the surface of my mind. He is not looking at me but downwards, with the serious, rather stern expression he used to have when he was learning a new chord sequence on his guitar. Conor often looks serious when he's happy. A flood of longing fills my mind. If only I could see him, just for one moment. If only I could know he was all right. I could make the Crossing without him, as long as I knew that he was safe. Just for one second – please, Conor, please—

"Don't!" cries Faro. "Stop your thoughts! I can't hear her!"

"Faro, what is it?"

"Elvira is there! I feel her! I hear her! But your thoughts are too strong for me, they are blotting her out."

"You can sense Elvira?"

"Yes, she is there. I am sure she is there. Let me hear her, Sapphire!"

If Elvira is there, then Conor may be there too. I wrench my mind away from my brother.

"Think of something else!" says Faro urgently.

I think of the whale. My dear friend the sperm whale, who

saved my life in the Deep, and who risked her life to protect us and bring us back safely after we had fought the Kraken. I think of her rough skin and her gentle spirit. Her awful jokes and the way she longs to see her daughter who has gone to the bottom of the world. The whale says: *You please me, little one.* She doesn't expect me to be any different from what I am. Whenever I think of the whale, I feel safe. She's hundreds of miles away – maybe thousands – but it feels as if part of her presence is with me now, supporting me, telling me that there is hope. We will find the others; I know we will. We'll all go to the bottom of the world together, and I'll find the whale's daughter too.

"She is there," says Faro.

I'm so deep in thoughts of the whale that for a second I expect to see her huge body swimming towards us.

"Elvira," says Faro. He straightens his body and throws back his head. His face is pale, but triumphant. "I've found her. She is far away from us, but she hears me too."

I move my lips although I can hardly bear to form the words.

"And Conor?" I manage at last.

"Conor is with her."

The next moment we've grabbed each other by the elbows and are shaking each other as hard as we can, as if it's the only way to believe something as wonderful as this. Faro's sharp, perfect teeth gleam as his smile widens. "Stop it, little sister! You are too strong for me!"

"Faro, they're coming! They're OK! We're going to see them!"

The wave of relief is so powerful that I feel as if I've been lifted out of myself. I grab Faro tight, hug him and start a clumsy underwater jig. But you can't dance a jig in Ingo – the water won't let you.

"Quick, let's swim to them, Faro. Which way are they coming? From the south?"

"No, we must stay here. Calm down. My sister knows where we are now. I have made a picture for her in my mind and I will send her a stream of thought until we are close enough to join hands. If we move we could confuse her. Be patient, there's only a little time to wait."

I am no good at being patient. My heart pounds. Staying still is torture.

"We'll see them soon," says Faro. Even though he's been telling me to be calm and patient, his tail lashes with tension as he strains forward, peering into the green depths.

I start to count, but when I get into the high hundreds the numbers blur and dazzle in my head. "Seven hundred and seventy-seven... seven hundred and seventy-nine..."

Faro's face is drawn with concentration. "She is coming... they are coming slowly, Sapphire, they are very tired... they are closer now..."

At long last, a speck appears and then another. A few seconds later, the specks have grown into moving, wavering shapes that might be...

"It's them!"

We shoot forward. An explosion of bubbles hits my face as

Faro powers his way through the water faster than I could ever swim. I plunge after him. Faro swerves sideways, and I see them at last. Conor lifts a hand on greeting, slowly and wearily. He and Elvira are hardly swimming at all now as we rush towards them, and then with one last stroke I'm in my brother's arms. The force of my stroke pushes him backwards.

"Whoa, Saph, don't knock me over—"

He sounds just the same as ever. He feels just the same as ever, real and solid. I pull back and put my arms on his shoulders so I can see him properly. He's pale and there's a bruise on his forehead, but he's smiling. And there's Elvira, smiling too.

Something completely unexpected happens inside me. Instead of joy and relief, I feel overwhelming anger. It's the sight of my brother and Elvira together, looking so... so *normal*. So composed. How can they look like that when I've been desperate, thinking they were dead, fearing that I'd never see Conor again?

"Where have you been?" I demand furiously. "We thought you were dead. Why didn't you stay close like we said?"

The smile vanishes from Conor's face. "Calm down, Saph," he says coolly. This is the last straw. I pummel his chest with my fists.

"I thought – I thought you were – *dead*!" I gasp out. "And you're just – *grinning*!"

Conor's expression changes. "Hey, Saph, I'm all right. Come on, you eejit, take it easy."

"You're the bloody eejits, you and Elvira, scaring everybody to death, making us think you were dead."

Conor frowns, as if he's just woken up and is trying to remember a dream. "Did you really think we were dead?"

"What else were we supposed to think?"

"Anyway, it's great to see you, sis, even if you do beat me up the minute I get close enough."

The storm inside me dies away. Conor's back, my own brother. Alive, solid, real. Nothing else matters. I become aware of Faro and Elvira clasping hands and looking at us.

"You will be able to take on Ervys and Talek and Mortarow all at once if they catch up with us, little sister," says Faro with a wicked grin.

"I'd put my money on Saph," agrees Conor. Elvira, however, seems slightly shocked by my violence. I decide to ignore both her reaction and Faro's.

"So what happened to you?" I ask Conor eagerly. His smile fades. Suddenly his face is weary, and there's a look of pain and bewilderment in his eyes. He glances quickly at Elvira and then back to me. At once I know something's gone wrong. Something important. Faro catches the glance too, and cuts in quickly.

"We must move on. We have lost days already, and these two look exhausted. We must save our strength for swimming, until we find safe shelter where Conor and Elvira can rest. The four of us are together again; that is all that matters. We can tell all our stories as we travel north."

CHAPTER FOURTEEN

We're sheltering deep inside a cave in the flank of an iceberg. The iceberg is drifting very slowly south, which isn't the right direction for us, but we had to hide because of the killer whales. Faro was the first to hear them. A few minutes later we all picked up the eerie clicking and whistling. I knew it was whales but didn't know which kind; Faro did, though. He said, "Orcas! A big pod, and they are hunting. They sound hungry."

"Can't we talk to them?" I asked.

Faro frowned. "We can't risk it. Listen to how hungry they are. They are still distant, but they are coming closer." I listened. The clicks and whistlings meant nothing; it was just a forest of sound.

"Listen harder," said Faro. "Remember you are Mer, little sister." That was when I realised I was trying to pick out words, instead of letting the waves of meaning vibrate against my ears until they became sense. How many times did I have to remember to let go of the Air, let go of my human way of seeing and listening? The water was suddenly flooded with the whales' conversation. Faro was right. The orcas were hungry and desperate.

Ferromir is starving... I have no more milk for him

Hold on, sister, we will find food for you and then you will have milk

My belly hurts, mama, my belly hurts

The whales' voices were full of anguish, love and concern for one another. I remembered what I'd learned from Faro long ago: orcas may stay in the same pod for more than forty years. They will do anything to nurture and protect the members of their pod. Their voices swelled in my ears.

Soon we will find food...

Soon... soon...

Do you feel that vibration, my brother?

Seals! Fur seals!

Follow me, there is food! This way!

"Quick!" said Faro. "Into the ice mountain!"

We all turned as one and dived for shelter. The first cave was too big, and Faro thought the whales could get into it. The second was hard to enter, even for us. We had to squeeze through the narrow gap between pillars of ice that guarded the cave entrance. We huddled in the back. The light was so dim we could see almost nothing, but we could hear the whales questing up and down. Their echolocation had spotted us and then we had vanished and now they were savage with hunger and frustration.

"They will not hear that we are Mer," whispered Faro.

"Or human," I whispered back.

"Don't talk," muttered Conor. "Keep dead still. If they sense we're in here they could ram those pillars of ice to get at us."

No one moved. No one spoke. My ears hurt from the battering of the whales' noise. They were very close, maybe right outside the cave's entrance. One of the weakest young was in trouble: two of the orcas were struggling to support him. They were all maddened by the pain of hunger. The sound surged around us, deafening us. At long last, it began to retreat. The orcas were giving up hope. Their desperate cries grew fainter. They were gone, following the faint hope of another hunting trail. I shifted position from where I'd been cramped against a wall of ice.

"I think they're going," I whispered.

"They'll come back if they feel us moving."

We hung still in the water, waiting and listening, until we were sure that the pod of killer whales had gone.

We've all agreed to stay in our cave until we're quite sure that the whales won't come back. I'm happy with that. I like the safe feeling of being surrounded by thick ribs of ice. Nothing can attack us from behind here. If any creature tried to squeeze in through the gaps, as we did, we'd be able to fight it off.

We've been out in the open ocean for so long, exposed and vulnerable. This is like having a little rest in camp when you are climbing Everest. I smile to myself. The four of us are safe again, and together. Soon we'll have to travel on, but for now I'm not going to worry about that.

"You can't help feeling sorry for them," says Conor thoughtfully.

"What?"

"The orcas. It's not their fault they've got to eat."

"You can think that now, because you are not between their jaws," answers Faro. "Have you ever seen two orcas playing with a seal pup, before they kill it?"

"No."

"They toss it high and catch it, and snap at it again, until they get tired of their game. Usually the pup is dead by then, but not always. The first thing every Mer mother teaches her child is how to convince a killer whale that he is not a plump, blubbery little seal."

"But we can't blame them," says Elvira, backing Conor as always. "Hunger drives them and they must feed their young."

"Hunger is driving me too, but I'm not about to take a bite out of Sapphire's leg," says Faro. Elvira takes the hint and opens the bag of tightly woven sea grass that she wears around her waist.

Oh, that bag of Elvira's! I am sick of the sight of it. Every time she opens it I feel a faint hope that this time she's going to bring out something different; but no. It's always the same vile tasting compressed tablets which Elvira assures us are made of exceptionally nutritious seaweeds, and will enrich whatever other food we find on our journey. Fortunately Elvira only expects us to swallow a couple of tablets each day.

I start thinking about food, while Faro nibbles his seaweed tablet with apparent relish. It is just as well that I don't feel hungry as there's rarely much to look forward to here. No more sea grapes or other delicacies: we are too far north for them now. Just what Conor calls "Elvira's pemmican" as he makes a face and swallows it whole so as not to have to taste it too much.

The long night passes slowly after the whales have gone. I think about the Mer, and food, and war. I wonder if one reason why the Mer seem to be able to live in peace most of the time is because they aren't always fighting for food supplies, as humans are. But then there's Ervys. He couldn't be any more aggressive if he were starving, so the argument doesn't really work...

Faro is restless too. He and Conor talk for a long time, in quiet voices. Then Faro turns to me and starts talking about this current that we've got to find. He's sure that there's a very strong current not far from here. Once we've rested, and are completely sure there are no orcas close by, we've got to find it and ride it northward.

"How do you know, Faro?"

"I can feel it."

"You can't feel currents when you're not in them."

"You have a lot still to learn about Ingo, little sister. Do you remember when we smelled land from far away? It is like that."

Faro's self-confidence can be provoking, but when you are sheltering inside an iceberg, not even knowing which way is south and which is north, it is very comforting. I touch the *deublek* on my wrist. We must move on. We can't hide for long inside a cave of ice. Ingo needs us.

After a while, Faro drifts into sleep. Elvira is on the other side of him, curled up around her tail, while Conor is on my other side. So he and Elvira are as far away from each other as possible... interesting. I've already noticed that they haven't talked to each other much since they came back to us. No long intimate chats which mean nothing to anybody else. No significant glances. No ripples of laughter from Elvira. At last I've got the chance to talk to Conor privately.

"Conor?"

"What?"

"Tell me what really happened after you and Elvira got separated from us." Conor and Elvira have already told us a bit about what happened. They were thrown against the wall of an iceberg – probably the same berg that nearly ran down Faro and me – and then Elvira had concussion, Conor thought, and she hadn't been able to remember anything. They travelled on very slowly, fearing that we were dead. It was only because Elvira spotted Nanuq that they'd discovered we were alive and which way they should go to find us.

This is the story Conor and Elvira told us earlier. Every so often they glanced at each other as if they needed confirmation. The story didn't sound quite right to me. There were too many gaps in it. It sounded like something they'd agreed on rather than the truth.

But Conor doesn't seize the chance to talk openly. "What's wrong, Conor? What really happened?" I have a sudden flash of insight. "It's something to do with Elvira, isn't it?"

"Yes," he says reluctantly.

"You can trust me, Con."

"All right. You know we said Elvira was concussed?"

"Yes."

"She wasn't. We were both shocked and we've got loads of bruises, but Elvira didn't hit her head. She just changed completely."

"What do you mean?"

"It had started before, as soon as we headed north. I don't know if you noticed?"

I think back. Yes, it's true. Elvira seemed more – more *real*, somehow. Not calm and perfect and a little bit passive. Her eyes sparkled and she was full of energy and she didn't seem afraid of the dangers. But what was wrong with that? "I thought she seemed... Well, better, really. More alive."

"*More alive!*" said Conor in a harsh whisper. "You should have heard her. She was *obsessed*. It was as if she wasn't Elvira any more. All she cares about is the North and how amazing it is. She loves it here, Saph. She says she belongs here. She kept on saying, "I've come home, Conor, at long last I'm home where I belong."

"Weird."

"She even *looked* different. You know how gentle Elvira is. That's what she's like, isn't it?"

"You mean all calm and beautiful?" I ask tentatively.

"Yes! I mean, Elvira's really brave and strong but she's not pushy. At least, I always thought she wasn't. But, Saph, suddenly she was like a different person. Even her eyes were glittering in a sort of – well, a sort of way that you'd think was crazy if you didn't know Elvira. We were lost in the middle of nowhere and she didn't seem bothered at all. I wanted to talk about you and Faro, and Elvira kept going on about ice mountains and the Northern Lights and eternal winter and eternal summer. It was like she'd been hypnotised. She wouldn't let me rest for a second. She kept pulling my arm and making us keep going north. And she's strong, Saph, she's really strong."

Conor sounds outraged. The idea of sweet, beautiful, bewitching Elvira ruthlessly dragging my brother along in her wake nearly makes me laugh, but I suppress it. The great undersea romance of the century certainly seems to have hit a rock. "That doesn't sound too good," I say in as neutral a voice as I can manage.

"The worst thing was that she didn't seem to mind that we'd lost you. Not *really* mind. She just kept saying that the North would look after you and we'd all be reunited *when it was the right time*. It was creepy, Saph. It was as if she'd been taken over."

"I expect she'll change back again," I say, hiding my anger at the idea of Elvira being so calm and philosophical while Faro and I were desperately searching for her and Conor. I also have to suppress a desire to punch the water and yell, *"Yess! Hallelujah! Conor has seen the light!"*

"Maybe she will," says Conor gloomily.

"So who talked to Nanuq – you or Elvira?"

"I did."

"Weren't you afraid?"

"No. You could tell straightaway Nanuq wasn't going to harm us," says Conor confidently.

"I wasn't quite so sure when I met her," I murmur.

"Apparently I have a personal spirit guarding me, that's what Elvira says. It's a northern thing."

"You mean – do you mean your Atka?" I ask cautiously.

"How do you know?"

"I had a sort of dream. And Nanuq said something like that to me too. You can't die until your Atka stops protecting you."

"Don't you start, Saph," Conor groans, then for several minutes he is completely still and silent.

"What is it, Conor?"

"Nothing." After another long pause he says quietly, "Sorry, Saph, I was just remembering something."

"What?"

"You know how Granny Carne got us to press our thumbs together?"

I haven't thought of that since we came to Ingo, but I

remember instantly. *Think of what's strongest for you here on Earth. Let it come to you. Don't force your thoughts.* I wonder again what it was that Conor chose to remember, but it's not the kind of thing you can ask.

"Oh well," says Conor, sounding a lot happier, "At least we're together again. If we find that current Faro was talking about, we'll be back on our way. I hate all this getting lost and not going anywhere. It's like one of those dreams where you run and run and you're exhausted but you've hardly moved at all."

"Yes, but..." I grope for the right words. "...but maybe all the getting lost and meeting strange creatures is all part of the Crossing – just as much part of it as when we're actually moving, I mean."

"God, Saph, I felt so sorry for Nanuq. Swimming on and on like that and finding nothing. She can't keep swimming for ever."

"She might be dead by now," I say, and in my mind I see Nanuq swimming a last few weak, jerky, desperate strokes before her sodden fur begins to drag her down. Her muzzle vanishes, and then her eyes. Polar bears can swim a long way, but they can drown too. The icy waters close over Nanuq and she sinks like a shadow into the depths of Ingo.

CHAPTER FIFTEEN

I t's the middle of the brief Arctic day when we first see the current. I knew that Faro was looking for a powerful current, but when I see it I am stunned. It is awesome. There is not much light. Ingo glimmers with the faintest of blues, as if it were dawn. We can't be near the North Pole yet, because it will be dark all day long there at this time of year. Maybe that's where this current will take us – to the top of the world, under the polar ice cap.

The current cuts sharply through the blue of the water. It shines jade green, the colour of a glacier in the highest Alps. But this is water, not ice, and it's going so fast that anything caught in it would vanish out of sight in half a second. The current stretches wider than the widest motorway I've ever seen. Just to look at it makes me feel dizzy. I don't see how we can survive inside that force. Even Faro looks shocked, but he quickly recovers himself.

"Greater than the Great Current, and we shall ride it!" he announces triumphantly, as if the current ought to feel honoured. But the current just keeps rushing past, terrifyingly sleek and strong.

"How are we even going to get into it, Faro?" I ask him.

"We'll have to find the right angle of entry," says Conor in the judicious voice he uses when he's talking about a problem in maths.

"We certainly will," I say with feeling. "How fast do you think it's going?"

Conor assesses the speed of the current. "We'd have to throw something into it and measure how quickly it travelled between fixed points to be sure." He smiles. "But since that's impossible, I'd say it was travelling at over two hundred miles an hour. Maybe more. Just look at it."

We all just look. Even Elvira's passion for the North doesn't seem to extend to tackling this current.

"We'll need to float parallel with it," says Faro. "Diving wouldn't work. The force of the water would break our necks. But if we floated at its edge, then the current would suck us in."

"Are you sure?"

Faro shrugs. "I've done it with other currents when they're too dangerous for me to dive straight in."

But not with one like this. The same thought occurs to all of us, but nobody speaks. Maybe we'd still be there, watching the snake-like northward rush of the current as if hypnotised...

But then a dark speck floats into the corner of my vision. I blink, but it's still there. The others are all staring in the same direction.

There's a dark, torpedo-shaped creature way off in the distance, growing rapidly bigger. Faro tenses. Maybe he thinks it's a shark. For a few seconds my stomach tightens with fear. But no, the shape is wrong for a shark. It must be a whale. I can't hear any whale sounds, though, and as the creature comes nearer I realise that its shape is wrong for a whale too. The dorsal fin is too rigid as well as too far back on the body. The flippers look wrong too. The body glistens dully, but it doesn't look alive. My brain refuses to make any sense of what my eyes see. Faro is quicker. His expression changes, and he clenches his fists.

"Metal," he says in a voice of such contempt and fury that I flinch. "One of your human machines. That *thing* does not belong in Ingo."

"It's a submarine," says Conor. "I recognise the outline."

A submarine. Of course, it makes sense now. It looks like a child's drawing of a whale, but it has its own power. Why would it be up here in the Arctic?

The submarine moves no closer. It seems to hang in the water, the way a whale does when she's resting. It looks so alien. I glance sideways at Faro and Elvira. Their strong, smooth seal tails are the most natural things in the world to me by now. This thing of metal, engineered to slip through the water with the least possible resistance, is a complete stranger. Faro is right. It doesn't belong in Ingo.

"It's got to be Polaris," says Conor.

"What's that?"

"A nuclear submarine. I've seen programmes about them. They travel under the polar ice cap. It's like a ship, Faro, only it sails underwater instead of on the surface."

"You mean that there are humans inside that metal thing?" demands Faro.

"Yes. And enough missiles to vaporise half of Ingo," says Conor grimly. We all stare at the submarine in silence, trying to absorb what its presence means. "It's a thousand times more deadly than any shark, Faro," adds Conor.

Faro's nostrils flare with revulsion. "Only humans would bring such a creature into Ingo," he says.

I was wrong when I thought the submarine had stopped moving. It's coming closer. If there were windows on a submarine and the people in it could look out with binoculars, we'd be within range...

Radar. How sensitive is the radar on a nuclear submarine? They must have all kinds of other tracking devices too. Maybe they are tracking us already. Someone might have just picked up our images on a computer screen. We'll show up as four living, pulsing dots. Maybe their technology is so advanced that they'll even be able to hear our heartbeats. What if they were able to pick out our arms and legs – or our tails...

Take a look. You ever seen anything like this before?

Increase the image magnification immediately. Alert the bridge.

"Conor! What if they can see us on radar, or pick up our body heat or something?"

Conor's eyes widen. He turns quickly to Faro and Elvira. "It could be able to hear us and see us, the same way a whale can. The submarine has all kinds of equipment inside it. We've got to get away before it spots us."

Faro turns aside and spits in disgust, just as he spat when he told me about Mortarow's spear.

"Faro!" exclaims Elvira, sounding horrified, but Faro ignores her. Instead, he seizes my right hand and pulls me forward towards the current. The submarine swings slowly, probing the water. What if the people on board suspect we're enemies?

"This time, keep close to us!" Faro shouts over his shoulder to Conor. One by one, we manoeuvre ourselves into position. We're beside the current now. I feel the force of it tingling on my skin, although it's not even touching me. A first faint nudge comes through the water, and then another, stronger. Suddenly I'm not afraid. My blood races, like the current. The suction seizes hold of my right hand, and I am gone.

We speed through the dark, beneath the ice. I don't know how long we've been in the current. Ingo time ebbs and flows so strangely that I've almost given up trying to understand it. Sometimes what I'm sure is only a minute turns out to be an hour. I'm sure we've travelled a long way. Hundreds of miles, maybe thousands. I know that Faro is close, because I can hear his thoughts beaming out towards me.

I am here, little sister.

Sometimes I feel a wave of Faro's exultation. He is loving this current, riding it like a surfer riding the biggest wave in the world. I know how he feels because the same exhilaration courses through me. Behind Faro's thoughts I can pick up the shadow of Elvira's. She's in touch with Conor somehow. She assures us that he's safe.

I can't feel any bubbles against my skin. The current seems to have crushed everything into a river of speed. It's not jade green any more, but black, because there is no light at all. I know that we are under the ice because we glimpsed it above us, before the dark swept over us.

I keep thinking about Dad. Not Dad as he is now, but Dad as he was a few years ago when he kept getting such terrible headaches that our doctor sent him upcountry for an MRI scan on his head. Dad said when he was in the scanner it sounded like a huge hammer being hit very fast, over and over, inside his brain. The current is like that. I thought it would be a smooth rushing sound but it's a thundering noise, as if all the atoms in the water are flying apart and then being smashed together again at high speed. I wonder where the current is taking us, and how long we've got to travel like this? I can't see anything; I can't taste or smell anything. All I know is the roar of the current, and the pulse of elation inside me.

I think I've been asleep.

Are you there, little sister? Faro sounds worried.

Wearily, I put out a tendril of thought. *I'm OK. What about you?*

I'm fine. No exultation any more. Maybe he's just tired, like me. I wonder how long I've been asleep. I reach out for Elvira, and sense her presence close by, but not what she's thinking. She's relaxed, peaceful. Conor must be with her.

Conor? Elvira, is Conor there?

We're fine, Sapphire. Don't worry about us, Elvira replies.

It's obvious that Elvira doesn't suspect that there's any problem between Conor and her. The word "we" is so proud and happy in her thoughts that I feel a bit embarrassed... and a little bit ashamed. Quickly, I hide my thoughts from Elvira. But just as I break contact, the steady roar of the current breaks up into sudden chaos. There's a confusion of giant waves charging together, surging, crashing, smashing on my ear drums until I cry out with pain. Just when I think I can't bear it any longer and my head will burst, the noise disappears. Silence sweeps in. My ears are still ringing with the bludgeoning of the waves, and for a moment I wonder if I've gone deaf.

Conor? Faro?

I'm here. It's Faro's voice.

Are we still moving, Faro?

I think so.

The thunder returns, but it's distant now. It's up ahead, and although we're not in it we are moving towards it. It reminds me of something that I know from the human world. My blood prickles uneasily in my veins as I reach for the memory.

A waterfall. That's what the distant roar sounds like.

"Faro!" I shout as a thrill of terror races through me.

At that instant the current jackknives. I am thrown forward, then back, then I'm tossed upside down by raging water. The current convulses as if its back has been broken. The next moment it's hurtling forward again as the thunder swells. I reach out desperately for Faro with my mind. We can't be separated now. *Faro! Where are you?* I stretch every fibre of my thoughts, searching.

Faro's there, trying to get through, his thoughts reaching out for me. I haven't lost him. *Sapphire!*

Where are the others?

A pause. Faro's mind will be sweeping the wide dark current, trying to pick up a sign of his sister.

She is there, he tells me at last. The flood of relief in his mind pours through me too. "They are just behind us. The *deublek* on Faro's wrist brushes mine, and I grab his hand and hold on tight. I don't want to lose anyone ever again.

I'm not prepared for Faro's blaze of elation. I don't understand. What's happened? What is so wonderful?

"South, Sapphire! We're heading south!" He is wild with excitement. I still don't understand. We don't want to go south. The southern route is blocked by the sharks and by Ervys. We've come all this way and risked the northern route because it's our only chance of outwitting them.

"Come back, little sister."

It's Faro. He is speaking right into my ear. "If we were not in this current, I would turn a hundred somersaults for you, Sapphire, and then you would smile."

"I don't see that there's anything to smile about if we're going south."

"Don't you understand?"

"There's nothing to understand. We need to go north, and we're going south. We've failed."

He is laughing. He is actually laughing.

"You humans! I think you believe that the world is like a flat rock, and when you come to the edge of it, you fall off. No. We have gone as far north as it is possible to travel, little sister, and because the world is round we must go south again. I have heard of it before, but never thought I would feel it through my own body. You must have felt the current turn. Did you not feel the North spin away from you?"

I hardly dare to believe him. It sounds too good to be true.

"But I don't know which way is north, Faro."

"Of course you do," says Faro impatiently. "That's the one thing everyone *always* knows." He makes it sound as obvious as hearing your own heartbeat.

"I think that knowing where north is might be 'a Mer thing'," I say, quoting his most annoying expression. "We could be going east or west for all I know."

"But how do you ever travel without knowing where north is?"

"We use maps, and compasses and sat-nav. You know about maps. You're always saying they're rubbish."

"You will have to tear up all your human maps which make the world as flat as a rock, because they are wrong," says Faro gleefully. I don't bother to argue. It's not worth resisting Faro when he's in this mood of glittering excitement. I almost believe I'll see the flash of his eyes through the enveloping gloom. "You're not going to fall over any cliff. Hold on, little sister. We are heading for the bottom of the world."

South. *South*. As we travel on I keep testing the word. Maybe the current carried us all the way to the North Pole, beneath the polar ice sheet. Now we're rushing southward, still in the darkness, still beneath a thick sheet of ice.

The Antarctic is land surrounded by ocean. The Arctic is ocean surrounded by land.

We'll have to find a different passage south through the land mass that hems in the Arctic Ocean.

Dad's globe swims into my mind. In my imagination I make it spin, as I've done so often. The strange thing is that although I'm on the longest journey through Ingo that I've ever made, it's easier to think of Air and the human world than it's ever been before. It feels as if they are connecting somehow, inside me, rather than fighting each other as they have always done. It doesn't feel dangerous to make the globe turn. Maybe this is what Saldowr meant by peace. Peace inside me, between Mer and human. Peace outside, between Ingo and the human world, because the two of them can connect at last...

I remember now. There *is* a passage. It's a narrow strip of sea between the far west of the United States – Alaska – and Siberia. Two huge continents almost meet there, but not quite. That's the passage we'll have to find. I can't begin to imagine how we're going to do that.

I'm not afraid. I'll think about that problem when I have to. For now it's enough to be travelling, close to the others even though I can't see them. It's enough to be lulled by the hypnotic drumming of the current, and to be carried onward, onward, wherever it chooses to go.

I sleep for a long, long time. When I struggle up again through layers of dreams, it feels as if I've been unconscious for days rather than hours. I was dreaming about Dad, and about my baby half-brother Mordowrgi. In my dream he was swimming with us, and we kept telling him that he was much too young to make the Crossing of Ingo, but he only laughed and swam faster inside the circle of my arms.

I push the veils of dream away and open my eyes. At first I'm not surprised to find that it's light. A very faint, ghostly grey light, but light. Then I remember the blackness in which I fell asleep, and the thick crust of ice between us and the surface. I look up, and all I can see is water. I turn sideways, and there is Faro, within touch, smiling at me quizzically.

"So you've come back to us, little sister," he says. And there are the others, Elvira still drowsing with her long hair wrapped around her like a cloak, Conor wide awake.

"It's amazing to see you again, Saph, after all that time in the dark," he says. The current isn't too loud now; we can hear each other speak. "I kept telling myself you were safe, and I knew you had to be because Elvira said so. But it's so different when you can see someone with your own eyes."

"*You* look different, Conor."

"How do you mean?"

"I don't know... Yes, I do! You look older."

"So do you, little sister," observes Faro.

Maybe we've all been asleep for years, like in that fairy story where two children fall asleep on a mountain and then return to their home villages and find all their friends are old and grey with long silver beards. I examine Conor's face more carefully. It's his expression that makes him look older, not lines or anything like that. I wonder if Faro's right, and I've changed too.

"Wow – we'll be able to say we've been to the North Pole," I tell Conor.

I visualise Dad's globe again, and am glad I used to study it so carefully. Geography can be useful; more useful than Faro realises, I think rather smugly. "We need to find the passage between America and Siberia," I tell them.

"*America. Siberia,*" repeats Faro sarcastically. "But we are making the Crossing of Ingo, not ripping the Air apart in one of your *aeroplanes*. What use are human names to us?"

I'm about to snap back at him, but Conor angles his body

against the thrust of the current and swims up beside me. "We'll never find a fifty-mile-wide strait when there are thousands and thousands of miles of land south of us, Saph. We'd die trying. Faro says that a strong current like this will know its own way south. There's nothing else to guide us. We've got to go with the current, and trust it."

Elvira is awake now. With both hands she pushes back her hair from her face. "Why is it light, Faro?" she asks sharply.

"We are no longer under the ice."

"We must leave this current and find another. We've got to keep going north!" Elvira sounds scared, almost panicky. Her eyes are like wide black holes in her face. I can't help feeling a pang of sympathy for the shock she feels, waking into a different world.

"We have to go north!" Elvira swims to us, and grasps Conor by the arm, looking into his face. "Don't you understand?"

"It's all right, Elvira," he says soothingly, "we're heading in the right direction. We had to go north to get to the top of the world, more or less, and now we go south."

"But—" Elvira breaks off, looking from one of us to the other. Her hand goes to her mouth. Her eyes are desperate. I remember my brother's words about how Elvira seemed like a different person as she urged him north: *She wouldn't let me rest for a second. She kept pulling my arm and making us keep going north. And she's strong, Saph…*

She doesn't look strong now. She looks anguished, and I can't help feeling sorry for her.

"The North," whispers Elvira, "I have to go there. That is my journey, don't you understand?"

Now Faro is beside his sister. "Elvira," he murmurs, "I cannot make the Crossing without you. Stay with us."

Elvira puts out a hand, testing the strength of the current. Her tail lashes. Is she going to try to force herself out of the current? But it's already carried us hundreds of miles south – maybe thousands. She'll be alone, and lost. Easy prey for the first polar bear or orca that chooses to forget she is Mer. Or she'll die of hunger and exhaustion.

"No, Elvira! You mustn't!"

Elvira looks startled. Maybe she didn't think I cared that much about her. "But, Sapphire," she says, her voice tight with pain, "I belong there, in the North. I never knew it before. I can be happy there."

"You will be happy alone," says Faro harshly.

"No, not alone, I am sure of it. There are Mer in the northern waters, I have seen them."

"I haven't seen any," says Faro.

Conor stares at Elvira. "We didn't meet any Mer, Elvira."

"But—" Elvira starts speaking, then stops. I have a flash of insight. The Atka. Maybe Elvira has an Atka too. Maybe Elvira saw her Atka, listened to her, even touched her. Maybe Elvira really did meet those northern Mer with their silver hair and skins as pale as the moon, when Conor was sleeping. Something has happened to fill Elvira with such conviction that she belongs in the North.

All this time, the current is sweeping us south. Elvira realises it, and gives a sudden, despairing cry. "Faro! What am I going to do?"

Faro puts an arm around his sister and her hair swirls, covering both their faces. They murmur together, privately. Conor and I swim away a few metres, not wanting to eavesdrop.

"*You* could persuade her, Conor," I whisper. Elvira would do anything for Conor... or at least, I thought she would...

"Not about this," says Conor. "Let Faro do the talking, Saph."

Faro and Elvira talk for a long time while the current bears us along at a speed so quiet and effortless that it hardly seems like speed at all. At last Faro swims across to us. "Elvira will complete the Crossing with us," he says.

Conor nods quickly, but his colour deepens and I know how relieved he is. He must have thought there was a real risk she'd leave us. Faro throws back his head in his old gesture of pride and resolve. How pale he looks, in spite of his dark skin. And how stressed.

"I have promised her that when we return home, she will have her choice. If she still wishes to go to the North I will not stop her. I will help her."

He stares straight at us, daring us to comment or to pity him. The current is the only thing that moves; Conor and I are frozen. I want to say something or do something, but I know it won't help. Elvira is Mer and the forces that are pulling her to the North are beyond my understanding. I remember the Atka gliding towards me on her ice floe and I shiver. The North wants

Elvira and it's powerful enough to take her from us.

"But why now, Faro? Why has Elvira suddenly changed like this?"

"The North has touched her, and Elvira's spirit has answered it. Her fate lies there."

It will tear Faro apart to help his sister to leave him and everyone who knows and loves her, but he will do it all the same. Faro keeps his promises.

I touch the *deublek* on my wrist and feel Faro's eyes on me.

"We two are joined together, little sister," he says, as if we're alone and Conor cannot hear us. "No one can separate us, until we choose to part."

CHAPTER SIXTEEN

First the ice disappeared, then the light returned, and then the colour of the water began to change. The jade greens and sharp blues of the Arctic are far behind us now. We are in the south. There is dazzling white sand on the sea bed beneath us, and if we look through the skin we find blue skies and a high brilliant sun. The water is a rich, tropical blue, with bars of turquoise above the sand.

We have come thousands of miles, changing from current to current to find the fastest, always heading south. The things that I thought would be the most difficult have turned out to be easy. The current that brought us from the Arctic knew its way to the narrow straits between Asia and America and brought us safely through, riding on its back.

We're in the heart of the Pacific now. We've learned to trust the currents, and have faith in our journey. It was hard, when the current which had brought us safely all the way from the Arctic suddenly lost power, and spread out, losing its force as a river does when it flows into a lake. We had to swim for miles and miles before we picked up another current, and it was much slower. It felt a bit like travelling on a rusty old cargo steamer, after a voyage on a gleaming ocean liner. "At this rate," Conor said grimly, "we'll have grey hair before we finish the Crossing."

I knew that Ervys was in his mind, too. His followers would be sharpening their spears. Everyone would be waiting for the young Mer to return from the Crossing. If only I could still feel Saldowr's presence.

But things got better. We learned never to stay with one current when it slackened speed, but to keep moving towards the fastest water. At first it was only Faro who knew how to find the best currents. We asked him how he did it and he frowned, struggling to put his knowledge into words. *You don't look for the current itself,* he said at last. *You look for the effect of it and then you know it's not too far away. You have to notice everything. How the fish swim and how the kelp forest sways. How the sand is forced into channels on the sea bed, and where the dolphins are travelling. You have to listen to what Ingo is telling you.*

Conor and I hadn't picked up the signs before. We hadn't even known that they *were* signs, but once Faro told us, we soon saw how water moving at speed changes everything for miles around.

That's one of the best things about this journey. I feel more part of Ingo than I've ever been. I'm learning all the things that a Mer girl would pick up some time in her childhood without needing to think about it.

Elvira swims by herself a little way behind us. She follows passively whenever we change currents. It annoys me that she won't try to help. She knows as much as Faro does; maybe more. She can change direction with one effortless flick of the tail. If I could swim like Elvira and had her knowledge of Ingo, I'd want to lead, not drift along in our wake.

Every so often Conor or Faro will fall back to keep her company and try to talk to her. After a while they give up. Elvira is lost in her own world, and she doesn't want anyone else there. She looks so sad. Her eyes gaze at nothing. She swims as gracefully as ever, but usually when the Mer swim they look as if they love the feel of the water against their bodies. Elvira looks as if she doesn't care where she is. Her body is with us, but her spirit is elsewhere.

I am sure now that her Atka has touched her. More than touched her: caught her in a cold spell that Elvira doesn't even want to escape. If it wasn't some kind of northern magic, how could she change so completely? She *was* happy before she went to the North; I know she was. At least, I think I know she was. But maybe with everyone, even with your closest friends (and Elvira's certainly not that), there are things hidden so deep that you never see them.

I *thought* she was happy, anyway. She was proud of her skill as a healer. Everybody respected her; Saldowr allowed her to look after him when he was so terribly wounded after the Tide Knot broke. I used to feel envious of Elvira because things seemed so easy for her. She was Mer and she was at home in Ingo. Even though she and Faro are brother and sister, Elvira doesn't seem to share the human blood that causes Faro so much doubt and anguish. Faro's right: their ancestors' blood must have mixed differently in them. Elvira isn't curious about the human world, like Faro. She's always been so sure of her place in Ingo. Suddenly, everything's changed. Elvira loves Faro (yes, and Conor too, although I prefer not to think about that). But you wouldn't guess it now. She hardly speaks to either of them.

I'm thinking about all this when I hear singing. It's Elvira, crooning words I can't quite catch. I scull with my hands against the current, to slow myself as much as I can. Elvira drifts closer, and the song becomes clearer. I recognise the words with a shiver of fear.

Alatuk alatuk Atka, Atka amaluk alatuk...

I scull more strongly, waiting for the current to bring Elvira alongside me.

"Elvira, where did you learn that song?"

"In the North."

"I thought it sounded like a northern song," I say neutrally. I don't want to scare her off by mentioning the Atka straightaway. "But won't it make you feel worse, singing it?"

"You don't understand, do you?" I feel a rush of annoyance. I'm only trying to help, and besides, I hate it when people say "You don't understand" in that self-pitying way, as if their feelings are much more complicated than anyone else's.

"No, I don't, and I can't unless you tell me," I say crisply.

To my surprise, Elvira responds. "Then I will try to explain, Sapphire. I don't *want* to feel like this. I have not chosen it; it has chosen me. My Atka has touched me and now I know I must live in the North. I will find my people there. I have already seen them and spoken to them. I will find my happiness. The North is pulling me – so strongly – and I must go to find it again."

Her words strike a chill into my heart, because it's like listening to myself. Ingo has pulled me like that, so powerfully that I haven't wanted to fight it. It has taken me from the human world to the Mer. Elvira's right. You can't resist it, because it's not just outside you, it's within you as well.

I touch her arm gently, in a kind of apology. "I do understand, Elvira. I'm sorry. But can you – I mean, will you really be able to leave behind everything you know? Even Faro?"

"I don't know," says Elvira soberly. "But if I cannot live, then I will die." This is such typical Mer fatalism that I want to shake her.

"No, you won't, Elvira! You can't just die when you want to, you're much too young. Besides," I add slyly, "what about Conor?"

Elvira blushes, then bites her lip. "I think Conor will never come to live in the North," she says, looking sad again. There's no point lying to her. Conor would hate a world of darkness, ice and atkas. Besides, he belongs here…

Here? asks an inconvenient voice in my head. *And where exactly are you so sure that Conor belongs?*

I'm not going to think about all that now. I make up my mind and say, "I'll help you, Elvira, if you really do decide that you want to go back to the North, once we've made the Crossing."

A faint smile touches her lips. "Thank you, Sapphire."

"But you've got to try to be happy until then. We really need you to come back to us, Elvira."

Elvira shrugs. "I came with you. I am here, aren't I?"

"We're not the four of us together making the Crossing any more. I didn't know how important it was that we were together until we came apart," I say.

"I did not think you cared so much if I was with you or not," says Elvira. Now it's my turn to blush, because she's right. How often have I found Elvira irritating, or wished that she would just go away and leave my brother alone? But now she has gone away, with her mind and spirit wandering elsewhere while her body follows us listlessly, and I hate it.

"I'm sorry, Elvira. We do need you. Please."

"Then I will try."

"Elvira..."

"What is it, Sapphire?"

"Couldn't you try and somehow block the North out of your mind?"

"I wish I could!" Elvira bursts out passionately. "Don't you think I would do that if I could? Everything I thought would be my future has been taken away from me. It is like a Tide Knot breaking in my life. But I can't fight the pull of the North, Sapphire. It is too strong for me. It's like a call which goes down to the bone and into my heart. I know that my brother and – and Conor – they are both angry with me. I wish I could explain it so that you all understood."

"I do understand," I say slowly. "It was the same for me when Ingo called me for the first time. You're right, you don't even *want* to fight against it."

"And now you are here, in Ingo," says Elvira.

"Yes."

"So you see how it is for me."

"Yes. Yes, I do, but… I don't think it's simple, Elvira. If you could just make one decision and then it's finished, it would be easy. I'd be here in Ingo, I'd become more and more Mer, end of story. But it's more like… Oh, I don't know, Elvira, it's like a tide that ebbs and flows inside you, just as real tides do. Sometimes it's so strong you can't do anything but go with it; and then you have a chance to think, and you remember everything you've left behind."

Elvira shivers. "I could not live like that."

"You might have to. Besides, it could be the way forward." I'm thinking aloud now, trying to convince myself as much as her. "I think that's what Saldowr's been trying to teach us. I don't want to offend you, Elvira, but the Mer can be a bit rigid – I mean, *certain*," I correct myself hastily. "But Saldowr seemed to be suggesting that certainty isn't always such a good thing. People who are totally certain about who they are and where they belong can become like Ervys, thinking that his way is the only way, and the Mer are the only ones who have rights…"

"But I want to belong somewhere," says Elvira. She looks so strained and unhappy that I stop trying to express my theory.

"You do – you belong with us," I say, and it's true. I've always secretly thought that it would be great if there were just the three of us, Conor, Faro and I, but now I know that I would miss Elvira. We would all miss her. She balances us.

Elvira smiles again, faintly, and looks a little comforted.

"What would we do without you if we were wounded or ill?

We've got to stay strong. We've got to finish the Crossing," I continue, and although she makes a little dismissive gesture, I think she is pleased.

So much to do... too much. And too much depends on it. I remember the stain of blood spreading out from Faro's tail. Everything's changed now that the Mer have taken up weapons. One death leads to another. That's how it happens in war. An attack, and then a revenge, and then another attack until Ingo is torn apart. Sometimes it feels as if there's only the faintest thread of hope, but I cling to Saldowr's words. *You carry something within you that is stronger than the divisions between our two worlds. Mer and human can become one, reconciled. The wounds that tear the Mer can be healed.* But we must hurry.

"Do you think we might be nearly at the bottom of the world, Elvira?"

"I don't know. We are a long way south, I'm sure of that." Visibly, she struggles not to get upset.

"I want to find the whale's daughter so much." I haven't talked to Elvira about this before, but I want to distract her. "If only I could see her, and tell her mother how she is."

"We will ask every whale we see," says Elvira gently, and now I don't know if I'm trying to cheer her up or if she's trying to comfort me. But it feels better that there are two of us.

"Come on, Sapphire," she says. "We must swim faster; we are way behind the others!"

I smile to myself as we plunge forward. I never thought I'd be glad to be bossed around by Elvira.

"Have you ever seen so many different coloured corals, Faro?"

We are floating above a reef. Small, brilliant fish flicker in and out of pink coral branches. I've already seen a fish which is shaped like a bat and a fish with wide, stripy fins that look like wings. Some of the fish are so brightly coloured and weirdly shaped that they remind me of little kids' paintings. But the colours are far too alive for paint. Earlier on Faro and I saw thousands of tiny bright green fish scudding away from a barracuda. We've seen tiger sharks too, and giant rays. None of them has threatened us.

We are resting for a while before we search for the next current. Elvira has taken Conor off to search for plants which she thinks she may be able to use in medicines.

Faro dives to look at the corals more closely. Suddenly he calls, "Sapphire! Come here! This reef is made of metal."

I plunge through the clear turquoise water towards the shaggy mass of coral, weed, darting fish and sea anemones. Faro is right. I can see metal too. A steel-grey curve, almost obscured by the living things that have made their home on it. We swim along the reef.

"I think it's a shipwreck, Faro."

Faro points along the sea bed. "There's another." And another and another. We stare through the transparent water as wreck after wreck appears in the distance, half buried in white sand.

"I wonder why there are so many? Where did they all come from?"

The water is not that deep here – no more than thirty metres – and very clear. I can't see any rocks on which all these ships could have foundered. In spite of all the brilliant, teeming life that covers them, the half-buried ships look eerie. I focus on one of the smaller wrecks. There is something wrong about it. It doesn't look like a ship at all.

"I'm going to swim up for a better view," I tell Faro.

I swim up until I'm a few metres from the surface, in the sunwater, then gaze down at the wrecks. Immediately, as if a jigsaw puzzle has put itself together before my eyes, I see the blunt nose, the tail, the broken wings. It's a plane. And there's another, with its fuselage shattered into coral-covered pieces.

"I think there's been a battle," I say to Faro as he swims up beside me. "Those ships didn't break up on rocks. They were sunk by something. Torpedoes or bombs, maybe," I go on, forgetting that Faro probably won't know what I'm talking about. "Maybe the planes were bombers."

"You mean that all these wrecks destroyed one another?" asks Faro.

"Yes. They were enemies."

"But now they are together."

"Yes." A school of crimson and orange fish shimmers above the wreck of a plane. "I wish I knew more about aeroplanes, then I'd know when all this happened. Which war it was, I mean."

Faro shakes his head incredulously, looking at the wrecks which litter the sea floor. "So much metal," he says.

"It must have been a huge battle."

Faro nods. I'm expecting an attack on the ways of humans, but he surprises me. "We will have to fight a battle, too," he says.

"What do you mean?"

"Ervys will not yield easily. We escaped the sharks, and his anger will be deeper and stronger than ever if we succeed in making the Crossing. He wants us to die."

"I know. But no one seems to have followed us so far."

"That doesn't mean that we are safe."

The reef is so beautiful and rich with life, but there will be bones buried deep in that white sand. My mind fills with planes roaring down the sky, guns blazing, oily smoke streaming behind them. They smashed through the skin of the water, and Ingo swallowed them. The shattered metal and shattered human beings would have sunk slowly to the floor of the ocean. After all the thunder of battle it would have been silent.

No one has ever wanted to kill me before.

"You always told me that the Mer didn't have wars," I say. "You were always saying that the Mer knew how to sort out their arguments without fighting."

"I thought it was true," says Faro grimly, "but it turns out that when we want something enough we will kill for our purposes, just like humans."

"I want to go," I say. "Let's find the others."

CHAPTER SEVENTEEN

We're skirting the edge of a huge kelp forest. Its dense, tangled mass sends a shiver through me. Faro doesn't mind exploring a little way into the kelp, but I never go with him and I count the seconds until he swims free again. I wish he'd stay out in the clear water, but he only laughs at me and says he's been swimming in kelp forests since he was a baby. Not forests like this, though, I'm sure of it. This one goes on for miles, dark and brooding. Anything might lie hidden in its depths. Even Faro has drawn away from it now, and he's swimming up ahead with Elvira.

Suddenly Conor is at my side. "Saph! Look to your left."

"What? Where?"

"Just between those two clumps of stems. There," Conor whispers as if someone – or something – might hear us. "Turn your head slowly. Don't make it obvious."

I steal a look sideways. Nothing. Or was that a movement? The back of my neck prickles as I peer into the gloom, trying to make it look as if I'm just glancing casually at the kelp.

"There, Saph! Can you see it?"

I catch a glimpse of a shape flitting between two thick stems of kelp.

"What is it, Con?"

"I don't know. Look, there's another! Don't let them know you've seen them."

The shape moves again. And there's another. There's a head – a flicker of an arm – a tail…

"Conor, they're Mer!" I exclaim much too loudly. Elvira and Faro hear me, twist round and are with us in a couple of powerful strokes.

"Mer! Look in the kelp forest. Not there, Faro, there!"

We can all see them now. A face glints through the gloom, then vanishes. A figure flickers into sight, then another and another. How many are there? I can't see clearly through the shadows.

"They are Mer," says Faro decisively. "I shall greet them."

"But, Faro, do you think you should?" asks Elvira anxiously.

"They are not likely to be followers of Ervys. His influence can't have spread this far. Of course we must greet our brothers and sisters." He raises his voice and calls out, "Greetings and good wishes to you, friends. We are travellers making the Crossing of Ingo."

Silence. Nothing moves. Perhaps they don't understand. *Don't be stupid*, I tell myself. Faro is speaking full Mer. Of course they'll understand. Even Conor does now. He's been in Ingo so long that the language has poured itself into him.

"Greetings, friends!" calls Faro, more loudly this time.

Again there's no answer. A long pause, and then a stir among the stems of kelp. A single figure emerges. He is Mer, but much smaller than any Mer I've seen. The sheen of his skin is a deep, tropical blue, like colour taken from a butterfly's wings. His hair is cropped as short as stubble on his skull. It's the first time we've seen a Mer person, male or female, with short hair.

He swims towards us, cutting the water with the ease of a dagger. His face is calm, but his eyes are wary.

"Greetings," he says as he comes up to us. His tail flicks lightly from side to side, holding him in place. He looks from me to Conor and I see his eyes widen with astonishment. I'm used to this look from Mer I haven't met before – when they encounter a human being in Ingo, not drowning but living underwater like one of the Mer. This man controls his surprise well.

"Greetings," we say one by one, and hold out our hands, palm open, to show our friendship.

"You speak our language," he says to me.

"Yes. I have Mer blood."

His look of interest quickens. "I have heard stories about such as you," he says. "In our childhood we believe such tales, but then we grow up and put them from our minds. So there is truth in the legends."

I smile at him self-consciously, not sure whether or not I like the idea of being a legend. Suddenly he jackknives, whips round and flickers in and out between the four of us so fast that his body is a blur of blue. Before we have time to react he is back in place, his face impassive. It's a display of skill that even Faro couldn't match.

"That was amazing," says Conor. The man doesn't smile, but perhaps his face softens a little.

"My name is Sapphire," I say, and point to the others in turn, "Faro... Conor... Elvira..." But the Mer man does not respond with his own name.

"We come as friends," says Faro, with an edge to his voice. "Do the Mer of these parts not wish to learn one another's names?"

"If I give you my name, how shall I get it back?" says the man reasonably, whisking his tail as if he longs to make another circuit. He is so fascinating that I can't help watching every move he makes. Somehow I've drifted round so that my back is to the kelp forest.

"Saph," says Conor very quietly, "look behind you."

I glance over my shoulder, and freeze. There are figures appearing at the edge of the kelp forest. Ten of them – twenty – no, more are coming from behind every thick stem and out of every pool of shadow.

"My people," says the Mer man calmly. They are all small, like him, but just as lithe and sinuous. They could surround us in half a second.

"We come as friends," repeats Faro, and I realise that he has also seen the crowding figures. "Know that we are making the Crossing of Ingo."

All the Mer recognise the Crossing of Ingo as the greatest journey they will ever make. Faro always told me that even those Mer who were never chosen to make it were bound to give any assistance they could to those who were on the

Crossing. But that was never entirely true, was it? Look at Ervys. He did everything in his power to stop us. Maybe there are other Mer who are equally hostile, for their own reasons. Maybe we've just found some of them.

"We have heard of the Crossing," says the Mer man. "We tell our children stories about that, too."

Faro stares at him in disbelief. "But you are Mer. Surely..."

"We are the Mer of the kelp forests. Our blood is older and truer than any other. Before the oceans divided from the land, before Ingo came into being, we were."

"But... but to be Mer and not to make the Crossing of Ingo..." says Faro slowly, as if he can't take it in.

Fortunately, the Mer man doesn't seem to be offended. "Our place is in the kelp forest," he says. "The forest is our mother and our home and gives us everything we need. Why should we travel?"

The other figures are edging forward a little. Mer children peep from the shelter of the thickest kelp stems. All of them have the same shorn hair. Their eyes shine through the gloom, bright with curiosity. The children's skin is an even darker and more beautiful blue than the adults'.

"We should like to meet more of your people," says Faro boldly.

Faro, why did you have to say that? There are hundreds of them. Why does Faro have to be so reckless? Maybe he thinks he'll be able to convince them that they should make the Crossing too.

"I will speak to them," says the Mer man. Without warning he flashes away from us into the shadowy border of the kelp forest. A group gathers around him, but we can't hear what they're saying. With a swirl, he is back with us.

"Our children would like to meet you," he announces, looking directly at me. "Our little ones have never seen a human being in Ingo."

"Let them come out here, then," says Conor quickly.

"They cannot leave the forest."

"Then I'll go with my sister. I am human too."

Elvira looks desperately anxious. Faro puts his hand on my arm protectively. "Our friends might lose themselves in the kelp forest," he says.

"They will remain on the edge of the forest where you can see them," says the Mer man with a touch of anger in his voice. "Our children are only children. You say you come as friends, yet you seem to suspect us."

"We'd be glad to meet the children," I break in to stop Faro arguing. I'm not sure why it's so important to these Mer that their children meet us, but there are only four of us, and hundreds of them. They swim much faster than we do, so escape isn't an option. They could easily surround us and carry us off into their forest. If we do what they want, maybe they'll help us. I want to find the whale's daughter so much, and talk to her. Perhaps these Mer know where the whales go.

The forest is a maze of thick stems, tangled roots and weaving strands. The light from the surface breaks up into a confusing camouflage net of shadows. If I went even a hundred metres into the forest, I'd never find my way out again. The stems would cage me like prison bars.

Conor and I swim to the edge of the forest. Adult Mer watch us closely, without moving. I have the feeling that there are many more pairs of eyes watching me than figures that I can see.

"Keep still. The children will come out soon," says the Mer man. I wait, my skin tingling with suspense. There is a stir in the shadows, and then another. With incredible swiftness, two tiny figures dart towards me, stop dead, quiver in the water and then swim on very slowly. They are young children, maybe six or seven. Four girls and four boys. Behind them more children emerge from their hiding places. They swim around us with the same dazzling speed as the adult Mer, skimming the stems of kelp. Now I see why they cut their hair short. The kelp is so thick that they'd get tangled in it a hundred times a day if they had long hair.

There's a light touch on my back. I turn and a little Mer girl snatches her own hand away, giggling.

"It's all right," I say. "I'm not going to bite you." She gives me a gap-toothed smile. She's so sweet I'd like to give her a hug. The rest of the children are shyer. They circle us, diving down to stare at our feet in wonder. One little boy puts out a tentative finger to Conor's big toe, but he's not brave enough. Conor wriggles his toes in the water and the Mer boy shoots up and away. The children aren't really scared of us. They're thrilled and inquisitive and a bit overcome by their own daring. They cluster together, their arms wrapped around one another. They whisper excitedly, turn around for another peep at the amazing sight of our legs and feet, and then burst into high, shrilling laughter.

"I feel like a circus freak," says Conor wryly.

The Mer man watches the scene with proud indulgence. I wonder if one of the children is his, but I don't ask. He might suspect I've got some ulterior motive. After ages of giggling the children get bored with us and they all shoot off together like a school of fish to play in the kelp forest again.

The faces of the adult Mer relax. None of them comes forward, though, or even meets our eyes. As soon as I look at them they glance away distrustfully. It's just as well I didn't try to hug that little girl. The parents would probably have thought I was trying to strangle her or something.

"Our children are happy that they have met humans in Ingo," says the Mer man.

"We are happy to have met them," says Conor blandly. For someone who rarely lies, Conor is very convincing. Seizing the advantage, he inquires, "Do you know where the nearest continent is?"

The word "continent" sounds strange in Mer. The idea won't quite translate. But I know what Conor's trying to find out. We were talking about it last night when the others were sleeping. We think we must be close to Australia now. Conor is sure that is what the Mer mean when they describe the great land that they have to journey around at "the bottom of the world".

At first I thought they must be talking about Antarctica, but Faro says that the sea around this great land isn't frozen.

If we're near Australia, then we'll be turning for home soon. I wish the whale had been more specific about where her daughter lives now. The oceans are so vast. "The bottom of the world" could mean anywhere in thousands of miles of water.

It's eerie that we might be so close to Mum and Roger. We might pass within a few miles of them without ever knowing it. Mum and Roger are staying on the Queensland coast. Roger might even be diving now, not that far from us. What if we saw him in all his dive gear slowly swimming around a reef? What if he saw us?

At first I thought that maybe, somehow, we could visit Mum, but Conor's sure that we can't. I suppose he's right. Imagine the shock it would give her if we suddenly appeared on the beach when she believes we're safe at home, thousands of miles away. "She might think we're dead and these are our ghosts. She could die of the shock. People do," Conor said seriously. Besides, how would we find one particular part of Queensland in all the length of Australia's coast?

I'm so lost in my thoughts that I start when Conor breaks the silence by repeating his question. "The nearest continent – the nearest land mass – which direction does it lie in?"

"We live in the kelp forest," says the Mer man at last, rather evasively it seems to me.

"We know that. But even from within the kelp forest you must communicate with other creatures of Ingo," says Conor.

His certainty surprises me, but it seems to convince the Mer man, who shrugs. "We speak to the whales when they rest in the sunwater close to our forest. They talk of land but it does not concern us."

"But they do talk of it."

"They say that whenever they want to follow the setting sun, a great land lies in their way. They must go far, far south to avoid it. There is so much land that Ingo chokes on it."

"Australia," murmurs Conor.

"You speak our language but you put into it words which we do not know," says the Mer man. "Are you trying human tricks on us?" There is aggression in his stance and in his voice. The goodwill from our meeting with the children seems to be dissolving quickly.

"Conor, we need to go," I murmur. I'm starting to feel claustrophobic in the kelp forest's crowded, shifting shadows. I have a vision of dozens of Mer children grabbing my arms and legs, wrapping me round and round with strands of kelp and pulling me into the forest. I can still hear the ghostly echo of their giggling, deep among the kelp. They would love me to come in for a game of hide-and-seek where I never found my way out again. What if their parents suddenly thought that it would be nice for their children to keep us here as playthings?

"We must leave now," I say more loudly.

"Very well," says the Mer man. "If you insist on finding land, ask advice of the whales. They are always travelling," and he smiles a little pityingly. I don't know if it's us he pities or the whales. Maybe both, for not having the good fortune to live in the kelp forest.

"Won't you tell us your name?" I ask impulsively, but he just regards me coldly for a while and then says, "No." Conor nudges me. It means *Time to get going, Saph*. He's right. I feel the eyes of a hundred watchers on my back as we swim back to Faro and Elvira.

"Not very forthcoming, was he?" says Conor.

"Don't, Con. He might hear you. He was very, very *strong*, wasn't he? Even though he was so small."

"Arrogant, I thought. And quite scary," says Conor cheerfully. Conor never minds admitting that he's scared.

"How did you know that they communicated with other creatures, Conor?"

"Deduction, my dear Watson. Otherwise how would they have heard stories about humans and the Crossing of Ingo?"

Faro and Elvira are just as eager to get away from the kelp forest as we are. We swim in a close group, not too slow, not too fast. It mustn't look as if we're afraid. I *am* afraid, and I don't know why the fear is so sharp. They didn't hurt us or threaten us – and I'm sure they've got nothing to do with Ervys. They seem cut off from all the other Mer.

"I am ashamed that he was Mer. There was no Mer spirit in him," says Faro.

"You don't have to be ashamed, Faro. It had nothing to do with you," I say gently.

"They are my blood. They shame the traditions of the Mer."

"I think they think they *are* the traditions of the Mer. It doesn't matter, Faro. They didn't do us any harm."

"Or help us." Faro tosses back his hair furiously. "It seems as if wherever we go, Mer are forgetting that we are all brothers and sisters!"

"At least we found out that Australia's to the west of us, and not that distant," says Conor.

"Great," I snap. "That's as good as having a map, isn't it? We've got to find the whales. The sperm whales, I mean. They'll help us; I know they will."

I don't know why I am so sure about this. The currents have brought us safe so far. But everything's about to change. Soon we won't be going outward: we'll be on the voyage home.

"We are wasting time," says Faro. "We must travel on until we smell the land or until we meet dolphins. They will know better than anyone where the whales are."

"The dolphins!" My heart leaps. When the dolphins travelled with us Ingo was truly home. "Can we call them, Faro?"

Faro smiles at me. Yes, he looks older. The Crossing is changing him. Faro will be a man soon, but I don't want to think about that. I want us to stay as we are, Faro and Sapphire, joined by our *deubleks*, free to wander in and out of each other's thoughts. A pulse of current washes my hair over my face, blinding me. Gently Faro pushes it back.

"If *you* call, little sister, I am sure that they will come," he says.

CHAPTER EIGHTEEN

The dolphins came when I called to them, just as Faro said they would. I opened my mind and heard the echo of dolphin language far in the distance. A wave of longing swept from me, as if I were a dolphin stranded on shore and they were my brothers and sisters, waiting to rescue me. I knew that the wave would break against their bodies, and they would come.

Of course they are not the same dolphins as the ones who helped us before, but as soon as I heard the high-pitched whistling of air from their blowholes and the first intricate clicking of their voices, I was back with my brothers and sisters.

I'm riding with a young female dolphin. She has already taught me her recognition pattern. Up until now I've only known dolphins by name, but their recognition patterns go much deeper. You can change your name, but you can't change the essence of what you are. Her name is Seiliko but her recognition pattern means "Quickest of the dolphin daughters in her age group and first in understanding the water".

Seiliko is about my age, I think, by dolphin reckoning. Understanding the water is an amazing thing. When I first got to know dolphins back home in Cornwall, I thought they were fast because of their muscles and their sleekness. I didn't realise how sensitive their skin is, or how they adapt to every tiny change in the flow of waves and currents so that they can work with the water and not against it. Seiliko angles herself so perfectly that nothing holds her back. Even with a human being on her back, she soars.

Seiliko asked me what my recognition pattern was and I said I didn't know, and then she laughed and said, "I will discover it by the end of our journey together."

I've ridden with dolphins before and I know you have to relax, stop being separate and let yourself become part of the dolphin's journey. But Seiliko taught me much more. She said, "You must feel with your skin. You must let the water flow over you. You must learn how the water parts to let you through it." I couldn't get it at first. My skin wasn't sensitive enough and all I felt was the way I slowed Seiliko down. After a while I began to feel what she meant. For a few seconds at a time I became part of Seiliko's understanding of the water. It didn't last, because I'm not good enough yet. But I've learned something about moving through Ingo which I'll never forget.

Seiliko can go faster than the other dolphins who are riding with Faro and Conor and Elvira, but she's always careful not to get too far ahead. I'm sure she would if she were hunting. She'd use all her speed to bring down her prey. But now, if she pulls too far ahead of the others she'll surge to a stop, or whirl around in a circle so that the water and the other dolphins become a racing blur. Then she'll stop dead and each time I think I'll be thrown forward over her head, but it never happens. I think Conor and Faro were a bit jealous that I'm riding with Seiliko, but it wasn't my choice. You don't decide, with dolphins: they do. She came up alongside me and said: *We'll ride together.* Elvira didn't care; she never minds about things like that. She was already deep in conversation with the dolphin who had chosen her. Probably asking him if he had any cuts that needed treating. Elvira still vanishes into her dream of the North for hours on end. Her body is making the Crossing but I think her spirit is always travelling backwards.

I slept a little during the night. Seiliko and the other dolphins plunged on tirelessly, always heading westward. Sometimes they breached and we saw the night sky with a big golden moon and millions of stars. I looked up but I couldn't recognise the constellations. All the stars were in the wrong places. A second later, we dived back through the skin.

"Dawn will be here soon," Seiliko says to me. She's right. The darkness begins to thin. The sea takes on a tinge of grey. We breach again and the moon and stars have disappeared. Seiliko keeps close to the surface, skimming at speed, sending up plumes of spray. Exhilaration pours through me.

"Sunrise!" says Seiliko. The sun explodes from the sea's grey rim, flooding it with colour. The huge ball of the sun is scarlet, then gold, then a pulsing yellow so brilliant that my eyes hurt and I have to look away. Streaks of fire shoot across the sea's surface. My face is bathed in flames.

"Sunrise!" cry all the dolphins exultantly, thrashing their tails on the surface so that the spray catches rainbows. Seiliko gathers herself and leaps clear of the water, then crashes down. She's going at full speed now, the others are falling back and I wish we could ride like this for ever.

At that moment Seiliko throws herself sideways. The jolt hits me like an electric shock. I'm hurled forward, then back. I'm not part of her any more. My skin peels away from hers. The next moment I feel myself slipping. I scrabble to hold on but her skin is suddenly slippery. Seiliko bucks again and I pitch sideways. As I fall, I hear her high-pitched warning cry: "Nets! Nets! Nets!"

I'm on the surface, pushing my hair out of my face. My lungs are burning. I'm not in Ingo any more. When you're riding with a dolphin you stay in Ingo even when they breach, but now I'm on my own. I have to breathe, and the pain is so terrible that I would scream if I had enough breath. Immediately Seiliko is alongside me again. I can hardly see her through a haze of pain. It only lasts for a second and then I'm back in Seiliko's protection. She eases herself under me, and I cling to her, exhausted, as Ingo flows back over me and into me. I don't have to breathe any more. The pain ebbs and I can see clearly again.

"Where are the others?"

"Below us," Seiliko reassures me. "They stopped before they hit the nets."

Seiliko plunges beneath the surface, and I see what she's already seen. Loose nets hang swaying in the water. If we'd driven on at such speed, the nets would have tangled round us so tight we'd never have got out. Slowly, cautiously, the dolphins skirt the nets. There's no sign of a boat. Maybe these nets have been abandoned, or ripped loose in a storm.

There's a shadow ahead of us in the water. Seiliko quickens her pace, then her body shudders to a stop. Her voice rises, keening. Behind us, the other dolphins respond with answering wails. My blood chills as I realise that the shape hanging from the net ahead of us is a dolphin.

We come closer. It's a young male dolphin, caught by his pectoral fins. He must have struggled and struggled until he drowned. There are gashes in his skin where the net has cut.

The dead dolphin lies on his back. His mouth is slack and the eye that we can see looks milky.

"He has not been dead long," says Seiliko. Her voice is harsh with distress. "The fish have not come to him yet."

"Can we free him? Faro, could we cut the net?"

"We have nothing to cut it with," says Faro, staring at the dead dolphin.

"Humans have been here," says Seiliko as if that's all there is to be said.

"I'm sorry," I say. "I'm so, so sorry."

"You did not put the net here, Sapphire," says Elvira.

"But humans did."

The dead dolphin and the net sway a little in the current. I wish we could cut him free. If we had a knife or even a sharp shell…

"His body understands that we can do nothing for it," says Seiliko. "His spirit is free to ride the waves."

I wish I could believe that too. The dolphin lolls there, so dead and so helpless.

"We must get away from this place," says Seiliko.

I'm glad to go, but I can't help looking back over my shoulder until the dead dolphin becomes a shadow again, and then disappears.

Seiliko knows where the sperm whales are. They were logging not far from what she calls the Great Land. One more day's journey, she says, will take us there.

Seiliko says nothing more about the dead dolphin, and nor does anyone else, but the memory of it hangs over us all. I've known for a long time about dolphins getting caught in nets and drowning there. But knowing is not the same as seeing it with your own eyes. I feel heavy, sad and responsible. The dolphins and Faro and Elvira don't seem to blame us, but in their hearts maybe they do.

The journey seems endless. I am longing for night to come so that I can sleep, and maybe then the image of the dead dolphin will leave my mind. The sun is low in the sky now, and it feels as if we're travelling straight into the sunset. My eyes dazzle until I can hardly keep them open. Even Seiliko must be growing weary. I listen to the hiss of water curling away behind us, and to the scream of seabirds when we rise above the surface. I don't really believe that we're ever going to see land. The ocean stretches endlessly ahead of us, and endlessly behind...

I must have fallen asleep. I open my eyes. We are logging on the surface. Swell moves beneath the skin of the water, and moonlight shines on the black humps of the three other dolphins. Everyone's resting. Dolphins don't sleep deeply; they drowse for half an hour or so, but on some level they're always alert to danger. I've been asleep for a long time. I stretch one leg and then another. Water clucks softly around Seiliko's body. I don't want to wake her but I feel much too alert and alive myself to stay still. Maybe she won't notice if I slip off her back and go and see if Conor's awake. Stealthily, I slide one leg over Seiliko's back.

"Where are you going, Sapphire?" she asks me, her voice the quietest possible outbreath of clicks and whistles.

"Oh! I thought you were asleep, Seiliko." I raise my head to look around. Beyond the dark swell of the sea there is a more solid, opaque line. I stare, and as I watch a few lights open along it, like eyes. For a moment I can't think what it is. A ship? A huge liner on its way across the world? A smell catches in the back of my throat, sharp, mineral and unmistakable. *Land. I can smell land. Those lights are human lights.*

We must be close to shore. Not more than a few miles at

most. There are people living there, in houses. How strange that seems after we've been so long in Ingo. Maybe children are going to bed in those houses at this moment.

"Seiliko, I think I can see land."

Seiliko's body tenses. "Where do you see it?"

"Over there, ahead of us. Look at the lights." Seiliko does not respond.

"Can't you see it?" I ask again. Suddenly I am seized with longing. "Seiliko, do you think that is the Great Land that you were talking about? My mother could be there. One of those lights could be shining from her window."

Still Seiliko says nothing. Maybe she's angry because of the nets.

"Could you take me there?" Seiliko could cross that stretch of water in a few minutes. We could be there and back again before the others woke. Imagine if Mum really was there, and I could see her and speak to her. Of course it's crazy to believe that out of all the thousands of miles of Australian coast, those lights show the place where she is. It's crazy but maybe this is one of those nights when the million to one chance comes true. Those lights are like a signal. *Here I am. Here I am.*

I don't care what Conor says, I know Mum isn't going to die of shock if she sees me. She'd want to see me more than anything. There's so little time. Tomorrow those lights will be gone. We'll travel on and we might never come so close to the coast again. And I know deep in my heart that there's danger waiting ahead. The closer we get to completing the Crossing, the closer we are to breaking Ervys's dreams of power, the greater that danger will grow. My Atka said, *You must stay in your world and fight its battles.* Ingo is my world. Ingo's battles are my battles. If something happens to me – if Mum never sees me again –

"*Please,* Seiliko!"

If there's the faintest chance of seeing Mum I've got to take it. It might be our only chance and there is something I must ask her. Deep inside me a question is forming, as huge and shadowy as a whale beneath the surface of the sea. I don't know exactly what it is yet. I only know that those lights have appeared for a purpose and I'm not meant to ignore them.

"I cannot take you," says Seiliko.

Her rejection sears through me. "But Seiliko..."

"I cannot take you," she repeats.

"I've got to see my mother, Seiliko."

Seiliko doesn't ask me why I think that Mum is there. She believes me, but she's still not going to help me. "Then I will swim," I say.

"No," says Seiliko, "that land is much farther away than you think." I think I sense a change in her voice. Maybe she's about to yield. At last she says reluctantly, "I cannot take you to land, Sapphire, but there is one who may be willing."

"A dolphin, you mean? Can you ask him for me? I'd be so grateful, Seiliko. You don't know how important it is."

"If you are sure."

"Yes, yes, of course I'm sure."

"Then climb off my back."

I slide off Seiliko's back and sink into the water, where I won't have to breathe air. But if I go to shore I'll have to breathe, and it will hurt…

I'll face that when I come to the shore.

A soft, mysterious whistling fills the air, like drops of music. Seiliko is calling. The sound fills the water, spreading out in wider and wider ripples. It's a sweet, wild, urgent sound. If I were a dolphin and I heard it, I'd have to come. I look up towards the surface of the water, but none of the other three dolphins or their riders has stirred. They still float on the surface as if they're enchanted. Slowly the whistling fades away. Seiliko dips beneath the surface and says, "He is coming. Wait here and he will ride you to the shore. Don't speak to him or ask him any questions and he will take you safely and return you safely. Promise me."

"I promise, Seiliko."

She melts into the shadows of the water. I wait tensely. I hear nothing, no clicks and whistles, no dolphin greeting, but suddenly the dolphin is at my side in a silent swirl of water. Moonlight streams on to the curve of his back. For a moment he looks transparent, like a trick of the light, and then I touch his flank and swim up on to his back and of course he is real and solid. But he doesn't speak to me. He waits until I'm in position and have sealed myself against him, and then without warning he leaps forward.

He is no faster than Seiliko but when he breaches he leaps even higher above the waves, so that he seems to hang in the air for seconds before diving so steeply that he enters the water with hardly a ripple. He dives deep, where the moonlight can't reach, then up to the surface to skim it like a stone skipping across a lake. He doesn't splash like the other dolphins. If I couldn't feel the solid roundness of his body I would think he had no weight at all.

I hear the thunder of swell breaking on a reef. I look ahead and see the white of foam where the water pounds. The dolphin doesn't hesitate, but heads straight for the wild water. I brace myself, but before I've had time to be afraid he finds a gap and we slip through into the calm of a lagoon. The water is shallow here, and so transparent that I can see moonlit crabs scuttling on the sea bed beneath us. As I slide off the dolphin's back, Faro's words from long ago ring in my mind. *As long as you are with the dolphins, you are in Ingo.* My feet touch the sandy bed of the lagoon. The water is chest deep, and suddenly I'm aware that it's warm. The dolphin slides away a couple of metres. Now I am in the Air. Now I've got to breathe. I brace myself, clenching my fists.

But it doesn't hurt. The air slides into my body easily. I can hardly believe it. Cautiously I take another breath and wait for the shock and pain of harsh air on my Ingo-smooth lungs, but my breath comes as easily as if I've never been in Ingo at all. A breeze caresses my face, carrying heavy, tropical sweetness. It reminds me of the palm trees in St Pirans when they come into flower, but the night here is much warmer than the hottest summer night in Cornwall. I look up. The night sky is rich blue velvet, and the stars are huge and close. The dolphin rolls over in the shallow water of the lagoon. I'm afraid that he'll strand himself, but he sculls lazily into deeper water, and floats there. I can see one of his bright eyes watching me.

It's very strange that he doesn't speak, but I don't want to break my promise to Seiliko by trying to make him talk. I'm confident that he'll wait for me.

I wade inshore, waist-deep, thigh-deep, then splash ankle-deep through the shallows on to dry, warm sand. I can't see the lights of the houses now because a little ridge ahead of me hides them. Leaves hiss, and there's a rattle and then a crack as if something's treading on dry twigs. Thoughts of snakes, poisonous spiders and crocodiles crowd my mind. I hold my breath and tiptoe forward. Sand sifts between my toes, and then I'm on a path.

There's a light shining ahead of me. I can see a vague dark shape that is probably a house. It looks too low for a house, though, more like a shed. There's only one storey, and the roof has a dull metal gleam. A wooden verandah runs around the house. I creep forward silently, praying no dog starts to bark. The light is coming from a window on the left-hand side of the building.

The ground prickles my bare feet. I put them down cautiously and noiselessly. I'm about ten metres from the verandah steps when the door opens suddenly, spilling light. An outlined figure stands there, looking into the dark.

It's a woman, wrapped in a dressing gown. You know how you can recognise people without ever seeing their faces, just from their shape and stance? I would know her shape anywhere. My eyes burn and her figure blurs.

"Mum!" I whisper. She freezes, then turns slowly towards me. I expect her to cry out for Roger, but she doesn't. Very quietly, as if any noise might scare me away, she says, "Sapphy?"

"Yes."

Mum seems to fly down the verandah steps and across the prickly grass. She stops just short of me.

"Is it really you, Sapphy?"

"Yes."

Slowly she stretches out her hands and puts them on either side of my face. She turns my face towards the moonlight and looks at me for a long time.

"It *is* you," she breathes at last.

"I had to come and see you, Mum. I had to ask you something."

"What is it, lovely girl?" Her words pierce my heart. I'd forgotten that Mum used to call me that, long ago when I was little.

"Mum, do you think that Dad is dead?"

Mum doesn't answer straightaway. Her fingers stroke my face, very gently, like the warm breeze. I can't see her eyes because she's got her back to the moon.

"Mum?"

"Yes," she says, "he's dead, Sapphy. Do you think I'd ever have gone with Roger if your dad was alive?"

"No," I say, "I know you wouldn't." And I do know it, because

Mum's not the kind of person who would just change from Dad to another man, unless she was sure it was right.

"Can I ask you something else?"

"You can ask me what you want, Sapphy."

My dark, shadowy questions have come to the surface, and now I know what they are.

"Why are you so afraid of the sea?" Mum's fingers go still. She takes a quick breath.

"What I was most afraid of has already happened. The sea has taken your father."

"But you were afraid before that."

"That's true. I always told your father it was because of what a fortune teller told me."

"Wasn't that true, then?"

"Yes, it was true in a way, but there was more to it than that. I can tell you now, lovely girl, seeing as we're both asleep and dreaming. When I was a little girl I was crazy for the water. Your grandma always said I could swim like a fish before I was two years old. She could throw me into the sea and I was never afraid. I'd laugh, she said, and dive in and out of the waves. Then one day I must have thought I could breathe underwater like a fish."

My body tenses. I can hardly believe what I'm hearing. Mum thought she could breathe underwater! Mum was so at home in the sea that she played in the waves, laughing! It seems incredible. I can't connect it with the mother that I know.

"Could you, Mum? Could you breathe when you tried?"

Mum laughs harshly. "I nearly drowned. I went down and down and the water was so rough that no one could see me. Your grandad had to dive in and feel around until he caught hold of me by my hair and dragged me out. I fought him, he said, and he told me that people who are drowning always fight their rescuers. He said I cried for days afterwards. I kept saying that the sea wanted me. Wanted to drown you, more like, he said, because he wanted to frighten me in case I did it again. That's when the fear started. I wouldn't go near the water any more."

"Do you remember what it was like, Mum, when you went down under the waves and they couldn't see you?"

"No. Only what they told me. I do remember one thing which I think was real, not just remembering what they told me. There was a pain like fire in my chest, and then just as it was getting better, that was when I was pulled out. That's why I was so afraid for you, Sapphy. As soon as you were born you loved the sea. Before you could even walk you'd stretch out your arms and cry to go in it. Mathew said you used to wriggle to get free when he took you in the water. I always thought the same thing might happen to you as happened to me when I was little, and maybe this time we wouldn't be in time to pull you out. You were always wild for the water. I was more afraid for you than for Conor."

"You don't have to worry about me, Mum." Mum laughs. Her hands drop to my shoulders.

"Look how tall you're getting," she says. "Nearly as tall as me.

It's right you ask questions now you're getting to the age when you can handle the answers. You ought to ask more questions at school, Sapphy, then they wouldn't say you're such a mazeyhead." Mum lets go of my shoulders with a final loving little shake. "Do you know this is the longest dream I've ever had that makes sense."

"I've got to go now, Mum."

"I know. I've got the feeling I'm going to wake up in a minute. Let's say goodbye before I do."

"Goodbye, Mum." I try to keep my voice calm. Mum doesn't know I've got half the world to cross before I'm home again, or that Ervys would spill my blood without a qualm, just as Mortarow spilled Faro's. Mum believes I'm back in our cottage, sleeping.

"Goodbye, lovely girl. Go on then."

She watches me go down the path. I turn to wave goodbye and she looks like a ghost in her white dressing gown, standing in the moonlight until I disappear from sight. I step behind a big spiky plant, so that she'll think I've gone. Mum waits a little longer, then she turns and goes back up the steps. It's so still that I hear her bare feet patter on the wood. She opens the door, goes inside and closes it again.

Mum doesn't think I'm really here, I remind myself. She would never close the door on me if she thought I was real. I know that, but I still feel empty as I stare at the closed door. I could always go and hammer on it with my fists until Mum and Roger both come out and then Mum will know that it can't be a dream because Roger sees me too, and I'm solid flesh and blood...

For a few seconds I contemplate the scene that would follow. Mum's disbelief, Roger's logic homing in on me. Once they knew it was really me, they'd never let me go. I'd never complete the Crossing. I'd have to go home on a plane with Mum and Roger. The others would face the spears without me, and Ingo would never be healed.

The door glistens faintly in the moonlight. *Leave it*, I tell myself. *It's much better like this.*

The dolphin is still there. I wade out into the warm water of the lagoon, and as soon as it's deep enough to swim I plunge in, dip down, and take a deep breath of Ingo. I am home again. The little building with the tin roof and the rustling, rattling scrub around it was alien. I'd have been scared to be trapped there.

I swim up to the dolphin, but I don't greet him because I remember my promise to Seiliko. I touch him gently on his flank instead, and he turns to me. He dips down for me to climb on to his back, and waits for me to settle against him. I keep my promise and don't say a word, but I can't help stroking his side gratefully. I can't imagine what I'd have done if he hadn't waited for me.

Slowly the dolphin eases forward towards the gap in the

reef. Soon we'll be out of the lagoon and back in the wild Pacific. I shut my eyes, feeling exhausted. The noise of water thundering on the reef grows louder and louder until it's on all sides of us, and then we are through. I open my eyes again to moonlight on the free-surging ocean.

This time the dolphin leaps higher than ever when he breaches. His whole body soars, makes a perfect arc high in the air and then plunges down and down into Ingo, beyond the moonlight. Phosphorescence pours off us as we rise through the skin of the water, and we dive back into an ocean of silver-green light.

At last the dolphin slows. Our beautiful, strange journey is almost over. There, logging on the surface, are the other three dolphins and their riders, still sleeping. Seiliko is a little way apart, and awake.

The dolphin dips down in the water so I can float away from him. I kick backwards a few strokes, and then he rises again. He is very close to me now, but somehow he looks less solid. Phosphorescence still clings to him, outlining his body. And what are those marks on his flanks? I didn't notice them before, but now I see a pattern picked out in light. A criss-cross pattern, cut into the skin, as if…

…as if he's tried to fight free of a net, struggling while the mesh cut deep into his flesh. Phosphorescence burns around him more and more brightly. The shape of the dolphin shows brilliantly, and then, as if a light has been switched off, it vanishes.

I wait for the slap of his wake against my body. Nothing. No sound of farewell. But then he never spoke to me, and I didn't speak to him. Seiliko made me promise…

"Seiliko!"

"What is it, Sapphire?"

"The dolphin! Where is he? Where's he gone?"

"Which dolphin?"

"You know which one! The one you whistled for."

"He is gone."

"Could you whistle again? Would he come back? I never thanked him."

"No," says Seiliko. She seems to be smiling, but then dolphins often look as if they're smiling.

CHAPTER NINETEEN

Faro is worried. "We are travelling too slowly. Taking the northern route has cost us too much time. We must travel fast and surprise Ervys."

"I've got to find the whale's daughter first."

I'm afraid Faro will argue, but he doesn't. "Yes, we owe it to her mother," he says thoughtfully. It's good to have a chance to talk to Faro on our own. The dolphins have been off hunting for fish, and now they're taking one of the short rests that seem enough to fuel them for hours of travelling. Conor is playing sea snap with Elvira. They're both laughing and they don't seem to care that sea snap is way too young for them.

"Elvira's a bit better, isn't she?" I say cautiously.

Faro glances at his sister and his expression clouds. "She will go to the North, all the same," he says. "We won't be able to stop her."

"But look at her with Conor."

Faro raises his eyebrows. "You think so? I thought so once, but no, they are friends and that is all. She will go away."

"Faro, don't be so – so fatalistic."

"We Mer see things as they are."

"Now you're being pompous too."

"Am I?" He smiles at me with a touch of uncertainty.

"Yes, you are. But I don't mind; I'm used to it."

"We are used to each other, little sister."

"I'm really sorry about Elvira, Faro." She's his only sister. Faro hardly ever talks about his parents, but I know they're both dead. Saldowr's his guardian, of course, and you can see that he loves Faro like a son, but Elvira is Faro's own blood. I can't imagine what it would be like if Conor suddenly told me that he was going away, into a strange frozen world, because he felt more at home there than he did with me.

Faro will never beg Elvira to stay. He's much too proud for that. Perhaps something will happen to stop her going. Saldowr might be able to persuade her…

"I don't think so," says Faro.

"Get out of my thoughts, Faro!" I swipe at him and he ducks away, laughing.

"Why? They were nice thoughts, Sapphire. I liked them."

"The dolphins are stirring. We'd better go."

It's Seiliko who spots the pod of whales. Her echolocation picks up their vast shapes. "Whales are close now," she tells me. "They are logging on the surface." I strain my eyes, but can't see anything.

"Soon you will see them," promises Seiliko, and she swims

faster, skimming beneath the surface and then leaping high so I can see far away over the calm dark blue water.

"There they are!" calls Conor.

I'd have thought the glistening dark bumps on the horizon were rocks if Seiliko hadn't been so sure they were whales. Seiliko reaches into the distance with clicks and whistles.

"They are your friends; they are sperm whales," she announces.

All the dolphins stop. After the rush of our passage the water feels eerily silent, but then we get used to it and far in the distance we can all hear the whales. I recognise their voices: Seiliko's right. They sound just like my dear friend.

"Why are we waiting?" asks Conor.

"I think your sister would like to talk to the whales alone," says Elvira in her silvery voice. I don't know how she guessed, but I'm grateful to her.

"Would you, Saph?"

"Yes, I – I think so. If that's OK."

"You should not go alone, little sister. I'll come with you," says Faro.

"She wants to go alone," repeats Elvira.

I do. I feel as if there's already a relationship between me and the whale's daughter, although we've never met. It's almost as if we're sisters. If I go on my own, I'll be able to talk to her properly. I am sure she is there in the pod.

"I can't let you go alone," Faro says to me.

"No, Faro, I want you to dive with me," insists Elvira. "There are pearls in the Southern Ocean, and ground pearls are precious for healing. I'll need your help to find them. Besides, Seiliko will be with Sapphire. She won't be alone."

Faro hesitates, glancing from me to Elvira. I know how much he wants to come with me. I close my mind so that he won't see my longing to go alone and be hurt by it.

"Come, brother," says Elvira. Faro shakes back his hair. It's the word "brother" that convinces him he should go, I'm sure of it. He won't risk refusing Elvira when he's so afraid of losing her.

"Be careful, little sister," Faro says to me, and dives after Elvira. As I swim away with Seiliko I turn and see Conor shading his eyes, following me into the distance.

Whales look very strange from beneath when they are logging. The top of their heads and parts of their backs are above the surface, while the rest of their bodies are submerged. As Seiliko and I approach them we see their vast tails hanging down. Seiliko swerves and makes a wide circle to bring us round to the front of the pod.

"It's very bad manners to approach a logging whale from behind," she observes. "Besides, there's a risk they will lobtail."

"What do you mean?"

"They strike the water with their tails, not only when they are angry but also when they want the rest of Ingo to knows its place."

The whales' echolocation will have sensed our presence long ago. They don't seem bothered by our approach, but Seiliko still slows down courteously as she rises to the surface and breaches in front of the cliff of a whale's head.

Everything I see is so familiar. A rush of homesickness for my dear friend the whale almost overwhelms me. I long to see her and hear the happiness in her voice as she recognises me.

Greetings, little barelegs. How long it seems since I've seen you.

But this whale doesn't know me. I look up at the vast box-shaped head, the skin that is so rough and creviced that it's like the skin of a giant prune, and the jaw that hangs a little open, relaxed. Teeth show in the whale's lower jaw.

Slowly she swings her head and then raises it clear of the water. The sea makes a waterfall as it streams down her brow, and then she submerges herself again, like a hippopotamus sinking into the mud. She regards us with one eye. Behind her, to the left and right, the other whales are stirring.

"Greetings," says Seiliko.

"Greetings," rumbles the whale, "but what creature is it that rides on your back?"

"A new kind of creature," says Seiliko boldly, although I can feel tension in her body now. "One who has human form and Mer blood, and is at home in Ingo."

"Are you sure it is not a human being? It looks human enough to me. Are you sure that it hasn't deceived you? Humans are full of deception. Once humans find our logging places, they come with ships and harpoons."

I think of how comfortingly my whale friend greeted me when she first met me in the Deep. I was afraid of her, but she put me at ease. She called me "little barelegs". What if she'd held me responsible for the killing of sperm whales by whalers? If she'd felt the same way as this whale feels, she would have left me to die in the Deep. I've got to convince these sperm whales that I'm not an enemy. I haven't deceived Seiliko, and I would never betray them to the whale hunters.

"I am a friend," I say aloud. "We came to find you because we are looking for the daughter of a whale – one of your kind – who lives on the other side of the world. She sent her daughter here to avoid the sickness that killed so many sperm whales in the oceans back where I live. Do you know her? Have you ever heard a story like that?"

The whale dips her great head so that she can examine me more closely. It's not a friendly inspection. "Come closer to me," she says at last. "You will have to leave this dolphin if you want to speak to me. She claims that you can swim alone in Ingo. Show me." The whale's head rises. All I can see is her scarred, mountainous flank.

"I'll have to go alone, Seiliko. You go back to the others," I whisper. I can feel Seiliko's hesitation. She senses the whale's hostility and she's not happy about letting me approach her alone. I lean down until my lips are against Seiliko's skin and whisper again, more urgently, "I've got to do it, Seiliko. She won't trust me otherwise."

Seiliko's answer is the softest murmur. "Are you sure?"

"Yes, I'm sure."

I don't feel very sure as I slide off Seiliko's back and she turns with a graceful twist of her body and dives. I swim towards the whale's vast, rugged side. It towers above me, making a heavy shadow through the water. There are tentacle scars deep in her flesh, and a healed slash that probably came from a giant squid's beak. She's been attacked while hunting in the Deep. As I swim close the shadow seems to darken even more. I peer around through the water. The other whales are drawing near, as if they want to talk to me too. *Or maybe they're just curious and they want to listen*, I tell myself as I try to calm a mounting sense of unease.

Through a gap between the whales I see a calf in the middle of a protective circle of adult females. All the whales in this pod seem to be female. The calf is afraid. Its anxious cries echo through the water, answered by booms of reassurance. But it can't possibly be afraid of me. I'm tiny, even compared to a baby whale. I've got no weapons. Something that my dear whale friend said once tugs at my mind. *The water turned red with our blood.* She was talking about a whale hunt. Maybe whales teach their babies to be afraid of humans.

"Come closer," booms the whale. I wish she sounded more friendly. The voice of my friend calling me "little one" or "little barelegs" echoes in my head. I never even thought about how she could crush me with one blow from her tail.

These whales loom over me, ominously. I remember how Dad taught me never to go into a field of cattle when the cows have their calves with them. *Even a cow that knows you can kill you if she thinks there's a threat to her young.*

How huge these whales are. None of them is logging quietly on the surface now. They've moved so that I'm cut off from the dolphins by massive walls of whales' flanks. I'm not scared; of course I'm not. Whales are not our enemies. I clench my hands and will my heart to stop beating so fast.

"Closer, closer," orders the whale. I'm barely swimming now, but they are still moving. They are drawing closer around me, in a circle that tightens second by second. The free water between their bodies is shrinking. There's barely a chink left to swim through.

Way behind me I hear Seiliko's voice, muffled by the whales' bulk, calling to me, "Swim back, Sapphire! Swim back to me!" It's when I hear the fear in her voice that for the first time I'm truly afraid.

"Saph," says a calm, familiar voice immediately behind me. I turn, and it's Conor.

"Con, how did you get here?" I'm so relieved to see him that I want to clutch him tight in case he disappears again.

"Dived under the whales. I knew something was wrong when I saw them crowding together."

"Con, you shouldn't have come! It's dangerous. They don't like us being here."

But even if Conor wanted to go back, I don't think he could now. In the few seconds he's been here, the whales have moved even closer. We are surrounded by rugged walls of flesh. The only space is above us. My heart pounds in my ribs, almost suffocating me.

"I'm going to speak to them," says Conor.

"Quick, before the gap closes." I stare up the steep, pitted side of the whale who told me to come nearer. *She* deceived *me*, getting me to do that. But if we swim straight up, then maybe there's still a chance of escape…

The whales are all around us. If they even jostle us a little, we'll be crushed to death like swimmers caught between a giant liner and the quayside.

"It's the calf that's making them nervous," Conor murmurs.

"Another human," rumbles the whale warningly as she sees Conor clearly for the first time.

"She's got to listen to us. She's got to," I mutter. "Conor, let's go for the gap now."

The space between the whales is narrowing. I kick as hard as I can, and we shoot through the gap above us just before it closes. The water beneath us shudders as the whales' vast bodies nudge together.

"Up to her head," calls Conor. "Higher, Sapphire!"

I swim past the whale's jaw. There is her eye, watching us as we come. Conor stops swimming, and sculls himself into position near the whale's eye.

"You don't need to be afraid of us," he says to her. In spite of the danger, I almost laugh. We're surrounded by whales who are all at least ten metres long – apart from the baby – and who seem to hate us, and Conor's telling this whale that *she* doesn't need to be afraid. "Don't be afraid. We haven't come to hurt the little one. We are not hunters. There is no ship."

The whale's eye is unreadable. "Why should I believe you?" she says. "Our blood has turned the water red too many times."

"Not this time," says Conor. "We come with a message from one of your sisters, who stayed on the other side of the world when her daughter left to escape the sickness. What's her name, Saph?"

"I don't know," I say. I call the whale my dear friend, but I don't even know her name. "You know I've always just called her 'the whale'…"

"Not particularly helpful, Saph," says Conor aside to me. "Quick, say something that'll make them recognise her."

My mind is blank. She is huge and gentle, and she calls me "little barelegs" and she says I please her. These whales won't want to hear any of that. "She – um – she…"

"You seem to know very little about our sister," observes the sperm whale coldly, "even though you claim to come with a message from her."

"She…" Light breaks on my mind. "She tells jokes! That's what she does. She tells lots of jokes."

"Tell me one of them."

"Oh no, I couldn't. They're too – too…" I hesitate, torn between the truth and loyalty to my friend.

"Too what?" demands the whale.

"Too – well, they're too bad, really. They're not funny at all. They're the kind of jokes you try to forget."

"*Saph*," groans Conor. Already the whale's body has started to move. She's going to crush us against another whale. We won't be able to stop her. Conor will be killed because of me.

Quivers run through the whale's body.

"Con!" I grab hold of him. I've got to protect him. He's only here because of me. The water billows. The whale's trembling grows stronger. A rumble begins somewhere deep under her blubber. It grows stronger. Tremors ripple under the scarred, hoary cliffs of her sides. The cavern of her mouth opens and waves of sound rush into the water, deafening us as we cling together.

"Conor!" In the distance I can hear the dolphins filling the water with desperate calls to us. The water shakes and we are thrown from side to side.

"Saph! *Saph!*" Conor's hands grab my shoulder. "It's OK! It's all right! They're laughing."

"Laughing!"

The thunderous belly noise swells from one whale to the next. They are moving apart a little now. There's free water between the whales and the vast bodies with their box-shaped heads are all quivering and booming with... Yes, Conor's right. It's not a roar of anger. They're laughing. All of them except the baby, and he's swinging his head from side to side eagerly, as if he wants to find out where the joke is.

At last the whale closest to us calms down enough to speak.

"It is our sister. You describe her truly. She has not changed."

"Were you laughing because you remembered one of her

jokes?" I ask hesitantly. Relief floods me, although I can't quite believe that we're safe

"No, my child. You know my sister and that it is impossible to laugh at the jokes she tells. We are laughing because we are happy. Our sister is alive and has sent us news of herself. That dolphin was speaking the truth. You are a new kind of creature that we have never met before. Your shapes are human, but your hearts are whale's hearts."

Conor is back beside me. "Just as well they're not really," he murmurs in my ear. "A whale's heart is twice as big as a man."

"Shut up, Con, my hands are still shaking."

"That's nothing. Look at my knees knocking together."

"Now, let us talk," booms the whale magisterially. "We are all hungry for news of our sister. Her daughter is hunting in the Deep, but she will return soon to feed her baby. Imagine what happiness she will feel."

But when the whale's daughter does at last return, she doesn't seem to feel quite so much happiness as the rest of the pod expects. She goes straight to her baby and we hear her mutter irritably, "I can't think about anything else until I've fed him." After the calf has fed she fusses over him for a long time. It's as if she doesn't *want* to talk to us. The other whales are obviously taken aback and disappointed that their wonderful surprise isn't working. They keep whispering to

Conor and me about how stressful life is for new mothers, and they hope we'll understand. I mutter as if I do, and Conor just looks embarrassed.

At last the whale's daughter finishes being busy and swims slowly towards us with her calf at her side. The other whales have already told her that we know her mother. She doesn't even greet us (too stressed and busy for that, obviously).

"How do you know my mother?" she asks abruptly.

"She helped me in the Deep the first time I went there – when I was lost. And then she took all of us back to the Deep to defeat the Kraken. We'd have died if she hadn't rescued us. She carried us to safety inside her mouth. She was amazing..." Words pour out of me eagerly. I want her daughter to know just how amazing her mother has been.

"*Inside her mouth*," repeats the whale's daughter. The other whales' tails start to swing. I'm afraid they'll begin lobtailing, but luckily they subside.

"We have heard that the Kraken woke."

"News came to us."

"We did not know of our sister's action."

"My mother should never have gone anywhere near that Kraken," snaps the whale's daughter. "It was a terrible risk for her to take."

"She wanted to help us."

"Help *humans*? I wish humans would help *us*."

"I mean, help Ingo."

"Hmm. From what you say my mother put herself in danger

quite unnecessarily. She's a grandmother now. She should be thinking about her family. I don't know why she's getting mixed up with humans."

"Sister," remonstrates one of the other whales.

"Why pretend?" demands the whale's daughter angrily. "When have humans ever brought us anything but death and misery?"

I am seething at the way the whale's daughter speaks of her mother. What right has she got to be so critical? But I've got to be careful. Conor and I are still surrounded by the whales, and I don't want them getting angry again.

"Your mother will be glad to have news of you. She misses you very much," I say, trying to change the subject away from humans.

"I know how my mother feels, thank you very much." The calf has been edging out to take a good close look at us, but the whale's daughter nudges him back into place protectively. "As if I need humans to tell me about my own mother," she goes on in one of those mutters that is meant to be heard.

She is jealous. I realise it in a flash that makes everything clear. The whale sent her daughter away to the other side of the world so she'd be safe, but still it must have felt terrible. She lost her mother. My dear friend doesn't even know that she's a grandmother yet. And I come here saying to her daughter how kind the whale has been, and how she's helped us and looked after us and even rescued us. Of course she is jealous. I can't really blame her.

"Your calf is beautiful," I say.

"I don't know about that. He's certainly hard work," says the whale's daughter with proud grumpiness. The calf butts against her, looking up, and she looks down into his eyes. It's obvious that she thinks he is the most beautiful creature in the world.

"Can I tell your mother about him?"

"I suppose so. Tell her…"

I wait. At last the whale's daughter says in a quite different voice, "Tell my mother I was thinking of her when he was born."

It's a long time before the whales will let us leave. Each of them has a message for our whale, and I have to keep repeating them to be sure I've got them clear. After that they start giving us advice about the best route home. One whale thinks it's best for us to take the Deep Current, then another argues that our bodies will never be able to stand the pressure. A third suggests we go due south, then we will be able to catch a current that will sweep us past the Southern Land – which I suppose means the Antarctic. More and more voices break in, all making suggestions and all contradicting one another. My head feels as if it's about to burst with advice.

"Which route do you use?" Conor asks.

Silence. Maybe they don't want to tell us. At last one of them says, "We are happy here. The hunting is good."

I hide a smile. The whales remind me of people who watch loads of travel programmes and can tell you everything about foreign places, but never go there themselves. Dad used to call them sofa travellers. The whale's daughter has travelled, though – she came all the way from the other side of the world. She's feeding the baby again, and it's clear she doesn't want to take part in the discussion. She never wanted to travel after all. She was forced to leave her mother, and her home.

At last the whales seem ready to let us go. Each of them says farewell to us in turn, formally. Just as we are about to swim off, the first whale we spoke to swings her head in our direction again. "You have friends among humans," she says.

"Yes," I reply.

The whale pauses, as if it's hard to put into words what she wants to say.

"Do you know the humans who power the ships that hunt us?"

"No! No, I told you, we've got nothing to do with them!" The whale sighs.

"We thought perhaps you might speak for us. Remember us, when you are back among humans."

CHAPTER TWENTY

Faro's lips are tight and his face stormy. He blames himself bitterly for pearl diving with Elvira while I was in danger.

"But I'm fine, Faro. Really fine."

"I was a fool ever to let you go. I forgot what our *deubleks* know. We are stronger together than apart. If the whales had hurt you, little sister, I could never have forgiven myself."

It doesn't matter what I say, he keeps brooding over it. I hate to see Faro so unhappy.

"Leave him," whispers Seiliko.

"But I want to make him feel better."

"He feels what he feels. Sapphire, I think I know your recognition pattern now."

"Really? Do you?"

I'm intensely curious, and a bit flattered. I never thought I'd have a recognition pattern, like a dolphin. And then I remember that Seiliko told me she would know my recognition pattern by the end of our journey. "Seiliko, you aren't going to leave us!"

"No, Sapphire. *You* are going to leave *me*."

So often I come to love someone and then they go away. Now Seiliko's going.

"Don't you want to know your recognition pattern, Sapphire?" asks Seiliko.

"I suppose so. I mean, yes, of course I would," I answer. I can't summon up much enthusiasm now.

Seiliko doesn't seem to notice. "Then I will tell you," she says. In spite of myself I feel a prickle of interest. I can't help hoping it will be something good, like Seiliko's own recognition pattern. I would love to be first in understanding the water – or first in anything, really…

"Friend of Ingo," says Seiliko as if I should be thrilled and impressed.

My moment of expectancy dissolves. Friend of Ingo! Is that all? It sounds so – so *weak* somehow. So *nothing*. As if all that's recognisable about me is that I'm not an enemy. I can't see why Seiliko thinks I'll be pleased.

"Oh."

"Sapphire, you do not understand," says Seiliko severely. "The pattern honours you. We dolphins honour you for it."

"Oh. I mean… Well, thanks, Seiliko."

"There is no need to thank me," says Seiliko rather haughtily. I've clearly ruined a moment that she's been looking forward to. I lean forward on her neck and embrace her. "Seiliko, I'm sorry. I can't think of anything better than being Ingo's friend. I've always tried to be."

"I forget sometimes how human you are," says Seiliko. She

sounds mollified, so I decide to ignore that fact that she's also being rather patronising. We've drawn ahead of the others, as usual.

"Soon you will leave me," she repeats.

"Are you sure you can't come with us?"

"No. It is decided. You will travel with other dolphins. We dolphins want to help you. You have braved the ice of the North, and journeyed many thousands of miles to what you call the bottom of the world. Because you are a friend of Ingo, Sapphire, we have agreed to send you home on a flight of dolphins."

"But Seiliko, four dolphins can't take us halfway round the globe. It's impossible. They'd be exhausted."

"You are right. You do not understand a flight of dolphins, and why should you? We do not turn our speed to human use, or even for the use of the Mer. We use flight only when there is urgent news to be taken on a long journey."

"But what do you mean, Seiliko? Dolphins don't ever fly, surely." I'm half prepared to believe that perhaps they do, and that this is yet another of the mysteries of Ingo. Dolphins flying! It would be awesome.

"We borrowed the word from the birds that spend weeks on the wing without ever stopping to rest. The swifts and swallows travel fast, but we travel faster – much faster. Each group of dolphins who carries you will send out a message when it begins to tire, and the strongest dolphins who hear it will rush to meet them. When they tire, the next group will come to carry you. Even if a dolphin flight dives through a shoal of sprats, we will not stop to feed. We dolphins know the currents as not even the Mer know them. No current is too strong for us to enter it. Sapphire, you will discover why it is called a flight of dolphins! You will go faster than Mer or human have ever travelled in Ingo."

Her excitement makes my blood tingle. It'll be like a relay race, and we'll be the batons that are handed from one group of dolphins to the next. Imagine a race like that, on dolphins, riding on currents so strong and fast that the water blurs. Faster than anyone has ever travelled in Ingo. Wait until I tell the others…

A disturbing thought crosses my mind. I must not tell it to Seiliko: it would be throwing her generosity in her face. "I'm so grateful, Seiliko," I say quickly. I look round and there's Faro, his body sealed against the dolphin he rides on, his long hair streaming through the water. I'll talk to the others. They'll understand.

Faro and Elvira can't understand what I'm worried about. Seiliko has left us now, with the other dolphins who have brought us this far. She's promised that the first relay of dolphins will be with us at dawn. Faro seized on the idea of the dolphins helping us straightaway, and so did Elvira. Conor was like me. He was afraid that when we returned, Saldowr might ask us, "Did you truly complete the Crossing?"

"And I wouldn't know how to answer," Conor said. Faro became impatient. He said that the only thing that mattered was to cross Ingo, and prove to Ervys that he hadn't defeated us. Elvira backed Faro. We seemed to be arguing for hours. At last, when we were all exhausted, Conor challenged Faro.

"You're Mer. The Crossing of Ingo is a Mer thing, not a human one. We have to trust you. Can you swear to us that it's right to travel with the dolphin flight?"

Faro threw back his head proudly. "You do not understand how greatly the dolphins have honoured your sister. I will swear," he said. "I know that we must defeat Ervys, or his following will grow until it splits Ingo like an earthquake under the sea bed. We must seize every chance of help that we're offered. Do you think I would agree to it if it were laziness or cowardice? No. The dolphins' offer brings hope for Ingo."

I was so impressed by this that it surprised me when Conor probed further. "What will you swear on, Faro?"

Faro's gaze moved to me. He smiled, swam to my side and took my hand. He lifted our joined hands high, and *deublek* touched *deublek*.

"I swear by this," he said. "The *deublek* that binds me to your sister and makes each of us stronger than if we were alone."

Conor nodded. "Then I accept what you say. But Saph's decision is what counts. Seiliko chose her. What do you say, Saph?"

"I accept it. We'll go with the dolphins."

It seems a long time until the arrival of dawn, and the first dolphins. No one sleeps much. I want to tell Conor about Mum but I don't, because I'm sure that he'll say it was a dream. I'm beginning to believe it was a dream myself. And yet what Mum told me had the feel of truth. It made sense of so many things. And I keep thinking of the tenderness in her voice when she called me "lovely girl".

How huge the stars are down here at the bottom of the world! We're resting just a few metres below the surface and it's so calm I can see the constellations clearly. I try to remember how long the stars have been there. To them, all our generations must look like less than a day.

It's comforting to think of the stars. I'm not really afraid of being dead, but I'm afraid of dying. It must hurt so much to die. I'm afraid that Ervys has set the sharks to watch out for us again and more and more of the Mer will have gone over to Ervys's side. The last thing they want is for us to return. They'll be hoping that we've been trapped in the ice or caught in a net like that dolphin. What will they do when we come back and they realise that in spite of our human blood, we've completed the Crossing of Ingo?

To calm myself I watch a shoal of tiny fish, like electric blue needles, shimmering about a thumb's length from the surface. I don't know what they're doing – probably feeding. Most creatures in the world seem to be either hunting or being hunted, most of the time...

I must have fallen asleep. I wake to Conor gently shaking my shoulder. "Saph! Wake up! The dolphins have come."

The water around us is ghost grey with dawn. Even the dolphins, solid and powerful as they are, don't look quite real. Elvira is already mounted, and Faro too. Faro smiles across at me.

"Time to go, little sister."

CHAPTER TWENTY-ONE

I'm in the heart of Ingo. The dolphins are taking us somewhere human beings have never dreamed about. I'm sure that even Faro could never survive here, if he weren't riding with the dolphins. The world outside the current goes by in a blur. We can't see or hear or feel anything except the pressure of the current sweeping us along with it, and the strong, supple backs of the dolphins that carry us.

Most of the time we can't talk, and the others are hidden by surges of foam. I have to trust that Conor, Faro and Elvira are still with me, racing alongside but out of sight. Sometimes, if the current we're riding starts to slacken, the dolphins swerve sideways, searching for the pulse of faster water. For a second or two we're slow enough for me to catch sight of Faro, his hair swirling in the tumult of water as his dolphin shoots past on my right. Conor is always looking out for me. A smile of relief breaks over his face when he sees that I'm still close to him and still all right. I smile back and try to wave, but the water's too strong. My hands are plastered to the dolphin's sides.

I catch a glimpse of Faro, but he doesn't look at me. He

doesn't seem to know I'm there. His hair streams across his shoulders as he rides low down on the dolphin's neck. The outline of his tail melts into the dolphin's body as they plunge forward into the heart of the next current. He doesn't look like my Faro any more. He looks like a different being, part Mer and part dolphin. I try to call his name, call him back to me, but the current stops my mouth. Beyond Faro, Elvira is flying along on a dolphin that quivers like a racehorse when it sees the finishing post.

I don't know how many times we've changed from dolphin to dolphin. Whenever they feel that they're beginning to lose speed, the dolphins sweep the water ahead of us, calling for other dolphins to leave everything and take us onward. To us, the dolphins seem tireless, but each time we slip on to the backs of a new group of dolphins, we feel the change. The new dolphins soar up through the water as if our weight on their backs means nothing.

The dolphins rarely speak to us after the first greeting. It feels strange because dolphins love to communicate, but there's no time or energy for it. Their task is speed. Suddenly I am sure that every second counts. Ingo needs us now, and the dolphins know it. Every time, they find the strongest currents and dive into them at such a perfect angle that we never hit the buffeting of the water. And then they fly. I understand now why they called it a flight of dolphins. My dolphin stretches out his body so there's the least possible resistance, and powers along the current so that miles stream behind us like moments. If the current slows even for a heartbeat, my dolphin races. While the current is fast, he steers into its speed and lets it fly with us.

All that's real is speed, and becoming more and more one with the dolphins, travelling deeper and deeper into the mystery of Ingo. I've always dreamed of being truly part of Ingo. I'm not Sapphire any longer, with my human body and my Mer blood, not quite belonging anywhere. I'm as much a part of Ingo as the sea bed flowing away beneath us, and the water surging with bubbles as it rushes away behind us.

We skimmed a coast where huge breakers thundered on black-fanged rocks. The current whipped inland and the dolphins risked everything for speed and took us within metres of the rocks. I saw jagged spikes of rock reach out for us, and then we whipped past. They couldn't get us. The water widened between us and the heave of sea throwing itself against land. Seabirds screamed and dived down past our heads. The dolphins plunged through a cauldron of bubbles and then we were heading out into open water again.

We passed schools of porpoises that leapt to ride our wake, but we were faster and they fell back. A pod of whales crossed our path and we dived down, down, down into the darkness under their bellies and then we shot up again towards the light before the dolphins swerved into a current so fast that everything vanished behind a curtain of rushing water.

So many dolphins, so many currents. Every muscle in my body aches. I can't begin to guess how long we've be travelling and I don't even care any more. All I can think of is the next change of dolphins and the next plunge forward into the unknown. One more dolphin dipping down for me to climb on to his back, his body sleek and glistening with muscle, his spirit burning with purpose. And just when I think I can't take any more, there's another dolphin, a female this time, and yet another current...

The others seem so far away. We have to keep together, but I've forgotten why. This is my life now, travelling on and on with the dolphins until I become one of them. Look at my hand, there, curved inward to the curve of the dolphin's shoulder. Surely it's almost the same colour as her skin. And the outline of my fingers seems to be blurring, melting into the solid flesh of the dolphin...

"Saph! SAPH!"

I jolt awake. Something's wrong. Something's different. I stare around me at the smooth grey water. Nothing's moving. We've stopped. And there's Conor, not on the back of a dolphin any longer, but swimming slowly and stiffly towards me. And there's Faro, staring into the distance ahead of us. Elvira is by his side.

"Conor." I look down at my hand. Each finger shows distinctly. Slowly, reluctantly, I peel my hand away from the dolphin's shoulder. As I do so, I think I hear a sigh from deep inside her body. She doesn't want us to separate either.

"It's all right, Saph. It's all over. We're there. Can you climb off?"

"I don't know. I don't think I can move."

I don't want to move. My dolphin dips down gently in the water, and the bond between us dissolves. I float away from her a little, then swim around to her head. Her small, wise eyes stare into mine.

"You felt it too, didn't you?" I whisper.

"You are one of us, little one," the dolphin whispers back. "Whenever you wish, you may ride with us. But now, go to your brother."

I push my hair out of my face and turn to Conor. "Where are we? Oh Con, I feel so weird."

"You were on the leading dolphin for too long. No one realised. We should have changed places. You must have taken a pounding."

But it wasn't like that. The water felt smooth and silky. I didn't even realise we'd pulled ahead of the others. "My legs are like jelly. Isn't it strange not to be… not to be going so fast?"

"I'll be OK in a minute," I mutter.

The four dolphins circle us, like athletes cooling down after a race. One of them, another female, nudges close to me. "How are you, little one? Are you sick?"

Little one. These dolphins are like my friend the whale. I hold out my arms to them and they press close, nuzzling and rubbing against me.

"Thank you, dear dolphins."

"Saph, are you really OK?" Conor sounds worried.

"I'm fine. It's just that I've never travelled so fast."

"It was wonderful, wasn't it?" says Conor, his eyes shining.

But just then Faro shouts, "Sapphire! Look ahead! Do you know where we are?"

I peer through the grey water. It must be very early up in the human world. The sun hasn't risen yet. There's something solid rising from the sea floor ahead of me. A wreck, maybe, or an underwater reef. No, it's too big for that. Minute by minute the water grows lighter and the outline clearer. I see low humps of drowned hills. Ruined stone buildings. A long line of wall that curves protectively around what must have been a harbour once.

"The Lost Islands!" shouts Faro joyfully. "Look, there they are! We are almost home, little sister!"

Almost home. Then that means we have almost completed the Crossing. It feels too sudden. Too easy. I ought to be elated but I'm not. There's a knot of fear gathering in my stomach, and I don't know why. Elvira turns, her sweet smile lighting up her face.

"Isn't it beautiful?" she calls. Conor and I glance at each other.

"What is it?" asks Conor, and I remember that he's never seen the Lost Islands before.

"They were islands once," I explain, "but then the sea level rose and covered them. Faro took me here once. You can even see the church, but it's all deep underwater."

"Did the people drown?"

"I'm not sure. I – I think some of them must have." I can't help shivering. The Lost Islands are so sad. All the life in them was wiped away, maybe in a single day, when the sea swallowed them. Maybe some people had time to escape in boats, but most of them must have drowned along with the cottages and the church which has lost its tower.

"Poor souls," says Conor. "You can't help thinking about how they must have struggled."

"I know." The knot in my stomach tightens. I try to steady myself. Faro's right that we're close to home. The Lost Islands are only about twenty-five miles from land. Soon we'll start to recognise every reef and every half-buried wreck. We'll swim on until we come to the Groves of Aleph, and there we'll find Saldowr.

I still can't really believe it. I expect to wake up any minute and find I'm still flying through Ingo on the back of a dolphin. I close my eyes, squeeze them tight and then open them again. The Lost Islands are still there, beneath deep swaying water that's changing from grey to green and turquoise and ultramarine as the sun rises. And there's Elvira, rummaging in her sea-grass bag for those disgusting tablets of seaweed.

"Swallow it, Sapphire. It will give you strength."

The dolphins move away a little, probably in case Elvira starts dosing them too. Besides, their task is complete. Tired as we are, we can easily swim home from here without them. We only need to catch the gentlest of currents and drift to the Groves of Aleph, and to Saldowr. Three of the dolphins want to leave now, but the dolphin who was carrying me says she will travel to the Groves with us before she rejoins her brothers and sisters. She wants to see Saldowr. She tells me that her recognition name is *She who carries our story across the oceans*, but we should call her Byblos.

I'm glad Byblos isn't leaving us just yet. Already I'm imagining our arrival at Saldowr's cave and how he'll welcome us. It's right for Byblos to be with us, because without the dolphins we'd still be travelling. It would have been weeks, maybe months, before we got back from the bottom of the world.

We have made the Crossing of Ingo. I daren't say it aloud: I can still barely believe it. I just wish that nagging knot of fear would dissolve and let me relish this moment. A thousand memories of our journey swirl in my head so powerfully that they almost hide my view of the Lost Islands. Nanuq, holding me between her paws. My Atka, gliding on her throne of ice. The marks of the net, cut into the side of the dolphin who carried me to Mum. I thought the Crossing of Ingo was just a journey, but it's more than that. I am not the same Sapphire as the girl who set out so hopefully on the southern route, before the sharks crossed our path.

"Look out! Look ahead!" Faro's cry cuts through the water. "Sapphire!"

I jolt out of my dream. The Lost Islands are changing. Moving. They look as if they're alive. As I gaze in horror, the swaying curtain of weed that grows from the drowned cottages and the church begins to move upwards. It looks as if a shaggy monster is rising from the Deep. The weed parts, and I see shapes shouldering their way out of hiding. The moving weed isn't weed at all, but long, streaming hair. One after another, figures rise from the weed bed. They are Mer, with broad shoulders and powerful seal tails. Their skin gleams blue as they turn with powerful strokes to form a line across the water. Some of the figures look familiar but they're too far off for me to recognise them. And they're holding long poles – sticks…

"Ervys," says Conor.

My heart lurches. It's as if I've always known that this moment would come. I strain forward and pick out Ervys, in the centre of the gathering Mer. And there's Talek – Mortarow – and Hagerawl – more and more of Ervys's lieutenants, each with a band of Mer forming around him.

Ervys and his followers have been lying in ambush. We've come so far. We have almost circled the globe, but it wasn't quite far enough. They knew we would have to come back this way.

CHAPTER TWENTY-TWO

"They've got spears," says Conor. Light glints on metal. Now I understand exactly why the Mer hate metal, and despise humans for depending on it. Those spears can kill so easily. I glance down at the healed scar on Faro's tail. Every third or fourth Mer man is carrying a spear in his left hand. I've never realised before this moment that the Mer are left-handed. I should have. Elvira is, and Faro. Maybe a few Mer are right-handed, just as a few humans are left-handed – my thoughts scuttle blindly.

"Faro," I say.

"I'm here, little sister. I will defend you with the last drop of my blood."

Dear Faro. Only he could say such a thing and make it sound completely natural.

"I'll defend you too. We'll all fight for one another."

"We will never be separated," says Faro sombrely. "We will die together."

The islands are alive with Ervys's followers. I try to count them but have to give up as more and more appear from behind ruined walls.

"I should have thought of this," says Conor. He puts his arm around my shoulders. "I promised Mum I'd look after you."

"We couldn't know, Con."

"Ervys was never going to let us complete the Crossing."

The ranks of enemy Mer sway like the weed they hid among. They've ambushed us so easily. I should have listened to what that knot of fear was telling me.

We're going to die here. No one will even know that we almost made the Crossing. Saldowr will give up hope of seeing us again. Mum won't ever know what's happened to us – nor will Dad—

I can't think of that now. I clench my fists as Sadie's puzzled, loving face rises in my mind. She will wait and wait and she'll never really believe that I'm not coming back.

There are only four of us, and Byblos. But Byblos mustn't die. She can still escape – there's just time. As if she hears my thoughts, Byblos nudges close to me. "Don't be afraid," she murmurs. "We will fight together."

"No," says Faro. His face blazes with sudden conviction. "Take Sapphire. Take her to Saldowr. He'll know that we didn't fail. She has crossed Ingo with her human blood."

"I won't go!" I say furiously. "I can't leave the rest of you."

And then Elvira breaks in, her voice as sweet and silvery as ever although her face is blanched with fear. "None of us should go. Byblos will travel faster alone. Go, Byblos, rouse Ingo. Tell Saldowr. Carry the message to all the Mer who are faithful to him."

Byblos swirls round. "I can take Sapphire on my back," she says.

"You'll be faster alone. Quick, Byblos, before they strike!" I urge her.

"Thrash the water," Faro tells us all. "Make it white with foam so they don't see which way she goes." He and Elvira smash the water with their tails. Conor and I can only kick, but even so the water churns, hiding Byblos as she escapes.

I'm afraid that Ervys will choose this moment to attack, but when the water clears again I see that his forces are still massing. I don't know why they bother. It's so obvious that they can wipe us out in a few seconds. Some of them are facing us, others turn north, east and west. They're not in range of us yet. If they hurled their spears from that distance, they'd fall harmlessly to the sea bed.

"Why are they waiting, Conor?"

"I don't know. Maybe Ervys wants to enjoy the moment."

We all stay very still, as if the least movement might provoke the Mer ranks to charge us. Yes, Ervys will enjoy making us wait. Ever since we witnessed his humiliation when he looked into Saldowr's mirror, Ervys has longed to punish us. He probably wouldn't admit it – he'd say that he's been forced to destroy us to protect the independence of Ingo, Mer blood and Mer rights. But he's got more personal motives too.

Faro scans the ranks of Ervys's followers intently. "Some of them are not so happy," he says.

"What do you mean?"

"Look. You can see it in their bodies. They are uneasy. That one there, next to Mortarow – yes, it's Teweth! – he doesn't want to be there."

"Faro, they're starting to move!"

It's just a ripple of movement to begin with. We watch, fascinated, frozen. The advance halts. Ervys is giving a speech, rallying his men. We see his arm go up, and the point of his spear catches the sunlight refracting through the water. A cheer rumbles through the water towards us. They are coming. They raise their spears in their left hands as their tails power them through the water. Ervys is in the centre of the front rank. I can see his face clearly now. It's set and scowling, as if he's facing an army of hundreds.

There's no army. Only us, the four of us, shoulder to shoulder. Faro on my left, Conor on my right, and then Elvira. Conor's face is calm. I hope mine is too. Ervys's men are coming closer. Soon they'll be within a spear's length of us. Perhaps spears travel more slowly through water than they do through air. We'll have more time to swerve out of their way. We shouldn't really be so close together because it makes us an easier target. But it gives me strength to feel the others beside me. Faro is right: we'll die together.

Ervys halts again, about a hundred metres away, and all his followers stop swimming too. They hang back a little as he moves forward. Another twenty metres, and then another twenty. He is a huge, dominating figure. He tosses back his shaggy mane of hair in a gesture which reminds me oddly of Faro.

"Come forward!" he commands.

"Why should we put ourselves within range of the metal you have stolen from the human world?" Faro calls back defiantly. Ervys's face grows thunderous. I brace myself for the order, and the advance, and the first shower of spears, but nothing happens. Ervys holds up his hand.

"Enough of this. We have no wish to shed blood."

This is so ridiculous that I would smile if my face didn't feel so frozen.

What are you here for then? I want to ask. *Why did you send the sharks to kill us?*

"We have a duty to cleanse Ingo of this human contamination," goes on Ervys. "These – *humans* – have tried to usurp the Crossing of Ingo, which is for the Mer alone. The old fool Saldowr encouraged them, in his blindness."

I feel Faro start forward, and grab hold of his wrist. "Wait. *Wait*, Faro," I whisper. The lines of the Mer move uneasily, as if some of them, too, don't like hearing Saldowr insulted.

"For this reason they must die," says Ervys, as calmly as if he's describing the weather. "But because we have no wish to shed blood unless it is absolutely necessary, we will spare you, Faro, even though you are a traitor to Ingo. And your sister, we believe, has been led astray. If you will humbly confess your fault, you may return to us and re-learn what it is to be Mer and to belong truly to Ingo."

Faro's body quivers with anger. I reach into the tumult of his mind. *Don't let him provoke you. We need time. Play for time, Faro.*

But I'm afraid he won't. Faro is so proud. I've got to make him understand that we must fight for time, never mind what Ervys or anyone else thinks of us. Every precious second gained will take Byblos closer to Saldowr's cave. She'll be rousing the Mer as she goes, and the other dolphins. Everyone who doesn't already belong to Ervys will hear Byblos' message. I pour my thoughts into Faro's mind, fighting past the waves of anger and defiance that are rushing through it. *Listen to me, Faro. You've got to listen to me.*

Faro pulls his wrist free of my hand and folds his arms. He stares straight at Ervys.

"So you mean no harm to me or my sister?" he asks.

Conor turns to Faro with a furious, disbelieving expression on his face. I try to signal to him that it's all right, Faro's got a plan, but I'm afraid of Ervys's sharp eyes. Surely Conor can't believe that Faro's trying to negotiate with Ervys so he can save his own skin?

No. Almost immediately Conor realises that Faro's playing for time. His expression relaxes, and he turns back to face Ervys with apparent calm. Elvira faces ahead too, her face very pale and her eyes glittering.

"If you yield to us now, you will come to no harm," says Ervys. "We have no wish to shed Mer blood." Very deliberately, Faro looks down at the scar on his tail. Ervys follows his gaze and says, "That is in the past. We Mer must fight together. We cannot be divided against the enemy. Join us, and you will become part of our strength."

"And yet you taunt me for my blood," says Faro. I'm stunned. Faro has brought up the subject that he hates so much. Not only that, he's brought it up in front of Ervys, who tried to shame him for having any trace of human in him at all.

Ervys frowns. He leans forward, scanning Faro's face. "You forget nothing," he says.

"Isn't our nature as Mer to hold on to our memories and pass them to our children's children?" demands Faro. It's like a sword fight, only here the blades are words.

"I tell you," Ervys insists, "if you come to us, we will build a nation in Ingo that will last until our children's children's children are ready for Limina. Your sister's descendants and yours will look back and praise the choice you make today."

Suddenly Elvira swirls forward. "Do not speak of my children!" she snaps imperiously. Both Ervys and Faro look at her open-mouthed.

"Any children I may have one day are no part of your bargains or of your battles," she goes on. I have never seen Elvira like this. I'm proud of how bold she is and how fearless. Neither Ervys nor Faro seem to know how to answer her. In one graceful stroke she returns to me and Conor.

"Fantastic, Elvira," I whisper, and a small pleased smile curves her lips.

Seconds are adding up to minutes. How long can we delay the spear charge? How long can we hold on, waiting for help to come? I look beyond Ervys to where his ranks of supporters hold their bristling spears. There are so many of them. Strong, full-grown Mer men, and youths who will make up in speed what they lack in muscle. Their faces are stern and they're all listening intently. I sense that they want Faro to come with them. They will want him because he will draw other young Mer to his side. And they won't want to spill his blood or Elvira's unless they have to. There is such a deep taboo against it among the Mer. Ervys sent the sharks to tear us apart, well out of sight of the Mer. If we're killed, all these men will be witnesses.

"You have a choice," says Ervys. "Choose Ingo, or choose the human world. One choice brings life and the other death. You will make a fine warrior on my left hand, Faro, and your human blood will be forgotten. You will purify yourself fighting for Ingo."

"Fighting for Ingo?" asks Faro. "But tell me, Ervys, what if I believe that I am already fighting for Ingo?"

"Then your human blood is deceiving you," says Ervys smoothly. How clever he is – much cleverer than I thought. "Ingo needs every last one of us," Ervys continues. "She cries out for you to avenge the wrongs done to her. Poison and murder, the theft of our ancestral places, the pollution of our world, the death of our kindred."

A low growl of agreement ripples through the Mer ranks as they hear Ervys name their grievances.

"Humans have desecrated Ingo. Humans want to tear the heart out of Ingo. Humans value nothing unless they can use it for their own ends. I am offering you a chance that will not come again. Do you choose to fight against us or to fight with us?"

Faro is silent. For the first time, I'm not sure what he is thinking. His thoughts are closed to me, his face unreadable. None of us had expected this. We knew Ervys wanted to destroy us but we didn't think he'd try to do it as subtly as this, by separating the four of us, Mer from human. Faro's talked to me so many times about the harm done to Ingo by the human world. Ervys is offering him a powerful temptation. I know Faro won't take it, I'm sure he won't give in, but there is still a cold knot of fear in my stomach.

"But if I fight with you, Ervys," says Faro slowly, as if he's working something out as he speaks, "If I fight with you, Ervys..." He draws out the words, lingering on each one. And just when the knot in my stomach seems to be rising into my throat and choking me, he glances sideways, eyes lowered, and slips me an almost imperceptible wink.

"You see, if I fight with you, Ervys, if I become one of your followers, like..." He breaks off to scan the lines of Mer. "...like Talek there – or Mortarow – and is that Hagerawl I see there? Greetings, Hagerawl! And you, Morlappyer – and Mentenour. It's a long time since you and I swam with the dolphins, Mentenour. And Bannerys, my friend, we two faced the orca side by side when he forgot that we were Mer—"

"Yes, yes," says Ervys impatiently. An uneasy stir runs along his ranks. They don't like Faro naming them and the past they've shared. It makes us all seem too real and too close. I suppose it's easier to kill people if you can pretend to yourself that they're not really people at all. But if they know your names, you can't pretend any more. Faro is even cleverer than Ervys.

"As I was saying," Faro continues, "if I were to fight with you, then there would be a difficulty which I cannot find my way around. No matter how hard I try, I fail."

"Perhaps I can help you," says Ervys. His teeth show, but I don't think he's smiling.

"I would have to fight against my friends," says Faro. His voice quickens. He's not playing with Ervys any longer: this is real.

"Understand me, Ervys, I am Saldowr's *scolhyk* and his *holyer*. I will never become a *clopen* for you, or a *harlotwas*. Saldowr says that human blood must cross Ingo to bring peace and healing to Ingo and to the Mer. I say it too."

I have no idea what a *clopen* is or a *harlotwas*, but I'm pretty sure these are not compliments. Ervys's face is thunderous. Without another word to Faro, he turns to his followers and shouts, "You have heard him refuse my offer of fellowship. He rejects Ingo, and the Mer are witnesses to it."

Some of the followers raise their spears threateningly. A low rumble of voices comes from the massed ranks. In a moment, Ervys will give the signal, and they'll advance on us. They will kill us now. I know it's going to happen but I still can't believe it. I've always been alive. I don't know how to imagine anything else.

"When they start coming, dive. It's our only chance," murmurs Conor.

It's not a chance at all, and he knows it. If we dive they'll rain the spear down on our backs.

Ervys surveys his followers and then swims a little closer to them. Slowly he holds up his left arm and stretches out his hand. He beckons Mortarow, and for the first time I realise that Mortarow is carrying two spears. One for him and one for…

Yes. Mortarow lifts one of the spears, balances it above his shoulder, draws back his arm and sends the spear soaring through the water towards Ervys. The spear does not travel fast, but its aim is sure. Ervys moves aside. The muscles of his arms and shoulders ripple as he reaches forward, catches the falling spear by its shaft, lifts its weight and holds it high in triumph.

He wants to be part of the killing. He isn't going to leave it to his men. If there is blood guilt for Faro and Elvira's deaths, they will be able to put it on him. How clever Ervys is. The answering roar from his men is much louder now. He is their leader and they will follow him, as soon as he gives the signal.

Ervys turns, balancing the spear's shaft across the palm of his hand. He controls its weight perfectly.

"They've been practising," mutters Conor.

Suddenly Ervys jabs the spear towards us. I can't help flinching away. Ervys catches the spear again, and laughs. He's playing with us.

"Not so brave now, when it comes to it," he taunts.

"You have more to fear than we do," calls Elvira. "Death is better than living with the curse of having shed your brothers' and sisters' blood."

"You're no sister of mine!" shouts Ervys angrily, but I see his tail twitch, and another ripple of unease among his followers. I am mesmerised by the dull gleam of the spear's point. It sways a little in the water as Ervys changes his grip on the shaft.

"I wish he'd get on with it," mutters Conor. "Listen, Saph, I'm going for the shaft. If I can drag it down he won't be able to aim."

"No, Con, he'll kill you!"

"He's going to kill us anyway."

Ervys's muscles are bulging. He is lifting the spear. His powerful tail lashes from side to side. He isn't going to throw the spear. He's going to charge us, with all the power and weight of his body behind the thrust—

"Ervys!"

A voice slashes through the tense, waiting silence.

"Ervys!"

We all turn. To the right of us, leaping through the water, comes a dolphin with one of the Mer riding on its back. There is something in the Mer man's hand: a three-pronged weapon with a short shaft. A trident. I can't see his face because his hair swirls across it as the dolphin leaps again. But I know the dolphin – I am sure it's her—

"*Ervys!*"

The voice is hoarse, desperate but commanding. All over my body the skin tingles. Ervys hesitates, spear in hand, looking at the dolphin, then quickly at us as if to judge whether or not he has time for the charge, then back at the dolphin which is almost on him now.

Yes, it's Byblos. Dear Byblos, coming back to our rescue with one of the Mer on her back. She swoops down through the water and at that instant Ervys makes up his mind. He raises his spear and plunges it into the dolphin's breast. The next moment he has disappeared in a thrash of foam as Byblos arches, trying to pull herself off the point of the spear.

I see Ervys's arm, bulging with muscle, still gripping his weapon. There are a few seconds of tumult, and then Ervys is free. He has his spear in his hand and it is crimson up to the shaft with Byblos' blood. I stare, horrified, as the crimson dissolves into the water. A plume of blood is pouring from Byblos' wound. Her body convulses.

The man on her back has slipped off and has his arms around her. He clings to her side as she heaves and shudders. I think he's trying to whisper into her ear. His back is to me and I still can't see his face. There is uproar among Ervys followers and his voice rises above it, shouting them down, rallying them. But dolphin blood fills the water and we can hardly see them. Byblos arches one more time, heaving for breath and life, and then collapses.

"Ervys!" shouts the man once more. "You have killed the dolphin!" and he swings around so that we all see his face.

"Oh my God," whispers Conor. "Saph, it's Dad."

CHAPTER TWENTY-THREE

"*D*ad"

Dad doesn't even glance at us. He has his back to us and the trident raised, ready. Dad's tail lashes as he edges sideways. Ervys is moving into position too. They start to circle, prowling through the bloody water. Byblos' body is already sinking away to the sea bed. Some of Ervys's followers hang back, raising their hands to their foreheads in the traditional sign against evil. But others are gliding forward, spears at the ready.

"Sapphire, they're coming!" says Elvira.

"I know." I can't take my eyes off Dad. He must have sprung on to Byblos' back as soon as he heard we needed help. He came straight to our rescue. For the first time, his Mer body doesn't look strange and alien to me. Dad belongs here in Ingo, but he is still my father. He's ready to battle with Ervys for our sake.

Their circling has brought them round so that Dad is facing me. His eyes track every shift in Ervys's position. I can't see Ervys's face now, but muscles bulge threateningly in his arms and shoulders. My heart thumps with tension. The spear is so much longer than the trident, but Dad is moving in, challenging Ervys.

"Look, Sapphire, look!" Elvira clutches my arm and points, and I tear my gaze away from Dad and Ervys. "Our people," cries Elvira triumphantly. "I knew they would come."

Our people. Mer men and women plunge towards us, hair flying through the water. Dolphins stop dead, flinging their riders straight into battle, and then the dolphins themselves charge, hurtling into Ervys's men from behind before the spears can turn to strike them. Bull seals rear up, showing teeth and claws. Far behind them comes the lumbering shadow of a basking shark and ranks of jellyfish. A herd of seahorses skitters through the water and around the heads of Ervys's warriors, half blinding them. Velvet swimmer crabs advance, snapping their claws. Byblos has roused Ingo. Oh Byblos. That plume of blood – the way you arched in the water…

"All Ingo is on the move," murmurs Elvira. Her eyes glow. "More will come, Sapphire!"

But we're still heavily outnumbered. Where is Saldowr? Surely he'll come soon. He's got to. Ervys's followers have swung round to face the new challenge, but they haven't hurled a single spear yet. The dolphins and bull seals fall back again, waiting. Even the sea horses retreat and hang in a cloud by the head of the basking shark. An eerie silence fills the water.

"Forward!" yells Ervys. "Forward! Attack them, you fools! Use your spears!"

But still no one moves. It's as if Byblos' blood has cast a spell

317

on them. Or maybe they're hypnotised by the slow circling of Ervys and my father. Maybe the battle is suspended until those two have finished their duel.

My father has his trident and Ervys has his spear. But a spear has a longer reach than a trident. They are not equally matched. Dad never takes his eyes off Ervys's face. He anticipates every move Ervys makes. Each time Ervys jabs with his spear, Dad has already slipped sideways. He's waiting for his chance. He needs to get close in, under Ervys's spear arm, in order to thrust the trident into him. Ervys knows it too, and he keeps parrying Dad's trident with the shaft of the spear to hold him off.

Suddenly the spell breaks. One of Ervys's army rushes forward in a thrash of foam, spear at the ready, poised to attack Dad. Conor and I hurl ourselves forward, but Ervys is too quick for us.

"Leave it, you fool! Get back! He's mine!" he yells, and the Mer man falls back.

Conor's still pushing forward, but Faro grabs his arm, "What are you doing?"

"I've got to help Dad."

"No. You'll get in the way and Ervys will kill him under your arm. Sapphire, don't move. Your father will take his eyes off Ervys. Wait."

The two men continue to circle each other. Thrust, parry. Thrust, parry. The muscles on their arms stand out in knots. Their faces are drawn with concentration. The Mer stand watching, fists clenched, lips drawn back so that their teeth show. Suddenly I recognise Mellina among them. Her face is anguished and she's clutching a lump of rock, with which she clearly intends to smash Ervys's skull if she gets half a chance. For the first time, I like her.

I don't even see the shark coming. It's behind me, and all I hear is a strangled cry of warning, I don't even know where from. A split second sixth sense makes me turn. It's a single shark, and a small one, aiming straight for my chest. I hurl myself sideways, and the shark just fails to turn in time. I'm thrown aside, my arm and shoulder seared by the shark's skin, but I'm alive. The next second the shark whips round, seizes me in its jaws and starts to shake me like a puppet. I'm so shocked that my brain stops telling me what's happening. There's another blow, so close that my head snaps back and the water explodes around me. I'm falling down and down, helpless.

Faro and Conor catch me. My eyes are full of blood, but I feel both my arms being grabbed. My vision clears and I see them, Faro on one side, Conor on the other. Through the turmoil of the water I see four dolphins attacking the shark, beating it off. There is blood in the water: my blood, and maybe the shark's too.

"It's all right." Elvira's voice drifts out of the blackness that is filling my head. "She's not badly hurt. They're just surface wounds."

"She was lucky that it was a bull shark, not a Great White," says another voice, Faro's I think, but I'm so sick and dizzy now that I can't be sure.

Surface wounds... a bull shark... The words echo as I come back to consciousness. But where's Conor? Faro is beside me, supporting me. Elvira's binding thongs of weed around my arms. Where's Conor?

"Can you swim, Sapphire?" Faro demands urgently. "Help her, Elvira, I must get to Conor," and with a powerful swerve of his tail, he disappears into the boiling mass of water, blood, Mer, seals, dolphins and spears.

Ingo echoes with cries and screams and groans. A long bellowing roar explodes above my head. A bull seal staggers back, blood pouring from his flank. I cling to Elvira and we swim as fast as we can, back to where Dad was before.

But there's no sign of Conor. I stare desperately through the mass of fighting bodies, searching. Somehow I'm sure that wherever Dad is, Conor will be with him. A spear glides through the water in front of me, its force almost spent. Elvira darts forward, grabs it, then hurls it to the sea bed. A dolphin surges past me and charges into a knot of Ervys's supporters, scattering them. A seal rears up and rakes its claws across the chest of the man Faro called Mentenour. Blood springs out in bright crimson stripes. I turn away.

"Elvira, where are they?"

"I don't know."

Two of the bull seals charge towards us. Even though I know they're here to help us, I can't help being frightened of them. They press in, one at my left hand, the other at Elvira's right.

"We are the Guardians of Limina," says one in a deep, gravelly voice.

"We will guard you as we guard our dead," promises the other.

Ahead of me, two Mer men sink down towards the sea bed, arms and tails entwined, still wrestling. Through the gap where their bodies were I see a three-pronged flash of metal.

"Dad!" My sickness and fear vanish as adrenaline surges through me and I hurl myself forward. Before the gap closes, I'm through it. I see Faro and Conor in the distance, riding dolphins into battle, their hair flying and their hands reaching out to seize an enemy spear in the swoop of their passage.

Dad has done it. He has got in close. With one hand he fends off Ervys's spear, while with the other he struggles for space to thrust with his trident. He's going to do it! Little by little he forces his trident round. Ervys's face is set in a snarl of battle. I don't know if he even sees Dad any more. His muscles bulge with the effort of trying to free his spear, but he can't do it. The angle is wrong and all the force of Dad's tail drives down against him. The trident's prongs gleam again as Dad twists it a little more, ready for the final thrust.

"You tried to kill my children," he says to Ervys. Ervys doesn't reply. He's looking over Dad's shoulder.

At that instant three things happen. I look beyond Dad, where Ervys is looking. A Mer man bearing a spear charges out of battle, his yell of triumph cutting across a scream from one of the watching Mer women.

And Mortarow stabs my father in the back with his spear, before Dad can thrust the trident into Ervys.

The woman's scream is cut off. The attacker's yell of triumph ends in a grunt. My father slumps forward, and the trident falls from his hand. As it does, one of the dolphins wheels round. Faro is on its back. In a long dive he swoops under the trident, catches it and holds it high. His face contorts with rage and he charges straight at Ervys.

"No!" A cry rings out, and the dolphin swerves. "No! He is mine, Faro. Give me the trident!"

It's Conor. My frozen terror melts and I plunge forward towards Dad. He has fallen through the water, but the Mer are there to catch him. Four women surround him, supporting him. Mellina is one of them, holding my father's head.

"Dad! Dad!"

Dad's face is pale, but he's conscious. "Sapphy," he mutters, "get Conor back."

"Are you all right, Dad? Are you badly hurt?"

One of the women is packing sea grass into the wound, but it keeps on bleeding. Dad coughs, then tries to smile. "I had him. I'd have killed him. It was a dirty trick."

"I know."

"But you're all right, my girl."

"I'm fine. Don't try to talk, Dad."

"Where's Conor?"

"I don't know. He's somewhere up there with Faro…"

I daren't tell Dad that Conor's fighting Ervys. I'm desperate to get back and do anything I can to help Conor, but I can't leave Dad. He looks so pale.

"You go, Sapphy," says Dad, as if he understands everything. "I'm all right here. Mellina – these others – they'll look after me. But come back."

"I will, I promise."

Mortarow's blow seems to have ripped the heart out of the battle. Some of Ervys's followers have stopped fighting altogether. Their spears hang from their hands and their faces are blank, as if everything they were fighting for has been taken away from them. There's no sign of Mortarow, but the bull seals and the dolphins are chasing off a group of Mer men who are still fighting hard in retreat, jabbing and thrusting with their spears.

But Ervys still has supporters. They stand behind him as Conor faces their leader, trident in hand. I swim as close as I dare, not wanting to distract Conor. Faro is there too, waiting and watching, ready to plunge forward.

"So, is it to be a fight between us, Ervys?" calls my brother. "Or have you got another of your supporters ready to stab me in the back as you did my father? A coward's trick if I ever saw one."

"It was no trick of mine," growls Ervys, and his tail lashes like the tail of a tiger when it's roused.

"Prove it then. Spear against trident, and nothing else."

"Spear against trident," agrees Ervys, and a small smile licks around the corner of his lips. He's a fully grown Mer man, armed with a spear, and my brother is a boy armed with a trident that he doesn't even know how to use.

I won't let him kill Conor. I don't care about all the "spear against trident" stuff. Ervys isn't going to come close to hurting Conor if I'm here.

"Careful, Sapphire."

"We've got to fight, Faro! We can't let him pick us off one by one."

"The Mer have got to see Ervys defeated. They're already turning away from him because of what Mortarow did."

"I can't watch my brother get hurt."

"He won't. He's going to defeat Ervys. And if he doesn't I will fight until every drop of blood has left my body. You can fight alongside me then, little sister."

I wish I had Faro's confidence. Ervys looks so menacing as he measures up to Conor. His shoulders are massive. The arm that holds the spear quivers with muscle. His face is so… so *threatening.*

But Conor will be quicker. Faro's thought floats into my mind. Yes, he's right. Conor is much lighter than Ervys, and because he's younger he's faster too. He'll have better reflexes. He jinks from side to side in the water, the trident flashing. He's trying to confuse Ervys and get him off balance. It won't be easy.

"Go, Conor, go. You can do it," I whisper.

The trident flickers. Ervys jumps back. One of the prongs has nicked his skin and shed blood. How I wish the sharks would come, just for Ervys. But they're his creatures now. It's a miracle that only one bull shark has appeared so far. Something must be holding them back.

Ervys swears, shaking his wrist, and then lunges at Conor, who dances out of range. A moment later he's there again, jabbing Ervys in the tail.

Ervys is getting angry. *Get angrier, Ervys. Lose control.* I can tell from Conor's face that he's angry too, but it's a cold, deadly rage that drives him on rather than clouding his judgement. He wants revenge.

With a lightning curve of the wrist, Conor brings the trident in again. Ervys snatches at it, but misses. The prong pierces his neck, and Ervys can't help clapping his hands to the wound.

It's not a deep wound, but that doesn't matter. Ervys's spear is turning over and over as it falls down through the water, gathering speed. Ervys stares after it, his face twisted with fury and indecision. He's wondering if he should dive after it, but he can't because Conor's pulling the trident back, ready for the next thrust. Ervys will have to swim back out of reach.

But he doesn't. He grabs for the trident again, and this time he gets it. The two bodies lock, swaying and struggling, then there's another jab, a cry from Ervys, and Conor breaks free, still holding his trident. Light gleams on the three metal points. They are razor sharp, honed for battle. Without warning, Conor jackknives, swims down, comes up just in front of Ervys, and feints with the trident so that Ervys lunges to his right, uncovering the left side of his body. It happens very slowly and also very fast. One moment Ervys is lunging with all the force of his powerful body, and the next moment Conor strikes.

The points of the trident bury themselves deep in Ervys's flesh, where the heart is. Ervys's body arches backwards as Byblos' did. He thrashes in the water, tearing at the trident with his hands, as Conor swims back out of reach. A sound between a cry and a groan comes from the watching Mer, but no one moves to help him. Ervys's eyes bulge as he stares from one face to another without seeming to recognise anyone. A harsh grunt comes from his throat, and then a gout of blood comes from his mouth. He doubles over, and begins to sink down. Immediately, four of his followers dive after him. They seize hold of him by his shoulders and tail and support him. He does not move, and his head lolls back so that his long hair streams down in the water.

"He's dead," says Faro as Conor swims slowly towards us.

"I killed him," Conor says to me, and his whole body shudders.

"You did well," says Faro, but Conor shakes his head. The trident is still in his hand, already washed clean of Ervys's blood.

"Where's Dad, Saph?"

"With Mellina."

"Is he all right?"

"Yes, he was talking to me."

"Thank God for that. I thought that spear thrust had killed

him." Conor's words open up a dark well of doubt in me. Dad's going to be all right; he's got to be.

"The battle's over," says Faro. I look around and see that he's right. The Mer are dispersing. Four of his followers bear Ervys's body away with them. Only one group still holds firm, some of them with spears. Suddenly, as if one thought has entered all their minds, they raise their spears high and then plunge them with all their force down into the depth of the water towards the sea bed. But I haven't got time to think about what that means. I've got to get back to Dad.

CHAPTER TWENTY-FOUR

I recognise the figure bending over Dad. Long grey hair, swirling cloak. No one else has a cloak like that.

"Saldowr," I say. My heart fills with bitterness. Why didn't he come earlier? Byblos is dead and my father is wounded. I don't know how many others have suffered. If Saldowr had come in time, surely he could have prevented some of it. Ervys would have defied him face-to-face, but Saldowr could have used his power to stop the other Mer from joining in the attack.

"Greetings." Saldowr smiles at me, but I don't feel like smiling back.

"How's Dad?" I swim forward, and Saldowr moves aside for me. Mellina is pouring a few drops of bright liquid into Dad's mouth. Even though they fall through water, the drops remain whole.

Those drops will make Dad stronger. He's still very pale, but he must have heard my voice because he opens his eyes and says, "Hello, *myrgh kerenza*," and he smiles. It's exactly like the smile he used to give me when I came racing down the track after school. Conor, behind me, says, "Hello, Dad."

"What happened, my boy?"

"I killed him."

"Good." Dad closes his eyes again. Maybe he's gathering his strength, because when he speaks again his voice is louder. "You outwitted him. You got in under his arm."

"Yes."

"Perfect."

Dad is quiet for a while. I notice that Elvira is there too, watching Dad's face. She bends down and puts her fingers on his wrist.

"What are you doing?" I ask.

"Feeling his pulse."

"Why don't you try and heal him, Elvira? You remember how you put your hands on my leg when I got hurt in the flood? Can't you do that?"

"I don't think so," says Elvira.

I look around wildly. All the faces are the same. Set and serious and somehow – *watching* – as if they know something's going to happen. But I don't know what it is. Even Conor suddenly has that look on his face.

"Conor, we've got to get help. Dad! We've got to fetch someone!"

Saldowr draws himself up and puts his hand on my shoulder, but says nothing. Dad opens his eyes again. His lips move but I can't hear any words, and then suddenly I realise that he's not trying to talk at all. He's trying to sing. I take hold of his hand and hold it in mine, pressing tight.

"*O Peggy Gordon...*" His voice is very quiet, not like the voice that used to ring around the pub and make everyone put down their glasses to listen. But the notes are still just as true.

...you are... my darling...
Come sit you down upon my knee
And tell to me... the very reason
That I am slighted so by thee...

Dad told me what "slighted" meant once, because I didn't understand the word. It means to scorn someone, to put them aside, not to want them any more.

I thought Dad had done that to us.

Maybe he thought we had done it to him.

We are coming to the chorus now. I squeeze Dad's hand again and there's the faintest answering pressure. He knows I'm here with him. I bend down so he can see my lips and I sing along with him.

I wish I was... away in Ingo...
Far across the briny sea...
Sailing over deepest waters
Where love... nor care... ne'er trouble me...

The song is finished. Everything's quiet, and Dad has closed his eyes again. Saldowr bends down over him. He puts his head against Dad's chest and listens. Slowly, he straightens up.

"He's gone," says Conor.

Saldowr lays his hand over mine, which still clasps Dad's. For a long time there is nothing else in the world but our joined hands. At last I look up. Conor's head is bowed, and his eyes are closed. Everyone else has moved away.

"Why didn't you come?" I ask Saldowr very quietly so Conor won't hear. "You could have saved him."

"I could not come, Sapphire. I had to hold back the sharks. Ervys's promises had crazed them, and they smelled blood. If they had got to the battle, everything would have been lost. Only one slipped the net I held over them."

I glance up. "The net?"

"Not such as humans use. I held them because even though Ervys had clouded their minds with bloodlust, they still remembered who I was. And then they remembered who they were, too."

I want to keep on being angry with Saldowr. I need to blame someone for Dad's death, but I can't. Ervys is dead, and Saldowr's face is ravaged with grief. His eyes search mine. Suddenly I realise that he needs to know that I believe him. It's the strangest moment. Saldowr has always seemed to know everything.

"No, you couldn't leave the sharks," I say, and Saldowr bows his head. We're silent for a while, both of us gazing down at Dad's face.

"Your father made his choice," Saldowr murmurs at last.

"This is as he wanted it. Ervys is dead, and you and Conor are alive."

We swim behind the dolphins as they bear Dad to the borders of Limina. Faro, Conor, Elvira and I are all together. Saldowr leads us. I understand now that he couldn't have stopped Ervys. He guards the Tide Knot and he's a great teacher, but he's not a magician. He can't prevent people from making the choices that they make – not for ever. He held Ervys back for as long as he could, until Ervys's hunger for power grew so strong that nothing could have stopped him. Once the battle started, he held back the sharks who would have wiped us out. He did all he could.

The battle seems a hundred years ago. Ingo is radiantly calm. It's a clear, perfect day and you can see every grain of sand on the sea bed, even though the water is deep off the Bawns. The guardian seals are back at their task, patrolling the borders of Limina.

The dolphins swim very slowly and smoothly. Conor holds my hand. Everything seems real and not real at the same time. Dad looks as if he's fallen asleep, and although I know he hasn't, the knowledge hasn't reached all of my mind yet. Conor says it's the same for him.

We're nearly there. The dolphins hang still in the water, and I wonder what's going to happen now. Maybe there's some kind of ceremony that I don't know about. I should have asked Faro. Maybe Conor or I ought to say something.

But all that happens is the dolphins begin to move forward again, very slowly. They cross the border of Limina, which none of the Mer can cross until they are dead, or ready to die. The plain of sand stretches out ahead of us, between the mountain range of underwater rock and the deep ocean.

"I can hear that music again," says Conor.

I listen, but I can't hear anything. It's a gift Conor has: to hear the song that the seals sing when they welcome one of the Mer to Limina. Even Faro can't hear it.

"They're singing for Dad," says Conor.

With all the grace and gentleness of their species, the dolphins lower Dad's body to the sand. His hair sways in the slight current. My vision blurs. I don't want to look any more.

"Time to go, little sister," says Faro, taking my elbow.

I don't look back. I don't want to see that it really is Dad, lying on the sand, in his Mer body. I have the strangest feeling that he's not really there at all. He's not in the human world and he's not in Ingo. Maybe he's somewhere out on the water, whistling as the waves slap the *Peggy Gordon's* hull. He'd like that.

CHAPTER TWENTY-FIVE

It's two days since Dad's funeral. I've been sleeping for most of the time, and so has Conor. I'm too tired to wonder what Faro and Elvira have been doing while we're asleep; I know that they check on us because sometimes I wake to find Faro watching me. His face is so sad and anxious that I always say, "It's all right, Faro, I'm OK," even though I'm not and he knows I'm not. Elvira doesn't watch over Conor, and he doesn't seem to expect her to be there. They're always very friendly, but the spark between them has gone.

When Conor and I are awake, we talk about little things that happened on our journey, not about Dad. Dad never leaves my mind, and I know it's the same for Conor. I can't believe that I will never see him again. The worst thing is that there's some kind of block in my memory. I can't remember what Dad's voice sounded like. Even when I try my hardest, I can't see his face clearly. You wouldn't think that could happen, would you, with your own father whose face is probably one of the first things you ever saw in your life? But when I try to picture him, everything is blurred, like the time I tried on Charlie Pascoe's glasses in junior school. I haven't asked Conor if he can remember what Dad looks like. It would sound too weird, and besides it makes me feel guilty that I can't see Dad's face, as if I didn't love him enough.

Last night Conor told me that he still wanted to kill Ervys.

"But you *have* killed him," I pointed out.

"Yeah, I know that, what I'm saying is *I still want to*, even though he's dead. Crazy, isn't it?"

"It's not crazy at all. He killed Dad."

"*Mortarow* killed Dad."

"You know what I mean, Conor. Mortarow held the spear but it was Ervys who killed him."

"God, I hate feeling like this. I just want to go home."

Conor feels so guilty too, even though I keep telling him that he had no choice. If he hadn't killed Ervys, Ervys would have killed him, and then probably the rest of us as well.

"I know all that, Saph. But I keep on thinking about what it felt like when I stabbed Ervys with the trident. It's so hard to do it, Saph, even when you hate someone. He's there in front of you, and he's flesh and blood. It's not like those films where the knife just slides in and someone's dead and you walk away."

"I know. Well, I don't know, obviously, but…"

"I'm glad you didn't have to kill anyone, Saph."

"But I would have done if I'd had to, so it's just as much my responsibility as yours."

Conor shook his head. "It's not. You know something, Saph – those guys who walk around thinking it's so cool to carry a knife, I wish they could feel what I'm feeling now."

"*You're* not a criminal, Conor! You were incredibly brave. You had to do it. You didn't fight Ervys for yourself, you did it for all of us."

Conor shrugged. "Maybe."

"Not maybe. Definitely."

Conor wants us to go home as soon as we can, but I can't face it yet. The thought of bursting through the skin of the water and taking a first breath of dry, harsh air feels like drowning in reverse. We've been so long in Ingo. It feels natural to be here.

The cuts and grazes that I got from the shark attack are starting to heal. Conor has bruises all over his arms and shoulders from the shaft of Ervys's spear. Elvira said that the best thing was rest and sleep. Faro found us this hollow to rest in, protected by rocks on both sides, and sheltered by a swaying curtain of angel weed. The sand is fine and soft, and Faro has made us pillows of sea grass. He must have slipped mine under my head when I was asleep.

On the third morning, Faro comes to fetch us. We're both awake. Conor is idly watching a starfish curling and uncurling its fingers. I'm lying still, feeling the water rock me gently.

"Saldowr asks you to come to his cave. He needs to talk to you."

Conor groans. "Can't we sleep a bit longer?" He rolls over and closes his eyes again.

"It's only a short distance," says Faro patiently. Normally he'd be angry if we didn't rush to do Saldowr's bidding. "Take my wrist, little sister, and I'll swim for both of us."

I shake my head. It's not the effort of moving that bothers me. I just don't want life to start up again yet. "I'm fine, Faro. I can swim."

"At least the shark attack did not rip off your *deublek*."

"No." I look down at my wrist. It seems amazing that it is still there, and safe. It seems so long since we each cut a lock of our hair with the sharp edge of a shell. The strands seem to have grown into one another. I can't tell which is my hair and which is Faro's. They were pretty much the same colour to begin with. Faro said it would protect us. Well, it did; we're both still alive.

"Don't cry, Sapphire."

"It's all right, Faro, I'm not really crying. I'm so glad we're still together. What if one of the four of us had been killed too..."

"But Conor says you will go back to the Air soon and rejoin the human world. We will no longer be together."

A pang of alarm shoots through me. The thought of leaving Faro is like abandoning a part of myself.

"We *have* to go home," says Conor. He stretches sleepily. "Just resting my eyes a minute," he adds drowsily.

I can see that Faro's about to snap that Saldowr needs us *now*.

"Yes, I need a minute too. I feel a bit weird," I add hastily. With an impatient flick of his tail, Faro comes to my side. Conor's eyes are already closing.

"Are you ill, Sapphire?" Faro demands.

"No. Just thinking about – you know – going home." *Home*. I test the word in my mind. I don't know how much time will have passed in the human world. It feels like years and years since we left, but it's quite possible that half term is still going on and everybody still believes we are upcountry with our imaginary cousins.

But life will go back to normal. Mum and Roger will return from Australia. Sadie will come home from Granny Carne's. (I can't think about Sadie now. It makes me want to kneel down and put my arms around the soft, warm folds of her neck and never, ever let go.) I'll go back to school. I'll be with Conor, and then there are my friends – Rainbow – our cottage – everything…

Everything? That's never going to be true. Even with Sadie in my arms, I'm going to feel empty in the human world. There'll be no Faro. No whale. No dolphins. No Saldowr. No wild racing currents that you can catch whenever you want to. No freedom to journey across the whole world. My future here is just waiting for me to discover it. In Ingo, I'm at home. I belong. I am Saldowr's *myrgh kerenza*. I'm my dear whale's *little barelegs*. The Mer have a place for me – they respect me. Now that Ervys is dead, they dare to speak out. Faro has brought me message after message from Mer who were just waiting for him to be overthrown. They offer their sympathy, and thank us for what we've done. They say, "Now you are truly one of us, *myrgh kerenza*."

It's not that there aren't dangers and difficulties here. It's just that I feel part of everything. I'm not tormented by the longing to be elsewhere that comes over me so often when I'm "home" in the human world.

"I'm not sure about anything any more," I say to Faro.

His face softens. "Shall I let you into my thoughts, Sapphire?"

"All right. No, Faro, maybe you'd better not," I add hastily.

"Then I'll tell you what's in my mind. I don't think I should call you 'little sister' any longer. You are not so little. And besides, you are not my sister!" Faro's face sparkles. For a moment all the sadness and heaviness of our memories falls away. "And I think you never will be. Elvira and Conor are apart now."

"I know."

"But *we* are joined, Sapphire. I knew it the first time I saw you, and now I know it more than ever." He smiles with a touch of mischief and a touch of triumph, but he's not quite the old teasing Faro. He looks not exactly more serious, but more... purposeful. With a shock, I realise that soon he won't be a boy any more, but a man.

"We belong to each other, Sapphire," says Faro with such confidence that I can't help smiling.

"Call me it one last time, Faro."

"All right, little sister. And now it's time to wake Conor, before Saldowr sends those guardian sharks to fetch us."

"I heard Saldowr was re-educating them."

"They certainly needed it."

We're in Saldowr's cave. It seems for ever since we were last here. Everything looks the same: the walls, the white sand, the soft filtered light from the entrance and the green glow of the sea worms which cling to the walls. Only Saldowr has changed. He swims to greet us, his body strong and youthful, his tail gleaming and seal-powerful. The wound he took when the Tide Knot broke has completely healed at last. Even his hair seems to be darkening as the grey loses its hold. Saldowr stretches his arms wide and his cloak flows back from his shoulders in an iridescent swirl. For a second he folds his arms around me, and I feel as if I'm held safe in a circle of power. He releases me, puts his hands on Conor's shoulders and looks into his face.

"So you have completed the Crossing of Ingo," he says, as if this were the first time he'd seen us since our return. No one has talked about the Crossing much these past few days. So much else has happened to crowd it out of our minds. It seems a hundred years since we swam under the ice.

Saldowr lets go of Conor's shoulders, swims back a couple of strokes and studies our faces thoughtfully. This reunion with him is so different from everything I imagined when I looked forward to the end of the Crossing. No grand return cheered by thousands of Mer. No sudden, dramatic transformation. The battle overshadows everything. We can't think about success or happiness when we see Ervys's spear every time we shut our eyes.

"So, you've completed the Crossing of Ingo, my daughter,"

says Saldowr. I jump, partly because I was miles away in my thoughts, and partly because of the word "daughter".

"Human blood and Mer blood have crossed Ingo together, not divided, not separated, not fighting one another. You have brought great healing to Ingo."

"Have we, Saldowr?" I ask dubiously.

"It looks as if we've brought war, not healing," says Conor.

Faro's eyes flash. "Saldowr sees farther than we can see! His understanding is as far beyond ours as the Deep is beyond the sunwater."

"You need not defend me, Faro," says Saldowr mildly. "Those are good questions and they require answers. Blood has been shed. Children have been left fatherless."

I look away. I can only cope with Dad's death if I think of it a little bit at a time, and not for long.

"I can't console you for that," goes on Saldowr. "All I can say is that you are children of Ingo too, and as much my son and daughter as Faro is my *scolhyk* and my *holyer*. No part of Ingo is closed to you now. Did you notice, when you were on your journey, that the human world remained sharp in your minds, as it has never done before while you were in Ingo?"

He is right. I've been able to relate one to the other, with both worlds alive and active in my mind. From Conor's expression, I think he's felt the same.

"Your Mer and human blood are no longer fighting within you," says Saldowr. "You're released from all that, as I hope Ingo and the world of Air will be one day. I told you long ago that Ingo

341

needs you, and those like you, because you belong neither to one world nor to the other. You are the future; you are part of a change that has to come, although it is painful. Ervys scorned and hated your mixed blood, and wanted to destroy you because you were a threat to him. He made pure Mer blood his rallying call, and some of the Mer answered it. But never as many as he hoped.

"You have the freedom of these two worlds which you have joined together. That's not to say there will be peace," he adds quickly. "Nor is it to say that the work of reconciling Air and Ingo is finished. No." He pauses, and an expression that I can't read settles on his face. "The work has barely begun. But it *has* begun. It may be as small as the moment of conception in the belly of a whale, but it will grow."

He smiles. A vision of my friend the whale flashes across my mind. I must find her. I must tell her about her daughter.

"But what about Faro?" asks Conor abruptly. "And Elvira? Are you saying they can move between two worlds as well as us?"

"You will have to ask them," says Saldowr.

"I have no wish to explore the world of Air," says Elvira. Her voice is as sweet and calm as ever, but now that I know her better I can hear the steely determination that's in it too. "I want to go to the North, Saldowr." I see Faro flinch, but Elvira carries straight on, "That is my destiny. My Atka has touched me and shown me my future. I can be truly myself, and I can become a great healer among the Mer of the North. I am sure that the North will welcome me."

Well, no one could fault Elvira for lack of ambition. I steal a glance at Conor to see how he's taking this. His hands are joined, with the thumbs pressed together, and his expression is faraway. I'm quite sure he's not thinking of the North. I think – I'm almost certain – that I know whose face is in his mind.

Saldowr regards Elvira quizzically, but he doesn't seem very surprised. "So you have found where you belong?" he asks her.

"Yes," she says firmly.

"You will leave your brother behind, and all who love you."

"I will take them with me in my heart," says Elvira, even more firmly.

How can she say that? Does she think it's that easy? Doesn't she even know how much she's hurting Faro?

Apparently not. Elvira looks radiant, and whatever Faro's feelings are, he hides them well. Maybe I'm the only one who sees the shadow of pain in his eyes. I have the strangest feeling that in spite of all her healing knowledge, in spite of making the Crossing, Elvira still hasn't really grown up. She still thinks that you can leave people behind, and not suffer for it.

"You will all visit me," says Elvira, smiling around at us seraphically.

"But Conor will return to the human world," says Faro. It's a statement, not a question. Conor doesn't contradict him, and Saldowr's face remains neutral. A further question hangs in the air, but Faro doesn't ask it, and I'm glad, because I still don't know the answer. I wonder how much Saldowr knows, when he talks about the future. I know that he experiences time differently from us. He can move back and forward, as if time were a carpet, rolling and unrolling for him to walk on. Maybe there are many rolls, and many possible futures. Only one of them can unroll for us.

Suddenly we hear voices outside the cave. Saldowr raises his hand for silence and listens intently. After a few seconds his face relaxes. "Faro," he says, "go to the entrance and ask Talek and his friends to come in."

Talek! He was one of Ervys's followers. Why is Saldowr allowing him inside his sanctuary? I don't want to see the people who are responsible for Dad's death. But, as usual, Faro obeys Saldowr's order without question. He reaches the cave's entrance with one thrust from his powerful tail. I hear low voices, then Faro moves aside. Mer figures stream into the cave. I recognise Talek, and the ones whom Faro called Teweth and Morlappyer. There are six or seven others whom I don't know. More voices murmur outside the cave. The remainder of Ervys's army is with us. Even though we're under Saldowr's protection, I can't help feeling a shiver of fear.

"Welcome," says Saldowr. Talek bows his head. The others shift uneasily, glancing at us. "Greetings, Talek, Teweth, Morlappyer, Gwarier, Kenethel, Pledyer, Gweryn, Sketh, Hagerawl."

Now I recognise Hagerawl too.

"Greetings," they mumble, and then the one Saldowr named as Pledyer swims forward a little.

"Ervys is dead," he says, not looking at Conor. The Mer gift for stating the obvious clearly hasn't deserted them.

"And Mortarow?" asks Saldowr.

"He has fled."

"But many of Ervys's supporters are alive and unwounded," remarks Saldowr calmly.

"We have thrown down our spears," says Pledyer.

"Yes. I heard that you had done that. And the sharks did not fight for you in the end, I believe, apart from one rogue bull shark who was brave enough to attack a girl from behind."

"The sharks deserted us," growls Talek.

"No," says Saldowr. His voice doesn't grow louder, but it becomes more stern. "The sharks did not desert you. I spoke to them and they remembered their duty, which they had abandoned to hunt these young ones. You know that to the sharks, duty is everything, unless they are crazed by the scent of blood. We spoke, and I was able to remind them of what they had forsaken." I shiver, remembering the sharks' cold, pitiless eyes.

"We are here to say that it is all over," Pledyer says.

"All over?" Saldowr counters him. "Go to Mellina, who has lost the man she loved and her baby's father, and tell her that it is *all over*. Tell little Mordowrgi that it is *all over*, when he's old enough to understand that it has only just begun. Ask these children, whose father you killed, if it is *all over*." And he looks at me and Conor as if he really expects us to answer. But we can't do that. Dad's dead, not only because of Ervys but because of all of them.

The burly, broad-shouldered Mer men look at us too. Suddenly I am not afraid of them any more. Their faces are so defeated, so exhausted. They look as if they have no hope left. And yet they've come to Saldowr, when they could easily have fled or even kept on fighting.

"Why have you come here?" asks Conor.

Anger swells inside me. Yes, why? After everything that's happened, how dare they come to Saldowr's cave as if they've got the right to negotiate? They were defeated in battle. Ervys is dead and his support is melting away. *Now* they come, when it's too late and the harm has been done. If they'd come earlier and they'd been willing to talk – and to listen – there needn't have been any bloodshed. They closed their minds to us because Ervys was so sure he was right and no one else knew anything about what was best for Ingo. And so Dad had to die. I wish Saldowr hadn't mentioned Mordowrgi. He's just a little baby who smiles at everyone and doesn't even know what death is. He'll keep expecting Dad to come home and pick him up for a cuddle.

"We have come because of the dolphins," says Talek in answer to Conor. His voice is rough. He sounds angry but I don't think it's anger than makes his voice so harsh. His shoulders are bowed, as if a heavy weight oppresses him.

"The dolphins?" asks Conor blankly.

"They are our brethren. They have been one with us since time began. Their sorrows are our sorrows, and their children are our children too. Saldowr knows this."

Saldowr nods. "But Byblos died on Ervys's spear," he says. The Mer look at one another. Nothing they say or do can change that.

"We never thought any of this would lead to shedding dolphin blood!" cries Talek. The other Mer men rumble agreement from their deep chests. "Even our own wives and daughters shun us now, for killing Byblos. They say we have brought evil on the Mer. We have got to atone for the crime, and make peace with the dolphins again. And with you, too," he adds quickly.

Dad's death is an afterthought; it's the dolphins that count. The Mer can't live without their relationship with the dolphins. Talek is honest, at least.

Another Mer man speaks up, "We must cleanse ourselves of Byblos' blood."

"And how are you going to do that?" asks Saldowr. He speaks quietly, but his voice rings around the cave. "Are you asking me to travel back in time and undo what you did? That is impossible. You have torn Ingo apart and that wound cannot be healed with a few words. I told you that you must accept these children, with their human forms and their Mer and human blood, but you refused. You sent the sharks to kill them. You were prepared to do anything rather than let them make the Crossing. You scorned my *scolhyk* because he has human blood in him too, from far back, and because he is part of the healing of Ingo, like these children."

Saldowr is awe inspiring. I've never seen his full authority before. His eyes flash, and I can hardly bear to look at the sternness of his face. His power fills the cave, and makes Ervys's followers seem like children. All the Mer men bow their heads.

"But they have made the Crossing," he goes on more quietly. "They are fully Mer now, and fully human too. You must accept them. You think that you hate them. You are Mer, and it is in your nature to hate change. I don't judge you for that. I judge you for your following of Ervys, your breaking of the laws that forbid weapons, and your greed for power in Ingo."

"You could have stopped him, Saldowr," mutters one of the men, head still down.

"I am not a magician," says Saldowr, even more quietly. "Ervys was free to choose, as you are free to choose now. Your mistake was to believe that your freedom was my weakness." Saldowr stretches out his left arm and points to me and Conor. "Look at them. Do you recognise them? Will you accept them? Say nothing unless it is true in your hearts."

The nine Mer men raise their eyes and stare at us. It's not a comfortable feeling. Each of them is far stronger than I am, and they've only recently stopped wanting to kill us. I know they won't hurt us while Saldowr is here, but it's still frightening to be with nine people who are full of hatred for you and who just want you to disappear and never be seen again.

I gather up my courage, and look Talek in the face. He is staring at me intently, but not with quite the expression I expected.

"Saldowr," he asks, "may I ask her a question?" Saldowr nods.

"Tell me," says Talek, "how you returned from the bottom of the world."

"With the dolphins."

"We saw that you were accompanied by four dolphins when you came to the Lost Islands. But how did you travel before that?"

"We were with the dolphins all the time. They called it a flight of dolphins." A ripple of sound runs down the line of Mer.

"A dolphin flight," repeats Talek. "And the dolphins offered that to you freely?" he asks, as if we might have blackmailed the dolphins into it somehow, or bribed them. But this doesn't seem like the time to take offence.

"Yes."

"To you, or to Faro and Elvira?"

I think back to Seiliko's words. *Because you are a friend of Ingo, Sapphire, we have agreed to send you home on a flight of dolphins.* "Seiliko – one of the dolphins – told me my recognition pattern. She said it was 'friend of Ingo'. That was why they agreed to take us home."

There is a long silence. I expect Saldowr to break it, but he doesn't. He has moved back a little in the water, as if to say, *I'm not going to interfere. Whatever happens now is for you to decide.*

The Mer are drawing closer to me and Conor. I want to shrink back but I don't move, and nor does Conor. Their gaze rests on our faces, piercingly concentrated. At long last, one word breaks the silence.

"Chosen," says Talek quietly.

In a rush like a breaking wave, the rest of the Mer take it up: "*Chosen... chosen... chosen... chosen...*" Nine voices repeat the one word until Saldowr's cave echoes with it, and then one by one the voices fall silent and the echoes die away.

My heart beats hard. I have a question now, and their answer will be the proof that they truly accept us. "A long time ago," I say to Talek, "Faro told me that your people had many names. Mer, Meor, Mor, Mare. But he said that there was another name, that only the Mer know, and which they keep secret from all who do not belong to their people."

Faro starts forward. "I will tell you now, lit... Sapphire. You have earned it."

But Talek holds up his hand. "No. I shall tell her. It is her right. Do you agree, my brothers?" There's a deep murmur of agreement. Talek smiles wryly. "It has been our name since time began. Each Mer mother whispers it into her child's ear, just as the child's personal name is also whispered into its ear. But to say it aloud now is... sad. We can say it but no longer feel it." He pauses and looks at the others, as if for support. To my amazement, I'm feeling sorry for him. Whyever can't the Mer use their name any more?

"We called ourselves *neshevyn lowenna*: the happier kindred."

Happier than what? I wonder. *Happier than whom? Happier than human beings, perhaps.*

"But as time went on only one word was used: *lowenna.*"

Happier. More joyful and more fortunate. It sounds bitterly ironic now, after the blood and betrayals and deaths. I understand why Talek said the Mer might not use their name any more. We are all silent. The sadness of it creeps through the water like a cold current. Impulsively, I stretch out my hands to Talek and the others.

"*Neshevyn lowenna,*" I say carefully.

"Very good, *myrgh kerenza,*" says Saldowr, and with a swirl of his cloak he turns to the entrance again. "Who is darkening the mouth of my cave now, Talek?" he demands. "How many hundreds of your men are waiting out there for you?"

He's right. The sea worms glow brightly, shedding their green light on the walls; but they only look so bright because the light is fading fast.

CHAPTER TWENTY-SIX

"Dear whale. Dear, dear whale."

"I came as soon as I could. I was hunting in the Western Ocean, in the trenches of the Deep. One day when I was logging – the hunt had been good, little one, and my belly was full of giant squid – I had word from the gulls that two human creatures had completed the Crossing of Ingo, and that a terrible battle was being fought among the Mer. I knew it was you they were talking about. I set out at once to find you, little barelegs. My heart was full of fear in case you had been hurt."

"No, I'm not hurt."

The whale turns her huge, box-shaped head. "Swim closer, little one. Swim in front of me so I can see you clearly." I swim around her jaw, and kick upwards until I'm level with her eyes. There's a fresh scar on the side of her head.

"A squid caught me with its tentacles. It was a hard battle, but his beak will never stab a whale's flesh again, nor will his tentacles sear a whale's skin."

"Did you eat him?"

"Of course. What greater pleasure is there after a battle than to eat the enemy you have defeated?"

I can't help smiling. Imagine if we'd tried that with Ervys.

"Why do you smile, little one?" asks the whale eagerly. "Have you thought of a joke?"

"Not really." Suddenly I realise that in the excitement of seeing the whale, I've completely forgotten about her daughter. "Dear whale, you know that I promised I'd search for your daughter at the bottom of the world?"

The whale's eyes fix on me. Her deep voice trembles with hope, doubt and fear. "You found her?"

"Yes. She's well, and she has a baby. A calf," I correct myself quickly.

There's a long moment of silence, as if the whale hasn't even heard me. Then I hear the deep, pulsing rumble of her voice: "Little one, little one, rise with me!"

The water swirls as the whale's vast body powers upwards, dragging me in its slipstream. We tear through branches of oarweed. A shoal of pilchard falls apart like a spun kaleidoscope as we surge through it. In a churn of bubbles the whale's body breaches, and she blows.

I stay beneath the skin, tossed by the waves of her rising. Slowly, the pounding of my heart eases. I swim backwards a little, away from the whale's shadow. A few minutes pass, and then she sinks down beneath the surface again.

"I had to do that," she explains. Her voice bubbles with emotion. "My daughter has a child! I am a grandmother."

"It's a boy – a male."

"Aaah," sighs the whale, as if there is still some air left in her, "and I was not there to help my daughter during the birth."

"She wasn't alone. Her sisters in the pod were there," I say quickly, and then wonder if the whale will want to hear that.

"Good. Good," booms the whale heartily, but I'm sure I detect a note of wistfulness in her voice. Of course she'd have liked to be there. It seems so wrong – unfair – that I've seen the whale's grandson and she has not. But she can go and visit him, of course she can.

"No, little one. It is too far. I am too old. One day, when he is old enough and strong enough, he will travel the world and then perhaps he will come in search of his old grandmother and I shall see him."

"Oh." It sounds bleak to me, not even meeting your grandchild until he's grown up. "That'll be good," I add quickly, in case the whale guesses what I'm thinking.

I tell the whale every single thing I can remember about her daughter. Every word she said, how she looked, exactly what the little one looked like. I give her all the messages from the other whales. She keeps getting me to repeat things, especially the message about how her daughter thought of her when the calf was born. It's quite boring, but I don't mind. I don't say anything about how the whales were hostile to us and might even have killed us.

"I don't suppose they've named the calf yet," says the whale.

"No, I don't think so."

The whale is silent for a while, obviously lost in her own thoughts. I understand why she's so absorbed, but at the same time I'm slightly hurt. I've come halfway across the world with her message – I've crossed Ingo and nearly been killed and met polar bears and Atkas and those strange Mer of the kelp forest – and all my whale wants to hear about is one little calf.

And then I realise something. I'm exactly the same as the whale's daughter. I'm jealous. I want to be first in my whale's heart. You idiot, Sapphire Trewhella. "He's really beautiful," I say.

The whale rumbles contentedly, but then she says, "You have changed, little one. You have grown older. I see marks of suffering in your face. Everyone who makes the Crossing is changed by it."

"It's not really the Crossing." I pause. I'm not sure I can talk about Dad without starting to cry, but the whale's attentive silence is so sympathetic that soon I'm telling her everything She is the easiest person to talk to that I've ever met. She never seems to misunderstand, or criticise. I even tell her about not being able to see Dad's face any more, and how bad that makes me feel.

"I was the same when my daughter left for the bottom of the world," she says. "I felt as if I had betrayed her. But after a long time it all came back. I could see every detail of her. I could remember everything we used to do together."

"Dad said that once," I say slowly. "He said he hadn't forgotten a single thing from our childhood."

"I'm sure that he hadn't. When you have a child you can't ever stop thinking of her."

"Whale?"

"Yes?"

"You know I have a little half-brother? He's Mer. His name is Mordowrgi."

"I believe you told me once."

"He won't even remember Dad. It'll be as if he never had a father."

"You could remind him, little barelegs."

"I suppose I could."

I lean against the whale's rough, corrugated skin that always reminds me of a giant, wrinkled prune. She is so comforting. I'm glad the others went back to the cave once they'd greeted the whale. Talek and Pledyer and all the Mer have gone too. I saw them out of the corner of my eye, swimming strongly away from the cave mouth into the glass-green distance. I was glad to see them go. Even though they've accepted us and we've accepted them, it still hurts me to look at them. Their faces make me think of the spears they made that killed Byblos and theyn Dad. I rub my face against the whale's skin.

"Careful, little one," she booms. "You will hurt yourself. We whales are not dolphins."

"I know."

"We do not have their quickness or their grace or the brilliance of their minds."

"You always say that. I like you as you are, dear whale. I wouldn't want you to be a dolphin."

The whale rumbles again. It's a bit like the sound Sadie

makes when she's drowsing by the fire and I'm massaging her head with my fingers, in just the place she likes—

"My brother wants us to go back to the Air," I say abruptly. "You know, back home to Mum and her boyfriend, and our house and everything."

"Back to the human world..." muses the whale. "Well, it's a long time since you saw your mother."

"Not all that long." I tell the whale the story of my journey through the reef to Mum. I remember every detail, but the strange thing is that the more I describe it, the more unreal and dreamlike it sounds. When I finish the story, there's silence.

"Don't you believe me?" I ask after a while.

"Oh yes. Your spirit met your mother's spirit," answers the whale confidently, as if she's quite used to such things.

"But what does that mean? Do you think I didn't really meet Mum – not in real life?"

The whale chuckles. "I did not say that, little one. You met your mother truly. No dolphin would lead you on a false journey."

But I want the truth. Did I meet Mum or didn't I? Did she really call me lovely girl and tell me what happened to her in the sea when she was a little girl of two? And then suddenly I remember something that I ought to have thought of long before. Why would Mum be in a wooden bungalow with a verandah anyway? She told us that Roger's friend was taking them on a trip way up north into wild country where they wouldn't even be in phone contact. They were going somewhere out in the bush. Would there be proper bungalows with verandahs?

My mind whirls. The more I try to sift out what's real, the more the layers of reality melt into one another. But I can hear Mum's voice, and it rings with truth.

"And will you go back with your brother into the human world?" asks the whale in a voice which sounds as if she's carefully keeping her own opinions out of it.

"Yes," I say.

"Ah." A sigh of disappointment – or even of grief – ripples through the vastness of the whale.

"Not in the way you think, dear whale," I say quickly. "Not for ever."

"You will come back to us?"

"Yes, I'll come back. I belong to Ingo now."

CHAPTER TWENTY-SEVEN

There's the entrance to our cove, up ahead of us. Conor and I swim together, not far below the surface. We've already parted from Faro. He wanted us to say goodbye out in open water: free water, he calls it.

I hated saying goodbye to him. I just wanted to get it over quickly. Now I'm worried that he'll think I didn't care, because all I said was, "See you, Faro," instead of all the things I could have said. It didn't seem real that we were going back to separate worlds after so long together. Faro was going to Saldowr's cave. Conor and I were going back to our cottage, where the washing-up would probably be piled in the sink where we'd left it.

The water is calm. Conor swims with the speed we've learned from the Mer. I swim a little way behind him. When I was little I was always trying to keep up with Conor, but not now. Once we're through the entrance to the cove, it'll be almost time to rise and break through the surface. I dread the thought of it after so long in Ingo. Conor's full of anticipation He can't wait to be there.

Slow down, Conor. The rocky entrance is so close now. As if he hears my thoughts, Conor turns. He looks a bit anxious. He hasn't said anything, but he's been watching me closely since last night. I think he's afraid I'll make a break back to Ingo at the last minute. "Come on, Saph!"

"I'm coming."

I'm not going to desert Conor; he doesn't need to worry about that. It's bad enough for him to leave Ingo knowing that Dad will never follow us home. I couldn't bear to see Conor with that blank, shocked look Faro had when Elvira told him she was leaving for the North.

"You're so *slow*, Saph."

"I'm swimming as fast as I can."

It's true. I'm swimming against a strong tide that wants to keep me in Ingo. It presses against my arms and legs. It wants to pull me back into the deep water. I'm not scared, because it isn't like a rip tide that wants to drown me. It's a tide that pulls my blood in the same way that the moon pulls the sea.

"It's not because I don't want to come with you," I whisper. "But not now. Not yet."

The tide relaxes its hold as if it understands. The rocks loom closer. Weed clings to them, below the tide line. The tide is rising now, and we're going home on it.

Soon I'll be able to wrap my arms around Sadie. Soon I'll be in our cottage again – picking duvet covers off the floor, doing the washing up, getting everything shipshape for when Mum and Roger come home. Mum won't be back yet – at least, I don't think she will. I have to trust that not too much time has passed in the human world while we've been away in Ingo. *The Call will make its own way through your lives.* I have to trust that the Call can still do that, and that Mum will know nothing about our absence. Maybe she'll remember a strange dream she had, which was so vivid it seemed just as real as the waking world.

Everyone in Senara will ask us if we've had a good time up in Plymouth with our cousins. Everyone except Granny Carne, that is. Her fierce amber owl-eyes will sweep my face, and then Conor's, searching for traces of what's happened to us. "You came back to us, my girl," she'll say, and then she'll scan my face again and she'll add so quietly that no one else can hear, "For now." Sometimes it can be frightening how much Granny Carne knows without ever being told. And then she'll smile at Conor and say, "I must tell my bees you're back."

Conor said last night, "It'll be so good to feel solid ground under our feet again." His view is that Ingo gave us a task and we've completed it. We've made the Crossing of Ingo, we've done what Saldowr hoped we would do, and we've defeated Ervys. Logically, our place isn't in Ingo any more, but in the human world.

Maybe that's true for Conor. I wish I could see into the future, like Saldowr and Granny Carne. I'm almost sure that Conor's future lies in the human world. Maybe Ingo will fade from his mind. He'll never forget it, but the gateway between Air and Ingo will close in him, like a scar growing paler and paler until it disappears. Last night he said, "You think I can't wait to leave Ingo, don't you, Saph?"

"It's true, isn't it?"

Conor frowned. "No. It's more complicated now that Dad… It's like part of us always being here."

"I know."

"You remember those whales, the ones who nearly attacked us?"

"Quite hard to forget really."

"You know what they said when we were saying goodbye? I've been thinking about it."

"You mean about the hunters?"

"Yeah. They wanted us to help them. They must have thought we'd have influence just because we're human."

"But we don't."

"No. They don't know about politicians and profits and stuff like that. But all the same they might have a point." Conor paused, then quoted: *"Remember us, when you are back among humans."*

"No one would listen to us, Conor," I said quickly. "Humans don't care about Ingo."

"You do. *I* do. You can't be so – so fatalistic, Saph! You sound like the Mer."

"I can't help it, Conor. I am Mer."

There. I'd said it without even meaning to. But Conor didn't react as I expected. He put his arm round my shoulders and gave me a tight, big-brother hug. "Poor old Saph," he said. "It's tough, isn't it?"

Suddenly I knew that Conor understood everything that we had never talked about. "I'm not saying I'm going to start ramming whaling ships," he went on, "but as far as I can see it's a battle, just like the one with Ervys. If we destroy the oceans, everything's gone. We can't give up without a struggle. People *can* change, you know they can."

I wondered if he was thinking about Elvira. Maybe he was, because he squeezed my shoulder so tight it almost hurt. "Anyway, it doesn't matter what you are or what I am," he said. "We'll always be together."

"Will we?"

Conor smiled. "Of course we will. You're not like Elvira."

"I know. It's quite scary when someone's as…" I was going to say "obsessed" but out of respect for Conor's feelings I change it to "as… er… as single-minded as that. Do you think she'll really go to the North and leave Faro?"

"A hundred per cent."

"Conor… Are you – I mean, about Elvira, do you…"

"No. I'm all right about it now, Saph."

"Good. I'd have hated her if you weren't."

"It's OK for you to hate her a bit if you want. Be my guest." We both laughed. Conor always seems to find a clear way through things that are as dark and tangled as a kelp forest. *We'll always be together….*

Darling Sadie. Dogs don't live in the past or the future; they've got more sense. They live in the present. There'll be hundreds of long walks over fields which smell so intoxicatingly of rabbits that Sadie won't know which way to run first. We'll have hundreds of nights by the fire, with me doing homework and Sadie curled against my legs, thumping her tail on the floor.

People have to leave home when they grow up. They get jobs, or they go away to uni. They're never coming home for good, even if their mums keep their bedrooms just the same, waiting for them.

Mum has always wanted me to go away to uni. She dreams of me becoming a doctor. *You could do it, Sapphy! You mustn't throw away your opportunities*. Oh, Mum. You make me want to cry sometimes, like when you blame yourself for the way things are and I want to tell you that none of it is your fault. You wouldn't ever have let Roger into our lives unless you'd believed Dad was dead.

I'll never be able to tell you how strange and solemn it was when the dolphins bore Dad's body into Limina. We didn't even cry; it was too deep for that. I kept thinking that Dad died trying to protect us. I wish you'd seen him flying forward on Byblos' back, with his trident in his hand. You thought he died for nothing, all that long time ago, in a stupid, random accident. You were so angry with him for leaving us. I wish I could explain to you what really happened. Dad made his choice, and it was for us.

I don't want to leave you yet, Mum. I think I'll even be able to cope with the way you keep going on about maths and science, and refusing to recognise that I'm not all that good at either of them. It must be quite hard when you're a parent and you find out that your children's dreams are nothing like the dreams you've had for them. I never thought I'd be glad that you've got Roger, Mum, but I am.

Last night, after I'd talked to Conor, I went to find Faro. He was close by, waiting for me. We swam to one of our favourite places, about a mile from the Bawns. Faro and I didn't talk much. It was so good just to be together, not endlessly travelling, not looking out for the shadow of a shark in the distance.

Faro didn't seem worried about me going away, back to the human world. We didn't even talk about it much. Faro told me that he was going to meet Bannerys and some of his other friends who'd followed Ervys. Faro didn't want to see them again – Bannerys was a traitor, he said – but Saldowr persuaded him. *Interesting,* I thought. *A year ago Saldowr wouldn't have tried to persuade Faro, he'd have commanded him.*

So things are changing fast. There's going to be an Assembly, Faro told me. It's to bring together all the Mer, whether they fought for Ervys or for Saldowr. It's got to happen soon, before the wounds harden, that's what Saldowr says…

"Saph!"

"I know, I know. I'm coming, Conor."

Granny Carne will help me. Mum will listen to her. Granny Carne will explain. I'll still be me, Sapphire Trewhella, and I'll still be Mum's daughter. I'm not going to suddenly grow a tail and stop speaking English. I'm Mer and human, but the thing that has changed since we made the Crossing is that my Mer blood isn't fighting with my human blood any more. There was a barrier in me too, and I've crossed it. I'll never have to throw away my human self, as Dad had to, in order to survive in Ingo. And I'll never, ever reject my Mer self.

Another minute, and we'll be in shallow water. It'll take less than half a stroke to swim to the surface, and then we'll burst through the skin into sharp, dry Air. The racket of the gulls will batter my ears as I struggle for my first breath. The air will go down into my lungs like a razor blade. Conor will support me and in a few minutes I'll be used to breathing again. We'll wade out of the water, shivering. As soon as you're out of Ingo, you feel how cold the ocean is. Your clothes cling to you, soaked with salt water. It's like being a newborn baby, all wet and vulnerable. You need food and fire and shelter.

I'm not even sure that my legs will remember how to walk. We'll come to the boulders at the back of the beach, and the cliff we've got to climb. Gulls will swirl around the rocky ledges, screaming out the story of our return. I'm sure they won't try to attack us this time. They won't be Ervys's spies any longer. They'll have gone back to snatching pasties in St Pirans. And maybe, even though it's daylight, an owl will swoop down too. She'll sail on broad, soundless wings, her amber eyes scanning the surface of the sea, waiting for our heads to break the surface.

Conor grasps my arm. "Saph, we can't hang around here too long. The tide's rising. It'll be dangerous once it covers the sand."

He's right. The rising tide always grows rough as it funnels through the mouth of our cove. Even on calm days you'd get thrown against the rocks if you tried to swim in at high tide.

Side by side, we swim on until the water is only a few metres deep. Beneath us the pale sand is ridged by the pull of the waves. We'll have to rise. I brace myself for the tearing pain in my lungs. It won't hurt for long. Don't be such a coward, Sapphire Trewhella. Think of Sadie. Think of Rainbow. I bet Conor's thinking of Rainbow...

At that moment Conor shouts, "Look, Saph, look!"

He's twisted round. He's pointing back towards the mouth of the cove, where late autumn sunlight glitters through the water. There's someone out there. A figure which might be a boy with a wetsuit pulled down around his waist...

The boy is diving now. As he dives, his body arches and he swings round in a tight circle. Refracted sunlight flashes on his body. Broad shoulders, long dark hair, a tail as smooth and powerful as a seal's. He turns one somersault and then another and then another and another, so fast that he becomes a blur of speed and foam and glitter. *Faro*.

"I thought he'd gone back to Saldowr," says Conor. "Look at that! How many somersaults do you reckon he's going to do?"

"Hundreds, probably."

"It's an amazing way to say goodbye." But I know Faro better than that. He's not saying goodbye at all. He's making a pattern as he weaves and twists through the water. Suddenly I realise that our journey has made a pattern too. It has bound Ingo and the human world close in ways that I don't fully understand yet, even though I feel the power of them. Granny Carne said there were others like Conor and me and Gloria Fortune, who share Mer blood and human. There always have been, secretly, and

367

maybe now that the Crossing of Ingo is complete our numbers will start to grow. I'm going to find as many of us as I can before I go back to Ingo again. Maybe, one day in the far future, Ingo and Air will be united…

Faro's teasing voice floats into my mind. *Those are beautiful thoughts, Sapphire, but why don't you watch me instead? You won't find anyone in the human world who can turn a thousand somersaults without stopping.*

I'm watching, Faro. I touch the *deublek* on my wrist. I understand the pattern Faro is making, and what it says to me. *Two together are stronger than one.* And something else, too, which is that everything that's happened has joined us together so tightly that we'll never really be apart. We'll be away from each other for a while, but it won't change the pattern that joins us. Faro and I, my dear friend the whale, Saldowr and the dolphins, the currents and the kelp forests, the seahorses and the crabs, the clear turquoise water and the wild black storms, Dad's voice calling out to warn me before the flood rushed in over St Pirans, even Ervys and the cold fury of the sharks… We're all woven together now. The future's there too, waiting to unroll.

I wish I was away in Ingo
Far across the briny sea
Sailing over deepest water…

I can hear Dad's voice as clearly as if he were still singing. *You don't have to wish for anything now, Dad. You're safe.*

I am in Ingo. I am at home.